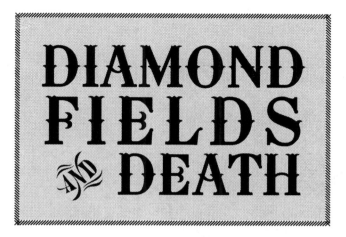

DIAMOND FIELDS & DEATH

THE FRAMING OF TOM HORN

Bob Jourdan

iUniverse, Inc.
Bloomington

Diamond Fields and Death
The Framing of Tom Horn

iUniverse books may be ordered through booksellers or by contacting:

iUniverse
1663 Liberty Drive
Bloomington, IN 47403
www.iuniverse.com
1-800-Authors (1-800-288-4677)

ISBN: 978-1-4502-9453-9 (sc)
ISBN: 978-1-4502-9454-6 (dj)
ISBN: 978-1-4502-9567-3 (ebk)

Library of Congress Control Number: 2011901446

Printed in the United States of America

iUniverse rev. date: 04/15/2011

CHAPTER 1

A cold chill hit Jim Keaton as dusk settled over the streets of Denver. Even in the warmth of summer, the mile-high city changed dramatically when the sun dropped behind the mountains. He pulled his vest together, buttoned down the front, and continued his stroll along the streets.

He had never been in a city of this size before, and he found everything about it interesting, charming, and curious. Plateglass windows fronted every shop, and buildings extended as far as the eye could see, all brick and stone, many several stories tall. Streets were paved in places with the same bricks and stones, with carriages and wagons clattering about. And of all things, streetlamps lit every block. Turn-of-the-century progress had invaded the Queen City of the West, and Jim wanted to take in all he could in the short time he would be there. People strolled along every avenue, apparently doing the same thing. Many of the men were dressed in city suits and ties, escorting ladies in their long, full skirts, often carrying umbrellas even though there was not a cloud in the sky. He enjoyed sights never seen back in his hometown of Del Rio, Texas, a sleepy border town along the Rio Grande, pressed hard against Mexico.

A few folks glanced fleetingly at Jim, who was obviously not a city fellow. His six-foot frame was taller than most, and his dark bronze complexion showed that he was a Southwesterner, one accustomed to working out on the open range. His raven-black hair would have caused some to mistake him for a Mexican, but his soft blue-gray eyes would give him away. And then, of course, his relaxed attitude did not seem to fit in with the hustle and bustle of scurrying city dwellers, always in a hurry to nowhere.

Most shops along the streets were closed or closing, with the exception of the saloons that seemed to be on every corner. In the businesses that were still open, lamps burned, and their soft golden glow lit the interior just enough to allow the last customers to gather their goods. A leather shop caught Jim's fancy. The windows were filled with items familiar to him from his work with livestock. He was intrigued with the dozens of bridles and bits, spurs and saddles, all lined up for display. In the remote villages where he had spent his life, it was unusual to find more than a couple of these items in any one store.

As Jim studied the various goods through the glass, he noticed the proprietor moving toward the door, apparently just closing for the night. The door swung open, and out stepped a trim, nice-looking young lady, not at all the usual tired and matronly type most often seen running businesses. She appeared to be in her early thirties, probably of Spanish descent, with long black hair and typical dark-brown eyes that often flashed black as ebony, with a bright sparkle.

"Come in and look around. Still have a few minutes before I have to lock up. Got lots more good things inside." The lady was genuinely interested in her business and wanted to give Jim a chance to see what she had, things that most working folks seemed to always need or want.

"Oh, no … I don't need anything. Just looking," Jim said. "More things here than I've ever seen in one place."

"Well, you come on in while I get things settled down for the night. There are some new things not shown in the window."

Jim stepped toward the door and then hesitated. "Will you be open very long?"

"Open just as long as you might need. I'm the owner, so I don't have any set time for closing. Let me show you something I've just taken in, something you might be interested in."

Jim moved inside, taking notice of things not in view from out on the street. There were heavy coats, wool blankets, shirts, boots, slickers—things he had not brought along with him from Texas, but things he might need if he stayed north very long.

"Oh, I'm Jody Quintana. And who are you?" the lady asked.

"I'm Jim … Jim Keaton. Came up from Texas for some business with the lawyer down the street. Got to meet with him first thing in the morning."

"I thought you might be from out of town, Jim. And since you are looking at things in my store, I'd guess that you are a stockman, not a miner?" Jody observed as she moved from table to table, squaring things up, making them look nice for tomorrow's opening.

"I've always been around livestock, Miss Jody. Never been a miner. But that's part of why I'm up here. Lost my brother 'bout three months back to a mine cave-in. Got to take care of his will. Maybe you know the lawyer … Mister Douglas Fitch?"

"Why, yes, Jim. He's a really nice man. His office is just a couple of blocks away. He does all my legal business for the store. You'll like him. Honest fellow too. But, Jim, let me show you what I just got from a spur maker down your way in Texas. His brother came up here a few days back with a gunnysack full of spurs. Name was Boone. Ever hear of them? Both make spurs, but what I want to show you is the best of them, marked B. Boone, the brother that didn't come along. His work is something to see!"

Jim knew he might have to buy a set of spurs if he stayed around very long. When Jody took him to a table toward the back of the store, he saw the best-looking spurs he had ever come across. Most were common, but several sets showed Mexican silver inlays, copper lines, highly polished steel, various types of rowels, and finely cut straps with bright buckles. Jim's old spurs back in Del Rio were plain and somewhat rusty with well-worn straps. The Boone spurs looked like they would last a lifetime.

"Look 'em over, Jim," Jody encouraged. "Try some on. I know you'll like those marked B. Boone. You look while I close down before going over to Antonio's for supper. Best eating place in town!"

"I'm staying at the Brown Hotel, Miss Jody. Food's pretty good, but I've been on the stage a few days, eating at stage stops," Jim said as he looked over the fine B. Boone spurs.

"Jim, if you'd like, you can go over to Antonio's with me. Best steaks around! Besides, it will be dark, and I'd appreciate having you with me. Sometimes those rough miners get out of hand, you know, just rowdy, but sometimes drunk."

Not only were the Boone spurs something Jim really liked, but here was an offer from a very nice-looking lady that he could not pass up. "I'll just take you up on that, Miss Jody, after you box up these spurs fer me. And I'll buy you a steak too. Maybe we can talk a bit about that there lawyer friend of yours."

The evening flew by, filled with delightful discussions, the kind Jim could not get in dusty stage stops. Jody was knowledgeable, intelligent, and, the best-looking lady Jim had seen anywhere. Although she was a solid business person, she displayed a quiet, soft side not seen out in distant settlements. She was single and had built her business with the few dollars left by her parents, who had literally worked themselves to death a few years earlier on the old homestead out on the dry, dusty prairie. Jody and her younger sister sold the homestead and moved to Denver to escape the drab life on the poor farm.

"Jim, I've had a wonderful evening with your company. But I've got to get back to my place over the store. It's late, and I have to open up early in the morning. Walk me back to the store, and you will only be a couple of blocks from your hotel. When you get done with Mister Fitch tomorrow, drop over and tell me how it all went. Maybe we can find time to go to Antonio's again."

Jim watched Jody walk up the flight of stairs to her home over the leather shop. They exchanged waves, and Jim walked on to the Brown Hotel.

The last few days had been eventful for Jim, to say the least. He arrived in Denver following a long, rough stagecoach ride of several days, all the way from the Texas-Mexican border. He had received notice from the Denver lawyer that his brother, Billy Keaton, had lost his life in a mine cave-in somewhere in Colorado. Billy had set up his will with the law firm some ten or twelve years earlier, realizing that his lifestyle as a drifting miner constantly on the move was rather precarious. The will directed the firm to contact Jim if he died and to hand over to Jim any and all proceeds of investments made by Billy through the law firm.

As soon as the state posted the death certificate, Douglas Fitch verified the death and sent the notice of Billy's will to Jim. Billy's investments had done very well, and now Jim's inheritance was worth thousands of dollars. The simple way to handle the entire process would be for Jim to travel to Denver to close out all details of the will and take possession of the proceeds.

Jim met with Douglas Fitch the morning after his arrival in Denver. Fitch was a quiet fellow, average looking from any aspect, thin gray hair, small mustache, and deep-set inquisitive eyes, the kind that caused folks to open up and talk plainly with him. He was a listener, doing just what good lawyers had to do. But today things were different. He had to fill Jim in on how his brother, Billy, had come to retain the small law firm to hold all his investments along with his will and power of attorney.

"I first met Billy back in 1888 or so, after he came out of the Rock Springs country where he had been involved in that famous diamond hoax of '72. When he filled me in on all the details and set you up to be his legal heir, he also said he had kept most of the story of his part in the scam from you, but he did tell it all to your folks. I understand they passed away about three years before Billy contacted me. That right, Jim?" Fitch asked as he arranged several files before him.

"Well, yes, they both passed on while I was still in school. I do remember Billy coming home and telling me some of th' things he had been doing. I was just a school kid back then, Mister Fitch. That was way back in maybe '73, '74. I was in th' second grade or so, going to that one-room school there in Del Rio. Billy did tell our folks all about what he had done, and after he left, we talked about it enough over th' years till I sure did know some about it all."

"Let me quickly run over some of the details so you will know how this inheritance came to be, Jim," Fitch offered. "You see, Billy had been drifting around the gold fields of California for a while, getting nowhere, when he partnered up with a couple of fellows named Arnold and Slack, Philip Arnold and John Slack. The three hit it off pretty good and soon made a gold strike. When a group came along and offered to buy them out, they took it. It was the best money they had seen since starting their gold prospecting. Now, this Arnold and Slack were not criminals as such, but they had a little streak of shrewdness in them that sometimes got them in trouble. No doubt, they were bright. But after getting a little money and becoming disgusted with how some prospectors hit and some didn't, they figured it was time to try to pull the wool over some of the big-time financiers. They planned to salt a bogus mine with diamonds and various gemstones and then have them look it over with the expectation that in the end they would buy the thing at some ridiculous price. They were thinking big, Jim. Thinking of roping in fellows like Horace Greeley, the Rothschild family, old General McClellan, and a few others that might be fooled into thinking they were ripping off a couple of ignorant prospectors.

"So, before leaving California, Arnold and Slack took a big part of their strike money and quietly went around buying all sorts of rough gemstones, diamonds, rubies, emeralds, and sapphires. Billy wasn't in on what they planned at that time, but he knew they used up most of their share of the money. Then they all boarded the train and headed east to Wyoming Territory, getting off at the coal-mining town of Rock Springs. Arnold and Slack knew the country south of the town—there were very few scattered ranches and lots of wild, open country. And because the area was so unknown, those two bright, roguish fellows hatched the plan to use their gemstones to salt a small place out in those remote mountains."

This all fit together with what Jim had heard over the years. But he never knew how it had started. And never knew Billy's involvement, at least not in detail. He had learned from his folks that Billy had a part in the famous salting of the so-called diamond field somewhere in northwestern Colorado on the Wyoming line and that Billy was paid a handsome fee for staying out near the diamond field as a watchman.

Fitch continued with more details. "Now, Jim, your brother really didn't learn of the salting plan until the three of them headed out from Rock Springs, heading south into that unsettled country. It was only then that Arnold and Slack told him just what the plan was. And since Arnold and Slack had bought the gemstones, Billy would not be a primary partner. But if he wanted to go along, they could use him. They offered to pay a good fee if he would make a camp and stay somewhere near the salted field as a sort of watchman while they went back to San Francisco to let the word out about the diamond strike. Billy jumped at the offer. When they picked out the right spot on that low bench off what's now called Diamond Peak, Billy pitched in and helped spread those various gemstones around. They worked for several days, punching holes in the ground and dropping a stone in each and then stomping the holes shut with their boot heels. Some were put into the fissures and cracks in the flat rocks that covered large areas of the bench. The weather would cover any sign of their work after a few weeks or months."

Fitch pulled one file from the stack in front of him and opened it, removing a few sheets, some flat single sheets, some folded. "I've got a pretty good description of just where that old diamond field ought to be, Jim. And there's a crude old map here somewhere that Billy drew up too. Shows the diamond field and the trail over to where he put up a one-room cabin and stayed on as watchman till it was all over."

Fitch shuffled through the papers and pulled several from the stack. "Yes, here's the old map and some of the papers that show a lot about the diamond hoax. That thing sure set the financial world in a spin, Jim. Those two fellows succeeded in duping dozens of prominent men from all over—California, New York, even reached over to Great

Britain. Most of them are named in these old newspaper reports. That Rothschild fellow must have been hit pretty hard; he committed suicide not long after. Seems the group paid Arnold and Slack something like six hundred thousand dollars. The first thing the general public heard about a diamond mine out there was when it hit the headlines as a diamond hoax, catching all the big shots in losses. It was exposed by a fellow with the national mapping outfit, or maybe he was with the railroad mapping outfit. Anyway, when he exposed the deal, it didn't take long for folks to drop any idea of going out there to strike it rich in diamonds."

Jim looked over the old papers and took notice of the hand-drawn map, the sort that an unskilled prospector would render. It showed several mountains and streams, some with names but most without. Jim was accustomed to using maps made by the military when he served in the army in General George Crook's outfit in Arizona during the last of the Indian wars. He had been assigned to a scout group as a teenage private when the last Apaches were rounded up. Then he was transferred to Fort Concho, back in Texas, where he continued scouting. Since the Indian wars were about over, he was sent on routine patrols from Fort Concho across to Fort Bliss, staying in outposts like McKavett, Lancaster, Quitman, and others. He soon resigned and headed back to Del Rio to make his living repairing windmills and filling in with cowboy work.

"Jim, if you would like to go through all these files, they are all yours," said Fitch as he passed a few pages of the records to Jim. "We've been handling Billy's affairs for many years, making the first investment with his money from the big hoax. Then we moved the investments around when it looked like a better return could be made. Actually, we about doubled the value for him. With Billy's inheritance you will be quite well off. There's maybe around twenty-five thousand dollars by now."

"Did you say twenty-five thousand dollars? You don't mean twenty-five hundred or maybe just twenty-five dollars? Why, Mister Fitch, that's more than I've made in my lifetime! Is this for real? Would it really come up to that?" Jim was startled by the amount.

"Why, yes, Jim. Of course, there will be some charges taken out for our handling of the will over these years. But even at that, the balance ought to be about that amount. You'd want us to open an account for you here at the bank. And if you plan to go out in those wild parts to maybe just see where Billy got started in all this, you might want us to make you a will, or maybe give us power of attorney just to handle your affairs just in case …"

"In case of what, Mister Fitch? Maybe me dying or something? I've been around too long fer that. I've lived through fighting Indians, chasing around over most of th' deserts, hanging off th' tops of them windmills to repair 'em, even outrunning a cattle stampede once or twice."

"Oh, I know, Jim. But you surely would want this money to go to the right people, wouldn't you? None of us ever plans to die. Billy wasn't planning to enter that mine shaft just in time for it to kill him now, was he?"

Fitch had a point, and Jim agreed. Before the morning was over, Fitch had completed the short will and power of attorney, opened a bank account, transferred the money, and handed over to Jim enough cash for his living expenses whether he returned home to his beloved Texas hills or headed out west. If he ran low on cash, a simple telegram back to the bank would bring him any amount of money he might need.

"There ain't no need in me worrying 'bout having to get back home and rustle up another windmill job now, is there Mister Fitch?" Jim asked as he let the facts sink in. "I always wanted me a little place back on Devil's River, but when I got back and looked around, all th' good places had been taken up. I might as well take th' time to go out and look at that place where all this started. How long does it take to get out to this old diamond field, Mister Fitch?"

"No trick at all, Jim," said Fitch. "All you do is catch the train or stage to Cheyenne and change to the train that will take you right out to Rawlins, Bitter Creek, and Rock Springs. From there you would sure have to get yourself a buggy or horse, and you would really need a camp outfit. There aren't many folks living out in any of those places. There are some rumors of minor range wars going on out in that country, but you should be able to stay clear of any of that sort of stuff."

As Fitch was putting away the official papers in their proper places, he rambled on about the old diamond hoax. "I got a lot of satisfaction knowing that your brother and his friends put one over on all those greedy financiers, beating them at their own game. They got beat so bad they never even filed any charges against Arnold and Slack. They never knew of Billy's part in it. Boy, what I'd give to have seen the looks on all their faces when they got that report proving the place was salted!" Fitch's laughter could be heard all the way down the hallway.

Jim stood up to leave and as he shook hands with Fitch said, "Thanks for everthing. I'll be headin' out first thing tomorrow to take a look at those diamond fields."

"Jim, I wish you well." Fitch put his hand on Jim's shoulder as he walked him to the door. "Keep me advised of your future addresses. And don't get yourself killed over something like a stockmen's war. And just wire me if you need anything."

Jim was more than pleased that he had made the long trip up from Del Rio. He liked everything about Douglas Fitch and knew he was in good hands.

It was not quite noon when he left the lawyer's office and dropped in to the barbershop just outside the bank's doors. He wanted his long, black hair trimmed just like he had seen on all the local fellows, the bankers, businessmen, even Mister Fitch. The sweet essence of the shop lingered with him as he hurried out to visit the proprietor of the leather shop.

"Jim! Wasn't expecting you back so soon, if ever. How did your meeting with Mister Fitch go?" Jody greeted him as he strode into the leather shop, taking in the smell of finely oiled and treated leather.

"It was like you said, Miss Jody. He turned out to be more than I expected. Took care of everything good and proper."

"Now, Jim, we've got to get something straight. You don't need to keep calling me Miss Jody. Makes me think you are a first-time visitor, a stranger. And you are not! You call me Jody, same as you'd call anyone back home. First name only, for friendship." Jody abruptly stopped working on the books at the counter. "And since it's noontime, we best close down and head over to Antonio's. And this time, I'm buying!"

Jim was caught in the rush but understood Jody's meaning.

Jody and Jim lingered over their lunch longer than they should have, with her owning a business and all. Jim eagerly talked of details of his great inheritance. The two had become captivated with each other's background and eventful past. But at the same time, Jim had to get on with finding his way to Cheyenne, and Jody had her business to run.

"Jim, do be careful. The drifters, miners, cowboys that come into my shop tell me that Rock Springs is a rough town. And there's always some killing going on out there, either over land or cattle or fighting between sheepmen and cattlemen, you know, the things you don't want to get mixed up in. When you've seen that place where your brother stayed that year, I hope you will come back here to see me." Jody's request was sincere, and Jim knew it.

"I'll be catching th' afternoon train to Cheyenne, spend th' night there, and head out to Rock Springs soon as I can. And sure, Jody, when I get done seeing that place and all, I'll head back here." Jim wanted to spend more time getting to know Jody better, but his mind was set on getting out west as quickly as possible.

CHAPTER 2

The train ride from Denver to Cheyenne was delightful compared to the long, dusty stage ride Jim had made from Del Rio earlier. Folks were rushing back and forth between the two high plains cities, doing business in mining and livestock plus hundreds of lesser things, such as selling pots and pans, farm equipment, barbed wire, and guns of all kinds for all purposes. The activity was more than Jim had seen anywhere in his travels of the past few years. Cheyenne was crowded with folks from the East trying to get out to the free land of the West. Homesteading seemed to be the central business, as far as Jim could see. And he could not help but think of how Texas was about all taken up and maybe this western country would be something he should consider for his own future.

The next day Jim boarded the train for Rock Springs and was on his way west. The big steam engine chugged its way up the grades, trailing a thick cloud of rich, black smoke. Every few miles they would stop to take on water, and sometimes a woodcutter waited along the rails selling wood or at least delivering wood contracted by the railroad. Jim thought that these must have been enterprising men, going out to the forest, maybe a mile or more from the rails, cutting ties and firewood, and hauling it back to await the next train. This sure wasn't Jim's idea of how to make a living. Even scouting for Apaches with the army would beat chopping wood.

After several long pulls up the grades, the train broke over the divide to roar quickly down into Laramie, Wyoming, a sleepy stockmen's town where the state had decided to build a university. Then a long haul out to Rawlins where the big state prison held any number of cattle rustlers, highwaymen, killers of all descriptions, and bunches of nondescript law breakers. A stop there was well received by all the travelers, a chance to eat and stretch, just to get out and walk around. For folks so used to the saddle, a train ride was hard on them in some ways, even though comfortable. Then it was off through many watering and fuel stations, out across the big desert to Bitter Creek.

Jim thought about leaving the train at Bitter Creek, but after looking it over for a few minutes, he knew there had to be a better stop farther down the line. Even the worker at the depot wasn't very encouraging about Bitter Creek.

"You from 'round here?" Jim asked.

The coarse, rough-looking man dropped the freight he was moving from the train, glad to have a reason not to handle it. "Ain't hardly from 'round here—from absolutely right here! Born and raised here. Strangers don't usually ask such questions."

"Well, fill me in on how to do some business 'round here. Looks like there might not even be a business house. Where's your livery, your stable?" Jim was just a little short with the character, not wanting to give an inch to him.

"You wantin' to buy a horse or maybe rent one? Now that would be jest like one of you fellers from back East, wouldn't it? What a beautiful day fer a gentle ride 'round th' countryside. Get to see all th' sights, th' lakes and streams, maybe take in a little fishing or swimming. Then drift back in at dusk fer a fine meal in th' meritorious, trimmed-in-gold Hotel Bitter Creek! Have a hot bath and a good cigar 'fore hitting th' hay in that there feather bed and be got up tomorrow 'round noon fer a stroll in th' Bitter Creek Park, jest 'round the block."

Before the smart-talking laborer could start in on his next buffoonery, Jim had him by the collar, stretching him out from his pitiful five-foot-seven-inch frame to more than six feet. He held him hanging there while glaring into his whiskered face and roughly telling him to talk straight when he talked to Jim Keaton or to get ready for the beating of his life! He didn't have time or patience to put up with nonsense. He was dead tired from traveling and really ought to just start by pistol-whipping him to within an inch of his life! Then with an overpowering shove, Jim sent the worker hard against the depot wall—hard enough to knock the wind from the shocked little fellow. He fell to the dock, gasping for air.

Quickly, Jim pulled the shaking man to his feet, and almost as though nothing had happened, he started brushing the little guy off. "Sorry, I didn't introduce myself properly. I'm Jim Keaton from Denver this week and Texas earlier. And I don't think I got your name, sir?"

"I … I … my name is Walt, Walt Bentsen. And I really didn't mean nothing by what I done, mister. It's jest that we get all kinds of dumb—I mean—questions 'bout things that jest ain't never here and ain't never been here. Jest don't know why folks think Bitter Creek might be a town like they must have back East somewhere. Really, mister, we ain't got nothing here."

Jim eased off. He saw that he had gotten out of hand, but he also knew the only way to handle this kind of fellow was with strong, decisive action. This little laborer would well remember Jim Keaton, and Jim would bet the man would always treat him very well if they ever met again.

"What if I need a horse? Are there any available?"

"Listen, Mister … Mister Keaton, I can get you a horse, but it might be a few days. We jest don't have regular calls fer horses. We depend on our friends out there somewhere on th' desert to bring us some once in a while. But I wouldn't want you to have none of them. See, they might have a burned-over brand or something like that. Jest not the kind you'd want. But, mister, if you could wait jest a couple of days, I would be more than happy to ride down to the Erickson ranch or maybe clear on down to the Rife and buy you a honest and good one! Even get a bill of sale."

"Walt, give me th' straight answer. Would I be better off to go on to Rock Springs? You know I'll need supplies, a camp outfit, good horse, some .30-40 shells and some .45s. I'm heading down toward Diamond Peak, looking fer a place maybe to homestead or buy. Maybe in Colorado or Wyoming or even over in Utah. Jest won't know till I look things over."

"Did you mean 'homestead,' like squatting, and all that?" Walt asked, looking very disturbed about what Jim had told him.

"That's what I said, Walt. And you can quit calling me Mister Keaton. To all my friends I'm plain Jim. Or is it that you don't plan to be my friend, Walt?"

Jim could see that Walt was siding with him, without really knowing it, and the shoving around had dividends already coming back. Jim knew he had Walt in the palm of his hand, and that just might come in mighty handy down the line. After all, Bitter Creek wasn't all that far from the diamond field or the livestock wars, if they really existed.

"Oh, mister, I mean, Jim. Uh, Jim, really now, I ain't one to hold no grudges. I had that little shoving coming to me. Sure, Jim. You can count on me. I really don't think you ought go 'round telling folks you might be planning to homestead over 'round Cold Spring Mountain or Diamond Peak. And that goes fer Diamond Mountain too. There's some mighty good folks over there. Thing is, they think there ain't no room over there fer no one else, 'specially folks they ain't kin to or don't invite. Why, hear tell of some prospectors never coming out of there. Now me, Jim—my mouth is shut. I jest never heard you say nothing 'bout that country. Even had a couple of good cowboys shot down there a while back. Jest don't know exactly why. 'Course, now, th' deputy and coroner are both living down there, and they always list th' official cause of any death."

"Walt, you mention Cold Spring Mountain. I'm new here, so tell me where it is. If there are problems there, I really need to know 'bout it 'fore I blunder into it, don't you think? Before you answer that, ain't there some place we can talk, out of th' sun? And what if I fool around here with you till I miss my train out to Rock Springs?"

"Oh, mister, I mean, Jim, I wouldn't let you do that. But today there will be another one coming on down th' line in jest a few hours. Not often done, but they got some special freight going and had to put on th' second train. Got some cool water inside."

Jim let Walt bend his ear long into the afternoon and had to get his ticket changed to catch the second train. Names and places fell out of Walt's head like sand from an hourglass. By the time he heard the lonely whistle of the oncoming second train, Jim had more than just a thumbnail sketch of the people and happenings all around the three-corners area, where Utah, Colorado, and Wyoming join. Walt had been out to the diamond field and knew the whole diamond salting story. Jim was careful in questioning Walt to learn that no one ever knew that Arnold and Slack had a secret third partner in the salting, Jim's brother, Billy.

When the train pulled away from the platform at Bitter Creek, Jim Keaton knew he had a loyal friend to whom he owed a lot. He had no idea how he could ever repay the man. He'd just have to let time tell. Jim marked the Bitter Creek area in his mind, something telling him he might need that out-of-the-way place or perhaps help from the only friend he had in that desolate country.

It was late at night when Jim arrived in Rock Springs. He went straight to the hotel, the Valley House, had a quick meal, and headed for his room. Before turning up the lamp, he took a look around, just a precaution and habit he had picked up over the years. The second-floor window looked out over a main street, now quiet with only the soft, golden glow of oil lamps coming from the saloon a few doors down. A walkway roof ran below the window, where a man could slip out on if he had to or someone could climb to from below. The door had a hook for security, a poor exchange for a loaded six-gun. Jim took note of the furnishings: chair, table, dresser with mirror, a couple of clothes hooks along the wall. Nothing unusual. The dresser could be pushed in front of the window, the chair could be braced under the doorknob. Looked like a good place to light for the next couple of days.

Jim checked his Colt .45 before hanging it on the bedpost, close enough to use if necessary. By then the bed was too inviting.

When Jim strolled around town the next morning, he found that Rock Springs was much larger than he thought it would be. The coal mines were in full swing with jobs for anyone. Shacks had gone up all along Bitter Creek and out every draw, spilling over the top on the plateau. There must have been two or three thousand people there, and they brought businesses in.

Jim had no trouble finding everything he needed. He was glad he had brought along his new Winchester Model 95 rifle from Texas, after seeing the price it would cost in the dirty, coal mining boomtown. There seemed to be plenty of new .30-40 ammunition. The shopkeepers said it was the best big-game cartridge to ever come along. Even better than the old .45-70, and lots easier to handle than the older .50 Sharps buffalo guns that simply kicked the daylights out of any shooter.

"Where you taking that good rifle, feller?" the mercantile store man asked Jim.

"Well, I'm sort of looking fer a little place somewhere down south of here fer putting in a few cows," Jim answered. He knew he best not let anyone know he was heading down to look over the old diamond field that had, in the end, furnished him the money for freedom for maybe the rest of his life. He remembered the warnings from Walt about the troubles down that way.

"Oh? You know someone down there, do you?"

"No, not a soul. Been kicking 'round since selling out a place down in Texas. Heard lots of things 'bout this country from some of th' soldiers I served with down in Arizona a few years back. Sounded like good ranch country, so I thought I ought to come see fer myself," Jim said in a hopeful, convincing manner.

"Well, if you plan on hunting much of anything bigger than deer, you ought to head up north. That's what that .30-40 is for, ain't it?" said the salesman, rattling off more than he should. "Besides that, feller, you ain't likely to find anything in the way of land south of here. There's been some bad happenings down that way lately, you know. You ain't from here?"

"No, but unless something stops me, I may jest be from here th' next time you see me," Jim replied with a great big Texas grin.

"Listen, feller, if you hear me straight, you really ought to head out north fer hunting anything. What I mean is, you need to know more 'bout what you're getting into by going south. Those folks down 'round Brown's Park are jest different. Why, when they come to town, they don't even spend no time. Get what they need and get out. Back to the Park. And the sort of goings-on down there, what with all them outlaws hanging 'round and all ..."

"My name is Jim Keaton. And since you seem to want to keep me out of some kind of trouble, I might like to know jest who you are?"

"Oh, didn't mean to sound out of place. I'm Andy Ewing," he said as he offered a hand big enough to hide a full-size Colt .45. "I have kin from Brown's Park. Kind of know what goes on down there."

"Why, Andy, you really are trying to keep my hide in one piece, ain't you? I've heard a bit 'bout that Park being outlaw infested. Is it really that bad?"

"Not if you keep clear of happenings. Don't try to get involved in much. And be sure to make friends with the right folks early on," Andy said as he went on about his business, stacking items on the shelves and dusting off the black coal dust that kept taking over everything in town. "You see, fellers like me can come and go down there anytime. They all know me, and lots of them knew my kin from the early days. So I'm okay. But guys that show up jest looking 'round, well ..."

Andy stood an even six feet tall but was somewhat slim. His golden hair wasn't real common, thought Jim. The suspenders Andy wore were never seen on a cowboy, so he was probably not a ranch hand. And he showed signs of some education, more than the common store clerk. Maybe he would be someone Jim could appreciate, even get to know.

"I'll be all right, Andy. I've mixed with those kinds before. They don't really jest up and go after a feller without any reason. What you're saying seems to be, don't give 'em any reason. Right, Andy?" Jim hesitated and added, "Don't worry 'bout me, Andy. I'll be dropping in to see you every time I'm in town. May need someone to set me straight on things."

"Sure, Jim … uh, Mister Keaton. I'll keep an eye out fer you. Now don't you ferget to get in here first, every time you get to town!"

Jim turned and strode out on the boardwalk, heading for the livery. He had all his supplies set aside, but he needed to get over to try out the horse he had inspected early that morning.

The gelding Jim purchased from the livery, a good sorrel with a blazed face, was six years old and well trained. Jim took him on a short ride out along the creek and across the rough draws and found him eager and willing to move out at any pace. Even after a mile run, full out, he was still ready for more. Grit, thought Jim. And that just might save both their hides some day.

A ten-year-old mare looked good for a light packhorse, gentle and broke to hobbles, lead rope, riding saddle or pack saddle, and even trained to pull a buckboard a little. What more could a man want? The deal was made.

Jim carefully packed away all the provisions in the panniers and tied the bigger items on top.Then he tarped down everything with a diamond hitch with new manila rope. Jim was eager to get started. The first few miles fell away quickly as both the sorrel and the mare stepped right along, almost as though they had been waiting for Jim Keaton to come along. There wasn't any real hurry, but it was always good to get away from town, any town, but dirty Rock Springs in particular. Coal dust and grime didn't fit in with wide open spaces and clean, crisp mountain air, at least not in Jim's way of thinking.

Jim knew that by keeping east of Quaking Aspen Mountain, the first big mountain out of town, he could set a course for Salt Wells Creek, some fifteen miles out. There would be a bit of a trail along the way, if he decided to use it. But why advertise the fact that he was heading out? A general bearing to the south or a little southeast would get him in sight of Diamond Peak within a day, so this would let him travel more cross-country and out of sight of perhaps most of the homesteaders and mountain folks, sheepherders, or cowboys. After all, just which group would he fit in with?

The first game Jim saw after leaving Rock Springs was a small herd of antelope, six or eight, standing off a hundred yards or so from the trail. How easy it would be to pop one with the .30-40 for supper. But then he would have to take time to handle the meat, and surely there would be others along the way, from what he had heard in town. No use being loaded down this early on the trip, he thought. Just enjoy the fresh air after all that coal dust back in town.

The country reminded Jim a lot of his days in Arizona: big, open country, not many trees, lots of grass and sagebrush, cactus, and sandy ground broken by rocky outcrops. Greasewood was mixed with sage in places, and up on the slopes there was a sparse sprinkling of cedar. The arroyos were dry and dusty, cut around many boulders and big, colorful rocks, pink and tan and gray. Water had not run here in many months, even looked as though it may never have run. Probably the best chance of moisture came from winter snows, melting to provide the country with enough dampness for the grass and sage.

The antelope had to have water, as did the other wildlife in the area. But nature provided for them, giving them the ability to smell out any water hole for miles. Back in the Arizona deserts, Jim had let the reins go on several occasions to allow his horse to find water. Invariably, the horse would head straight to water, often found in a sheltered place, under an overhang in the rocks where no one would likely find it on his own. He had even set snares at those holes, knowing that some small animal would have to venture in for water too, and he could capture himself a meal for survival. It was important, even vital, for anyone out in the wilds to understand his horse and to use it and its good senses. A horse would nearly always be the first to spot danger, sometimes only sensing it, but then zeroing in by pointing its ears alertly straight at it. Many a cowboy owed his life to his alert horse back in the Indian days.

The water in Salt Wells Creek wasn't too good, but it had to do. The creek was cut deep into the alkali flats, some of the small bluffs as much as twenty feet high and vertical. Only an occasional game trail gave access down to the water, plus the usual cuts from the arroyos that had washed deep entries down to the creek. The main traveled trail had to stay some distance from the stream in order to get around the steep washes. Down in the soft, sandy bottom, there were many signs of animal life of all kinds. They obviously made heavy use of this narrow, shallow stream for water, so Jim knew he could depend on having plenty of game along the way. The tracks indicated antelope with their little pointed toes and no dewclaws to show when the prints sank deeply in the sand and mud. There were larger deer tracks with deep-cut prints showing their dewclaws. Coyote and wolf tracks were plentiful, and occasionally he observed the track of a cat. This was the kind of country Jim could learn to like.

Jim couldn't help wondering why everyone he met cautioned him about moving down south of Rock Springs. Even back at Bitter Creek, Walt had talked about various cowboys, drifters, prospectors, and others being killed or simply vanishing in that country. And that good clerk in the mercantile store, Andy Ewing, had tried to talk him into heading out north. Andy did, however, mention that things would be okay if Jim tied in with the right people down south, without giving him any names, advising him to stay clear of problems, whatever they might be.

By the time Jim reached a spot where there were plenty of cedars and some oak brush down along the stream, the shadows were getting long. He had pushed the horses hard, considering they had been held in a small pen at the livery with little exercise over the last few weeks. They were a spunky pair, but there was no use overdoing the first day on the trail. Tomorrow would be a big day, what with the thought of reaching Diamond Peak and the diamond field—if he could locate it at all.

At midday of his second day on the trail, Jim knew he should turn away from Salt Wells Creek and try to cut east to intersect Vermillion Creek. Salt Wells headed in the pines four miles away, the first pines he had seen. If he continued in that direction, he would end up on the wrong side of Diamond Peak, according to the map made by Billy many years ago. Since Diamond Peak had been visible from all the higher points all day, Jim knew where he had to go. He was close now to his goal. It was within sight, only a few short hours away. He planned to hit Vermillion, follow it downstream into the Rife ranch country Walt Bentsen had told him about, and on until he came to the well-used trail heading south. He could follow the trail into Canyon Creek and then start watching for the long bench coming off Diamond Peak, where the diamond field ought to be. His evening camp might be made in Johnson Draw, maybe even in the remains of Billy's old camp.

CHAPTER 3

The cedar-rimmed bench coming off Diamond Peak had to be the diamond field bench, two or three miles away. A watered meadow meandered off to the east, and up its far reaches Jim thought he made out a slight trace of smoke. Surely no one would be camped way out here. Maybe it was a sheepherder's camp. In any case, he needed to know more about it, and he spurred the sorrel up the slight rise toward the smoke.

The long meadow had been used some in recent days. Here and there Jim picked up the broken-off tops of sage and grass. Whatever had been there had taken only the best grazing and moved on. There were game tracks showing, but no cattle tracks, maybe sheep. He crossed and continued on toward the trace of smoke that seemed to come from the next small valley beyond the first cedars. Entering the cedars, he knew he had best stay inside the cover offered. If the smoke was from a rustler's camp, he sure didn't want to be seen. Even if it was from a cowboy or herder camp, there was no point in letting them know he was around. The sorrel had pricked up his ears a couple of times, and even the mare was indicating something ahead, maybe livestock of some kind. The route took Jim away from the bench where he thought the diamond field might be, but he was taking no risk of being caught by a bunch of thieves or rustlers, the kind that would just as soon bushwhack a lone rider for his horse and pack animal as not.

After most of a mile ducking in and out of the cedars, Jim reached a high point that overlooked the entire upper meadow. He could see the makings of a nice, small stream. There were a few pines showing across the way, a sure sign that he had climbed up quite a way. He pushed his outfit back into the cedars a bit and stepped off the sorrel to have a look around. He took out the field glasses he had in his pack, tied the horses in a clump of dense cedar, and moved out to check the meadow.

Instantly Jim saw what the horses were trying to tell him. Not a quarter mile away, down near the little stream, stood a log cabin. It was a small thing, two rooms, maybe twelve feet square each, and with a stovepipe chimney emitting the trace of smoke he had first seen. There was a shed along one side, and nearby was a pen made from aspen poles, big enough for maybe a couple of horses. Not far from the entry was a wire stretched between two trees—a regular clothesline, not the normal sort of thing. Then off just a ways stood a well-built outhouse. No homesteader without a woman would spend his time putting in a quality outhouse and clothesline. But the haystack told the story: the place had to be that of a homesteader, preparing for the future, and there had to be a woman around. There were no signs of livestock, so Jim figured the fellow was out on the range somewhere checking his stock. And most likely the woman was with him. He felt sure he had not been detected, so he backed away, stepped up on the sorrel, and eased back deeper in the cedars. By cutting through the thickest part of the grove, he could cross a few draws and be back near the diamond bench, perhaps a mile away now.

It was good to know that someone was in the area who was not an outlaw—at least that is what he hoped. And if there was a woman living there too, it was a good bet that the outfit was straight. No rustling, just hardworking folks trying to make a go of a homestead.

As Jim rode through the shadowy cedars, a chill swept over him. He pulled the collar of his heavy coat up around his neck and ears to bring back a touch of warmth and hurried the sorrel along. It was getting late in the day to start trying to find the remains of a salted diamond field, especially since he only had the hand-drawn map to go by. Everything so far had been just as the map indicated, but there was no real scale to it, so anything might be way out of place. He broke out of the cedars onto the upper end of the bench he thought might hold the diamond field. He made a circle around, covering maybe a half mile, in hope of stumbling on to the signs of some kind of older activity. Directly toward the high point of Diamond Peak, there was a sharp-pointed knoll about a half mile from the bench. To Jim, this sure looked like it could be the knoll his brother had used many years ago to observe the diamond field. His pulse rate jumped as he thought how close he must be to the field.

Nothing seemed to show the possible old activity Jim hoped to find on the bench in his hurried look around. Good judgment told him to wait for tomorrow. For now, he needed to get situated somewhere for the night. He thought he ought to try to find Johnson Draw and drop down into it like his brother had done. After all, Billy had stayed most of a year out here, and this should mean that Johnson Draw had some good points for setting up housekeeping. He spurred the sorrel to a lope, with the mare right behind, heading for what he thought should be Johnson Draw.

In only a few hundred yards he came to the steep drop-off at the brink of a draw that rapidly became a full-blown canyon. The bottom appeared dry, but after dropping off into it, Jim drifted down to the first branch and found water. Obviously, the main fork would be the one carrying water, so Jim took a turn up the stream. The canyon was quite different from the country he had ridden through for the last couple of days: lush grass belly deep to the horses, some aspen, and lots of cedar, with pines up the slopes. Chokecherry and buckbrush was thick from time to time, and Jim could see why Billy might back up this canyon to put in a hidden shelter.

The game trail Jim followed led to another fork in the canyon, and there on the dividing point stood an abandoned cabin. He stopped his little troop for a look before moving ahead. As remote as this cabin was, any kind of outlaw might be in residence. Through his field glasses he determined the place was empty of humans, but it still might be occupied by varmints of the four-legged type. Regardless of how things looked from a hundred yards or so, Jim knew to approach carefully. He checked the ground for any tracks of shod horses or boots. None showed. He moved on in, resting his hand uneasily on the butt of his .45.

"Hello, in there," Jim called in a voice halfway between a call for an answer and of someone not wanting to be heard too far away. After a few moments, he called again. "Anyone home?" Nothing.

Jim stepped down from the sorrel and ground tied him to the spot. The cabin looked a little spooky, so he eased out the Colt .45 before moving inside. It was empty. It took a while to get used to the dim light filtering into the one-room cabin. He could tell that someone had lived there not too many years back. The logs were hewn partly flat on three sides, and the chinking between them was still in fair shape. The floor was covered with debris left by earlier visitors and recent animals. There was an old potbellied stove sitting in the center of the room and shelving along one side. The remainder of a table that hinged to the wall had no leg, so its one end was resting on the floor. On the opposite side of the room was a bunk bed, or what might pass for one. The remnants of the mattress showed that field mice had taken to it in a big way, leaving only bits and pieces scattered around. The door on a small cabinet on the other wall was closed and secured with a hasp with a hook hanging through it. Jim opened it and was surprised to find a lantern in working condition and a can of oil. There were odds and ends there too, but for the moment only the lantern held Jim's interest.

Out in the fading sunlight, Jim cleaned the lamp and poured in some of the oil. The wick was dried out, so he soaked it in oil before touching a match to it. The adjustments worked, and the globe was intact. He was beginning to feel right at home.

With that stroke of luck, finding the working lamp, Jim was elated. But he knew he had work to do in the brief time remaining before light left the canyon. It was already getting nippy, and he could see the chilled breath coming from both the sorrel and the mare. In the patch of aspens joining the cabin, he found the outlines of a corral where old tree branches had been utilized for fencing. The grass inside the small clearing was knee high, since nothing had used the place for years. Quickly Jim pulled together the useful limbs and added a few new ones and decided he had a good temporary corral for two horses. He led them down the few steps to water and returned them to the new corral for the night.

Next came the hurried cleanup of the cabin. In the fading light he made a hasty job of it, but he did find the old stove workable after cleaning out the hardened ashes of no telling how old. With a few dry branches from the pines and aspens, he had a cozy fire to knock the night chill from his new home. Out of his panniers came the tools for cooking, and before long he had bacon and pan-fried bread fit for anyone. Then he gathered pine boughs for a new mattress before spreading his tarp and bedroll on the bunk bed.

As a last move, he secured the plank door as best he could, bracing a log as thick as his arm from the floor to the center cross member. Then he checked his Colt .45, hung it handily, and blew out the old oil lamp. The night sounds of the canyon soon had him sound asleep.

The call of a pack of coyotes hunting their breakfast stirred Jim from sleep. For a few seconds he lay quietly, listening in the dim light of dawn for anything unusual. He heard the sounds of the sorrel and the mare grazing the deep grass in the hastily built corral. A few calls from magpies were letting all of nature know that someone had moved into the old cabin. The soft trickle of water in the nearby stream was reassuring. Maybe there would be trout in there for a varied menu, from time to time, he thought. They probably would have been stocked by a herder or cowboy if they didn't work their way up from Vermillion and the Green River when water was deep enough throughout the system. He would check for trout today, he was thinking, when a sound of footsteps on gravel brought him bolt upright in the bunk. He held his breath, not wanting to make a sound. Then he heard it again, with splashing sounds, like something or someone was crossing the creek. The horses were still grazing, so whatever was out there wasn't too interesting to them.

Jim slipped over to the door and removed the log brace as quietly as he could. He had the trusty Colt ready as he slowly pulled back the door. All sounds stopped. He could see downstream quite a way. Nothing there. When he turned to check upstream, he breathed a sigh of relief. A herd of mule deer stared intently at him, wondering whether to take flight or stand. They were grazing their way upstream to some secluded bed ground, probably a route they had been taking all their lives. Would the newcomer in the old cabin charge out to give them a chase, as would a mountain lion? Was he a threat to them at all? Or was he only another occupant of the canyon to live with? The old doe leader turned and silently moved a few yards up the slope, followed by several others. The only buck in the bunch quietly vanished into the thick cover. Jim then walked out the door, took a look around, and headed back in to start the coffee. A last glance back showed the deer standing, not much worried about his presence.

Jim spent the whole morning tidying up the cabin and reinforcing the fence around his corral. He found a good spring just upstream from the cabin a few yards, and this would be the place to fill his water bucket. He could run a short fence to the stream below the cabin to allow the horses to water there. A small meadow back up the draw just beyond the clump of trees around the cabin and corral would do for long-term grazing of the two horses. He would picket them first and then start using the hobbles, allowing him to find out just how close they might stay to the cabin. He sure couldn't afford to lose one of them.

Thoughts of the diamond field were hard to keep off his mind. He found himself hurrying on little jobs that shouldn't be hurried because of his desire to get on with the search for the field. He had even thought of possibly finding some of the salted gemstones, maybe enough to make the trip really pay off. By noon, he knew he simply had to saddle up and head for the lower bench, the spot where Billy had spent so much time placing the stones so that they would appear natural and then sitting on the knoll guarding the field until the trap was sprung.

In the discussions with Douglas Fitch back in Denver, Jim heard the details of how Billy, Arnold, and Slack had punched the holes down, dropped the rough stones in, and then covered them by stomping with their boot heels. The first snow or rain would wash out any evidence of man-sign. But just so the gullible moneygrubbers wouldn't miss finding some gemstones rather easily, they decided to pile up sand and fine gravel in mounds, looking a little like anthills. Into this mix they added very small gemstones. Anyone could kick over one of the mounds and sift through the loose material and, hopefully, find the "natural" gemstones brought up from deeper down by the ants. Those anthills were scattered over the area, and when Billy left that country, they were still there.

Now Jim needed that piece of information as one of the keys to the location of the diamond field. The ride out of Johnson Draw took only a few minutes. Then he crossed the upper end of the bench, jogging along, looking for any sign of unusual workings. He set up a grid across the bench, figuring that would be the best way. Otherwise, he could ride in circles for days and still not locate the field. He saw that he could scan about twenty-five yards on each pass across the bench, and since he knew the field was close to the cedars, he really didn't have to go all the way out on the bench. This would shorten his search considerably. The map of Billy's helped too by showing that the field was near the head of the bench where the cedars pinched out, for the most part.

The first couple of hours went by fast. The excitement of thinking he was close to the diamond field kept Jim's mind on nothing but the business at hand—the finding of the field. In particular, he should be able to see the fake anthills, if someone had not destroyed them to cover up the big hoax. The ground cover was sparse on the bench, with only a fair amount of grass and sage and no cedars, at least none out on the bench proper. He knew the men had used the nearby cedars for shade and firewood when they were showing the field to the financiers and mine owners from California while pulling off the hoax. So Jim decided to stay in the very edge of the cedars for a while and maybe pick up the site of some old campfire. To an Apache Indian tracker like Jim, the old camps would show up rather well for many years.

Then it happened: Jim came right out on top of an obvious campsite made dozens of years earlier. His heart skipped a few beats as he circled the spot, widening the circles on the upper side, out toward the bench top. In only a few minutes he found the first fake anthill. A quick look around showed dozens more, some kicked in, some not, but all washed mostly down by time. The general area was flat with sheets of rock making up most of the surface. The rocks had many narrow cracks or fissures in them. Jim was off the sorrel so suddenly that the horse shied back, taking the reins out of Jim's hand and prancing backward several steps before realizing that nothing was wrong. Jim quickly crouched over the best-looking anthill and started digging with his hands and boot heel. In only seconds he had it thoroughly torn apart and started sifting through the fine sand and gravel.

There before his eyes was a shiny, little green stone, not at all like what should be there. An emerald, if he was not mistaken. More scratching turned up a second small emerald and a beautiful red ruby. None of the stones was large enough to be of much value, but they proved the stories told by Billy those many years ago.

Jim spent the afternoon digging around in the old salted area, turning over rocks, scratching down in the cracks and seams, and finding a gemstone once in a while. Time had gotten away from him, and when the cool shadows started stretching over the bench, he noticed the cold seeping in around his neck. He turned up his collar and took a look around. He had done a lot of random searching. His find exceeded anything he might have dreamed of, about a dozen stones in all, mostly very small diamonds. None seemed to be of very good quality, but he wasn't much of a judge of gemstones. Maybe some were better than he thought. Or maybe they were all but valueless. After all, salting wasn't done with first-class stones.

Somehow, the ride back to the snug cabin in Johnson Draw seemed longer. He was tired, hadn't eaten all day in his excitement of the find, and was now getting cold. It was springtime, but up above seven thousand feet, it was still cold and not much different from winter, except for maybe a lack of snow. When he rounded the last bend in the canyon, he saw that the cabin looked the same. He thought of things that needed to be done to make it livable if he stayed very long. In the late twilight he noticed the dirt roof needed repairs and some of the brush up against the cabin walls should be grubbed back. Now that he had the diamond field located, he could probably take the time to make these improvements.

Jim spent the next few days scouting the country and fixing up the corral and cabin. He even found that trout did live in the small creek, so he made a crude seine from a gunnysack and proceeded to catch a dozen or so to fill out his bland diet. He found that antelope roamed all over the foothills of Diamond Peak, and they could be approached rather easily. The .30-40 made quick work of a young doe, which gave Jim fresh meat plus a hide to use for various things. He cut it into narrow strips and made excellent ties for everything around the cabin. In some of the seep-spring areas he found wild onions that would flavor up any meal, and he found a few piñon nuts that could be pounded into pemmican made with dried antelope or deer meat. This had been a favorite food in Arizona when traveling, and he had learned to make it from various items, all good.

Jim had been in the area for a few days, and he wondered why he had not seen any ranchers, herders, or drifters. Of course, there was the homesteader's cabin he stumbled on only a couple of miles from the diamond field. Andy's cautionary advice to stay clear of any of the rough fellows common to the Brown's Park country surely would not include this homesteader. But even homesteaders could be rustlers—or worse.

Out on the desert flats Jim made a discovery that bothered him a little: the tracks of a large herd of sheep. Ranchers were using this part of the country for winter sheep pasture. Where they might be, or where they might show up, was a question Jim needed to answer. If they moved up on the diamond bench, they would surely see that he had been around. If they found him, they would have some questions that he didn't want to answer. Someone might still hold a mining claim on the diamond field, and he could be called a claim jumper. Sometimes that got serious enough for a rope party, and he would be the guest of honor. No, he wasn't ready for all that. Maybe he had best get up on the high knoll that his brother had used and try to locate the herd or herder first. If they were still out there, they could be seen for miles from that high point. If no one showed, maybe they had just passed through. Precaution was what had kept Jim alive in the Apache days, and it should still serve him well.

For the next few days Jim's time was spent the same: up at dawn, saddle up and ride to the high knoll, picket the sorrel out of sight, set up in a secluded spot with a good view of the low country, search for anyone out on the flats, and then go down to the diamond field for prospecting. Then he would head back to the knoll to wait out the day, using his field glasses to check anything that moved in the lower country. He looked directly down on the diamond field, and this proved that no one was hanging around there. And he saw no more sign of any sheep herd or herder in the area.

Jim had been watching the country for a week when he came down from the high knoll one evening and found fresh shod tracks of a horse near his cabin. They meandered along the little creek and ended where someone had tied the horse near the cabin entrance. Around the cabin were fresh boot tracks, the heels all full and square, showing little or no wear. Someone had been in the cabin, but after a quick inspection, Jim could find nothing missing. There had not even been a meal taken, as might happen if the intruder was a drifting cowboy or traveler. Back outside, Jim took a close look at the hoofprints and found the shoes were in very good condition, little or no wear as might be the case if the horse belonged to a herder or someone who had to use horseshoes that were not necessarily new. Added up, this looked like someone of means had visited him, not just a common hand or drifter.

Although Jim had not met any of the local ranchers, he had heard enough about them from Walt Bentsen and Andy Ewing to know that several didn't have to work too much to get by quite well. Out toward Bitter Creek that would mean the Ericksons, maybe the Rifes, and a couple of others farther away. Then down toward Brown's Park there would be several, maybe the Jarvies, Crouses, Bassetts, Davenports. Then up out of the Park and down along Talamantes Creek was Sparks and in Beaver Basin was Cole, both with big sheep outfits. They would be the closest to Jim. It might be possible that they had found him while riding out to oversee some of their herders. Still, it could be anyone. Jim would have to be doubly cautious. Someone might not like his moving in. Maybe the cabin was on a homestead, all legal in someone's name.

The next day Jim had to go on about his business, even though he was concerned about the stranger drifting around the area. He took the sorrel back up to the high knoll, but this time he picketed him in a different place, a little more secluded. When he went to his lookout, he changed that spot a little too. Hopefully, he might see the stranger from this vantage point and determine who he might be. He decided to sit on the backside of the knoll looking toward Johnson Draw.

The day passed slowly. The sun was warm, making him drowsy. All the game animals had found shade and bedded for the day, except the antelope that he could see down on the flats. They must sleep at night, just like people, he thought as he gazed idly across the grassy, sage-covered country. The heat waves shimmered across the foothills, making some of the antelope appear to be floating above ground.

Jim had fallen asleep when the whinny of the sorrel startled him to reality. This was like a bugle call from the army days, a definite call to action. He quickly rolled over into thicker brush and brought his .30-40 up close. He checked his trusty Colt to be sure it was available too. He had listened for not more than a minute or so when the sorrel whinnied again, a bit more excited. Jim knew someone was around. He crawled through the cover, keeping the .30-40 in front of him. Then he saw the rider coming directly toward him, looking at the sorrel from time to time. It was as though the rider knew right where Jim was. But how could he? He had been in a good location, hard to see from almost anywhere. Had the rider been watching him? Surely no one could have sneaked up on him that easily, but that could happen when you allow yourself to doze off.

When the lone rider was still a full hundred yards away, he called out, "Hello, up there. Coming up to visit with you."

"Come on," replied Jim, for lack of any other response.

The horse and rider picked their way up the knoll, past the sorrel, and right up to Jim, who by now was standing uneasily, ready for whatever might happen. In his days scouting Apaches he had seen many a trooper fooled by this kind of approach, and now they were pushing up cactus on the Arizona desert.

"Boy! Ain't this a fine day!" called the rider as he stepped down off the good-looking roan. "I haven't minded being out a bit."

"Well, now, it really has been a nice day. You caught me dozing off a bit there. Kind of surprised me," Jim said, noticing that the rider wasn't carrying a handgun, but there was a Winchester in the saddle boot.

"Name's Ed Cole, up in Beaver Basin."

"Nice to meet you, Ed," answered Jim. "I'm Jim Keaton from down in Texas."

"Lord, man! What on th' face of th' earth are you doing out in this country? I always heard that Texas was like dying and going to heaven! And you jest up and left?" Ed asked as he scratched around in the dirt preparing a place to squat for a while.

"Oh, I had a place down there, but then I got a chance to sell it at a price I jest couldn't refuse. Back in my scouting days with th' army some of my buddies were from up this way. They talked so much 'bout it, I jest decided it was time to come see fer myself," Jim said, trying to be as convincing as possible. After all, he did know enough about ranching and about Texas to tell a good story. And he sure didn't want anyone knowing about his connection with the diamond field.

"How 'bout some coffee, Ed? I've got th' makings over in my

saddlebags. Jest my dozing off tells me it's time," Jim offered as he moved toward the wallowed-out spot in the brush where he had spent the day.

"Sure thing, Jim. Been in th' saddle most all day myself. Well, 'cepting th' time I've been watching you over here." Ed grinned a bit, knowing Jim didn't realize he had been seen.

"You been seeing me all day?" said Jim, startled enough that it showed all over him.

"Ye see, Jim, when I was cutting across Johnson th' other day to go out on th' Canyon Creek divide to check up on one of my herders, I dropped by th' old homestead cabin jest to see that it was still there. And guess what I found, Jim? Someone had done moved in!" Ed was enjoying playing cat and mouse with Jim, and Ed knew he had Jim at a bad disadvantage.

Jim went on with gathering a few sticks for a fire. He pulled his saddlebags from under a stunted cedar and prowled through them getting out the coffee pot, coffee, and his one cup.

"You're welcome to th' only cup I've got, Ed," he said as he handed it to Ed.

"No, no, Jim. I always carry one too. Might even have some jerky or something to go along with th' coffee." Ed stepped away toward his roan that was contentedly grazing nearby.

Jim had the fire going in jig time, poured water into the coffee pot from his canteen, dropped in a good handful of fresh ground coffee, and turned to watch Ed while he loosened the cinch on the roan, seemingly preparing for a longer visit.

"Hey, Jim, how do you like good elk jerky?" called out Ed. "I got this elk jest a couple of months back, down on th' Green River in th' snow. Not too many left there, you know."

"Don't know 'bout elk jerky. Tried most every other kind, but never elk," Jim answered in his easygoing way.

This Ed was sort of coming on to Jim, real friendly like. Maybe he wasn't such a bad fellow to know after all. But from past experience,

Jim knew not to be too quick to take to any stranger. Even at that, there was something about the man, something Jim just couldn't put his finger on.

"So you found my use of th' old cabin, did you, Ed? If it's yours and you'd rather me not stay there, I won't mind getting out any time you say," Jim said to turn the discussion to how or why Ed was down in Johnson Draw.

"No, no, Jim. That old place was jest a rundown shack, 'bout to fall in till a homesteader came along some years back. Thought he could make it out here with some cattle on th' claim, you know, after th' government decided to give 160 acres if anyone could prove up on it. Back East that would be a lot of country, but not out here! No sir! That would barely keep a feller alive. 'Course, th' feller didn't even seem to have any livestock when he first showed up. Then in no time at all, he had twenty-five decent-looking cows. Trouble was they carried someone else's brand," Ed waited for Jim's comment.

"You don't mean it? A real rustler, right out here?" said Jim.

"Sure thing. Nobody knowed much 'bout it fer a while. Then one day one of my herders came loping in on his horse, all sweaty and winded. Said that feller had cut out over a hundred head of my best sheep and was driving them way too fast toward Bitter Creek. Guess he was going to try to sell 'em 'fore we could catch up with him. He didn't make it." Ed paused long enough to let that point sink in with Jim. "Got th' sheep back to th' herd all right, only lost a couple 'cause of th' run he put 'em through. Kind of figured since he didn't really need th' few head of cows anymore, might jest as well put my brand on 'em. After searching fer th' rightful owner, you understand."

Ed was a pretty salty old fellow. Maybe that was why Jim felt slightly uneasy about him. Maybe it showed in the way he looked at Jim. Hard to imagine how folks really are, without knowing them.

"Th' coffee's boiling, Ed. Hand me your cup."

Jim poured each of them a full cup of boiling black coffee, the kind that could walk off alone, the kind anyone out on the open range appreciated. So strong it might last them till they came onto another batch, somewhere on down the line.

"Ed, what could you do with double-branded cattle and no real bill of sale?" Jim asked.

"Oh, that's not too much of a problem out here, if you know jest where to move 'em to. Over in Brown's Park there's several fellers always looking fer cattle, cheap. They don't ask 'bout brands. They move 'em across th' state line, jest a few miles, you know. How 'bout more jerky?" Ed said as he handed Jim the leather pouch.

Jim was thinking all kinds of thoughts. Is this friendly man a killer? Did he really just kill the sheep rustler out there in the sage and leave him for the coyotes? Would he do in just anyone or only those that needed done in? Maybe he was like so many others Jim had known in the past that wouldn't harm a hair on the head of anyone they took a liking to, but for others, watch out.

"Then I take it th' cabin may be open fer my use? Might jest be here a while, Ed. Need somebody like you to maybe steer me right, since I might need to locate some place to homestead fer myself. Or maybe buy, if th' price was right. From this cabin I could probably get around to seeing a lot of country. Any ideas on something like this, Ed?" Jim asked, wanting to get the subject back to more civil things.

"Well, from what I've seen, you've been more interested in th' diamond field."

Just how long had this Cole fellow been out there watching him? Jim thought he had been keeping a sharp eye out for anyone that might have seen him digging around in the diamond field. Until now, he was sure no one had. But then how could this fellow know so much about what Jim was up to?

"Oh? You've been watching me, have you, Ed?"

"Sure, Jim. Ever since I found you in th' cabin and trailed your horse out to th' diamond flats. You're not th' first to go digging 'round out here. And I'll bet you're not th' last, neither," said Ed with a twinkle in his eye. He seemed pleased that Jim had not known he had been watching.

"And if you don't mind my guessing," Ed continued, "I think I may know more 'bout you and th' diamond field than you'd ever think. Could I be right, Jim? You wanna hear me out? You ain't like most of 'em. Seems you got more interest in it than most. Like maybe you know more 'bout it than most, or even anyone. 'Course, I can see you ain't old enough to have been in on it. But it could have been your old dad, couldn't it? Or maybe that Arnold or Slack was your uncle? And after watching you come up here on this knoll every day, sort of watching fer something, just like you knew this was th' lookout point. Well, all I had to do was put two and two together, and there it was, plain as day! You was in on it. Least you sure do know more 'bout it than all them others put together. There always was a rumor that there was someone else involved, and some of th' stories even talked 'bout posting a guard or lookout up here, right where you headed.

"Gosh, Jim, I didn't notice how late it was getting," Ed said. 'Spose we ought to head down off here. Getting kind of cold, like maybe th' weather might change. Winter ain't over this time of year. Still might get a late blizzard. Could we head down to th' cabin fer the night? Got lots to talk about, Jim. I jest think you are going to be a real good neighbor."

Jim was confused. Here he had gone to a lot of trouble to keep his connection with the diamond field secret, and the first guy to meet up with him seemed able to read his mind. Was he that easy to figure out? Had he been too obvious?

The ride back to the Johnson Draw cabin was quiet. The hooves of the horses turned over rocks now and then, and they ran into a herd of mule deer coming out of the cedars for their nightly grazing. The sun dropped below the rim, and the first evening star shone brightly in the west. The cabin looked dark when they rode into the little corral, unsaddled, and saw to the horses. They then went in to fire up the old stove, cook up a meal, and talk.

They talked late into the night and covered any and all kinds of subject matter—horses, cattle, sheep, local folks, rifles, old days, and more. Both men seemed pleased to have the company of the other, but Jim thought Cole was holding back on something, maybe just the parts of his life that were best not discussed. Of course, that was nothing more than the old code of the West.

The talk drifted to the little cabin they were in and the corral and small meadow Jim was using for his horses. Ed described how he had first been in Johnson Draw back in the early '80s, not long after moving into Brown's Park, staying with the old-time family, the Bassetts, who were there to this day. He told of the little homestead Jim had discovered not far south and east of the diamond field. It belonged to a man and his wife who came out to set up several years earlier. Good folks. Ed told of how all the ranchers got out of the country back in '79 when the Ute Indians went on the warpath and how they went up to Green River City till it was over. Most folks were still concerned over another possible Indian uprising when Ed first entered Brown's Park, then known as Brown's Hole.

They moved on to discussing the homestead laws. Ed related how all the original settlers had to make claim on the country they had lived on for those many years, how some failed to protect what they all considered their land rights. Ed and others had their cowboys make claims, get title, and then sell the claims to their bosses, including Ed. He ended up holding most of the better water holes around Beaver Basin and Diamond Peak. When the rustler met his end over the sheep, the very cabin they were in became part of Ed's water hole plan. The so-called homesteader had fixed the cabin up a lot, making it tight and chinked good for the winters. Ed then sent his herder over to Hahn's Peak, the Routt County seat, to get a homestead set up. After the claim became final, Ed bought it from the herder for almost nothing, since the herder never fully understood what was going on.

Somehow, this bit of information disappointed Jim, without any real reason. Even though Jim had done a little work on the place getting it in shape to stay for a while, it had never entered his mind that it had grown on him. Jim had scouted it out enough to find that if he owned it, he could probably make a go of the place. It was well watered, had plenty of excellent grazing, had shelter for the winters, and was remote enough to keep strangers from dropping in unannounced. With the unsettling bit of information that Cole owned the cabin, Jim found himself tired out, ready to get in the bunk.

"Let's call it a night, Ed. If we don't, we might jest as well start breakfast!"

"Well stated, my friend. I still need to get on with my flock checking tomorrow. Could go along, if you jest want to see more country, you know," said Ed, leaving the obvious open invitation.

"Golly, Ed. I'd sort of like that. Didn't expect to have a guide fer seeing what was out around here. I believe I'll join up with you then."

CHAPTER 4

Their long, hard day caused them to sleep in the next morning, not getting the coffee on till well after sunup. The canyon was warming fast as Ed led Jim out toward the desert flats. They had put together a bit of grub, maybe enough for a couple of days, and rolled up a good bedroll and some cooking utensils. They didn't need Jim's pack mare because they didn't plan to be gone that long. Just going out to make the rounds of Ed's herders out on Shell and Dry Creeks, check the condition of the sheep, and then head on up to Cold Spring Mountain where he had moved an early herd from the winter grounds. They would probably be staying in the sheep camps and would share provisions.

"Ed, why did you move those sheep up on Cold Spring Mountain this early? Could still get some bad weather. Might lose some."

"Jim, you don't know jest what's going on out here. Got to protect th' summer grounds from outside crowders. Looks like they intend to push some of us off th' mountain, taking it fer themselves," said Ed as he drifted off into thoughts of his own.

Jim didn't fully follow what Ed was telling him, but he did know from talks with Walt and Andy that something sure might be going on in this part of the country. He had understood that it was maybe all happening down in Brown's Park, not up toward the Wyoming line. But if there was friction between the cattlemen and sheepmen, it had to include the country to the north of the Park. That's where most of the sheep always came from.

The first camp was at least fifteen miles off the mountain, out on the flat near Shell Creek. Water was scarce out there, and Shell carried mostly snowmelt or rain, with springs few and far between. Ed knew the country like the back of his hand and had every spring mentally marked. The herder had the sheep out a mile or so from his wagon, and after visiting with him for a while, they left a pair of border collies in charge of the herd and headed toward the camp. The two collies were responsible for keeping off the coyotes and wolves and took orders from the herder just like a buck private in the army. Ed had introduced the herder as Rudy, a herder that only came to him recently.

At the wagon Rudy made up a pot of black coffee while Ed took inventory of what was needed to keep him supplied for the next month or so. Together, they whipped up a meal while discussing the movement of the herd. Ed wanted the sheep moved to the mountain by the end of the month, so Rudy would start grazing them in that direction tomorrow. Then Jim and Ed stretched out on the ground under the shelter of the wagon for a rest, still talking about the job at hand. After too brief a time, Ed was up tightening the cinch on his roan, getting ready to move out. Within just minutes the sorrel and the roan were heading south into some of the most desolate country Jim had ever seen. It was called Dry Creek, a well-deserved name.

An eight-mile ride found them at the second herder's wagon, situated on a spring that the herder had dug out. In that country it was common for water to be in the watercourse, but underground. All herders knew just where to dig down to find it, almost always less than two or three feet. Sometimes there wasn't enough to supply the camp, and the herder had to move to a better spot. There were no trees out in Dry Creek, no shade, no wood for fires. Again, by digging a little, the herders could find underground roots of sage or greasewood to maintain a fire and could use dried buffalo chips when they might find enough of them.

The thousand or so sheep were only a few hundred yards from the wagon, and the herder had started for camp as soon as he saw Ed and Jim riding in. The horse used to pull the wagon doubled as the herder's riding horse and was hobbled nearby. It was an Appaloosa from some Indian's herd, no doubt, and was typically spotted across the rump. He had the Roman nose, big head, and probably even the crazy-looking pink eyes, Jim thought. A cowboy wouldn't be caught riding one of those, so they ended up as herder horses mostly.

"Hello, amigo," Ed called out to the herder as he walked around the wagon tongue.

"Buenos dias, Senor Ed," came the response. The herder was a Mexican, the same as Rudy, and this tickled Jim, who came from the Mexican border and spoke Spanish as fluently as English. Jim also knew that if this Mexican had been along the border, he could speak and understand English very well too. At times, however, the border Mexicans would indicate that they "no savvy English" in an effort to hear the gringos talk openly about their plans. This caused many gringos, Texans in particular, to come down hard on any Mexican, forcing him to admit his knowledge and understanding of English. Then all conversation would be conducted in English. This was the Texans' way of making all Mexicans use the English language if they were planning to work on this side of the border.

"Jim, this is Juan. He came to me from your country, somewhere along the Rio Grande," said Ed.

"Oh, good, Juan. I'm Jim, from down there too. And I know you'll use English! Right, Juan?" Jim replied quickly, a habit he had picked up over the years in dealing with border Mexicans.

"Si, senor ... I mean, yes, Mr. Jim, yes." The herder caught on fast. He was rather young, maybe in his early twenties, slim and trim, with a bright smile and the obvious look of intelligence.

Then Jim passed a few words with Juan in flawless Spanish to let him know he could understand anything Juan might say in that language. Both then knew right where the other one stood.

"Jim, I never even thought you could talk that lingo. 'Course, I should've knowed you could, coming from that part of th' country and all. You know, you might be more help to me than I thought. There's lots of times these herders get off together and get to talking that Mex, and I don't pick up but part of what they are saying. Why, they might even be planning a lynching party fer me, and I'd never even know," Ed said with a little twinkle in his eye.

The three then sat and discussed the condition of the sheep, the losses caused by a big gray wolf that got in among the herd a week earlier, and the hilarious story of how Juan ran out of the wagon in his long-handle underwear with nothing more than a table knife to chase the marauder away. The sheepdogs helped by barking, but they sure didn't want any part of that wolf.

"Juan, I guess I'll jest have to get you a rifle if these wolves keep coming 'round. We sure can't stand losing many sheep that way. Can you shoot?"

"Si, Ed. I shoot pretty well. Never had much ammunition to practice with, but did have a rifle in every camp I've been in," said Juan. "Mostly .32-40s, even a .44-40, once."

Ed did another survey of things Juan needed for the camp and helped down a big pot of coffee. The day was getting late. Jim and Ed had to plan on staying the night with Juan, or they had to hit the saddles in a hurry to get on up toward Irish Canyon. Ed knew there should be water at Irish Lake, a spot he often used for a camp before heading up to the top of Cold Spring Mountain.

It was almost dark when they arrived at Irish Lake, and they had to scurry around to get a fire going and make the open camp before the pitch-black night descended. The night was not too cold, but the fire sure felt good. They had been in the saddle too long for one day, but they had covered both the lower sheep camps. They only had the one on Cold Spring Mountain left to check.

"Jim, have you ever killed a man?"

"Why, uh, what do you mean, Ed?" came Jim's startled reply.

"Well, jest that, Jim. You been all over that Apache country."

"Oh, you mean an Injun, don't you, Ed? Sure, I got into it with them when I wasn't old enough to be doing it. Wasn't even out of my teens when I had to go out on a patrol, and we got hemmed in by 'bout a dozen Apaches up Cedar Canyon. Boy, I sure was scared! I'd jest seen my first soldier that was scalped only a couple of days before. He was a mess. Hung on a day or two and then died. So when we got cornered in that canyon, that was all I could think of … being scalped. The sergeant got an arrow in his leg right off, blood jest a-running. Then one missed me by no more than an inch, and somehow I knew my life wasn't likely worth much unless I took hold and did something to keep them savages back from us. Two troopers got killed in th' first attack, both shot with an old musket and then filled up with arrows. So, the next one that got close enough, I jest took a real calm aim, jest like you would do on a deer, and pulled th' trigger. I still remember th' blood spurtin' out his middle. Then he turned 'round, and it jest looked like his whole insides was falling out. He was dead right there. We fought 'em off fer two or three hours before they gave up and left. By then I guess I was what you might call an experienced Injun fighter. Killed three that day myself."

"What 'bout anyone else, like maybe a white man, or Mex?" asked Ed.

"Well, later—a couple of years maybe—I got mixed up with having to watch over th' captain's wife while he was out on patrol," Jim began to tell his story. "Somehow, he always thought I was th' only one to watch after her. Seems she told him th' other troopers sometimes looked like they jest might harm her, break into her place at night. Anyway, she put th' captain on to using me as guard.

"One night I was jest dozing near the front porch when that lady went to screaming fer all she was worth. I jumped up and started fer th' upstairs. That was where th' bedrooms was. Then all of a sudden she come flying out th' door, landed flat on her back, and didn't have hardly no clothes on, or maybe left on. That is, a tough older trooper had gone in and got her and tore away most of her clothes. Guess he was going to do something to her, if he could.

"Well, when I saw this, I didn't know what might be next, but I had my .45-70 cocked and ready, and when that feller lunged out that door after her, I jest yelled loud as I could. Hoped he would stop, but he didn't. He came fer me, all the while pulling his pistol from his belt. Before I knew what happened, I'd done gone and shot him, right through th' middle. Always was a good shot. He fell right across that poor lady, and she jest passed plumb out. Then th' night orderly was there. He just stood and stared. He didn't know what to do. Then some more guards showed up, and we started trying to get things straightened out. I jest knew I'd done something bad. Ended up getting a medal for being brave. Can you imagine? For being brave, when I was scared half out of my wits!" Jim stopped talking and stared into the campfire for a while.

"Didn't mean to get you all up over something that happened that long ago," said Ed. "I sort of thought you knew how killing went."

"Why'd you ask, Ed?"

"No reason, Jim. It's always good to know more 'bout who you're with."

The next morning they started the ride up the steep trail heading out of Irish Canyon toward the top of Cold Spring Mountain by way of Limestone Ridge. Jim rode silently, his thoughts on what Ed meant by asking if he had ever killed anyone. Was he possibly working up to something else? Did he need to know that Jim knew how to kill, even if it did happen during army times and in the line of duty? And since Ed had told him about killing the rustler, was he letting him know they were both of the same cut of cloth? Questions seemed to be piling up around Jim's new friend, and answers were not coming. At least not right now.

"Jim, I better tell you where we're headed," said Ed. "Seems some folks have gone to thinking they ought to own all of this mountain instead of sharing it like most of us have done fer many years. Th' trouble might have started when Goodman sold out his place to this feller up from Texas, feller named Matt Rash. He's always seemed to be a good sort, well, up till recently. Then a few months ago my herder told me 'bout seeing two fellers driving 'bout twenty-five steers pretty hard across Dry Creek. Looked like they was heading on over Limestone, right up on Cold Spring. 'Course, the herder couldn't follow to see, but soon as he told me, I cut out to try to pick up their tracks. Sure enough, there they were. And they went right over Limestone and on up past Bassett Springs and over toward N S Creek. By then I was sure I knew jest who it had to be. Since there was two of 'em, I knew th' other one too. Had to be Rash and his buddy, Isom Dart. He's sort of black like. The two of them come up together from Texas or there 'bouts. Both worked fer them Bassetts and stayed there, mostly. Isom uses a cabin on th' far end of Cold Spring, not too far from my place, and we really didn't think much 'bout it. He was a good sort too. Till recently."

"But, Ed, how did you know Matt was pushing those steers? And what of it? He's in that business, ain't he?" Jim pointed out in his quiet manner. He had seen others accused unjustly and knew he never wanted to be in on anything like that.

"Jim, I'm jest like you. I ain't going in on a feller without really knowing th' truth first. So I watched fer th' chance to visit Matt's cabin and corral while he was gone. Has a little cabin there on N S Creek, you know. Sure 'nough, in 'bout a week he packed up to go over to Ashley Valley, taking, of all things, some beef to sell. I slipped up to th' cabin and sure 'nough out near th' corral I found several hides with th' brands cut out. I jest knew th' rest of them steers was on down th' way at Summit Springs with ol' Isom. A few days later I rode through Isom's small bunch of cattle, and mixed among 'em was 'bout a dozen steers with strange brands."

"What's this got to do with me?" asked Jim.

"Once we get up on top, we jest might run into one of them fellers," answered Ed. "Matt's place ain't too far along Cold Spring. 'Course, then when they see you riding with me, they jest might get to thinking th' two of us is working together. Maybe even both running some sheep together. This is what I've been telling you, Jim. These are th' ones that are trying to push th' sheep off Cold Spring Mountain. They jest moved up here recently. Always before they kept all their stock down in Brown's Park. They joined in with some outsiders that come into th' Park a while back and even killed a couple of herders. Then they told th' sheepmen to get out of th' area, even though they were th' original homesteaders. Beat th' stuffing out of one sheepman. Even put a rope 'round his neck and sort of stretched him. Almost choked him to death."

Ed talked like he had never talked before, giving Jim details of things that were going on and were not any of Jim's business, at least till now.

"Ed, if I got caught having to take sides, you look like you're a good sheepman, doing your job, trying to make an honest living. That's what I've always done too. So if someone is fighting 'gainst that, then I guess they would be fighting 'gainst me, don't you think, Ed?" Jim said as they rode over the top to see all of Cold Spring Mountain spread out in front of them.

The top of Cold Spring Mountain was a big plateau, maybe three to five miles wide and more than fifteen miles long. Grass was belly deep to a good-size horse, and springs came up everywhere. Off the south and west side were solid cedar thickets running clear down into Brown's Park. The Green River was visible far below, maybe eight miles away. Ed pointed out the red cliffs plunging down over a thousand feet on each side of the river in Lodore Canyon, some fifteen miles away. This was a sight that Jim had often thought about, a closed-in, big valley with a river running through, meadows all across the bottoms, lots of grass, good springs. No wonder the folks in Brown's Park were jealous of what they had. Jim figured he would fight for it too if it was his.

They rested the horses for a while, just taking in the view.

"Ed, where do all these folks live? I don't see any settlement down there," Jim asked.

"Oh, you have to kind of know jest right where th' cabins are. They ain't in sight from here 'cause mostly they are right up against th' foot of this mountain, backed up in them cedars or part way up a draw. There are some across th' river, but not where we could see 'em. Can't see th' cattle. Too far," said Ed.

"Jim, I guess if we meet up with these guys, I'll jest tell 'em you are on your own, jest looking fer maybe a place to homestead or maybe buy. That way, if they have bad thoughts, they can be on me. I get along with them all right, long as they don't know I'm on to them rustling. They already told me and Sparks that we would have to give up some of this top country or leave. They intend to put more of their cattle up here."

"Sounds good, Ed. Besides, I probably ought to go down in the Park and get acquainted with most of them. Might want to live here fer a long time. If the right place was available, 'course," said Jim. And, he thought to himself, the right place just might be back in Johnson Draw, if he could get the rights from Ed.

Jim could not help noticing the game on Cold Spring Mountain: mule deer and antelope mostly and a variety of smaller animals and birds. As they rode along, Jim asked Ed about the wildlife, pointing out the many bucks they saw with their antlers heavy in velvet, still growing daily.

"You ain't seen nothing like was here a few years back," Ed lamented. "Why, we used to come up here and not even bring grub. Jest counted on shooting a deer or antelope fer every meal. Threw away what we didn't eat. Used to shoot 'em with .45s. Didn't need these long-range rifles. 'Course, every now and then we'd run into a bear. They are gone now. Maybe one shows up once in a while. Then way back we had a lot of elk around. They're gone now too. Sometimes I can still find one down along the Green River, and once in a while one will wander through this part of th' country, probably lost or crazy."

"Ed, where do you think your sheep are on th' mountain? Is your herder with them?" Jim asked, changing the subject to get back to their reason for being on Cold Spring Mountain.

"Oh, Jim, they might be anywhere. Should be pretty far along th' mountain, probably off th' north side, maybe up to th' top, maybe not. Th' herder will keep close watch on them. He has a couple of dogs too.

'Course, if Rash or someone had a mind to, they sure could chase 'em off. You know, they clubbed a bunch of sheep to death a while back," said Ed as he slapped the roan on the rump and stepped up the pace.

The ride out across the top of Cold Spring Mountain was varied, with stands of aspen mixed with buckbrush and chokecherry, all separated by expanses of sage, greasewood, and deep grass. They had to ride around rock outcroppings and made short detours around abrupt little draws that always had a few deer hidden in the brushy bottoms. From the higher ground the view ahead was open for one to three miles, still on the mountain, really a high plateau. The fast trot that Ed set up in the crisp early morning air caused Jim to pull his collar up against the chill, and steam rose off both horses every time they slowed a little.

"Won't be far to Bassett Springs, Jim. We'll let th' horses blow a minute there. If you followed th' drainage off to th' left there, you would end up in old man Bassett's yard. 'Course, that'd be a tough ride, what with all them thick cedar and rock ledges going off toward th' Green River. Stayed with them folks a while when I first come to this country. Got along fine. You might need to meet them sometime, since they seem to be th' kingpins of th' Park, or at least some of 'em seem to think so."

"Hold up, Ed!" Jim warned. "There's a rider up there. Looks like he's looking fer something!"

"Where's he at, Jim?" Ed asked. "I thought I could see most everything 'head of us. Been sort of watching fer anything out of place."

"He's jest off in th' aspens down to th' right, maybe most of a mile. See him ducking in and out 'round that big rock pile, Ed?"

Jim pulled his sorrel up just behind a spot of tall brush, motioning to Ed to move over with him to stay out of sight. From the saddlebags Jim took out his field glasses and started searching the country ahead. The rider had only been in sight for a few seconds, just long enough for Jim to see that he was looking alertly about him, watching for something or somebody.

"There he is, Ed. Just coming out from them rocks. What do you make of him?"

"Don't rightly know, Jim. That big horse sort of looks like it might belong to Charley Sparks. You know, th' feller I told you 'bout that lives down Talamantes Creek below me. A good sort of feller, runs sheep over here with me mostly. We divide th' country. Kind of early in th' year to see him up here if it is him."

"Take a look through these glasses when he comes out of the aspens, Ed. Don't really like to have folks ride up on me unknown like," said Jim as he handed the glasses to Ed.

"That sure 'nough is ol' Charley! Gosh, Jim, these things really help th' seeing. Why, I can even see th' markings on th' horse and th' kind of rags Charley's wearing! Let's hurry along and try to catch him. Looks like he's heading fer Cold Spring. We can veer off a little and ought to jest 'bout meet him up there. He maybe can tell us where my herder and flock might be. Don't think he seen us at all, Jim. Like he's looking fer some lost stock, maybe one of his horses. We're jest three or four miles above his place right now," said Ed as he passed the glasses back to Jim and spurred his roan.

Jim's sorrel felt the twinge of excitement when Ed's roan suddenly jumped out to a lope, and before Jim hardly knew it, the sorrel was right behind Ed's horse. Jim had no idea where the spring was, but he knew Ed had every nook and cranny of the whole plateau set to memory. Since Sparks was down a bit lower and in an aspen thicket, Ed and Jim would be out of sight on the flat top of the mountain.

In less than a mile, a patch of aspen showed up ahead, and Jim knew the spring would be there. They slowed to a trot before suddenly seeing the big horse and Charley Sparks standing in the edge of the trees staring out at them cautiously. They had surprised him. Ed waved, but Sparks didn't move. They trotted over toward him, closing the distance.

Ed hollered out, "Don't you give a friend a greetin' no more, Charley?"

"Why, if it ain't Ed Cole! You sure are a long way off th' desert to be a sheepman, Ed," said Sparks as he quickly put his horse to a trot to meet Ed and Jim. "And two of you too! Why, I could have mistook you fer rustlers or worse, Ed. Let's get over to th' spring and get down fer a spell."

At the spring the three men dismounted and checked their saddles, loosening the cinches to give the horses a breather. Then Ed introduced Jim to Sparks, and they found a place to build a fire and make coffee. The sun was getting high enough to warm up the country, and the shade of the aspens would be welcome.

"Jim here is new to th' country, Charley. He come up from Texas looking fer a place to set a few head of cattle on. Maybe homestead or something, I thought he must've got hisself lost to be way out here. Some of his old army troopers had told him how nice we was up here. Even said the land was good! Now, Charley, don't you go telling him no different," said Ed as he tested the coffee.

"Well, Jim, if you come all the way up here looking fer a spread, you deserve a good look around. Lots of this country is taken up, but there's always room fer a good man. There's been a couple of places left recently. Well, they are legally open. Just have to know your way 'round. Not too good an idea to plan on setting up on one if certain fellers are maybe using it," Sparks said, words trailing off under his breath.

Now Jim was hearing things similar to what he heard back in town about what might be going on in Brown's Park and on Cold Spring Mountain. And Jim thought maybe this new fellow, Sparks, might be easy to become acquainted with. He wasn't picking up the feeling that Sparks was keeping things back.

"What are you doing way up here this early, Charley?" asked Ed.

"Well, I might ask you the same. I jest thought it was time to get a few head moved up from winter pasture. Seems some other fellers are already moving some funny marked cattle up here from the other side, Brown's Park, you know. And I did see your herder moving some of your sheep a few days ago up Talamantes toward Beaver Basin. Now, Ed, don't you think it's a bit early?" asked Charley.

"Charley, we can talk open like, with Jim here. He kind of knows some 'bout what we're up against. See, he sort of took up th' old place down in Johnson Draw. The place where th' sheep rustler used to stay. Mine now since he don't seem to really need it no more. I took Jim out on th' desert to check on my herders, and he knows I moved a herd up on Cold Spring early. Did it fer th' same reason you did, Charley. Them two fellers up here are pushing us a little hard, don't you think?"

Jim stirred the fire and moved the coffee pot back into the coals. He was hearing some of the real goings-on, and he wasn't about to say anything that might slow down the talk. After all, if he liked it around here well enough to take up a place, he sure didn't want to walk into something over his head. Like Douglas Fitch in Denver said, don't get yourself killed over a dumb range war that you don't know anything about.

"It's been going on a long time, Ed," said Charley. "But looks like Rash and Isom are going a bit far now. Rash met up with me a while back with a bunch of cattle with different brands. Told me to keep still and not get too interested in checking the brands 'cause he had a bill of sale and the brands certainly weren't from anywhere 'round here. Said he railed them in to Rawlins and trailed them across the desert and over Limestone."

Jim thought this sounded like the herd Ed had told him about earlier, the one Ed tracked over Limestone and knew it would go on to the Rash cabin.

Charley continued. "Then he told me not to plan to move my sheep very far up on Cold Spring 'cause he jest might want to use most all of it. I mentioned that I'd always run my sheep up here, so jest what might he mean? He kind of got ugly, Ed, and then finally said it would be all right to move them up on th' slopes, jest not on up to th' grass on top. When I told him I'd be moving them jest like always, he dropped his hand down on that Colt .45 he always carries, but then he turned and galloped off. Never looked back."

"Charley, I'm jest a little ahead of you," said Ed. "I sent my herder up like you seen last week. Jim and I are on our way now to find how they're doing and where they made camp. Kind of wanted 'em high on th' mountain, maybe to make a show. Really thought they ought to be clear down toward Summit Springs."

"Wouldn't move too close to Summit Springs, Ed. Isom Dart has been staying in th' cabin up there and has several wild horses penned up to break. Sells lots of them now. Really good at handling them," commented Charley. "I did see a bigger number of cattle all 'round his place too. Actually, it weren't cattle so much as it was young stuff, calves. And you know, he ain't got th' same number of mother cows! Now ain't that strange, Ed? Must be those doe deers up there dropping cow-kind of calves 'stead of fawns! Now that would be a real hoot!"

Charley's and Ed's laughter echoed across the spring. Even Jim had to admit it was a rather funny idea, but it could lead to serious consequences.

As the day wore on, the talk turned to all sorts of things. Jim learned that Charley Sparks had come into the country back in the early 1880s from Missouri. He spent some of his early days with the Bassett family, but he soon moved on north over Cold Spring Mountain to set up his homestead. Sparks ran sheep along with Ed, sharing the public ground. The two sheepmen got around to discussing the rains that were needed, the fencing going up all over the country, the better houses thrown up here and there, the number of women out on the ranches, how the livestock wintered, and on and on. Jerky was brought out along with bacon and fried bread. More coffee was made, followed by the usual midday siesta while the horses grazed quietly nearby. The noisy black-and-white magpies flew in to sit on the near aspen limbs and argue over the food scraps.

"Jim, I hate to break this peaceful day in half, but we got work to do. We've got to find th' sheepherder and see if he still has any sheep left. Don't even know where he is at. Get this here campfire out and get to moving on." Ed got to his feet, raked dirt over the smoldering fire, gathered the cups and shook out the remains of the coffee, and then put them in the saddlebags.

DIAMOND FIELDS AND DEATH

"I'm ready anytime you are, Ed. From what I've heard here, I'd guess th' herder didn't go clear out to Summit Springs. If he did, he might be in trouble. Do you think that feller, Dart, would bother your sheep?" asked Jim as he shuffled around getting things ready for the ride.

Sparks cut in. "Isom might be a real outlaw, Jim, but he don't rough up folks. Seems his old background of jest being black is 'nough to keep him from getting on anyone direct. Sure, he'll drive off some of your cattle any time he thinks he can get away with it, 'specially if he has that Matt Rash telling him to. But he's got a good side too, if you can call it a good side. I'm sure he would intimidate any other cowboy or herder that ain't white, so if he saw your herder, yes, he would have sent him and th' sheep packing off th' mountain. But if th' herd was down on th' lower slopes, don't think he'd have done anything. Wouldn't do anything either if maybe your herder camped over near Cottonwood Spring."

Jim moved out to gather the three horses that had grazed back into the trees. When he returned, Charley motioned him to join them while he spoke to Ed about a spring party being planned down in Brown's Park.

"You know how it is, Ed. The kids is all moving back home after school is out in Rock Springs and Craig, so we jest got to have a little get-together down at th' schoolhouse in th' Park. And Jim here ought to be down there to meet all th' folks. Some of th' boys will barbecue up a young steer, and all th' women folks will bring in all kinds of good eating things. All th' music players will turn out too, so you best have your dancing boots on. Ought to try to get in there early and get settled in fer th' weekend."

"Sure thing, Charley. You know I wouldn't miss that shindig fer nothing," replied Ed as Jim passed the reins of each horse over.

"What's this all about?" Jim asked. "Sounds like something a feller wouldn't want to miss."

Ed put a sly wink out to Sparks and turned to Jim. "You ain't got no ties to no women, Jim, and it sure don't take long fer these ranch ladies to get that kind of word spread 'round. Jest 'cause them ranch girls seem too quiet at th' dance in front of all th' old folks don't mean they ain't little wildcats out in th' dark!"

"Jim, don't let that ol' Ed mislead you. You mix with th' wrong gal and all sorts of things can happen. You need to know 'bout some of them that gives and gets th' most attention, 'specially from th' full-grown cowboys, even some old-timers. Now, that Josie—she filed fer a divorce. Sort of a looker fer these parts. Not hooked up right now. But th' one you don't want to fool 'round with is her little sister, th' one that's coming home from some kind of back East school—Ann. Now that's th' kind that could get a feller shot, or worse," said Charley, trying to fill Jim in on right from wrong at these dances.

"She's keeping time with that Matt Rash, and he ain't one to take kindly to anyone sparking up to little Ann. But I can tell you that Ann might make up to you jest to see what Matt would do! She sure is a tease. Been known to go beyond a tease. Jim, she'll sure look good at th' dance, but she's as rough as any cowpuncher that ever rode th' range. Ride and shoot, throw a lariat, and even handle a hot running iron. She and ol' Matt get along 'cause both know how to increase their herds without owning any mother cows."

"There's another feller jest come in recently too, Jim," Ed added as he stepped up on the roan. "He don't look like anyone I'd trust to throw a small calf. Won't look you in th' eye. Shuffles 'round like he is interested in horses, but don't have ranch-like hands, if you know what I mean. No calluses. Name of James Hicks, I think. He fell right in with Rash. Even works with him some now. He's been all over the mountain lately. Over to see Isom Dart, down to Davenport's, over to Thompson's on the Snake River. 'Course, he visits th' Bassetts too. Thing is, Jim, you ought not trust him, and you need to know that he and Rash have something going. Stay clear."

"Nice to meet you, Charley," said Jim as he climbed on the sorrel. "Plan to see you over at th' dance. Third Saturday of May?"

Charley nodded, gave a wave, stepped into the saddle, and turned down the mountain heading toward home. He was pleased with meeting up with Ed and the newcomer, Jim. The long visit satisfied him that both he and Ed knew what was going on and both would be on guard. But both seemed ready to continue their sheep movements as always, in spite of Mr. Rash and Mr. Dart.

"Jim, I think th' herder will be up near Beaver Basin on th' slope of Cold Spring Mountain. Probably 'round Spitzie or Willow Spring. Maybe out on top near Cottonwood, though. We'll check all of 'em. Ought to get there in time fer fixing a camp with th' herder, maybe even get a good meal fer a change," said Ed as they jogged along.

As they rode, they took in the scenery, with a view of Diamond Peak just six or eight miles north. Far off on the horizon to the west, they could see snowcapped mountains in Utah, and off toward the south they could see Diamond Mountain across the Green River. Jim marveled at the peacefulness of Cold Spring Mountain.

The herder was set up at Cottonwood Spring. It was no problem for Ed to ride directly to it, having figured that the herder took his time grazing the sheep up Talamantes and across Beaver Basin. The herder was Joe Garza, one of the few born in the States. His command of English was equal to his family language of Spanish. He had set up a good camp beside the spring, leveled his wagon, and set out the washtub and buckets, shovel and axe, and other items necessary to living on the mountain. Ed and Jim unsaddled their horses and placed the saddles under the wagon to become part of their beds. They spread their bedrolls, and both pitched in to help Joe prepare a supper of fresh antelope steak, potatoes, and onions, topped off with lots of black coffee and canned peaches right out of Ed's cellar back at the ranch.

After they finished their chores, the three men sat around the campfire discussing the events of the day and the sheep movements in particular. Joe had noticed a rider up high on Cold Spring Mountain, thought to have been Isom Dart. He knew Dart had a small outfit at Summit Springs, but it had never been of concern in the past. Ed informed Joe that Matt Rash had warned Sparks not to move up the mountain with the sheep, but he held firm and told him he would move as always, meaning up on the mountain. He told Joe not to get into trouble with either Matt or Isom, but to let him, Ed, know if anything out of the way took place. And above all, he warned him not to get in the way of any stray bullets.

"Let's hit the hay, Jim. This has been one long day," said Ed.

"I agree. Maybe too long. All these things going on could make a feller tired without even doing any work. That dance you and Sparks talked 'bout. Does everybody out here show up? I mean, even those that don't seem to get along any too well?"

"Oh, yes, Jim. At these dances nobody brings too many grudges. And ol' man Bassett takes up any guns at th' door. Keeps 'em till th' party is over and won't let anyone that gets drunk have a gun till he sleeps it off. Usually, though, some young buck will have a little fistfight with another young feller over th' attention of some flirtin' young gal. Th' little gals all scream and carry on, but they all secretly enjoy being th' center of a fight. Ain't no likker allowed inside th' school building, so we all stash a jug out 'round th' wagons somewhere. You'll see them fellers all slip out from time to time to go look at th' moon," answered Ed.

"Well, what with that dance coming up right away, I may have to head to Rock Springs fer supplies. Boots getting kind of run down and don't even have a decent shirt fer a dance. Mine are all work shirts. Didn't ever have no plans to go to any dance, 'specially out here. Need some stuff for th' Johnson Draw cabin too. Grub supply wasn't intended to last ferever. Really thought I'd be drifting out 'round th' country and back to town, but what with th' looks of this part of th' world, I jest might hang 'round for a long time—that is, if you can spare th' cabin and all. Really like it down there," said Jim as he tossed out the last few drops of thick, black coffee on the dying fire. "Reckon I'd need a light wagon too, Ed, or load that pack mare pretty heavy."

"Sure, Jim. Me and Sparks both have a light spring wagon fer quick trips to town when we don't have too much to bring back. You're welcome to use mine any time. Think that mare would pull one?" asked Ed.

"The folks at th' livery told me she would. Guess I'd find out, wouldn't I? Is th' trail to Rock Springs good 'nough fer making fast time, or is th' trip in always a two-day affair? Must be over fifty miles to town," Jim asked.

"Good trail, Jim, if you jest stay on it. Don't try to cut across none. Lots of bad arroyos out there. On our way in tomorrow we can stop by th' place and get th' wagon. One of my men will drive it over to Johnson and then ride th' horse back. It sure rides easier than those ol' buckboards of th' old days. These new springs are th' stuff. And th' whole wagon don't weigh a ton like th' old ones. You can jest 'bout trot all th' way to town without stopping. Well, that might be stretching it a bit, Jim. Let's hit the bunk," Ed said. He crawled under the edge of the herder's wagon, slipped off his boots, and pulled the covers up around him.

At an elevation of eight thousand feet, the nights were always cold through spring and even into early summer. Jim snuggled into the heavy wool blankets and rested his head on the saddle, thinking over the happenings of the day. The clear, crisp mountain air carried the sounds of the night from down in the basin where a pack of coyotes were howling. Somewhere high in the aspen trees surrounding the spring came the low, lonesome call of the hoot owl, about to start its nightly hunting of field mice and cottontail rabbits. The stars were ice-clear, twinkling by the millions, seemingly close enough to reach out and touch. The Milky Way spread half across the sky. The Big Dipper and its North Star were clear, much more so than Jim had ever seen down in Texas. As the moon came up, it cast an eerie light across the sagebrush, leaving dark shadows mixed with highlights. There was not a cloud in the sky as Jim drifted off.

"Coffee's on! Get out of there, Jim. We got too much to do to be wasting time sleeping," Ed called out. "Light's already showing in th' east. Ain't going to chase 'round after any breakfast. Plan to be down to th' ranch fer that. Got to get that little wagon ready fer you. Hope one of th' herders is 'round to do th' delivering fer you. If not, looks like you may have to break that sorrel of yours to do some wagon pulling."

"I hear you, Ed. Be ready 'fore you get th' coffee poured," Jim replied from his snug bed.

The sun was just peeking over the rim of Cold Spring Mountain when Jim and Ed said their goodbyes to Joe and headed off the mountain into Beaver Basin. The ride to the ranch house took them out into the basin where they forded Beaver Creek and headed out toward the west end, not too far short of the timber and higher country.

"Put my cabin kind of out of th' way, up Two-Bar Creek from Beaver. Had a good reason back when I done it. Th' logs had to come out of that timber you see up on that western ridge yonder. By th' time I drug some out of there and got 'em to th' lower end of Two-Bar, I decided th' cabin would be jest fine right there. Built one room at first. Then over th' years, added a couple more. Don't need much when you live alone, Jim," said Ed, talking quietly as they trotted the horses within sight of the cabin.

Jim had no real idea what to expect of Ed's headquarters. The three-room log cabin was fairly neat, and the dirt roof had a good stand of grass on it to help prevent erosion and leaks. There was a crude fence of small poles around the place to keep out critters of all kinds. A barn, shed, and corral were set close by, and the spring was handy a few yards from the door. Inside, there were four bunk beds, some benches and a chair or two, a kitchen table with benches, and the luxury of two potbellied stoves, one in the kitchen and one in the bedroom, which seemed to also be the main living room. The third room was a tack and supply room, containing a couple of extra saddles, some harness and tarps, ropes, branding irons, spurs, branding paint, and other small items and tools.

The herder was out in the corral getting a horse ready to ride. Ed was having extra posts and poles cut in the upper forest, the job of the herder. Ed went out and had a brief talk with him about moving the wagon to Johnson Draw, and then he returned and cooked up a breakfast to carry them through till dark. Before long, the herder came in and announced he was ready with the wagon, all hooked up. Ed introduced Jim to Rueben Garcia, admonished him to hurry back to get on with the pole cutting, and sent them both on their way.

Jim followed Rueben on a dim trail leading around Bishop Peak and out on top of a windblown, sloping flat with a view out to the desert that Jim immediately recognized as the country he had covered on his trip from Rock Springs. They picked up the head of Johnson Draw, kept to the high flat on the north side, still on some kind of track leading down off the point a couple of miles away. Antelope scurried around, getting out of their way as they took an abrupt turn and ducked down into the trees to the Johnson Draw cabin. Rueben unhitched the wagon, mounted the horse, and immediately headed back to his assigned pole-cutting job.

Jim pulled the light wagon to a protected place, turned the sorrel out into the miniature pasture, and went to take his ease in the cabin he had not been in for several days. It felt like home, just comfortable, thought Jim. Comfortable enough to want to own it, improve it, and stock the surrounding hills.

CHAPTER 5

The trip to town was Jim's first venture on the main trail from just below the diamond field. It was much better than he thought it would be. The pack mare easily took to the harness and proved to be a good puller. They made more than half the trip the first day out and arrived in Rock Springs just after noon the next day. Jim left the mare and wagon at the livery, walked over to the Valley House Hotel, and moved in.

"You plan to be here long, Mr. Keaton?" asked the desk clerk as he studied Jim's entry in the ledger. "See you ain't from here, but I kind of remember seeing you a while back. Like lots of fellers, drift in, drift out."

"You got a pretty good memory there. I was here earlier, bought an outfit from th' livery, and traveled down south looking over th' country. Be here a couple of nights this time, I think. Got to buy some supplies," answered Jim.

"Been to the south, huh? Not down to Brown's Park, were you?" asked the clerk, obviously wanting to get into Jim's business. "That's nice country. Looking fer a place to light, are you?"

"Oh, I don't know. Sold out in Texas and jest come up here 'cause some of my friends said it was nice, like you say," answered Jim again, this time wondering why the clerk would be asking so many questions. Most hotel clerks seemed to be like this, though, he thought. "You must get acquainted with lots of folks passing through."

"Yes, but most jest keeps right on going. That's why I noticed you. Not many folks head south, at least not as far south as Brown's Park. 'Course, did have another feller kind of like you, looking at the country, maybe looking fer some horses to buy or something like that. Been in several times. Last time was jest a few weeks ago. Name was ... let's see, yes, here it is in the book. James Hicks, going all the way to Brown's Park. In from Baggs, Wyoming, it says here. Good guest. Paid with gold. Don't guess you've run into him down that way, have you?" asked the clerk.

"No, I sure haven't. Only folks I've run into have been Mr. Sparks and Mr. Cole, close to Diamond Peak," replied Jim, not seeing any reason to let anyone know he knew anything about this Hicks fellow. Hard to tell just who might be tied in with Rash, Dart, and Hicks, if they were all involved in cattle rustling as both Cole and Sparks seemed to think.

"You met Charley Sparks? He's a good feller. Don't much get involved with those shenanigans always going on in the Park. And ol' Ed Cole is one of the old-timers down there. Runs sheep, like Sparks," commented the clerk.

"What if I found a little place somewhere out here to buy? Who would I need to see 'bout money, finances, you know?" Jim asked, trying to change the subject from people, namely Hicks, down in Brown's Park.

"Oh, there's jest one feller to take care of all that in this whole part of the country. That'd be ol' August Kendall. Owns the bank. Makes them loans. Takes the collateral and then is quick to repossess too. That is, if you ain't got no way to pay. You jest need to get over to the bank and visit with him. He's there most times, if he ain't gone out to one of them ranches he owns or partners in. I can tell you, though, if you ain't got no bank account with him, you sure ain't going to get no loan," allowed the talkative clerk.

With that, Jim checked his room, dropped off his belongings, and walked out to the street to survey the town.

Nothing much had changed since he first arrived on the train from Bitter Creek a few weeks earlier. Same coal dust on everything, mixed with the usual street dust. The buildings were mostly just shacks, meant to be temporary till the coal ran out. Exceptions were those that were more closely related to the future of the railroad—the hotel, several eateries, a couple of better saloons, and a few fairly well-built boarding houses. There were several blocks of business houses that had boardwalks in front of them. And there was the mercantile store, perhaps the largest building in town. Jim headed straight in to pay a visit to Andy Ewing.

"Andy! You ain't changed a bit in warmer weather, you rascal! Man, it's sure good to see you again!" exclaimed Jim when he walked in and saw Andy behind the first counter.

"Why, why, oh, Mr. Keaton! Gosh, same here. How you been? You don't even look all shot up much! Golly, it's good to have you back. Didn't know if I'd ever see you again or not," Andy gushed as he stepped around the counter and grabbed Jim's hand. "Tell me all 'bout where you been and what you've got yourself into?"

"What do you mean, what I've got into, Andy? Told you I could take care of myself. Those folks I've met down south are great fellers!" Jim said as he pumped Andy's hand. "Disappointed, though, that I ain't even been shot at. And I've found some really nice land and all, not for sale or nothing like that, Andy, but sure may be a place I'd like to have. Even found th' owner."

"Gosh, Jim, we got to talk. Let me tell the fellers to finish up the day and do the closing without me, and I'll buy you a drink over at the Cat Claw—the best saloon in the West!" Andy said and then turned to find his helpers.

"Ain't much at drinking, Andy, but with you, I'll have one, jest one, though. Got too much important stuff to do to waste time drinking. Besides, it makes me lose my brains," replied Jim.

The Cat Claw was just like Andy said, the best saloon in town. The two took a table over in a quiet corner, ordered a whiskey each, and lit into one another with all the questions and answers necessary to cover the weeks since they first met. Jim mentioned that he had come to town mostly just to get a pair of new boots and a shirt for the upcoming Brown's Park dance.

"You're kidding me, Jim! You don't mean to tell me that you made such a hit down there they even invited you to the dance? I'm going to be there too. You must have captivated them folks with tall tales or something," said Andy. "Why, that's going to be the biggest dance of the spring, right before gathering too. All them school kids will be home, the cowboys will all come in off the range, folks from here will gather up and go down. How'd this invite come about?"

"Long story, Andy. You know how you told me to get acquainted with certain folks? Well, right off, I met up with Ed Cole and then Charley Sparks," Jim said.

Andy cut him off. "Oh, Jim, don't think ol' Ed is too good. He may treat you real fine, but if you ever think about cutting in on his range, he ain't any too nice. Did he tell you 'bout the sheep rustler? How he jest up and tracked him down and plain killed him? Sheep ought not be worth a man's life. Then there was the miner that got out there looking fer them salted gemstones a few years back. You know 'bout that? The diamond field?" Andy asked in a lower voice.

"Well, yes, Andy, I guess I ought to have told you a little something 'bout that. See, when I came here and met you, I was really looking fer that same field. Didn't want anyone to know. No idea how folks out here might take that. Found it too. But now I guess everyone out here knows th' story or at least most of th' story. Reckon maybe I know more than anyone out here 'bout certain parts of th' hoax. Better keep that to myself. No offense, Andy. Jest might get out to th' wrong folks. Nobody needs to know," answered Jim.

"Never mind what you might know 'bout all that, Jim," replied Andy as he swirled his drink around nervously. "The thing is, the last person to see that miner was ol' Ed himself. Miner never showed up no more 'round here, or anywhere else either. Then a year or two later a coyote dug up some bones. They still had some of the ragged clothes parts on 'em. Same kind the miner always had. A herder found the remains and reported it to Charley Sparks, down there. Nothing ever came of it. No one could identify the bones. Charley is sort of the acting deputy sheriff down there, at times."

"But, Andy, that don't mean Ed had anything to do with the death of that ol' miner now. Jest 'cause he might be th' last one to see him," said Jim.

"But, Jim, that ain't all! A feller went in, right into Beaver Basin, and filed on a homestead right where Ed kept his sheep in the summer. Took up the best spring there too. Next thing we knew, Ed filed charges on the poor feller fer rustling sheep. No evidence at all. Judge let him off. Ed told the feller to get out of the country, but the man was stubborn. Then there was a shootout, and Ed claimed the man drawed on him in an argument over a ram. No witnesses, no case, and Ed went on his way."

Now Jim had something to think about. Maybe that is why Ed questioned him out on the mountain about killing people.

"Jim, what I'm gettin' at is that Ed can be a nice guy when he likes you and when he wants to be. But jest don't try to move in anywhere 'round his grazing country. Jest ain't worth it. 'Course, on the other hand, ol' Ed has sure helped out some folks down there. Helps a little family now homesteading not far out of the diamond field. Think their name might be Finch or something like that. They think the world of Ed. Why, he rode all night last winter in a bad storm to get a doctor from town here and take him out to see 'bout that lady there, Mrs. Finch. She made it, but if it weren't fer ol' Ed, she'd have died." Andy stared out across the barroom floor, lost in his own thoughts.

"Andy, I may as well tell you, I've been planning on putting in down there, right in there with Ed, down in Johnson Draw. He sort of led me to believe that he would even appreciate me being down there. Seems to think I'd be a good buffer fer him 'gainst any bigger outfit from up here in Wyoming moving down there. Maybe using me? You know him. What do you think?" Jim asked.

"Sounds like Ed took to you, Jim. If he really did, you couldn't do no better. Like I said, he really takes care of the Finches. Jest don't cut in on anything he might be wanting."

"Hey, let's have jest one more drink," said Andy as he turned to look for the barmaid. "This kind of heavy talk is too much fer fellers like us! We're here to have a good time and welcome in summer and all that. And don't say no to me. I'm jest like you. Lose my brains too, but only after three or four drinks. We ain't going to have any more than two. Oh, Mary Lou, head over here fer me and my friend! We need another round before we give it up."

Mary Lou slipped around the end of the bar and moved slyly over to Andy's table, staying on Jim's side. "Andy, I don't know why I like you so much. You never stay in here long enough to get friendly. That's probably why I like you too. You're just not like those others. What'll you have?"

Andy ordered two whiskies, while Jim couldn't help noticing how nice Mary Lou looked. Not at all what he had seen in other towns and villages running saloons and bars. Most were always a hard-looking bunch.

"Well, Andy, I'd love to get you the two drinks after you tell me who the second one's for," said Mary Lou as she looked down at Jim and winked.

"Oh sure. Mary Lou, this here's Jim, Jim Keaton. He's a friend of mine jest in from down south. Came here and stayed over at the Valley House a few weeks ago, did his outfittin' through me at the store, and now jest came back to buy hisself a new set of boots fer the Brown's Park dance coming up," Andy answered. "Looking fer maybe a place to put in a few cows."

"You know, Jim," said Mary Lou in a quiet, soothing voice that showed the diction only learned in the best boarding schools, "sometimes it's just plain difficult to get things out of Andy, especially the kind of things a lady wants."

Jim looked up into Mary Lou's green eyes and was caught so off guard that he found himself totally speechless. Then he became aware of Mary Lou's arm around his shoulders. Her smile was genuine, and her touch was warm and friendly. He tried to push back his chair, but the rear legs caught in the rough floor, and he suddenly found himself falling over backward right against Mary Lou. She skillfully, cunningly, caught Jim, hugging his head and shoulders tightly against her bosom with a coy smile just to let him know she was all woman.

"Gosh, Jim, I didn't know you would be coming on to me quite so fast. I hardly know you!" exclaimed Mary Lou, with a mischievous sparkle in her eyes. "Andy, why don't you get Jim here to teach you how to get acquainted with a lady like he does? See, we could have been together like this for a long time."

Jim could feel his face reddening as he politely tried to get his feet under him and the chair back in place. Mary Lou's hold was no longer necessary, but she didn't seem ready to release him. He couldn't just push the lady away. He sort of liked the feel of such a beautiful lady holding tightly to him. He found his arms slipping around her, as though for support.

"Oh, ma'am, I'm jest terribly sorry 'bout that. Really didn't mean to fall all over you," Jim stuttered, still holding her close, as he glanced over at Andy to see him beaming, about to bust right out laughing.

"Gee whiz, Jim! The two of you! Didn't know you was that fast. Man, alive! You and Mary Lou right up there and friendly! Mary Lou, why you ain't never offered to hold me like that," said Andy, obviously enjoying every moment of the fun.

Jim stepped back away, picked up the chair, and replaced it sheepishly. "Miss, ma'am, I sure hope I didn't hurt you any. This jest don't happen to me every day!"

"I was getting to like the idea of just staying here, Jim. But now you just let me go, like you didn't like me catching you," said Mary Lou, thoroughly enjoying teasing Jim in front of Andy. "Guess I might as well go get those two drinks now that I know just who the second drink is for."

Jim and Andy stared at Mary Lou as she walked away toward the bar. She was dressed in the best of fashion, nothing at all like other women Jim had seen in saloons. Andy noticed Jim's curious look at Mary Lou.

"Jim, you jest met the owner of the Cat Claw Saloon. And I bet ain't never been another feller go through a meeting like that! Why, I even thought there fer a minute you wasn't about to let go of her! Maybe you sort of liked it?" teased Andy. "And she don't put up with no nonsense 'round here. That's why this here Cat Claw is the best place in town. Those other places are full of drunks fighting all the time. Busted up furniture, doors falling off, windows broke out—all sorts of stuff like that."

"Really, now, Andy. Surely she don't own this place? Why would she be waiting tables?" asked Jim in total surprise at Andy's comments.

"She don't wait tables, Jim. Jest certain tables," answered Andy as Mary Lou returned with their drinks.

"Buying new boots for the dance, are you, Jim? Have you seen the town? Know where to get those boots? If you wouldn't mind having a lady escort you around, I might take off tomorrow. Could take you to the best shop in town. That is, if you wouldn't rather have Andy's company," said Mary Lou.

"Jim ain't looking to me to show him 'round town none, Mary Lou. You jest go right ahead and get with him. You know all the places. Jim would like that, wouldn't you, Jim? Why, Mary Lou would even get you better prices, I'll bet. All the folks here in town know her," said Andy.

"Well, then, I ought to just come over to the Valley House and meet you there for breakfast, shouldn't I, Jim?" said Mary Lou. "Or do you have other things to do? Maybe we should get together after lunch? You name it, Jim. I can arrange to be with you just any time you say." She left the door full open for any thought Jim might have.

"Ma'am, ah, Miss Mary Lou, I do have some other business like finding that banker, Mr. Kendall. Jest to see 'bout maybe getting some money if I happen to find a place I could buy," answered Jim, still not knowing just how to address Mary Lou properly. She seemed too nice and refined to call her by her first name. She was a beautiful lady, not at all like what Jim expected to see in Rock Springs. And her friendliness set Jim back a bit. After all, who was he to command such attention from the lady owner of the best saloon in town?

"Jim, please call me by my name, Mary Lou, Mary Lou Garrett. Came here from Mississippi where folks are friendly and open with each other all the time. I hope you don't mind me calling you Jim, do you?" Mary Lou asked.

She quickly explained that she came west after her father died and her mother tried to set her up with a proper husband, a wealthy planter that Mary Lou found obnoxious. Mary Lou needed to get away and agreed with her mother that a visit with an aunt in California would help cool things off.

When Mary Lou got to Rock Springs, she became fascinated with the rough life of the cowboys and miners, rather enjoying their freewheeling ways of life. She found a building for sale, wired home to her private banker for family money, and put in the Cat Claw Saloon. Her first few weeks proved too rough for a refined lady from the South, and she closed down, did some rethinking, and reopened as a quiet, sophisticated, first-class saloon. Before long, she found she had captured all the better class of business and social people as regular customers. Her business grew along with its reputation, all resulting in sound profits.

"Well, Miss Garrett, er, Mary Lou, if it's jest th' same with you, I'll take care of business first and then call on you over here at your place. Might be late in the morning or early afternoon," said Jim.

Andy continued to give Jim a hard time over how quickly he set up a date with the most desirable lady in town as they finished their drinks and called it an evening. Jim headed over to the livery, checked on the mare and wagon, and then went to the Valley House for a thick steak, thinking all the while that the beef just might have come from rustled steers. After dinner he hurried to his room where he tumbled into bed.

All mining towns came to life early. The hustle and bustle out on the streets was a far cry from the peace and quiet of Johnson Draw at dawn. By the time the sun was up, most businesses were finishing their first trades for the miners who had to be in the mines early.

At breakfast Jim chatted with the waitress at the Valley House, finding out where the bank was and when it might be open. She allowed that Mr. Kendall really didn't have to open early like the storekeepers that made their living off miners. But he usually did get down to his bank not long after the miners cleared the streets. He always dropped in at the Valley House for coffee before opening the bank if Jim might like to hang around and catch him there. The waitress even offered to introduce him to Mr. Kendall, if he'd like. Jim appreciated the offer.

Within the hour Mr. Kendall strolled in, all dapper in his full suit with a gold watch chain across his front. He was immediately met in the entrance by the manager, who led him to the best table in the house.

Jim watched the proceedings, thinking to himself how pompous Kendall was and observing just how Kendall expected everyone to snap to attention when he glanced around at them. Several businessmen immediately paid homage to Kendall, much to his satisfaction. The manager sent not one but two waitresses to the table to busy themselves with minor straightening of this and that, giving the silverware an extra polishing, and providing him with coffee before he even ordered it. Jim was thoroughly impressed and a little disgusted.

Then Jim noticed several of the businessmen leaving, as though they suddenly had shops to open or appointments to make. Like maybe they were ill at ease being in the same room with Kendall. Or maybe they were in bad debt to him and didn't really want to be confronted by the man, particularly right out in public. Jim's experience in the past with unknown or bad-tempered broncos had taught him that when expecting a bad time, delay only heightened the problem. The way to handle it was to step right up to the bronco and get on with it. And he decided that was the way to get on with Mr. Kendall.

"Uh, miss, you mentioned introducing me to Mr. Kendall, and I think that must be him over there. Would you mind, that is, if you think it is right?" asked Jim of his waitress, who was standing and also observing the proceedings at Kendall's table.

"Sure," said the waitress. "He ain't God. Don't deserve all that flittin' 'round they do over him. Come on!" She got Jim's name and an idea of what he might want to discuss with Kendall and led him to the throne.

"So, you're new here, are you, son?" asked Kendall after the customary introductions. "What do you think of our fair little city? Just booming like a gold rush town, don't you think? Why, I'm so busy setting up folks in new, solid businesses here in Rock Springs, I hardly have time to look up. Being a visitor, you might not know it, but I own interests in about everything in town and lots of ranches out of town!" Kendall's vaunting, loud laugh echoed through the dining room. "Won't you have some coffee with me, Jim, boy? I'll pay. Miss! Bring my friend here your best coffee, and make it snappy! Just don't like to wait, Jim."

The waitress about jumped through herself, getting the coffee to Jim in no time at all. Jim made small talk, mostly just answering the statements Kendall made. He really wanted to get down to business, but he could see that Kendall first wanted to impress the newcomer with his importance in the community. From time to time, he stopped talking long enough to wave to someone or shout across the room to greet another. Finally, Kendall slowed down enough to focus attention on Jim.

"Now, Jim, boy, if you plan to do business or maybe to put down stakes here in Rock Springs, you just let me know. I'm the one you can turn to any time you need help—help with things like finance, maybe money for some cows or even sheep, or lease money. Just you name it, Jim, son. We can surely strike a deal that would be good for both of us. You know what I mean?" asked Kendall.

"Well, Mr. Kendall, that's sure what I need to discuss with you, if you don't mind," Jim replied, recognizing that a man of Kendall's nature was looking to be properly stroked before getting down to business. Jim knew very well how to get along with Kendall's kind, having learned some of the tricks back in his army days. He knew too that Kendall would be looking for an inside play, regardless of what Jim wanted to do. If it was livestock, Kendall would want a share. If land, he would want a partnership with all risk belonging to Jim. If things went bad, Kendall could end up with a ranch with little or no investment of his own.

"I've been down 'round Brown's Park with Mr. Cole, just looking 'round and gettin' a feel fer th' country. Really do like it down there. Now, I know if I ran across some little place to buy, an old homestead, maybe abandoned, I'd need money," Jim started explaining.

"Wait just a minute there, Jim. You been looking around the Park? You got any bank account here with my bank?" Kendall asked abruptly.

Jim could see Kendall's whole attitude swiftly change with the mention of Brown's Park. "Well, no, not at present, Mr. Kendall. But I could transfer what I've got over to your bank, maybe five hundred dollars. But that sure ain't enough to start ranching on," said Jim.

"Now, son, if you really want to start some livestock, why don't you go out north of here? Lots of good country up there. That Brown's Park country sure don't have no more room for newcomers … er … for folks that don't know anything about that country. I hold some of those places like that Davenport ranch, and Matt Rash and me are together on all his holdings. I sure don't want nobody interfering with what I got going on down there. Why, I'd be a fool to loan to an outsider to get in there and start competition against my own holdings, wouldn't I? You understand? You say you don't even have money with me, and you're asking me to loan to you? No, no. I jest don't do that. My advice to you is to get out of that Park country, get somewhere else. If you do, you can come see me then."

Kendall was through talking. "Waitress, put this on my tab. Even his coffee," he said as he got up to leave. "If you use your senses and go out north, do come see me."

Jim had really been burned. The gall of that pompous old dictator treating him like dirt. Calling him "son" and, even worse, "boy." Jim wasn't any son of the old coot, and he sure wasn't any longer a boy. But at the same time, he picked up that something sure might be going on between Kendall and all the rustling down in the Park, since he was underwriting Matt Rash, and this tied him to Dart and even that strange fellow, Hicks. This whole thing seemed to be getting bigger with the involvement of more interesting people. More reason to keep quiet about what he was finding out.

Jim was still smarting a bit over Kendall's treatment when he went over to the mercantile store to give Andy Ewing a list of supplies he needed. Andy took it, looked it over, and allowed as he had all the goods listed. Wouldn't take too long to get the list filled.

"Jim, I jest got to ask, 'cause you sure do look like a coyote that's jest been shot at and missed. Sort of like you tucked your tail and might be slinking away from something. Bet you jest talked with ol' Kendall, didn't you now?" Andy asked quietly, not wanting anyone to overhear his conversation.

"Oh, Andy, you know how it is. Being an outsider, ol' Kendall didn't quite treat me like he ought. Matter of fact, Andy, he indicated he didn't appreciate me even being down 'round Brown's Park. Acted like I might get into something he was controlling. Something maybe pretty big. Anyway, he sure ain't going to be easy to borrow any money from fer getting set up down there. What do you think?" Jim replied, also in a low, confidential voice.

"Well, Jim, you make me feel kind of guilty now. Should've told you more 'bout ol' Kendall. We jest sort of take him like he is, knowing bankers is all kind of strange. But then I should've let you know he was backing some folks down there and was taking some kind of kickbacks from them. Maybe it's jest normal collateral, maybe it's something more. Ain't our business, but we all seem to know," said Andy.

"Still have to hunt up a boot man, Andy. Thought I'd get something to eat at the hotel, do some jawing with the room clerk, and then go over to get Mary Lou Garrett. That looks like something worth doing, something to get a feller's mind off heavy stuff, if you know what I mean, Andy," said Jim as he turned to the door. "I won't really need the supplies till I get ready to head out tomorrow. Jest stack 'em somewhere till then."

When Jim arrived at the Cat Claw, Mary Lou was waiting. She passed a few words with her helpers and quickly had Jim by the arm, leading him out on the boardwalk and down the street to the boot shop.

The boot and leather shop was something to see. Jim had been in Jody's leather shop back in Denver, but she did not have the number of finished boots this one had. Most shops he knew from down in the Southwest were harness shops that might make some boots on the side. But here was a shop that made boots first. There were boots dyed in all colors—brown, black, gray, and even unusual colors, such as wine, olive, and red. They were stitched in every design, made as high tops and low tops, pointed toes, round toes, medium heels, and tall heels, some of everything.

"Now, Jim, if you plan to dance all night at the Park, you best get something that really fits right," Mary Lou suggested. "I've seen cowboys that sure couldn't walk the day after a dance, trying to get by in those bad riding boots. Sit right there, Jim, and let an expert fit you. Didn't know I knew anything about boots, did you? And maybe I really don't. Could be that I just want to play with your legs, cowboy," said Mary Lou, loud enough for the shopkeeper to plainly hear.

The shopkeeper's eyes got big. He turned away and was slipping out of the fitting room when Jim called out to him.

"Feller, don't you leave me here alone with this young lady! You jest get in here and do your job. She ain't up to nothing, I don't think. Get me them black boots over there with th' white insets and stitching."

The red-faced clerk fetched the boots as both Jim and Mary Lou enjoyed the fluster they had put him into.

"Do you have this same boot in his size?" asked Mary Lou.

"Oh, yes, ma'am, Miss Garrett. I always try to make up several sizes when I do them. Got jest what you need," replied the clerk.

Jim tried on another pair that fit just right. "I like 'em," he said. "How much?"

"Oh, you sure pick the best. This here pair is my top boot, jest fifteen dollars," tested the clerk.

"Now, sir," started Mary Lou, "you and I have done business a long time. You are always my special guest at the Cat Claw. You know you should treat Mr. Keaton here the same way. He's with me, my special friend."

"Sure thing, Miss Garrett. Jest for you, and you know, I wouldn't want folks knowing 'bout my pricing jest between you and me. Ten dollars," answered the clerk. "You do want me to box 'em up for you, don't you, Mr. Keaton?"

The boot deal was made. Jim was duly impressed with Mary Lou's bargaining for the right price, just like Andy had said. They moved on to make the shirt purchases, again with the right price obtained by Mary Lou. She then led Jim around town, showing him the nicer places to do business and impressing on him the fact that he needed to know whom to deal with and whom to avoid. She knew all the folks, both good and bad. Jim found her company very desirable, warm and friendly, and wide open. They spent time chatting about their ideas and the things they wanted to do in the future, discussions much deeper than normally carried on between new acquaintances or friends. And both seemed pleased to find that neither was committed in the way of any romance. They were independent, free to go and come, no ties.

"Jim, I really need to check on my place. Sort of just left it with the girls, you know. They always do a good job, but they need to know that I'm around too. My home is above the saloon ... that is, if you ever really needed to know. My personal friends enter from the outside stairway around the back. No need to go through the barroom and up the staircase. That's my shortcut to and from the business floor. Everyone in there knows who walks up that flight of stairs," Mary Lou said as she moved very close to Jim, looking up at him with her sparkling green eyes, not asking, and certainly not pleading, but obviously giving him directions to her private domain. "You'd surely come over before leaving, wouldn't you, Jim?"

For a moment Jim pulled back, and then he caught himself, leaned down close to her, and hesitated.

"Well?" said Mary Lou weakly as she reached up and put her arms around Jim. Both knew they had found something, or someone, as their lips met for the first time.

Jim was confused as they parted, each saying something about having things to take care of elsewhere. He was smitten in a way he had not known in years, if ever. And he knew Mary Lou was different, a business owner just like the nice lady, Jody, back in Denver. She was, like Jody, bright and intelligent. But she differed in that she was highly educated, a refined Southerner, light brown hair, just a bit taller than most women. And with unusual green eyes. Could it really be that she was actually interested in him? Could this be something with meaning?

Jim knew he had to get first things done first and try to forget about Mary Lou, at least long enough to finish up his reasons for coming to Rock Springs in the first place. Got to get the wagon over to Andy's place right away and have him pack the supplies on it, making it ready to go at first light tomorrow. Have a quiet meal at the Valley House, alone, time to think. Things had happened altogether too fast for Jim. Maybe get to his room early and turn in. But leaving without knowing what was really going on with Mary Lou? Of course, maybe only he, and not Mary Lou, was beguiled and captivated.

"Been out all day, have you, Mr. Keaton?" asked the desk clerk. "See you got some pretty big packages there. Got you a surprise, though. Not many folks land in here and get hand-delivered notes. Probably something to do with Kendall since you did visit with him on money and all, didn't you? Probably got yourself approval fer some kind of backing," continued the clerk as he turned to the mail slots, pulled out an envelope, and handed it to Jim.

"You're right. Long day, got my shopping done. Sure got some fine boots," answered Jim, taking the note and turning toward the stairwell. "Have my charges ready early. Got to get on my way at first light."

Up in the room, Jim put away his packages, gathered some things to carry to the wagon early in the morning, and finally stretched out on the bed to rest and open the note passed to him by the clerk. It had been sealed rather well, maybe to ensure that a desk clerk or anyone else would not pry into it without Jim's knowledge.

The handwriting was neat, concise. "Jim, I would like very much to visit with you tonight at my place. Would you like to share a nightcap? Come up the back way. I'll keep the night lamp on. Mary Lou." The note was that simple, and just that mysterious, from a stunning, desirable, and mischievous green-eyed beauty that Jim could not resist.

Jim got by the desk without the clerk knowing he left. He made his way to Mary Lou's back stairs in the dark without being seen. And the lamp was just as her note said, on but low. He knocked quietly and gently opened the door.

"Jim! I was afraid you might think my note too forward. Come in. I've been hoping you would come over. Bolt the door behind you," said Mary Lou in her calm, serene manner.

CHAPTER 6

Jim's return trip to the snug cabin in Johnson Draw was filled with mixed emotions. His plans of continuing his quest for the cabin were now overshadowed by his thoughts hanging back in town—Mary Lou. He couldn't let it interfere with his original goals, and he knew it. He had seen men throw caution to the wind over women, always ending up the loser. After all, he had learned that women were a nickel a dozen, or so said the good ol' boys out in the hills. They had never met Mary Lou. Still, he had to clear his mind of her, at least for the coming few days or weeks.

The sorrel was overjoyed to see Jim and the mare back at the place after being gone a few days. He whinnied and charged around the boundary of the small holding pasture, kicking up his heels and frolicking like a youngster. Jim turned the mare loose with the sorrel, and then he toted the supplies into the cabin, put them away, and tidied up the place. A quick meal and a pot of black coffee left just about enough time to hitch up the mare again, tie the sorrel behind, and make it over to Ed's place to return the wagon. He even could deliver the fresh jug of whiskey he had picked up as a gift to Ed for the use of the wagon.

"Hello, in there! Anyone home?" called Jim as he wheeled into the clearing around Ed's headquarters. No answer came and things looked quiet, so Jim unhitched the mare and put the wagon away under the shed. The afternoon sun was getting low over the sagebrush hills when Jim noticed the sorrel perk up and point toward the slope of Cold Spring Mountain. Sure enough, two riders were moving slowly along toward the cabin, still too far away to tell just who they might be. But it almost had to be Ed and maybe the herder, Rueben Garcia. The riders changed their pace as they saw the two extra horses near the barn and were soon trotting up to the hitching post with greetings to Jim. Ed and Rueben were returning from a trip up the mountain to deliver supplies to Joe, the herder near Cottonwood Spring.

"How'd it go off there in th' big town, Jim?" asked Ed as they stepped down and started unsaddling their horses. "Rueben has plumb finished th' pole cutting since you were here last. We jest might put you to work helping haul some of 'em in."

"Could I bribe my way out of that in some way, Ed?" teased Jim, winking at Rueben. "Would you let me off if I gave you a new jug of the best whiskey th' Cat Claw had to offer?"

"Boy! What a deal! You'd do anything to get out of work, eh?" answered Ed, teasing right back at Jim. "Let's get in and see what we can cook up. Jest might strike a deal. And put away those horses of yours too. Ain't no time to be heading back to Johnson tonight."

The oil lamps cast a warm glow across the room as the three men sat around talking late into the night. While Jim was gone, more cattle had showed up on top of Cold Spring Mountain, and Sparks had moved his first herd of sheep up near Bassett Springs. Ed had gone out to his desert country to tell his herders to move to the high country with all the flocks, and they would show up any time now.

"Ran into that Rash again while you were gone, Jim," said Ed after a lull had come over their idle talk. "Me and Rueben had gone up to take some supplies to Joe at Cottonwood Spring, and since we were there, jest thought we ought to sort of wander off toward Summit Spring and see if any unusual cattle had showed up, or really jest see if any were up there at all. It ain't far over to Summit, you know. 'Course, I knowed they was already doing their spring roundup. Sort of wanted to get an idea of jest how many cattle they might be pushing 'round, what effect it might really have on how me and Sparks would run our herds."

Jim set his cup down and looked curiously at Ed. "They round up all th' livestock on th' mountain, don't they, Ed? Then cut out each man's cattle for him?"

"That's right, Jim," answered Ed. "'Course, that'd give them th' chance to find any dogies and brand 'em fer themselves, don't you see? They ain't never going to do nothing fer free. Always something in it fer them. Sometimes they find nearly grown cattle without brands. But then it is a good way fer th' little guy to get most of his cattle rounded up and counted and cut out. They all know not to ever argue with Rash if they seem to come up short. Them that are part of Rash's good friends get treated really good. Sometimes even gettin' a few new calves branded with their brands.

"Well, we jest rode along and got over close to ol' Isom's cabin there at th' spring when we seen Rash and that feller Hicks and a cowboy gathered 'round ol' Isom. Then we seen what Isom was doing. Butchering out a bull. By then we was right up to 'em. I knowed they seen us ride up, but they was so ganged up in a big argument with ol' Isom that I don't think it registered on 'em that we was there. Boy! What a bunch of cussing was going on. That Rash was fit to be tied, yelling at poor ol' Isom 'bout th' bull belonging to Sam Spicer down in th' Park and all." Ed hesitated, letting it all sink in on Jim.

"Then when it looked like ol' Isom had 'bout taken enough, he straightened up from his work and lit in on Rash. Isom got to talking 'bout some money Rash owed him fer helping on a rustling job a few weeks back, 'bout eighty dollars, you know. That feller Hicks was sure taking it all in. Didn't act like he knew much 'bout it till then. Sure kept his mouth shut. Shows he was new to what was going on or that he knowed all 'bout it and was jest there to back up Rash, if Rash needed him.

"Me and Rueben thought sure a fight was going to get started, either with fists or even guns, knowing how tempers are sometimes. But we sure didn't open our mouths none. Jim, you should've seen us! We was keeping as still as a field mouse with a hoot owl circling above. Why, we heard things 'bout all th' rustling that'd been going on, things we hadn't even dreamed of before," said Ed.

"Finally, when Hicks sort of backed away like he knew it was over and all, Rash turned and started in on me and Rueben," Ed continued. "Wanted to know jest how long we'd been there and what we might've been hearing. You could see the scowl on his face. He was looking jest plain mean, Jim. I motioned Rueben back a little, seeing that ol' Rash jest might decide to pull out that .45 and start shooting. Things was hot, Jim."

"Gosh, Ed! Just look at what all I missed out on! And all that time I thought I was having more excitement in town than you'd ever have out here," Jim said in a lighthearted manner, trying to simmer Ed down a little, knowing he was all worked up.

Almost as though Ed had not heard Jim say anything, he continued on about the confrontation on Cold Spring Mountain. Jim knew Ed was too serious about it to stop now.

"Rash moved toward me. I was still on my horse, you know, and started in 'bout me moving my sheep up on th' mountain. I'd got Rueben here backed off a few steps and was thinking jest how to get at my saddle gun if need be. Then Rash started getting ugly 'bout my herders, my sheep, and me." Ed was showing great anxiety over the ordeal on the mountain. "Jim, you know a man jest can't take that and run away. Why, they'd be after you fer everything you did if you let 'em bully you jest once. I didn't have no choice. I had to show that Rash that I wasn't putting up with his nonsense 'bout what I could and couldn't do with sheep on th' mountain, th' country I'd run on since Rash was still wet behind th' ears. You been 'round, Jim. You know how it is."

Jim just nodded, knowing Ed wasn't looking for any comment but was eager to fill Jim in on how things went.

"I jest started berating that Rash right there in front of his men, Hicks, the cowboy, and Isom. Told him we had all got along too many years fer him to start acting like he owned all th' country. He would sure find my sheep right where I'd always had 'em, and if I even thought he was going to harm any of them or my herders, he'd pay a heavy and dear price! And if he got any closer to my horse, in the mood he was in, he jest might get trampled on or jest plain ol' stomped!"

Ed hesitated in his story, letting himself calm down. He knew he was getting too emotional, letting folks see how enraged he had been over Rash. After a few moments, he continued. "When I saw I'd buffaloed ol' Rash jest a little, I started my horse backing up. Sure didn't want to turn my back on that bunch. Isom went back to his butchering, Rash's cowboy had lost a lot of his color, kind of turned white-like, and that Hicks was off away from all of us, looking like he didn't want to know no more 'bout nothing. He'd been hired by Rash to help out on th' roundup, cooking, or something.

"When we'd got far enough apart so maybe we wouldn't be too easy a target, I turned my horse and walked him slowly over to Rueben, and th' two of us went on out of there. I knew I'd better go back to see Joe and let him know there had been trouble. Sure didn't want him mixed up in it. Don't want none of my herders ending up dead like those two a while back. Had to be sure Joe had a rifle and some shells. And be sure, too, that he had my backing if he had to do something like defend hisself 'gainst any of Rash's bunch, you know. Well, Joe had a really nice .25-35 rifle and one box mostly full of shells, but I don't intend him being up there without more. Be taking him a couple of extra boxes tomorrow. You might jest as well go along with me up there, Jim," said Ed.

"That's just what I need, Ed, a chance to get shot!" exclaimed Jim, all in jest, knowing the ride to Cottonwood would give him a chance to get a better idea of the country. "Headin' up at first light, Ed?"

"Sure thing, Jim, if we get some sleep. Take that extra bunk in there. Leave the mare in the pen. Rueben will see she gets some hay while we're gone," answered Ed.

Daylight found Ed and Jim away from the cabin, heading up Cold Spring Mountain in the frosty sagebrush. Deer were still out grazing and seemed to be everywhere. Now and then they rode up on a small antelope herd and watched them scurry off to different feed grounds, staying out of the way of the horses and riders. At the insistence of Ed, both men had checked their rifles, added to their ammunition, and carried Colt .45s with belts full of shells. The saddlebags held the extra boxes of .25-35s for Joe.

"With all this heavy artillery we could sure wipe out these deer and antelopes, Ed," Jim said as they trotted along.

The spring at Cottonwood created a very small pond where most of the wildlife in the immediate area always came to drink. Ducks occasionally flew in, and sage grouse stayed close by. The herders always set up their camps far enough from the pond to allow wildlife to continue its use, after getting accustomed to the new camp. Ed and Jim approached the pond, and off scurried a pair of ducks, quacking loudly as they climbed away. Joe was close to his wagon, feeding his dogs and generally getting ready for the day.

Ed called out to Joe, letting him know company was coming in. Joe waved, stepped into his wagon, and returned with a couple of extra cups for coffee. The big coffee pot was hanging from a steel hook over the dying fire. Joe filled the cups as Ed and Jim stepped down from their saddles, and Joe acknowledged Jim's return to his camp with a couple of words in Spanish. The two ground-tied horses quickly started grazing on the lush mountain grass.

"What brings you back today, Mr. Ed?" Joe asked.

"Brought you something I hope you don't need, partner," replied Ed. "Here's a couple more boxes of .25-35s for that rifle of yours. Jest can't never tell how thick or how big th' dirty, sneaking coyotes might get 'round your sheep in th' next few days. If some of them two-legged coyotes gets to giving you or th' sheep trouble, you sure got my permission to open up on 'em. Don't want to have to come up here and bury you, Joe. Be too much work," Ed teased as he accepted the steaming hot cup from Joe.

"Seriously, now, Joe, if you do see any of that Rash bunch heading your way, I want you to yell out to them to stop 'fore they get closer than maybe a hundred yards, you know. If they hear you and keep coming, I want you to pull out that rifle and fire a shot in the air to get their attention and let 'em know you mean business. Then if they jest keep coming, shoot 'em off their horses," said Ed, showing conviction to enforce what he was telling Joe to do.

Jim about dropped his cup. He couldn't believe what Ed was ordering his herder to do. How far would ol' Ed go, Jim wondered as he tried to regain his composure.

"Be careful not to jest wound any of 'em. If it comes down to it, we sure don't need no witnesses left to tell different stories. And come running fer th' cabin. If we ain't around, jest get in and block th' door and wait fer us. 'Course, I don't think them rascals have th' backbone to do anything now, since I gave 'em good warning not to. But, Joe, we jest ain't taking no chances, see?" said Ed as he swirled the coffee around in his cup.

"Mr. Ed, I understand. Mostly those fellows treat me nice. A few days ago a couple of th' roundup cowboys came by. Even left me a bag of dried apples. We had coffee, and they rode on, looking for strays. Mr. Rash has never been over here. When I see Isom, he's always way up on top, but even he waves to me. There ain't going to be no trouble, Mr. Ed, but I'll sure be on guard. I'm a real good shot," Joe answered.

Jim stood by, taking in all the comments, not fully understanding why so much animosity existed between the various ranchers. Seemed that in country where a person could see for three days in all directions, there surely would be room for an extra soul or two. But who knew just why men turn to hate? When one fellow had livestock on a piece of ground and had had them there for years without trouble, why would another want to just move in on top of him when there was plenty of room all around?

Jim had heard that Brown's Park was the best place in the world to raise livestock and make a living, with plenty of room right down there. The Park had never been overgrazed. Why would a man like Rash start moving his cattle to other areas, up on Cold Spring Mountain, when

he was making a perfectly good living down in the Park? It had to be
greed, plain greed. Seeing someone else happy and using the public
ground must have touched off something inside him that no one would
ever understand. Maybe just wanting to have control over other people
caused the greed in the beginning. After all, folks around seemed to
agree that anyone who got along with those greedy characters was
always treated very well. Maybe it was bootlicking. If the local folks
treated the greedy one with great respect and the proper amount of
bootlicking, the fellow would bend over backward to try to show them
that he was not all bad. He could afford to give them a helping hand
because they would never be a threat to him.

"Jim, I'm going fer a little ride out over Cold Spring Mountain.
Don't want no one with me, jest in case I run into anyone up there,
you know. I jest need to see what might be going on up there, 'specially
since that run-in. You can visit here with Joe fer a spell. Be back by
midday. Fix us up a big steak, will you, Joe? You're the best cook on the
mountain. Got any antelope steak?" Ed asked. He rechecked his rifle
and Colt, tightened the cinch on the saddle, and stepped aboard.

"Sure thing, Mr. Ed. Now you be mighty careful up there on that
mountain all alone. If we hear any shooting, we'll come a runnin'," Joe
answered.

Joe and Jim busied themselves around the fire until Ed was out of
sight. Jim noticed that Joe was very somber, watching after Ed every
step of the way until he vanished over the horizon.

"What's wrong, Joe?" asked Jim.

"Plenty! He's going to kill that man, Rash. When he came to my
camp after that run-in with Rash, he was still plenty mad. Hardly
greeted me. Muttered to himself, to his horse, to the sky. I made out
his plan to kill Rash. He was thinking out loud. Never a word about
it direct to me, but I put it all together. Now he's traveling armed. Not
much looking at the range like he used to do. Not looking at the sheep. I
tell you, Jim, he's going to do it. Maybe not today. Maybe not tomorrow.
But he will get it done," Joe said, very matter-of-factly.

Jim knew the entire situation was out of hand. How could things have gone so far wrong in the short time he had been gone? And was Joe right in thinking that Ed was really going to try to kill Rash? And if he did, then would that mean he'd have to kill Isom too? Seemed that any time this sort of thing got started, there never was an ending, at least not until all the main players were dead.

Then there were all those stories he heard back in town, that Ed was the last one with the miner who was looking for gemstones in the diamond field, and that shoot-out with the fellow over a homestead up in Beaver Basin. Was it self defense, like the deputy and the others around had declared it, based on the word of only Ed? No witnesses? Add to those stories Ed's hunting down and killing the sheep rustler and taking over the Johnson Draw cabin and the few head of stock belonging to the rustler. It was beginning to seem that what Andy had told him about not getting too close with Ed might be right.

Of course it was true too, like Andy said, if Ed took a liking to you, he'd do anything in the world for you. As an outsider, Jim knew he could get by for a time without having to take sides, just stay clear of certain happenings. Yet, he had already committed himself, in a way, to Ed. And word did seem to travel around the area rather quickly. Could it be that Rash and Dart, as well as that fellow Hicks, might have already checked off Jim as Cole's colleague, making him a marked man too?

When Ed returned, not much was said about what he had been up to. They chowed down with Joe, saddled up, and rode off the mountain to Ed's cabin. Ed was quite relaxed; nothing had happened up on Cold Spring Mountain, and he was talkative about making the Brown's Park dance, only a few days away.

"That Cat Claw jug you brought out from town will be enough fer th' both of us fer th' whole dance, Jim. That is if you ain't more of a drinker than I think," commented Ed.

"With all them folks from all over this part of th' world being there, Ed, I sure ain't going to make some kind of fool of myself. Nothing to gain. Maybe a lot to lose, if you know what I mean. Rash and all of them will be there too?" Jim asked as he gathered his few things and made ready to ride back to the Johnson Draw cabin.

"Like I told you, Jim. All these main differences 'tween us folks is mostly fergot at th' dance. Oh, you know, guys like Rash will maybe do a little intimidating 'round. Won't cause any open trouble. You jest plan on being yourself. Chase 'round with th' ranch ladies as long as you're careful not to be drunk. Otherwise, some husband might jest lead you outside. They usually jest tie th' drunks to a wagon wheel and leave them out till they sober up. Th' dance jest goes on," replied Ed.

Jim stepped up onto the sorrel, adjusted the mare's lead rope, and turned out across Beaver Basin toward Johnson Draw.

CHAPTER 7

Jim could no longer come in sight of the Johnson Draw cabin without a feeling of contentment washing over him. The cabin had become his haven of peace, a refuge and retreat from the daily problems of folks ranging livestock against one another, folks living too close together in dirty mining towns like Rock Springs. It was so quiet there—only the calls of the mountain jays and magpies, the yipping of the coyotes, and an occasional lonesome howl of a wolf. Mule deer herds were used to him living in the cabin now, and they paid him little attention as they came to the spring to drink or used the draw for their daily trek to and from their feed grounds. Within gunshot range of the cabin, deer and antelope, does and fawns made their home. The antelope stayed mostly up on the plateau, but they often came into the draw on blustery days to gain the protection of the aspen groves and enjoy grazing on their leaves. Once in a while they would use the groves for bed grounds, but never for long, and never deep into the undercover like the deer so commonly did. Coyotes used the draw as a regular run, and Jim often returned to the cabin to find their tracks printed inside his own, made only a short time earlier. At night the hoot of the owl kept the cabin company, along with the beautiful starry sky.

As he worked the sorrel and mare down off the plateau, through the brief span of timber and into the narrow draw, his attention was drawn to the possibilities of some kind of improved pasture for raising a little hay for winter use for his stock, starting with the two horses or later a few head of cattle. Until that point he had not entertained the thought of wintering in Johnson Draw. Why would the notion hit him now? Was this just another sign of how the cabin and country had grown on him? Was Ed's friendship making him feel so comfortable that his subconscious mind was moving him to accept the new country? Even to somehow overlook the problems over in Brown's Park—the rustlers, the pushing of some cattlemen against some sheepmen, the ideas of killing one another?

The quickened step of the sorrel toward the corral and grassy enclosure pushed Jim's attention back to reality, to getting the horses turned out and taking care of small jobs around the place that he had put off. He knew the place had been a homestead at one time, and as such, it surely had corners marked somewhere to show the true boundary. Did the lines run up or down the draw or bounce abruptly out on top of the plateau? Surely the original homesteader had given thought to this and marked his lines to take in things of importance. Obviously, the spring had to be included, as well as the small, crudely fenced corral-pasture for horses.

A 160-acre homestead couldn't be too hard to circle and locate corners. Jim started by searching close around the cabin, ensuring that the immediate area was not close to the boundary. Then by climbing up the canyon wall a few yards, he could get a better bird's-eye view of the possible homestead. Sure enough, he thought he could make out the old outlines of the boundary. Some locations seemed to be fairly well marked, but others left him guessing. It looked like the old place had been set out in a rectangle, or perhaps square, with the lower boundary located a hundred yards or so below the cabin in the main draw. That meant the homesteader had marked out the junction of the two draws, giving the place both draws to ensure more water, and the far back boundary would have to be out on top of the plateau. Thus, there would be shelter and water in the draws and open grazing on top.

Jim dropped back down into the draw and started walking along where he thought old boundaries probably were. When he arrived at what should have been the old corner, he searched around, and sure enough, there was a small, overgrown rock pile with an old rusted-out tin can set in the middle to mark the official corner of the property. By carefully observing the vegetation all around, he was able to determine where the old property line probably ran. Looking farther along it, he could see where a few old trees had been cut out, and now he knew the direction where he would find the next corner. Once it was located, the rest would be easy. His first move would be to rebuild the corner marker, making it big enough to see from a distance.

Within a few days Jim had the property well marked and was pleased with his efforts. He was also busy reinforcing his small corral and weaving tree branches together along the lines of the small pasture. The cabin required a little work on the sod roof, plus a bit of chinking, and he needed to build a lean-to on one side of the cabin to give him outdoor workspace in bad weather.

But this could all wait. Jim needed to pay a visit to his neighbors and get acquainted. After all, they were the closest folks to him, and if ever he needed help, they would be handy. Homesteaders did need help once in a while, whether simple or desperate.

Jim was glad to see no new tracks in the diamond field when he trotted the sorrel across toward the Finch place. The trip from the Johnson Draw cabin to the Finch cabin was not far at all. Jim wondered why they had not been over his way. Did they even know about him? That first day when he discovered their place, he had kept his presence unknown. Maybe he had done a perfect job of it.

"Hello, down there!" Jim called out as he came over the low ridge behind the Finch cabin, only a hundred yards away. He had seen that there were three or more horses in the corral, and this tended to mean someone was home. "Coming on down!"

From the shed stepped a man with a hoe in his hand, giving Jim a friendly wave. "Come on in," he called. "Margie, put the coffee pot on. We got a visitor coming!"

Jim walked the sorrel up to the hitching post and stepped down.

The homesteader hurried over, sticking out his hand as he introduced himself. "I'm Bill Finch. Let's get inside fer coffee."

"Well, Bill, I'm Jim Keaton from back over th' hill there in Johnson Draw," replied Jim. "Sure could use that coffee. Been making my own too long."

Bill led Jim through the plank door of the cabin into a bright, clean room, all finished out with window curtains, corner shelves with chinaware on display, benches with backs and arms, a rock fireplace with iron hooks for pots, three oil lamps, and other comforting things that made a house a home and showed the handiwork of a woman. From the other room came the aroma of fresh coffee and bread.

"Margie, this here's Mr. Keaton, Jim Keaton, from over in Johnson Draw," said Bill as he introduced Jim to his wife, Margie.

Jim wasn't ready to find a bright-eyed, young woman out in these hills, living in a cabin, even though it was the best cabin he had seen. "Ma'am, I'm sure pleased to meet you. Knew you folks was over here sometime back, but been jest so busy I ain't been over. Decided today jest to drop everything and head on over," said Jim.

"Why, Mr. Keaton, you should have come earlier. You're always welcome here. A few weeks back we saw a sheepherder that said there was a new feller living somewhere 'round here. He jest didn't know where. We been watching ever since," said Margie. "Do sit down and I'll bring you some coffee. And what kind of homemade pie would you like, Mr. Keaton? Got apple and apricot. Picked th' fruit myself down along th' Green River last fall. Canned it up and can't wait fer th' folks down there to have more this year."

"Ma'am, this jest sounds too good. I'll take th' one you've got cut," answered Jim, not expecting anything at all like homemade pie.

"Jest one more thing, Mr. Keaton. You can't have either kind till you start calling me by my name, Margie! Now, do I hear it that way, or do I hold up th' pie?" teased Margie.

"Oh, ma'am ... I mean ... uh ... Margie. And 'course, th' same here. Jim is what I go by." Jim stumbled and stammered, trying to find just the right words.

The pie and coffee went over real well, and before long talk started of things like the condition of the range, the livestock Bill was running, the garden he and Margie put in. They had been on the place three or four years, just about enough time to get it set up like they wanted. They had visited all the surrounding country and knew most everyone within a day's ride, and they were very fond of Jim's friend, Ed. Ed had not only helped them get the homestead, but he had even cosigned a small loan they had from Kendall, the banker in Rock Springs. Then, too, it was Ed who had fetched the doctor to see Margie through a bad miscarriage during the hard winter. They felt like they owed him a lot. Couldn't have made it without him.

Jim pushed back his chair and said to the couple, "Well, I've got to get back over to get some more things done in Johnson Draw. Never expected to find such good folks as you over here. Would've come sooner. I guess I should've come in or at least hunted you up back when I first arrived."

"Jim, I don't know if you can get that cabin and old homestead from Ed now, but you know if we can help, we sure will do it. He really never uses it, so maybe it can be got," said Bill as the three of them walked out to the hitching post.

"Oh! 'Bout fergot. Bill, are you and Margie going over to th' Brown's Park dance coming up?" asked Jim.

"Sure, Jim. Me and Margie jest don't miss one of them get-togethers. We hear th' little Bassett girl will be home from school and all. Lots of folks all th' way from Rock Springs, Green River City, Ashley Valley, Maybell, Craig, and other places make that dance. Boy! Does that old schoolhouse shake and rumble, what with all them folks stomping and carrying on. Have to build a new one, some day. You going over, Jim?" asked Bill.

"Got invited and Ed tells me I shouldn't miss it. Good chance to meet some of th' folks from all 'round. Went to town and bought some new boots fer it. Guess that alone is enough to tell you my answer, ain't it?" said Jim. "Don't know any lady out here at all, till today, that is. At least now I maybe can get at least one dance out of those new boots. That is if you don't mind my dancing with Margie, Bill?"

"Now, Jim, you may as well know right now. Me and Bill have an understanding 'bout th' Brown's Park dances. He can swing any of th' ladies he wants to, as much as he wants to. And I can swing any of them fellers. But when it's all over, we just remember who we're going home with!" Margie said with a twinkle in her eye.

"Best be on my way. See you there. Sure hope you see fit to bring along some of your homemade pies, Margie." Jim swung aboard the sorrel and reined him toward Johnson Draw.

Jim had always carried his .30-40 rifle in the saddle scabbard, never knowing when it might be called on or for what purpose. As he trotted the sorrel out through the cedars and up on the sagebrush flats, he spotted several small herds of antelope grazing for their afternoon meal. He remembered that his larder was getting low, and nothing would be much better than a tender antelope steak. He reined in the sorrel, pulled the rifle from the scabbard and placed it across the saddle in front of him, ready for instant use.

The .30-40 was one of the latest new cartridges, and Jim selected it because it would outrange the newer .30-30 but recoil much less than the old .45-70. It had gained a good reputation as a large-game caliber, even useful on grizzly bears. Grizzlies were something that Jim did not have to worry about locally because they had been shot out some thirty years earlier by the livestock men. In the constant westward expansion of the country, the conflict between man and beast had to be settled in some manner, or the movement would have been curtailed to a large degree. Since the grizzly was the most formidable enemy of mankind, second only to the Indian who had now been subdued, it had to be kept in check. If that meant total annihilation, so be it.

But this was not Jim's worry today. The rifle was now used against wolves and coyotes and as a provider of wild game for his food supply, and the antelope would easily come into range of the .30-40.

From the saddle, Jim saw a herd of antelope just over the skyline in a shallow draw a few hundred yards ahead. When within easy rifle range, he dismounted, leaving the sorrel ground tied, and slipped up to the edge of the draw with his rifle ready. In the herd he noted several young animals, this year's fawn crop. They were already over half the size of the does. With a deliberate aim, he fired one shot and collected enough antelope steaks and jerky to last the month.

With the field-dressed antelope across the saddle in front of him, Jim trotted on toward the cabin in Johnson Draw. The sun was getting low when he arrived and turned the sorrel loose in the corral. He quickly quartered the small antelope, cut out a choice piece to take to the cabin and hung the remainder from tree limbs in deep shade where it would cool out and keep for several days. Once in the cabin, he turned the lamp on high, stoked up a fire in the old stove, and felt contentment not known by city-dwelling folks.

For the next few days Jim worked hard on the cabin and grounds. He wanted the workshed finished first, and he spent long days cutting the poles, skinning them, and hewing some sides flat. He set uprights deep in the ground and notched the tops to take a matching notched crossbeam. Then with notched rafters set as close together as he could get them, he covered the whole thing with antelope hides followed by a layer of dirt. A large tree stump served as a worktable, and he placed his best-hewed poles against the cabin wall on posts set in the ground, thus providing a first-class workbench.

All the work on the cabin kept Jim's mind off the big dance, but when the day arrived, Jim was out early, before light. He packed his new boots and shirt, plus a pair of Levis that was not too worn. Then he made up a bedroll and checked the saddlebags for his regular cooking gear: cup, plate, and small pot for coffee, a bit of jerky and flour, and other tidbits. He rolled everything in a light tarp and tied it behind the saddle just as dawn began streaking the eastern sky with an orange cast outlining the few clouds. The sorrel looked eager as Jim stepped aboard and reined him toward Beaver Basin and Ed's headquarters. The ride out of Johnson Draw, over the divide near Bishop Peak, and across the basin only took a little over an hour, putting him at the hitching post just in time for breakfast with Ed.

"Won't take but a shake to have a good breakfast 'fore we start out fer that dance, Jim," said Ed. "We can go up to th' Cottonwood camp and let Joe know where we're headed. Won't reach th' schoolhouse till kind of late-like—maybe halfway through the afternoon. Rueben here can finish up th' kitchen fer us."

Jim noticed that Ed had already packed his roan for the trip, including his gun belt over the saddle horn. Every cartridge loop was filled, and the .45 looked as if it had been cleaned. The saddle scabbard held the rifle, and Jim wondered just how much ammunition Ed might be packing for it. Could it be that Ed was planning to take on Rash and the others at the dance? No, even Ed would hold off if he could. Maybe he was just being cautious.

Once out on the trail they visited briefly with Joe at the camp, just to let him know they were on their way to the Brown's Park dance and to be sure nothing out of the ordinary had been going on between Joe and the roundup cowboys. Then they were on their way up on top of Cold Spring Mountain.

"Figger we best go off down Goodman Gulch, Jim. Matt uses th' old trail down through th' cedars, so it is easy to follow. Can't jest go off Cold Spring anywhere. You ain't ever been over here, have you, Jim?" Ed asked.

"No, sure haven't been. This will be my first trip on that side of th' mountain. Since all this country seems to be used by them fellers with funny marked cattle, jest didn't seem to be much reason fer me to drift over. Least not without you along, Ed," Jim answered.

Within a couple of miles they broke out, overlooking the entire Brown's Park country. From some five miles away the Green River reflected the early morning sunlight. Off in the far distance they could see Lodore Canyon with its rose- and rust-colored walls projecting up over a thousand feet from the river. The skyline was dominated by

Diamond Mountain, where many of the Park ranchers ran their cattle. And a pure sea of cedar ran all the way down Cold Spring Mountain, from top to bottom. Jim could see no clear way through the jumbled rocks and thick cedars, so he reined the sorrel in behind Ed's roan and followed him in single file over the rim and down into the cedars.

Ed understood that Jim would want to know about getting down through the cedars and ledges. "Long way down there, Jim. We're 'bout eighty-five hundred feet up here. Them surveyors seemed to think th' schoolhouse was only like fifty-three hundred feet. What with all them red rocks all th' way down, ledges and stuff, we'll be a while 'fore we get down to th' valley. When we do break out, we'll go over by th' Sterling place and right out across th' clear country fer a few miles to reach th' schoolhouse. It's right over by them Hoy Bottoms."

Jim noticed how the horses slowed, picking their way along, while Ed continued explaining the country. "We'll be down where Vermillion Creek joins in with th' Green River. Ought to be lots of folks down there by now. Some been on th' trail fer a day or two. Somebody sure furnished a steer fer roasting. Maybe Matt Rash done that. Be no cost to him, if you get my drift. 'Sides that, ol' Isom Dart is one of th' best cooks 'round these parts. I bet it's him and some of them Bassetts doing th' cooking and fixing. With Rash being th' president of th' cattle association fer th' Park, it sure might be that he is th' one putting it all on, getting ol' Isom down here and all. Be kind of nice if it is that way. He'd be putting on th' dog, acting like th' nicest feller in th' world."

"Whoa up, Ed! Jest look at that big buck!" hollered Jim as they rounded a point in the cedars. "He's big as an elk!"

"By gosh, Jim, if you ain't right! That big guy is shore 'nough th' king of this hill if there ever was one!" answered Ed as he abruptly pulled up the roan in a shower of rocks and dust. "Why, I bet his horns go wider than any gun barrel, even wider than the whole gun! What do you think, Jim? Maybe three feet wide, maybe more?"

"Ed, he's th' biggest buck I've ever laid eyes on anywhere. Been all over that Arizona country. Never was one that big down there. That

head would sure look like something, mounted, and maybe in ol'
August Kendall's bank back in town!" exclaimed Jim. "Still in th' velvet,
Ed. Reckon he will still be here when he gets them horns all polished
out and all?"

"Sure, Jim. He'll be here all right. Thing is, you can't never find 'em
like that when you go looking fer 'em. 'Course, we could kind of mark this
spot and plan on sneaking back down here in a couple of months when
they is all polished and looking good. What do you think?" Ed asked.

"Oh, Ed, I'd sure go fer that! This .30-40 ain't never been sighted
on nothing like that, ever," commented Jim, knowing the odds of ever
seeing that king of the hill again would be slim. Then the buck seemed
to fade away into the dark cedars without making a sound.

"We best move on. Be noon 'fore we get out of these confounded
cedars, Jim."

Off Cold Spring Mountain and out of the cedars and rocks, the
going was easy across the Park bottom toward the schoolhouse. By
midafternoon they came in sight of the schoolhouse and could see the
crowd gathering. Wagons were parked all around the building and clear
down to the Green River, some two hundred yards away, and clear out
to Vermillion Creek, about a quarter mile from the school. Dozens of
horses were hobbled or picketed out in the lush pasture. As they closed
in toward the grounds, Ed and Jim could see the crowd around the
smoke coming from the barbecue area, indicating that their arrival was
just at the right time.

To Jim, the scene brought thoughts of his army days when he had
time on his hands and read every book he could find on the older days,
days back when the mountain men came down the Green River to the
first rendezvous ever held in these parts. That would have been some
seventy-four years back, in 1826.

Brown's Hole had been the wintering ground for thousands of
roving Indians and was even then known for mild winters and abundant
game. From 1826 until 1840 or so, Brown's Hole held the largest of
all the famous rendezvous with business exceeding that of Bent's Fort,

over on the Arkansas River, and even that of Taos, New Mexico. The rendezvous usually lasted several weeks in the early summer months. Then the trappers would again head out into the mountains to trap more beavers as the approaching cold weather made the pelts thicker and more valuable. Thus, the cycle was started again, and the next spring all the trappers would work their way back to Brown's Hole for the next rendezvous to trade and sell their hard-earned furs with the Indians and fur company representatives from the East.

The center of all activity at any rendezvous was gambling on skills of rifle shooting, horsemanship, knife throwing, wrestling, and other activities. Naturally, dalliance with the Indian squaws was a favorite pastime for all the mountain men, and often as not, they would head back to the mountains followed by the squaw of their choice. Watered-down whiskey was commonly brought in by white traders to entice the trappers and Indians out of their best furs, and this led to injuries and killings.

But the parties must have been something, thought Jim. Dancing all night and sometimes for days, stuffing themselves with roasted bear, elk, deer, and mountain sheep, the best of all wild game. The Indians always brought in dried buffalo as well as some meat taken right in the valley. And always there were dried berries and gourds, fruits and nuts, and various foods white men had never sampled. The trappers would often give up their tobacco and steel tools for soft tanned skins that all the squaws made. Then they would have to trade their beaver skins at a loss to the white traders to regain what they had traded away to those squaws.

By the 1850s, all this was gone. Jim would never get to see those major events of the past. But he knew the rendezvous were now simply replaced with settlement dances, just like the Brown's Park dance. So, perhaps nothing really goes away, but just changes with the times. The dances Jim had attended in out-of-the-way places still had the feasts, with beef replacing wild game. Gambling still went on, although not to the extent of losing everything one owned. There was still a little friendly competition with horse races and some rifle shooting and the like. Trades were still made and even a few squaws were available, although they were now white for the most part.

"Jim, we best get on down there toward th' creek or river if we intend to find a place fer our bedrolls. Got to hobble out these horses too, you know. First thing you know, there'll be too many folks wanting to stop us to visit, and we'll get caught short doing what we ought to," Ed advised as they rode into the crowd of people scurrying around. Ed was giving first one, then another, a hand wave and an occasional greeting.

"Ed! Jim! Hey, there!" came the feminine voice from among the crowd. "Wait, fellers! We been looking fer you."

Ed drew up and turned, looking all around. "Where'd that come from, Jim? Sounds like someone I ought to know, like maybe Margie. Margie Finch!"

"Why, sure 'nough is, Ed. Here she comes, over there near them wagons and things," replied Jim.

"Well, are you jest going to sit up there like a knot on a log? Or are you going to get down and give a neighbor a hug?" said Margie as she broke from the group and rushed over toward Ed and Jim.

"Margie! How good to see you. Been a spell. You know Jim here too?" said Ed as he stepped down from the roan and picked Margie up in big bear hug.

"Sure do, Ed. He was over jest a bit ago visiting. Jim, you get down and let me hug you if you ain't going to do it fer me!" exclaimed Margie as she pulled away from Ed and reached up to drag Jim down from the sorrel.

"Gosh, Margie, er, Mrs. Finch," stammered Jim, totally taken aback by the abruptness of Margie's friendly, unconstrained pulling on his arm as he left the saddle and found himself directly in the clutches of the only woman he knew in all the area. "How are you? How you been?" Jim asked, trying to get an answer of some reasonableness out to her.

"Don't you keep calling me Mrs. Finch no more, Jim! We agreed to my name when you was over at th' place, remember?" Margie said in a playful manner. "And we been sort of keeping you and Ed a place over by th' wagon. Got room fer both bedrolls right under th' wagon, and even have some room fer th' horses. Close to th' river too."

"Jim, sounds like our troubles is over, don't it?" said Ed. "Let's get things settled over there and get on to that beef I can smell too good."

Margie led them over to the wagon where Bill was tightening some bolts and checking over one wheel.

"Just knew you'd both be showing up here," he called out from under the frame. "Kept you a good place, if you like it. And you better hurry if you want some of ol' Matt's beef being served up by Isom over there!"

Ed and Jim took care of their horses and spread their bedrolls under the Finch wagon. Then they strolled over toward the cooking pit, following their sense of smell all the way. It took most of an hour to get there, as literally dozens of cowboys, ranchers, and families stopped them for introductions and brief chats, getting acquainted. Jim was very pleased at the reception he received from total strangers, thinking once more how nice it might be to be a part of this country, even though a little remote over in Johnson Draw. He met them all—the Davenports, Jarvies, Allens, Rifes, Hoys, Crouses, and so many others. He knew he would never remember their names over the coming weekend.

It seemed that all the folks had a pack of kids around. They were running and chasing, playing tag, throwing rocks at the river, which was much too far away but getting points for who could throw the straightest and farthest. The little girls were mixing in but usually just enjoying playing with each other. Some knew one another from school, but there were others who were from town and knew no one. Mainly, they were just full of energy and bubbling over to be out in the open at a big area gathering. And Jim could hardly hold back his broad smile, remembering back when he, too, was their age and off on some family outing, too many years ago.

"Hold up there, young feller," came a shout from over near the crowd at the cooking pit. "Don't you even have time to stop and see an ol' buddy, Jim? Ain't been all that long, now has it? Bet you jest thought you were never going to have to put up with th' likes of me again, eh?"

Out of the crowd came Walt Bentsen from Bitter Creek, waving his arms and acting like he had found a long-lost brother. Jim had not thought about Walt in days, or weeks.

"Walt ... Walt, why who'd ever think you'd be all th' way down here!" answered Jim as he stuck out his hand and literally pulled Walt over to him. "You sure are a sight fer sore eyes! The first feller I ever met in these parts, back when I first stopped off there at Bitter Creek on my way out to Rock Springs. Ed, you got to meet this here feller," said Jim as he turned to Ed, again pulling Walt around.

"Hi, there, Walt. Long time no see," Ed greeted him. "You don't get down this far very often, Walt. Might've knowed you'd be here fer th' big dance, though. How's things in th' big city of Bitter Creek?"

For a moment Jim was startled. But then why shouldn't Ed know Walt? They had both been out in this country for many years and had to associate in some manner from time to time. And hadn't Ed followed that sheep rustler off toward Bitter Creek and recovered his sheep up the trail and maybe even got up in Walt's country? If the rustler was planning to ship them out by rail, Walt might have been the very person the rustler had to deal with.

"Well, gosh, Ed, you best get that Jim on over to th' feed trough there. Ol' Matt and Isom sure ain't going to hold any back fer you," said Walt, all the time pushing both men toward the food line. "We'll all have to get together after a while. Got my bedroll off there below the riverbank. In case I miss you later, jest get on down there and spread out with me!"

Jim and Ed found themselves next to the best-smelling beef and beans and baked bread they had been around in some time.

"Man, ain't this something, Jim?" Ed said appreciatively as they started filling their plates to the rim. "Looks like we can jest stuff and stuff till we won't have to do any cooking fer days and days."

CHAPTER 8

"Hi, there, Ed! And Jim, no less," shouted Isom over the noise of the crowd. "Dive in, men. Ain't every day you get this here free Matt Rash beef! Don't let it worry you none, Jim, that I knows who you is and all. Everbody knows anybody that's new 'round here. Seen you up on th' mountain once with Ed here. We'll get to know each other good 'fore too long, being up on th' mountain with livestock and all. And, Jim, if you ever need a hand at anything, jest come on up and let me know. I'll help you. We sort of all pitch in fer each other, you know. Jest th' way we do things 'round here. Fer now I'm going to pick you out th' best, juiciest hunk of ol' Matt's beef we got. Here, jest you try that!"

"Isom! Nice to see you. Kind of knowed who you were jest from all th' good things I've heard 'bout you. Looks like you're having a grand ol' time here," said Jim. "You even got yourself a helper down there, ain't you? Ain't that ol' Matt at th' end of th' line, dipping out them beans? I guess he knows who I am too, Isom? Even if we ain't ever met straight out?"

"Sure, Jim. He's being real sweet-like today. Takes care of everyone out here, jest like he really enjoys it!" answered Isom, smiling all the time. "Jest act like you knowed him since he was born. He understands. We can all get in some talking and visiting later on."

This bothered Jim for a moment. Everyone around seemed to know all about him, but he didn't know them. But then he was the new man on the mountain. Sure, he'd be the talk of all the camps. And in this country they would all give him every benefit of the doubt about anything until he proved himself, one way or the other. It was just the ranching way.

"Ed, you sure was right 'bout all these guys getting along at these big dances and all. I really didn't know jest what to expect. I'm fixing to like all this," said Jim.

"Sure, Jim. Jest like I told you. Say, you ain't never met this James Hicks feller neither, have you, Jim?" answered Ed, motioning toward the back of the schoolhouse. "That's him, over there by the building. Looks like he's full up and jest trying to find a place to rest. Don't much socialize."

Jim turned and his jaw went slack. Could it be? Could that fellow against the schoolhouse be James Hicks? Ed must not mean the same person Jim saw, a tanned fellow that would most surely pass for a Mexican most anywhere, or even maybe an Apache.

"Ed, do you mean that feller over there, that dark-looking feller? Why, that ain't … I mean …" Jim stopped short, looked back toward the schoolhouse and then back toward Ed, thinking he best not say anymore. He could be wrong, but that was just not a man named Hicks!

"Sure do. Th' same feller from up on th' mountain with Rash when we had our little meetin' of th' minds. He's th' one that stayed clear of th' whole thing. Couldn't really tell jest which side he might be on, and sure didn't want to have to find out," answered Ed.

Jim was sure he knew the fellow from back in the past, back in the cavalry days. That's where he knew him. Not Hicks at all! Sure not anyone named Hicks. That had to be the scout from the old Indian fighting days in Arizona—Tom Horn! Ol' Tom Horn himself, the chief scout from back when Jim was a young soldier just trying to get started in life. Everyone at the fort knew Tom Horn, but Jim was too young and totally unknown to be recognized by anyone of the stature of Horn, a well-known Indian scout of no little fame. But why would he be out here in Brown's Park under an assumed name? James Hicks? No, not a chance. But why?

"Something wrong, Jim? You look like you got th' plague, er something. Don't take kindly to all this food?" Ed looked intently into Jim's face. "What's got in you, feller?"

"Oh … er … nothing. Nothing, really, Ed. It's jest that … Oh, sure … er … I mean, ain't this here beef jest 'bout the best and tenderest stuff you ever set your teeth to, Ed?" Jim finally stammered out, trying to recover from recognizing James Hicks as Tom Horn.

Now Jim's thoughts were spinning. Should he let Ed know that Hicks was really Tom Horn? And if Ed knew, would he keep still about it? Maybe Ed could figure something out about just why the man was using another name. Surely Ed would know what to do, how to react. But for now, though, Jim knew he had to just keep it to himself and not let on that he ever knew this man, Hicks, or Horn. There surely had to be something up, something too big to open up about. And if anyone introduced James Hicks to him, he knew he would have to be careful and not give himself away. Jim thought to himself, don't make a mistake and call him Tom Horn!

"Well, Ed, good to see you again. Been a while. See you got your friend here with you. My name is Bassett, young fellow, what's yours?" The little old man stuck his hand out to Jim, and through the heavy, gray beard, Jim could see a friendly twinkle in the old fellow's eyes.

"Oh, I'm Jim Keaton, sir. I've been staying in Ed's cabin over in Johnson Draw. Kind of helping him some with his livestock and all," answered Jim. He took in the courtly manners of the old gentleman, wondering just why he would strike Jim as different, intelligent, perhaps educated, and, of course, the Bassett he had heard about ever since his arrival in Brown's Park country. An old-timer, for sure. And the man that more or less ran the community dance, seeing to it that nothing got out of hand, even taking up all the guns at the schoolhouse door.

"Jim, you need to know Herb Bassett here. Takes care of things like being ex-postmaster and knowing things 'bout land deeds and titles and things. You may want to talk with him 'bout something like a land deed some day," said Ed. "You see, Herb, Jim here is sort of looking over th' country fer a little place to settle on. Getting to like this Park country."

"We'll visit later, young man. Right now you best get that beef finished and get ready for the dance. I've got to get over and see that all the music instruments are ready. And round up the musicians too!" said Herb Bassett as he moved off toward the building.

People continued to come by for introductions and to make small talk with Ed. They all treated Jim with great respect, something that seemed common with country folks. Not like back in town. But even though Jim met many likable folks, he simply couldn't get Tom Horn off his mind. Something was going on that struck Jim as not right, but just what it might be, he didn't know. But his mind was made up not to tip his hand, not just yet. He needed to get an idea about what Horn might be up to.

Jim remembered hearing that Horn had drifted down into Mexico for a while after leaving the cavalry, and then he was up in the Denver area where he became a detective with the Pinkerton agency. Just what he did there, Jim had not heard. There had been rumors that he had gone off to Wyoming for range detective work, but Jim was not sure what that might have included. There were stories drifting around that Horn had killed his share of men, both good and bad.

Dances started early out in the ranch country. Even though everyone lit up oil lamps and hung them in the schoolhouse and around the yard, they all liked to get things going before darkness set in. All the Brown's Park folks and visitors had changed to their best town-like dress, or at least the best things they owned.

The grown-up ranch women all had their hair up in French twists or buns and bangs curled into a frizz. The younger girls wore their hair in curls or braids tucked up with big bows of ribbon, and some even had on a bit of face makeup, much to the consternation of many of the older folks. The girls' dresses came to about three inches below the knee, and they had to wear slippers. The women wore dresses that were tight fitting down to the knee and then flared out and continued to the floor. They were allowed high-button shoes with high heels, and all were shown off among their crowd.

Cowboys and ranchers gathered along the walls and talked about livestock and horses, standing ill at ease in new boots and jeans. Then when the music started, the first of the dancers slipped out onto the rough floor. Within minutes old men, young girls, mothers and daughters, fathers and sons, little imps no taller than some of the boot tops were all out on the floor swinging with the music, most of which they had never heard and didn't care.

The first hour went off with everyone getting acquainted, or reacquainted, no one really letting down their guard. As the night wore on, however, things changed. By the second break in the music, a few young and not so young fellows were feeling the effects of the jugs they all had hidden outside, usually close enough to the building to be handy. And by then a few of the brazen young ladies, usually those from town, were making eyes at the sheepish, shy cowboys, especially those who just might have a secret, or not so secret, girlfriend in the crowd. As the music got faster and louder, the crowd got noisier, until they could be heard all up and down the valley.

Jim had no trouble getting acquainted with most all the ladies, since he was the new fascinating fellow of the party. Margie started it off, grabbing Jim before he could resist and swinging him around the room to the envy of the other ladies. Then it was Mary Crouse, happy to have Jim to dance with while her husband was off somewhere in the darkness with a jug and a few horse-racing friends, drinking a little too much, as usual. Elizabeth Erickson, from several miles north of Jim's little cabin in Johnson Draw, took him around enough for him to discover that some good-looking women were truly ranching and business minded with no designing thoughts on any man.

Esther Davenport was one of the first young girls to cut in on Jim, pleasing him to no end. Josie and Ann Bassett then made a couple of rounds with him. Josie was about to finalize a divorce, something almost never heard of or done. Ann had just returned from some school in time to saddle up her horse and go up the mountain with Matt Rash to help with the final part of the roundup. Jim found Ann interesting, even intriguing and fascinating.

It didn't take long for some crusty young cowboy to slip a jug of whiskey inside the hall, work his way to the punch bowl, and deposit half of it into the punch. It happened at every dance. Some say it was designed that way, just to help the older ladies loosen up and enjoy the night. Several of those ladies gathered in a tight circle, sampling the punch, pointing to the bowl, and then giggling a bit, turning, and walking away after refilling their glasses. The men all noticed that the punch got much better, and soon even the musicians were calling for punch. Joe Davenport's guitar took on a better tune, Sam Bassett's fiddle got louder, and even Josie's zither gained momentum. But the organ that Herb Bassett had hauled in by wagon stayed mellow. He played steadily throughout the dance, with hardly any change.

As the night settled in, Jim noticed that Ann was cutting in on every other dance, taking him from some other delightful lady. And he also noticed that she was beginning to hold him closer, to the point where several of the young girls stared, whispered, and turned away when he caught their eye.

"Jim, I've got to get some fresh air," said Ann as she wheeled him around on the dance floor and headed him toward the door. "Oh, don't get too excited. Matt Rash isn't looking. Besides, I'd kind of like for him to just try to stop me from dancing with you."

Before Jim could do anything about it, Ann had him halfway out the door. "Really, Jim, I just agreed to get you out here for someone else," Ann chirped coyly with a big smile and a twinkle in her eye.

When they stepped out in the semidarkness, with only the dim golden glow from a couple of lanterns to light the way, someone out in the darker area shouted at Jim.

"Jim, you ol' rascal you! Didn't think I'd ever get you away from all them women in there. Had to take charge of things by enticing this here pretty little Ann to fool you some! She can make anything work out," came the familiar voice just before the big hand of Andy Ewing reached out and pulled Jim from the clutches of little Ann.

"Andy! How long you been here? Where you been? I thought I'd surely seen everyone here. How'd I ever miss you?" said Jim ecstatically, overjoyed by the presence of perhaps the first friend he had in all the mountains. "All the way from Rock Springs and not even covered with coal dust. Must've shook it all off making the trip!"

"Jim, you're no different out here than when you were in town ... with that nice Mary Lou Garrett. Guess I'd best tell you, she asks about you all the time. Just what do you have on all them pretty girls across the country, Jim?" said Andy as they stepped away from the building toward the wagon camps.

"Oh, Andy, there sure ain't nothing out here like Mary Lou. Well, there's some here, but not the same. These are all outdoors types, you know? The kind that can sure 'nough fix fences and saddle horses and hitch up teams and things like all that. They even shoot game and rope steers. Now back in town there must be plenty that used to do these same things but don't have to no more. I'd be plumb embarrassed if ever I had to ask that Mary Lou to do any of that. Does she really miss me any, Andy?" Jim asked with a serious tone in his voice.

"Sure she does, Jim. I ain't never seen no woman sulk 'round over nobody like she did over you fer days and days after you left. She jest ain't never taken to no man before. Jest wish it were me, Jim!" Andy laughed. "I'd like to see something like that now, Jim. Me and Mary Lou ... Wow!

"But your love life ain't what we're here fer, now is it, Jim? I'm camped over near the creek there, jest past the last wagon. Got to get out of here tomorrow so I can be back at work not too late Monday, you know. So let's get back in there, and when you wear out, come hunt me up and let's talk. Bet you got lots of things going on, what with you making such good friends with that there August Kendall at the bank and all. Did you see him out here yet, Jim?" asked Andy.

"I thought I saw him at a distance, all close up with Matt Rash and some other folks I didn't know. Haven't got close 'nough to even say hello. Don't really care if I don't, Andy. And you're right. Let's get back in there and kick th' walls a little more. I was jest getting to know that little Bassett gal. Then you came along! Jest pulling your leg, Andy. You know I'd rather see you than hug up on that young thing," Jim said with a twinkle in his eye.

They turned toward the building just in time to meet Ed coming out.

"Hey, what you two doing off out here while things is going on inside? Oh, bet you been out to visit that jug now, haven't you? Don't know if I could handle it if th' two of you got skunked out on me tonight! How you been, Andy?" said Ed as he moved to ease Jim away.

"Jest heading back in, Ed. I'll leave this scalawag in your hands. I got to get back in there," Andy replied as he ducked away with quickened steps toward the festivities.

"Jim, do we need to talk 'bout something? Something eating on you, feller?" Ed asked as he proceeded to lead Jim farther out away from the music and crowd.

They walked slowly out to the Finch wagon, where their bedrolls were, before another word was spoken. Jim was turning things over in his mind, knowing that he should confide in Ed about this Hicks-Horn affair. After all, Ed seemed to be tied in somehow with all the goings-on, the trouble over grazing on the mountain, seeing Rash and Dart butchering out Spicer's bull, noticing how Hicks reacted to the problem. Could it be that Horn was some kind of detective? Maybe the rumors about Horn killing those rustlers without giving any of them a chance were true. Could be that if Jim didn't let Ed in on what he knew, Ed just might get cut down by someone, Horn perhaps, without really being a part of the things that were going on in and around Brown's Park. Maybe that was the answer. Just open up with Ed and see what he thought.

"Ed, I've got something you might ought to know. But I want

your word that you won't open your mouth 'bout it. It jest might get somebody killed. Do you see what I'm trying to say, Ed? This jest has to be stone cold and quiet," said Jim, not knowing just how Ed might react.

"Now that's better, Jim. I jest knowed you had something big on your mind all day. Sort of seen it clear back there when we got to the eating line. Even noticed you ain't cut out much fer th' jug we brought along neither. And ain't even tried to slip out with none of them pretty ladies that's been all over you all night. Well? Let's have it, Jim. I ain't out here fer my health. Could be in there having some fun, you know," said Ed, trying his best to give Jim every chance of getting the heavy burden off his chest.

"Ed, you know that Hicks feller you pointed out to me today? Jest how well might you know him? When did you first know he showed up out here on the mountain? And jest what does he really do? I think when we'd think 'bout it, we'd agree that he don't really act like a drifting cowboy or range hand, now does he, Ed?" Jim started off. "Do you really know anything he does for real, Ed?"

"Well, now that you bring it up, Jim, no. No, I can't say that I've known him to do much of nothing, but jest seems to be around. Hangs out kind of full time with Matt Rash, you know. Been all over this Park country, dropped in on jest about everybody at one time or other. Ol' Billy Rife tells me he even was way off up to his place once or twice. Talking 'bout buying horses, but didn't really seem interested in any details of a sale. You know, that does seem strange, now that we're thinking 'bout it, don't it, Jim?" Ed answered staring off into space, thinking.

"Do you know a feller by th' name of Tom Horn, Ed?" Jim asked.

"Sure, Jim. I 'spose most all th' folks out this way heard of him," replied Ed. "Been up in Wyoming working fer a bunch of money hounds, them ranchers that got more money than they can count and still wantin' more. Lots of talk they been paying him to handle rustlers, you know, without ever going to trial, no court hearings. None of that.

Jest gets them rustlers and gets 'em good. When he first showed up 'round Laramie, the story is he got right after some of them bad sorts and left them notes on their doors telling them to be gone in thirty days or else. Some of 'em jest up and ran out. Never seen 'em in these parts again, but heard they was way off somewhere like Texas, or maybe even clear down to Mexico."

"Any stories 'bout maybe him killing any rustler," asked Jim.

"Well, seems a couple of 'em didn't run, got found shot dead right after them thirty days ran out. Met a feller from Cheyenne a while back, told me 'bout being in th' saloon there one night when this feller, turned out to be Horn, got hisself all likkered up, drunk, full of whiskey talk 'bout how he done got rid of certain of them big rustlers 'round. Even said he jest plugged 'em with that new .30-30 of his. Sure 'nough, when this feller did some checking, he found that them rustlers was found shot dead by a .30-30. 'Course, Horn was fifty miles away at th' time. Till they added up th' time it might take a real hard rider to go that far. Then they sort of knowed it could've been th' work of ol' Horn. Jest lots and lots of stories going 'round 'bout that feller, Horn. Why do you ask, Jim?"

Jim hesitated. "Is he working over in this country, Ed?"

"Well, you know how that could go, Jim. We sure don't think he's over here. You know, we wouldn't likely know if he was or wasn't, now would we, Jim? Who out here would even know him? Could've been brought in by some big outfit like Haley, or even Ayers, Wilson. I don't know of no one that would really know him if he run smack into him. Why, he could be jest 'bout any of these drifters we see all th' time coming through here," Ed said. "'Course, he does carry a right new Winchester .30-30. None of them 'round here much. I think maybe ol' Tittsworth up north closer to Rock Springs might have one."

"Ed, jest what kind of rifle do you think Hicks might be carrying?" said Jim. "Do you have an idea jest where he might be camped?"

"You're getting at something, ain't you, Jim? And if it's what I'm thinking, we best get on over to his camp and take a look. He's staying over there at Matt's wagon. Saw him there jest at sundown. We can get over there, but if he catches us, we'd better have a good story. I got it! We'll jest carry this here jug with us, and if anyone catches us, we can sort of act drunk and jest keep moving on. Let's go!" Ed said with a vengeance.

Hicks's camp wasn't over a hundred yards from the Finch wagon, toward the cooking area. The dance was in full swing, and most everyone was either inside or at least close to the hall. Jim and Ed carried the jug out in plain sight, waving their arms a bit, leaning on each other some, just doing what any good drunk might appear to do. As they moved in near the wagon, they spotted Hicks's gear just under the edge of the wagon bed. Quickly, Jim motioned Ed to crawl under and inspect the rifle while he, Jim, stayed out on guard. In no time at all, Ed was up with a look of astonishment on his face.

"It's a new .30-30 Winchester! Let's get out of here 'fore someone comes along," said Ed, pushing Jim off toward Finch's camp.

"Okay, Ed," Jim started in. "I know Tom Horn. Served with him down in Arizona years ago. He wouldn't know me 'cause I was just a ragtag soldier and he was th' chief of scouts. We weren't there together over a couple of months. We both moved on in opposite directions. James Hicks is Tom Horn!"

The two men moved out into the darker area, quietly thinking things over. If Horn was here, who or what was he after? His reputation would mean he was on the prowl for rustlers, any kind, not just the big-time fellows. He'd take any kind he might come up with. And it wouldn't take much evidence to get the man killed. Even if it turned out to be Ed ... or even Jim.

After some thought, Ed came up with a dozen names of folks that Hicks, or Horn, had been to see. Some he only visited and asked questions of, but some he stayed with a day or two or more. While he visited Charley Sparks, he only stayed a short time and never came back. Same thing with the Rifes. But he seemed to always be in and out of the Bassett place, and of course, he almost lived with Matt Rash, even to the extent of staying in his bunkhouse and hiring out to him to help work the roundup. Most all the Brown's Parkers had been guilty of "finding" a stray calf or two or maybe more from time to time, so how would anyone ever pick out only one or two, or maybe a few more, to accuse of rustling? To get them all might mean wiping out all of Brown's Park.

"Jim, I see what you mean 'bout keeping quiet 'bout this. Must not be nobody else in all this country knows Tom Horn by sight. Could be, if anyone ever did recognize him, Horn jest might up and kill him. After all, that Horn sure couldn't risk being known. Why, no telling how many folks jest might like to catch him out on th' range all alone and do something 'bout him," commented Ed. "And another thing, Jim. Jest what if someone like that Rash might have a little grudge 'gainst someone like me. And might set that someone up jest so Horn would jump to conclusions and rub him out without no more evidence, you see?"

"That's why, Ed, this has to be kept jest 'tween us," said Jim. "From th' looks of things 'round here, nobody else has an inkling of who this Hicks really is. We sure ought to always know where Horn is all th' time. Guess, too, we might even not talk 'bout him as Horn. Always as Hicks, so we don't get ourselves in trouble. Jest trying to keep up with his whereabouts is going to be hard. He was 'bout th' best Injun tracker in th' whole West back in them days. Injun sign was jest plain to him, things nobody else could see. And when it came to slipping up on folks, Injuns or anybody else, he was th' best."

Both Jim and Ed became silent. Too much to consider. They knew that if Horn were pushed toward them, right or wrong, anything might happen.

Jim knew caution would have to be their watchword. "We ain't going to always know jest where he might be, but it wouldn't be such a bad idea to know if he ever vanishes fer a few days. And we need to know if he gets reported as being anywhere else, see? I guess, Ed, all that would mean we better become real live detectives, kind of like a stock detective. But more a man detective, watching out fer our own hide, so to speak," Jim said in a hushed voice, as though someone might be close by, listening. He really didn't quite know what to do next. But at least now he had a confidant, someone to talk to, a sounding board when things got too confusing.

"We been gone too long, Jim. Some of them ladies will be missing you. Not me, jest you. We don't need to set ourselves apart by this thing, you know. Got to look like nothing is up. Let's get on back inside and try not to look so gloomy. We at least have him in our sights fer now," Ed allowed as he turned Jim toward the dance.

CHAPTER 9

Jim and Ed both headed straight to the spiked-punch bowl. They needed a little relaxation, and maybe it was time for them to lean back and enjoy the dance now that they had cleared their minds of a heavy load. The ladies kept adding to the punch every so often, and just as often some maverick cowboy would replenish the whiskey additive. None of the ladies seemed to want to notice. Both fellows did notice that someone had stocked the tables with delicacies: cakes and pies, berries, nuts, and even some jerky.

The minute Jim spied the pies, he called out to Ed. "Ed, jest look! I bet that Margie brought along some of them homemade apple and apricot pies just fer us! Start looking, Ed. Margie's will be ten times as good as any of them others!"

"Bet you don't find any, cowboy." Margie's flirtatious voice came from behind a couple of folks browsing the treat table. She eased around them and moved right up against Ed. "But I bet I know jest where a handsome feller could get a piece, way out there in th' dark. And nobody would ever have to know." She looked over at Jim, winked, and continued. "Bet there's even two pieces. Saved them back when I couldn't find you two when th' feed trough was being filled. Where you two been, anyhow? Not out with some single gal now?" she teased.

"Golly, Margie. Didn't know you really cared," Ed replied. "You know we'd both be pleased to find that pie, even out there in th' dark. Wouldn't we, Jim? Jim? Now where'd that feller go?"

"Margie! Margie!" came Jim's urgent cry as he was dragged to the dance floor by none other than Ann Bassett. "Don't let that Ed get it all! Bring some back fer me! Please, Margie!"

Ann Bassett was demanding and possessive, always used to having her way. "Now, Jim, you've got some tall explaining to do! Just where have you been? Been looking all over for you. Even got caught by Matt and just right out told him I had my mind on you! Now what do you think of that, Mr. Keaton?" said the impish Ann as she spun Jim out across the floor right in front of Matt Rash.

Matt caught Jim's eye just enough to let him know that Ann wasn't to be fooled with by the likes of Jim. And Ann was all wrapped around Jim. This was a game Jim didn't want to play, but he had no choice.

"Now, Jim, the next time we go by the door, I just know I'm going to need some more fresh air. This dancing really gets a girl down, don't you think? Or do you think it's really supposed to be that cowboys get the girls down?" Ann whispered in Jim's ear.

Jim was just not used to having girls he hardly knew throwing themselves all over him, especially right out in public, right in front of the other ladies and right in front of their jealous fellows. Fellows who might already have reason not to want to get along with Jim.

"Ann, you are jest doing this to start something 'tween Matt and me, ain't you? I've been 'round long 'nough to know a thing or two 'bout this carrying on bit," Jim protested.

"Jim! Now would a girl like me do a thing like that to a fellow like you? There's nothing between Matt and myself, at least nothing serious with me. He knows I'll do as I please, when I please, and with whom I please! Enough of that. Tonight I'm with you. Matt knows it, and Matt's seen it before. If he can't stand the heat, he ought to stay out of the kitchen. That's just the way my mother used to tell me things were, and that's final. Besides that, there's the door coming up, and we're going out to cool off. I think it's you that needs to cool off now,

Jim!" said Ann as she skillfully maneuvered him right out the door into the night.

With just a little encouragement, she had him headed straight for the riverbank. "I know a place where we kids used to go to hide out, where no one ever found us. Hurry, Jim. It isn't far. We won't be gone long."

And Jim could feel himself giving in to this exciting young lady, not much more than half his age, with twice his audacity.

The two hurried out across the sagebrush flat, across the deep grassy meadow, and down the drop-off to the riverbank. Ann was leading and quickly had Jim around a bend and up a slight side draw to a spot where it narrowed to just a cut in the embankment. They were only fifty yards or so from the river with its cold, clear water moving effortlessly toward Lodore Canyon, only a few miles downstream. As best as Jim could tell, they were not far from the Finch wagon and camp. They could still plainly hear the music and frolicking from the hall as Ann directed Jim to the high grass in the very end of the cut. Just a small, hidden place where the soft grass made a really congenial place to lie down, snuggle up close, and get better acquainted. As Ann pulled Jim down against her, he found himself wanting her completely. He could no longer resist her.

Jim found Ann's lips against his, warm, sensual. Jim's earlier inhibitions crumbled into dust. Little did they notice the crystal clear mountain air, with all the stars bright as new diamonds, twinkling by the thousands, showing off the Big Dipper, Little Dipper, the North Star, the Milky Way, and millions of stars almost too far out to be seen. And time lost all meaning.

"Gosh, Jim! How long do you think we've been gone from the dance? I hardly remember leaving," said Ann as she righted herself and started to pull Jim up from their snug nest in the embankment. "Listen! Isn't that someone just over the bank there? Oh, what if we get caught?"

Both hurriedly began refastening buttons, tucking in their clothing, and brushing the grass and leaves from their hair.

"Really, Ann, I think we're pretty near my bunking grounds jest up there at that first wagon. That's th' Finch wagon … Margie …" Jim tried to explain but was cut off in mid-sentence by Ann.

"Oh, I saw that spunky little Margie over there at the dance with you! Thought she had you for herself, didn't she, Jim? Much as I like her, she just don't know how to get a man, 'cepting her own, Bill. And he's sure different too. Tried to get him to be friendlier with me at the fall roundup dance out here. He wouldn't even go outside the building with me. Can you imagine that, Jim?"

"We best get on back up there, Ann. I jest know someone will be looking fer us. Maybe ol' Matt. Can't say I'd blame him none either," Jim said as he gathered himself for the short walk back. "And there sure is someone at th' Finch wagon. Kind of late to try to dodge 'round 'em too, Ann. Jest have to go right by whoever it is. Maybe they jest might get up in th' wagon and not see us."

"Hey, there? Who's fooling 'round out this far from th' dance at this hour?" It was Margie's voice. She had gone to the wagon early to get things ready for bunking, since the hour was getting late for hardworking folks like her.

"Oh, why Jim … and Ann? You two together out here? Now don't go trying to tell me no silly stories 'bout jest what you been doing. Probably jest come down to get some air and rest from all that dancing. I wondered where you two might be, what with Matt and that feller Hicks both out looking fer you. Jim! Don't you dare go back in there till you get them jeans buttoned back up. Turn 'round here, Ann. Let me tie that back bow and get them leaves and burrs off your back. Why, them ol' biddies back in there might think you been lying out with Jim if they saw th' two of you like that! Could jest tell 'em you was out here helping me get th' wagon ready fer th' night, couldn't we? Come to think of it, we have been here fer a while, now ain't we, Ann? Jim?"

Spunky little Margie. What a jewel, thought Jim as he caught on to just what Margie was trying to do for him and Ann.

"Don't need none of them excuses for Matt, Margie," said Ann.

"He and I have this understanding. But as for that no-good Hicks, if he says anything more to me, I'll get that bullwhip off my saddle and cut him to pieces with it! And that Matt best stay out of the way if he don't want a whippin' too! All that Hicks is good for is bragging 'bout all the folks he's killed, all the Indians and all. Can't do nothing good. I really let him know 'bout me being raised by that Indian squaw, least being fed from her breast to keep me alive for most of my first year. Then him thinking he could get somewhere with me by bragging 'bout being an Indian killer. Get in my way again, might just find himself being killed. Or maybe at least hurt bad. No room for him in Brown's Park. Not on the mountain either," fumed Ann as she puffed up and even turned red at the mention of Hicks. "Don't mean to sound hateful, Margie. Just the way it is!"

Jim was set back by Ann's outburst against Hicks over such a trivial thing. Could it be she was on to Tom Horn? Surely not. She wouldn't take that kind of chance with a known paid killer. Or would she? After all, when she was home, folks said she seemed to run the Bassett ranch ever since the death of her mother some years back. And there were rumors about what all she might be up to along the lines of expanding her own cattle herd. But for such a warm, lovable, and beautiful young lady, it just seemed all out of place.

Jim was seeing for the first time just how complex the personality of the Bassett girl really was. It could also explain a bit about how a young lady such as Ann could pass her twentieth year and still be single. Maybe she scared all the local boys away, since they were at least somewhat aware of her dual personality. Or maybe she simply loved them until they became serious and then turned them out to pasture before anything could happen in a matrimonial way. Jim was getting deeper into this Hicks thing, and he sure didn't expect to get it all mixed up with Ann Bassett.

"Now, get on back up there 'fore they do catch th' two of you up to no good. I'll be along, soon as I get finished here with th' bedding in th' wagon. Bill and me ain't ready fer this much nightlife. Can't keep up with all you single folks," said Margie as she turned back to her business like nothing out of the ordinary had happened. "Oh, and don't cross me up none, Jim, you and Ann. If anybody ask me anything 'bout th' two of you, we three was together out here at th' wagon."

Jim was fit to be tied. Never had he run across anyone like Margie. Most women would berate the actions of any couple caught out as he and Ann had been, and before the night would end, everyone at the dance would know all about it. That little Margie was really first class in Jim's books. And he was ever in debt to her now.

Halfway back to the hall, they met Blanche Tilton, Ann's friend who came out from Craig for the big dance. She and Ann had been close friends for years, sharing confidences of all natures, including their men.

"Ann! Been looking all over for you. Now I see what you been up to, taking Jim out to keep him away from all the rest of us!" exclaimed Blanche. "You promised me you would introduce us soon as you got in the first few dances with him."

"Blanche, we've been out here helping Margie get the wagon ready for the night. Not stealing Jim at all. Jim, this is my friend, Blanche Tilton, from Craig. We been running around together for years, even to the point where I think I can turn you over to her for a while without having to worry much about what she might do with you. At least as long as I can have you two in sight!" said Ann as she slightly urged Jim forward toward Blanche. "Guess ol' Matt's been wondering about me too. It's time to give him a tumble. Been putting him off most all evening. Jim, you and Blanche get along to the dance floor. I'll be along soon as I find Matt. That won't take long. Here he comes now."

"Ann! Ain't you ever going to have time fer a dance with who brung you?" Matt said as he joined the threesome. "Been putting up with your flirting with all those fellers all night. And 'specially this new feller here!" Matt stuck out his hand to be introduced to Jim.

"Well, so you're Matt Rash, eh?" Jim replied, grasping Matt's hand in a hearty handshake. "We've spoke a time or two today, but this is th' first time we've met. What do you think of th' party so far, Matt?"

"Been a good one, Jim. Lots of folks showed up, and 'course some new fellers too, like yourself. See you been staying out there with ol' Ed Cole. Heard you was using his Johnson Draw cabin some. Intending to stay 'round these parts, Jim?" Matt asked in a friendly tone.

"Maybe, Matt, maybe. Seems the longer I'm here, th' better I like it. Jest grows on a feller, don't it?" Jim replied. He did not want to get into too much discussion with Matt until he had a better feel for the way things might drift. He had noticed someone, possibly Hicks, lurking back some distance in the dimness of the night. Just why Hicks would be around but not really in the open seemed strange to Jim. Was he watching out for Matt, just in case Matt got into something, a scuffle or brawl? Or was he stalking Matt, just keeping an eye on him for other reasons? Knowing that Hicks was really Tom Horn was a load to carry. But he knew he couldn't let it be known, at least not now.

"Would that be your new man, Hicks, back there a ways, Matt?" asked Jim. "Never met him, but some folks told me who he was. Don't seem to be too sociable."

"Oh, yes, Jim. That is James Hicks. Been helping me with th' roundup fer a month or more. He's from down in New Mexico. Got a horse ranch or something like that," Matt said. "He came up here looking fer horses to add to his place. Sort of like you, Jim. Got here and seemed to like it. Been visiting all th' folks fer miles around, checking on horses and all. Guess I'll be losing him right away. Says he's got to get back to see how things are going at home. We're going to miss that feller, Jim, in spite of whatever Ann might've told you."

Jim could see that Matt had been pleased to have James Hicks around, as he continued explaining just who Hicks was.

"See, Hicks there is th' feller that rode like th' wind to Vernal that night when ol' Jim McKnight got hisself shot. Er ... maybe you ain't never heard 'bout that?" Matt then tried to fill Jim in a bit about how Hicks fit in with the folks in the Park. "McKnight is Josie's husband, till later this week anyhow. A deputy shot him fer resisting arrest a few weeks back. Had to do with Josie trying to get her two boys and some property back from ol' Jim. They all thought McKnight was 'bout dead, so Hicks volunteered to make th' hard ride to Vernal to get in touch with McKnight's folks and all. Made that forty-five mile ride in less than five hours. Now, feller, that takes some kind of riding, don't you think, Jim?"

"Moves plenty fast when he has to, or wants to, huh?" Jim replied, not wanting to seem any too interested in Hicks.

"Let's get on back inside. Me and Ann has some dancing to catch up on. Looks like that Blanche has you lined up too, Jim!" Matt observed as he took Ann by the arm and headed toward the old school hall.

The dance went on past midnight, and sometime halfway to dawn the whole crowd took a break for breakfast, at least those who could stand the sight and thought of food. Some good-hearted, sober ladies had put on the biscuits and bacon, stirred up enough eggs for a small army, boiled up gallons of black coffee, and called out all the chowhounds. The hot food and socializing got many of the cowboys and ranchers thinking about just how tired they truly were. Before long many had drifted out to their bedrolls, calling it quits. Ed and Jim took on big helpings of grub. Long before the first light started to show in the east, they, too, headed to their saddles and bedrolls under the Finch wagon. The day had been almost too long.

CHAPTER 10

"Jim! Jim! Get out of there, man. You've 'bout slept th' day away, and things been happening 'round here. Jim! Come on, get up from there. Things you need to know 'bout. Sun's been up long enough to set off dust devils, and here you are still sawing logs!" Ed was excited as he pulled the blankets off Jim and started shaking him to life.

"Golly, Ed, I sure didn't know it was this late. Must've passed out there last night. What got you so stirred up, Ed?" Jim slowly came to life and sat up under the edge of the wagon.

"Jim, you know what we talked 'bout last night, on th' quiet-like?" Ed asked with a stern look on his face.

"Sure, Ed. You mean 'bout ol' Hicks and all, don't you?" answered Jim, feeling around for his boots and shirt.

"You got it, Jim. Be quiet till we get out away from th' wagon. Them Finches are still asleep in th' wagon bed. They had a long night, putting up with th' likes of me and you and all," replied Ed. "Hurry up and get dressed and get over to th' riverbank and wash th' sleep out of your eyes. Got something to tell you that can't wait ferever."

Jim hurried into his old boots, carefully putting away the new pair that now had lots of marks on them from most all the ladies stepping on them at the dance during the night. He rolled up his new shirt and placed it in what would become the bedroll to tie behind the saddle for the long ride back to the cabin. By the time he was dressed and headed

129

toward the river, he could see Ed fidgeting around nervously, tossing pebbles in the water, and anxiously awaiting Jim's arrival. It was all too obvious that Ed had problems on his mind. Could it be that somehow Hicks had discovered that they knew he was really Tom Horn? Or maybe Ed had found out the real reason for Hicks's presence in Brown's Park.

"Hey, what's up, partner?" Jim approached Ed at the riverbank. "You look like the nervous cat that jest caught th' lady's canary bird."

"Jim, he's left! He got out early and packed his saddlebags and headed out down th' river like maybe toward Maybell or Baggs. Left sort of quiet-like too. Even led his horse th' first couple of hundred yards from th' camp. I watched it all from my bedroll there under th' wagon. Been awake fer a while thinkin'. His stirring 'round must've woke me," said Ed.

"Well, Ed, you remember last night ol' Matt said something 'bout Hicks leaving right away to go back to check on his ranch down there in New Mexico. Maybe he jest made up his mind sort of quick-like and headed out. You don't think he might've caught on to us any, do you, Ed? Don't see how he could have any idea that we were on to who he really was." Jim bent down to dip a few handfuls of cold river water to splash on his face. Even though the sun had been up a good while, the chill still hung down on the river and in the shadows.

Ed also knelt down at the edge of the water after realizing that he had not cleaned up earlier because he was worrying over just what Hicks, or Horn, was up to.

"This thing jest might be making me jumpy, Jim. Didn't mean to rouse you too much over it, but still, if we intend to figger out what's going on with that feller and with Rash and some others, we got to be watchful. Like we said last night, jest need to know what they are doing 'fore they might be doing things to one of us. Been thinking 'bout how many stories been going 'round 'bout Horn jest up and killing folks with no warning, no nothing. But now with him maybe gone, I come up with an idea you need to be in on. With Rash staying here to finish up th' party and all, gives us a chance to get up on th' mountain with no one 'round and do some looking," Ed said as he continued washing up a bit, getting ready for the day.

Jim looked up, puzzled that Ed would have some plan already working to learn something about what was going on. "What's th' idea you've got, Ed?"

"We need to get our good-byes said 'round here soon as we can. Get something to eat with some of th' folks and then ease on out toward home," answered Ed. "But, Jim, we ain't going home. Least not direct. This thing gives us a chance to get to Matt's cabin up on Cold Spring without nobody knowing. If there's more sign he's been rustling, it jest could be that Horn is 'bout to finish him off. That'd explain why Horn, Hicks, is staying so close to him and all. 'Course, that don't mean that Rash is th' only one Hicks would be after. Got to count in ol' Isom and some more, like even some of them Bassetts and Davenports and ol' Crouse, and hell only knows who else, 'cluding you and me! If Rash planted the idea with Hicks that we was rustling too ..." Ed let the words trail off.

"Then, Ed, why don't I round up th' horses and get 'em saddled and all while you let folks know we're leaving. I'll need to let certain ones know, myself, if you get th' drift, Ed. Wouldn't want to jest up and leave without saying my good-byes to some like Bill and Margie. And maybe that Ann herself. Need to see ol' Andy and Walt too. 'Fore we mount up, I sure do want some more of ol' Matt's juicy beef," said Jim as they both turned and headed away from the clear, cold water of the river.

Within the hour, all the good-byes were said. Everyone invited both Ed and Jim over to their respective ranches at any time. The Finches insisted that they come over for more pie before the week was out, and even the reserved Elizabeth Erickson gave them a special invitation to her ranch. Ann made every effort to get Jim to go back to the Bassett ranch and stay over for a few days in the bunkhouse, where Ann could get even better acquainted with him. But, finally, both men were in the saddle and heading away from the Brown's Park schoolhouse.

Ed took the lead, heading right back toward the Sterling, the way they came the day before. After jogging two or three miles, Ed abruptly turned the roan back toward the Bassett ranch, leaving the main wagon road and taking to a cattle trail a little way off in the cedars and draws.

"Where we headin', Ed?" asked Jim as he quickly spurred the sorrel to keep up with the roan.

"Didn't want no one to know, Jim. We're heading over to take th' trail up Matt's Creek to Bassett Springs. You remember we were up in that country on th' trip from my desert camps a while back. Then we're going over to N S Creek to pay a little visit to Matt's mountain cabin while he ain't there. Jest no telling what we might find up there, Jim!" Ed said as he set the roan to a lope, heading higher up in the cedars, angling toward Matt's headquarters ranch.

The trail up through the heavy stands of cedar was tough to make when in a hurry. The branches whipped back and popped Jim and the sorrel often, as Ed kept the roan in a fast trot. They only took one short break to let the horses blow, and then they were off at a hot pace again until they reached Bassett Springs near the top of Cold Spring Mountain. From Bassett Springs the grass and sage slopes were all green, fully recovered from winter storms. Sage grouse were scattered everywhere around the spring, standing dumb-like, easy targets for anyone who wanted to take one. The herders commonly killed them with rocks any time they needed some variation in their larder. The young ones were very fine eating, but the old sage hens were so tough they could almost crack your teeth.

"Jim, it ain't far across th' top here to where ol' Matt has his summer cabin over on th' N S Creek. By gettin' up there without no one 'round, we got a good chance to look things over. What do you bet we find more remains of cattle hides without brands?" Ed said as both men cooled off and rested their horses in the lush grass near the spring. "If we do, you can bet that ol' Hicks found 'em too. He's been up there enough. Then if there's anything to th' stories 'bout Horn pluggin' all those rustlers, you might think he was aiming fer ol' Rash, wouldn't you?"

"Just don't know, Ed," Jim answered. "Hicks has surely covered th' country while he's been here. Sure hard to call him Hicks when I know he is ol' Tom Horn. Ed, if he visited all them other folks, wonder jest how many of 'em he plans to do away with? Wow! He could be a real busy feller! Guess I never will understand th' likes of his kind. Always liked to think th' law could handle rustlers. 'Course, now we sure know that all them kind jest don't get caught by th' law. Then what's a feller going to do? Go after th' bad men by hisself—no help, no backup? And not being much at killing folks, a common feller jest couldn't get it done. Maybe, Ed, we need fellers like ol' Horn."

Ed sat for a few moments and then tried to give Jim some kind of answer. "Don't need 'em at all, Jim. We jest always take care of our own, you know. And if you think 'bout it much, it's easy to get to seeing that if you was that rustler, you really might prefer being gunned down by your neighbors, your friends, you know, Jim? Now take us, fer example. What if one of us caught th' other one stealing, or maybe worse? Now wouldn't we rather have it settled 'tween us, jest us two? And if it came to gunning, don't you think you'd rather be gunned in a fair way, by one of us? No, no use bringing in an unknown gunman. Having him shoot one of us through th' guts from ambush, never knowing jest who done it. And maybe even while we was sleeping or feeding our horses. Maybe while fixing us some grub. Never even knowing nothing 'bout th' why. Never even knowing we'd been suspected. No, Jim. That ain't fer me."

This was something new for Jim. He had never thought about dying in that manner or dying in any manner. Now here his friend was talking about the benefits of maybe dying at the hands of friends, but in probably a violent manner, a shoot-out. What difference would it make to a fellow if he were caught and maybe killed by a friend as opposed to being caught and killed by a stranger? Death would be final in either way. But then maybe Ed had a point. A stranger, or hired killer, probably would just do the job and walk away, maybe in an ambush, in which case you would never know where death came from. It would suddenly happen, and you would not have any idea why. And before figuring it out, you'd pass on, never knowing.

On the other hand, if a friend in a direct confrontation did it, he'd be there, telling you why he was doing the deed. And if you sure enough were the guilty person, you would have to admit to the consequences taking place. And, too, if a friend gunned you, he'd take care of you till you faded away and then bury you away from the coyotes and magpies. Maybe ol' Ed was right. Maybe they really didn't need the likes of a Tom Horn or any other like him. They should maybe take care of their own, at least if the law wouldn't or couldn't.

The peaceful day was something to appreciate, thought Jim, lying in the cool grass near a quiet spring of pure, clear, cold water, listening to it murmuring over the rocks on its way to some place deeper down the canyon, maybe even reaching the valley, maybe clear down into the Green River and beyond. A golden eagle wheeled around overhead, taking in the sights of the two cowboys lying still on the ground below while their horses nibbled at the new grass seemingly without a care in the world. And off in the rocks, not fifty yards away, came the sharp whistle of the rock chuck, warning his friends that the cowboys were still there. How could a day like this have undercurrents like rustlers, gunmen, desperate men of all kinds, wandering around, causing all kinds of grief across the country? They must not ever stop to smell the flowers, Jim thought, or to watch the simple things in life that made it all worthwhile.

"Best get moving," Ed called from across the spring as he roused himself and started gathering in the two horses. "It ain't far to th' cabin. Get this thing behind us so we can maybe figger something out."

Matt's cabin was a simple affair, just one room and a small corral attached. It sat in the edge of an aspen grove and had a small spring near the entrance. Inside was a table, a couple of chairs, a potbellied stove, and a bunk against one wall. There was one small window and the one door. Just enough comforts to be called a cabin, at least for a single person. It was stocked with the standard provisions, enough to get a fellow by for a few days at a time. A sage flat extended two or three hundred yards out from the front of the cabin to a thick aspen grove, one that would hide a good-size herd of mule deer or perhaps a man just wanting to watch the cabin from a hideout. The other side of the cabin was actually in a grove and would offer an escape route to anyone wanting to get away from the place. The small corral would hold several horses, and there were some tools of the cattle trade lying around handy. Over the back fence hung several cowhides, something of real interest to both Ed and Jim.

"Stretch that first hide out some, Jim. Kind of looks like there ain't a flank on it," said Ed. "Looks like there might be a dozen or more 'round here, don't it, Jim?"

"Sure does, Ed. And this one back in th' corner has a perfect hole cut from th' right hip, right where a brand might ought to be. Ed, I've heard you fellers talk 'bout ol' Matt maybe being in on something like rustling, but this is th' first thing I've seen that kind of forces me to call it your way. If this ain't th' cabin of rustlers, then I sure ain't never seen one. What do we do now?" Jim said rather quietly, as though someone might be listening.

"Got to look 'round some, Jim. Figger out what jest might be done," answered Ed as he eased around from the corral, looking out toward all the aspens, thinking. Then he stepped up on the roan and rode a little way off, still looking over the aspen patches, the rock outcrops, downed timber—anything that might conceal a man. He made a big circle around the entire place and returned to where Jim was just finishing the inspection of the dozen or so hides. Not a brand was found on any.

Ed's voice was a little lower when he spoke. "Jim, we best get on out of here. We found what we expected. Now th' question is, jest what did Horn find up here? If he was here at all, and we know he was, he sure has all th' rustling evidence he'd need on ol' Matt. 'Bout all we can do is lie low, keep this all to ourselves, try not to tip our hand. And watch fer what's going to happen."

On the way off the mountain, Jim kept wondering why Ed spent so much time studying the lay of the land around Matt's cabin. If what Joe told him a few days back, about Ed mumbling about killing Matt, had any spark of truth in it, maybe Ed was planning to ambush Matt at the cabin. But why not just wait around and let Horn do the job, if Horn really was after rustlers, and if Horn had all the evidence he needed? Since Horn, or Hicks, had ridden off to somewhere earlier from the party in Brown's Park, maybe Ed figured Horn might not return to do the job. Only time would tell. But maybe time was running out. How long would it be?

"Ed, I'm going to head in to my cabin without stopping over. Tired plumb out. Need to get back there and rest up, catch up on a job or two. Would I make time by going down off th' mountain along here and circle out to th' wagon road, up to Finch's, and over to th' cabin?"

"No, it's lots closer down through Beaver Basin, Jim. Cut 'cross through th' gap, and you'd 'bout be to th' cabin. Since you ain't staying over, what do you think 'bout headin' in to town in a few days fer supplies? Could take th' spring buckboard, make good time. Maybe use my horse fer th' first half going in, and trail your mare fer changing out over 'round Erickson's place or so. Bet we could be in town by dark. Take all next day fer business, head home th' next. Jest three days lost. What do you think?"

"Wouldn't mind at all, Ed," said Jim. "Could use a day in town with not too much else to do. Getting out from these hills might do a feller some good. 'Sides that, Ed, I'd have a day to get back with th' finest lady in all these parts. You know, th' one Andy mentioned at th' dance—Mary Lou, Mary Lou Garrett, over at th' Cat Claw. Some kind of lady. Not like any of them others, not at all!"

"Jim, them ladies are going to be th' death of you. 'Course, maybe jest wishing it was me!" Ed replied as they rode down toward Beaver Creek. At the creek they split off, one heading up to the Two-Bar, the other out toward the gap and over to Johnson Draw.

Jim arrived at the cabin before dark, had time to check on the mare, turn the sorrel loose in the pasture, fix a bit of bread, and put on a pot of beans. After a simple meal of bread and fried steak, fresh from a young antelope, it was time to turn in. The past few days had been eventful for him, meeting dozens of folks in the Park, discovering that Hicks was really the old Indian scout from Arizona, Tom Horn, and having such a great time at the spring dance. Then there was that young, fresh thing, that Ann. Enough happenings to last a while, Jim thought, as he drifted off to sleep in his private domain, the snug cabin in Johnson Draw.

CHAPTER 11

Three days later found Jim and Ed pulling into the livery in Rock Springs after a fast ride from Johnson Draw. The two horses did well, neither showing signs of being worked too hard.

When they checked in at the Valley House, the clerk was all eyes and ears. "You sure ain't been gone long, Mr. Keaton. Maybe you ain't cut out fer that rough mountain life, after all. Jest teasing. Real glad to have you back … er … Jim. Even got a helper along, eh? I ain't seen Mr. Cole fer a long time. How you been?" The clerk hadn't changed a bit, still as curious and talkative as ever.

Before Jim could get in a word, Ed snapped at the clerk. "Jest get us a room apiece, and we ain't interested in spending th' night talking to clerks!"

Jim was taken aback, not expecting Ed to rise up in the face of a simple clerk. Why would he suddenly seem to be offended by this kind of clerk talk? Was Ed upset over something Jim didn't know about? Seemed to be as jumpy as when they were trying to figure out the Hicks-Horn affair back in the Park.

"Oh, yes, sir, Mr. Cole. Didn't mean no harm. Jest making talk. Let me give the both of you the two best rooms in the house. They overlook the main street. Can see all the goings-on and all. Even got new locks on the doors too. The maids put on new sheets jest today." The clerk was plainly intimidated, caught off guard by Ed. "And if you jest got in off the trail and wanted a hot bath, we could sure enough fix you up ... er ... fer two bits. Let me jest call the bellboy and git them two baths made up. You ain't getting this kind of treatment nowhere else in town!"

"Okay, okay, feller. You made your point. I ain't mad at you. Jest tired, dirty, and hungry. Don't mean to take it out on you. That hot bath did th' trick. We're heading over fer a steak. Be back fer that hot tub 'fore you know it." With that, Ed turned up the stairway with his duffle. "Well, come on, Jim! Ain't got all night."

By eight thirty both Ed and Jim were in their rooms with the lamps turned out. It had been a long day, and tomorrow would probably be another. Jim was thinking of only lounging around, maybe visit with Andy most of the day. And see Mary Lou. Sleep overcame him.

The knocking was quiet at first. Jim woke quickly, but he didn't stir. Then it came again.

The low voice of the room clerk called, "Jim? Mr. Keaton? Got a note fer you. Kind of urgent."

Jim felt around for his .45, always hanging at the head of the bed, even when in town. Carefully pulling it from the holster, he eased out of bed and moved near the door. At the next quiet knock, Jim answered in a low voice, "Anybody out there with you?"

"No, no, Mr. Keaton. Jest got handed a note from a boy from the Cat Claw saying it was urgent. Don't mean to wake you, but this seemed to be fer real," said the clerk in a nervous tone. "Don't need to open the door. I'll jest push it under the door fer you. If you need me fer anything 'bout this, I'll be right there at the desk. Jest holler."

Jim picked up the note, a sealed envelope, the kind that immediately brought back memories from the last note he received at the Valley House. He turned up the lamp and tore open the envelope and saw a neat, folded note in a very pretty handwriting he instantly recognized. It was from Mary Lou! But how? He didn't let her know he was in town. Didn't want to deal with her when he was worn out from the trail. He hadn't been in town a total of more than three hours. Well, three hours before going to bed. Now the spring-wound clock said ten thirty. Two hours of sleep seemed like forever.

The note read: "Heard you were in town. Thought you might like a nightcap at my place, Jim. You know the way. The lamp will be on. Missed you. Mary Lou."

It only took Jim a couple of minutes to be dressed and out the door.

The next morning Ed was out early and couldn't raise Jim for company at breakfast. By the time the sun was up, he had checked on the horses at the livery and gone to the mercantile store to order his supplies. He needed a few pieces of leather goods for the tack room, a keg of nails, and a spool of the new barbed wire, as well as some sheep-marking paint and a dozen burlap wool bags. After browsing around the store a bit, he came upon Andy, working in the back.

"Hey, there, Mr. Cole! Gosh, sure didn't look fer you in town fer a long time yet. Looks like you lived through the dance last week. Don't reckon that ol' hanger-on, Jim, come in with you, did he?" asked Andy all in one breath.

"Sure, Andy. You knowed I couldn't get out of that canyon without him now, didn't you? He's somewhere 'round. Said he only came in to visit with you. Couldn't even get him out of bed this morning fer breakfast. Must've really been sawing logs," Ed replied as he continued to look around.

"Oh, now, Ed, you and me both knows why he came along with you. And it sure ain't jest fer your company! Bet you anything he come in jest to see that pretty thing at the Cat Claw, Mary Lou Garrett."

"Well, it might jest be, Andy. Jest might be. Let's change to a better subject, like gettin' together th' things I need fer th' ranch. Found most everthing, but still need some .38-55 shells fer that ol' Winchester of mine. And while we're on guns, tell me what's selling best these days. Maybe the .30-30? Ol' Jim keeps th' coyotes off with that .30-40 of his. Won't part with it at all." Ed was making small talk, still checking over items on the shelves.

"Well, Ed, that .30-30 does sell good, but 'round here the folks still like that .38-55 like you got. Not too many .30-30s 'round here yet. Did sell one of those really nice Savage Model 1899s in .30-30 the other day. Went to a big rancher up north. Got one Winchester 1894 sitting up there in .30-30. Ought to get it sold 'fore long."

"Jest how much is a new Winchester .30-30, Andy?" asked Ed, even though he wasn't in the market for one.

"That being 'bout one of the newest calibers out, Ed, I'd have to get eighteen dollars fer it. Might throw in three boxes of shells fer 'bout two more dollars. Jest ain't as cheap as they used to be," Andy said as he moved along the counter, getting the few little things Ed pointed out.

"Set all this out fer me, Andy. Box it up a bit, 'cept fer them wool bags. I'll jest carry them with me. I'll bring th' spring wagon over some time today and pack it. Got to head back out at first light in th' morning. You can bet ol' Jim will be by to see you after a while. When he finally comes crawling out," Ed said and then moved out toward the street.

Ed's step quickened as he headed over toward the livery. It wasn't like he wanted to get away from Andy. Just that he had things on his mind, things that needed tending to. He had noticed a youngster hanging around the livery earlier. Just the kind of kid that made a good errand boy, something Ed needed real bad just now. He could find out if the boy would run errands, for two bits or so. And he might even get an idea of just how the boy would keep still about what the errand was for.

It was midmorning before Jim slipped quietly down the back stairs of the Cat Claw, glancing all around to see who might be back in the alley watching. Everything looked quiet, and Jim headed straight for the cafe at the Valley House. The same young lady who had introduced him to the banker, August Kendall, on an earlier trip was there to wait on him.

She remembered Jim and the treatment Kendall had given him and simply had to twist him around about it just a little. "The food will taste better now, Mr. Keaton, since ol' Kendall ain't here!"

From the cafe, Jim went straight up to his room to check things over. He noticed that Ed was gone, probably doing his shopping, something Jim had to get on with too.

He headed out over the town, first to one shop and then another, but by noon he was at the mercantile store looking for his friend, Andy Ewing.

"Taking off to eat, are you, Andy!" Jim exclaimed when he spied Andy slipping out a side door. "You can't do that without me! After all, feller, we ain't visited in several days. At least since th' big dance. Have you healed up 'nough to visit by now?"

"Been waiting fer you, Jim. Knowed you was here. Was told you had a hangover, or something, still in bed. Get a move on and we'll find one of our Chinese places I bet you ain't never been in out here. Food's good too!" Andy grabbed Jim by the arm and had him down the street in no time at all.

The little cafe was not much to look at, but it was clean, and Jim was willing to take Andy's word for the food. After filling up on foods Jim had never heard of before but found to be just as good as Andy claimed, the two leaned back to talk about the events of the day.

"Hey, Jim, what's with your buddy, Ed?" asked Andy. "Came in to get his supplies and asked all 'bout a new rifle. I knew that wasn't like him, wanting something new when he had something jest as good already. Reckon he's fixing to buy you a Christmas present or something? What's really funny is that he can't get the thing fer a while now, cause I done sold it jest before you came in. Sold it to jest a kid too. Paid me cash, right to the penny, fer the .30-30 and some shells. If ol' Ed slips back in here to get the thing 'fore you all leave, I'm sure going to give him a hard time!" And Jim knew Andy would.

But Andy was right. It wasn't like Ed to be thinking about any new rifle, if he was. Maybe he was just passing time. All the men around always liked to think and talk about new rifles. But why would Ed be curious about a .30-30? He always thought the .38-55 was better and that was what he kept handling. The only time Jim ever heard Ed mention a .30-30 was when the two of them were checking out the rifle owned by Hicks. Could it be ...? Surely Ed wouldn't be interested enough in the .30-30 to buy one for trying out. Why, he could always just stop by Billy Tittsworth's place and shoot his to see how it would do. And if Horn had the only one down in the Park, why would Ed want one?

In any case, Ed didn't buy one, and the only one in town was sold to someone else. Jim could put any thoughts of Ed owning a .30-30 out of his mind. Or could he ...?

Jim and Andy spent most of the early afternoon together before Andy had to get back to the store. As they approached the mercantile building, they saw Ed with the spring wagon pulled up to be loaded. He had already put on a couple of bags of corn for his special horse and was ready to pack the wire and nails and other items aboard. Jim hurried along to catch up and give him a hand.

"Don't need much help, Jim. 'Bout got everything, 'cepting those nails and that wire there. Saved a place fer both, close to th' end there," Ed said as he quickly took hold of the wire and placed it on the wagon bed.

Jim heaved up the nails and pushed them over toward one side, against the rolled up wool bags.

"Don't do that! Jim, I told you I 'bout had things where I wanted 'em! Don't want anything over on that side 'gainst them bags. Got stuff there that don't need things leaning on. Oh, don't mean to be so grumpy, Jim. Must be jest tired from all this. Don't pay no 'tention to this snapping 'round. I get over it." Ed looked sheepish after cutting off his best friend over nothing.

But Jim detected something different, something Ed didn't own up to. He put it aside for the moment. "Come on, Ed. We've had a hard week. Let me take you over to th' Cat Claw and buy you a real store-bought drink from th' prettiest woman in all of Wyoming," said Jim as he reached out and put his hand on Ed's shoulder in friendship. "Andy here will see to it that th' wagon is taken care of fer us. I'll bet

Andy can even get it back to th' livery fer th' night. Can you do that fer us, Andy?"

"Why, sure thing, fellers. Won't take up 'nough time fer nothing. You can get it before light too, all ready to travel."

With shopping completed and the goods all packed on the wagon, Jim and Ed headed over to the Cat Claw. Jim knew Ed had never seen Mary Lou because he never went into the higher-class establishments. Ed just didn't drink that much, so no reason to ever be in the Cat Claw.

"Jest you wait and see what I got to show you, Ed. And don't get to thinking 'bout running off with her neither!" Jim said.

The two were escorted to a special table off to one side in the best section of the place. The lady waiting on them simply said, "She'll be right out!" and left. Ed was dumbfounded. When he looked up and saw Mary Lou approaching the table, he was struck speechless, couldn't talk, and couldn't close his mouth.

"Well, who have we here, Mr. Keaton? A fellow as handsome as this surely wouldn't be running around with you, would he, Jim?" said Mary Lou in her most coquettish manner as she moved right up against Ed. "Matter of fact, we see so few fellows the equal of you, sir, the drinks are going to be on the house."

The sparkle in Mary Lou's green eyes was enough to shake Ed back to his senses, and he tried to introduce himself to her, but he stumbled all over himself until Jim rescued him.

"Mary Lou, this is my best friend on th' mountain, Ed Cole. Ed, this is more than my best friend in all of Wyoming, Mary Lou Garrett. And, Ed, you can talk now. She don't bite," teased Jim, to the full enjoyment of Mary Lou.

"Ed, I've known of you for several years, but you just never came by to see me. I felt slighted. Could have known you much better," Mary Lou said as she turned toward the bar to get the drinks.

"Ed, that sort of fixes things fer you so you got to come here to do business from now on, any time you're in town, don't it?" Jim enjoyed the idea of getting to pick on his friend, getting to see him completely set back by a lady.

Ed had never known what went on in the Cat Claw, always thought of it as being too good for him. He had always done his limited drinking at the little places on the fringes of town among the sheepherders and drifters. Those places seemed to always have enough easy women to go around too, if he ever needed the company, but he did have trouble believing any of them were worth being with. The Cat Claw, on the other hand, had a completely different class of girls. Didn't seem rough and tough, talked nice, not cussing full time, dressed nice, even smelled nice.

Jim noticed how Ed took in the whole place, looking it over in quick glances here and there, after making the customary sweep of the room as though watching for some hired gunman lurking in a dark corner. In the shanty-type saloons, Jim figured Ed knew to watch his back, never knowing when some drifter might decide he was carrying some cash that the drifter would have an interest in having. Many of the herders in town for the first time in perhaps a year or more would drink a little too much, fall in with one of the toughs, and be rolled in the dark alley. More often a barroom harlot would take an eager herder to a back room and easily discover just how much money he had. A sly wink toward one of the renegades that always hung out in those places would result in marking the unsuspecting herder for a hit later that night. Jim was sure Ed always sat in a corner, a wall to both sides of him.

"Okay, Ed, I saw you looking over my nice red-haired lady. If you think you might like to get to know her, I'll just assign her to your table. She asked me who you were," Mary Lou allowed as she set the drinks on the table. "Her name is Wanda. Been with me a couple of years, and she does not put up with nonsense, if you know what I mean. She's single, had to run off a husband that chased too much, so I hired her in here. Sure has been good. And if you two hit it off real good, I don't try to oversee what any of my help does on their own time. She has some time off coming, just in case she had reason to want off early tonight. It just might be that Jim and I might want to leave early too, so if you want company, don't count on us. Or, Jim, am I guessing wrong?"

With that, Mary Lou motioned to Wanda to come over and join them. Introductions were made, and the four enjoyed two more drinks before Mary Lou invited Jim to go to her place for late coffee.

"Wanda, if you need off early, just take off," Mary Lou said. "Ed might like to see the bright lights of Rock Springs tonight if you want to show him around. Jim and I need time to visit together, alone."

"Er … Ed, we don't need to meet up to go to th' rooms at th' Valley House. If you head out that way, you don't need to look fer me. I'll be along. Mostly we jest need to meet at th' livery at first light." Jim looked sheepishly at Ed and Wanda before turning to hurry along with Mary Lou, down to the end of the saloon, and up the interior stairway, a route to Mary Lou's that Jim had never taken before.

The cold, clear dawn came early in the dusty town of Rock Springs. Jim and Ed arrived at the stables just at light, tired, but trying to look alive. They hooked up and rolled out before sunup. Ed's horse made the first pull without much effort as Ed kept up a fast pace out around Aspen Mountain and up Salt Wells Creek. By noon they were nearly halfway back to Cold Spring Mountain without exchanging many words between them, as both Ed and Jim were lost in thought.

"We could take a break and change th' horses at Pretty Water or Gap Creek, Jim. What do you think?" asked Ed as they entered the narrow canyon and the Erickson country. "Been pushing this ol' horse pretty good fer a while. Even been pushing a couple of fellers that way too."

"Good idea, Ed. We could jest throw out them wool bags on th' ground and take us a quick nap. Seems like I ain't ever going to catch up on my sleep. Need to be back in th' cabin. Nothing ever bothers me over there," answered Jim.

"We ain't 'bout to pitch out no wool bags! Told you I got things packed like I want 'em in this wagon. Ain't changing nothin'! Don't get me started. Jest need to change out th' horse and exercise that mare of yours a while," Ed answered in a huff and popped the horse on the rump with the quirt, just to let off his own steam over the wool bags. "Don't mean to be so jumpy, Jim. Jest a bit too tired. We could use some grub. Brought along th' leavings from th' Valley House there in that bag under your feet. Biscuits and sowbelly, maybe some preserves and stuff like that. That little lady waiting tables there fixed it up."

Jim was startled by Ed's strong comments over the bags, as though there was some live thing inside them, something Ed was hiding. Or maybe it was just the way Ed had of protecting simple wool bags. Probably got used to having them stolen by various cowboys, herders, and drifters for use in camps, when they were in short supply. Old habits die hard.

The side creek coming into Salt Wells had good water in it, and the stop was restful to both men. They changed the horses, devoured lunch, and took time for some discussion of the events in Rock Springs.

"Did you hear anything 'bout th' whereabouts of ol' Tom Horn while you was makin' th' rounds in town, Ed?" Jim asked while they put up the remains of the grub and tightened the last of the harness on the fresh mare.

"Did some askin' 'round, you know. Don't want to cause no one to think we was interested. Didn't come up with nothin'. Most folks think he's over 'round Cheyenne. Some thought he hung out in Rawlins. Truth was, nobody knows jest where he might be. Didn't let on that we knowed Hicks was Horn neither. Got a look at the desk clerk's book, jest long enough to check on Hicks being in Rock Springs a couple of times, jest like you said. Sure 'nough, there he was, right there in th' book." Ed drifted off to his own thoughts as he stepped up into the wagon.

Jim swung up to the driver's seat, picked up the reins, gave a quick jiggle, and the mare moved out in a good trot. The trail was fairly good as it worked its way south out of Salt Wells Creek bottom and over into Vermillion. It was nearly sundown when they pulled up at Jim's cabin and unloaded his few purchases, unhitched the mare, and put Ed's horse into the harness for the short run over to Beaver Creek.

"Sure you don't want to stay here tonight, Ed? No fun traveling in th' dark over th' mountain," said Jim as Ed hurriedly tightened the tie-downs on the supplies. "You got no reason to have to be back there tonight."

"Got things to do, sheepherders to check on in th' morning, got to see jest what that Rash might be up to since we been gone. Need to get 'round a bit and find out if Hicks is really gone or jest maybe hidin' out. Bet Charley Sparks knows something. Going to see him first thing." With that, Ed went off into the twilight, heading home.

Jim stepped into the cabin, lit the oil lamp, fired up the old potbellied stove, and stirred up a short meal. Just being back in the cabin gave Jim a feeling of relaxation and peace for a change, but he still could not get Tom Horn off his mind. Wondering just why Horn would be using the name of Hicks had Jim worried. At least he had Ed to confide in, and maybe between the two of them they could find out just what Horn was up to. If Horn was working the Brown's Park country to find and eliminate rustlers, the evidence Jim and Ed found at the Rash cabin would surely point to Rash and his friends as the rustlers in question. All this left Jim with too much to think about, and he thought perhaps a day or two of work around the cabin and another trip to the diamond field would do him good.

A couple of days later, first light found Jim pushing the sorrel out of Johnson Draw and across the flats toward the diamond field. On arrival he set a camp and stepped out on the bench to start his usual casual search for any gemstones. After what seemed only a short time, he turned up a beautiful red ruby from the first anthill he checked. At first it looked like only more semi-red grit, the sort that might truly be brought up by ants. It was somewhat larger than most grains, and when he rubbed off the outer coat of weathered grime, the sun caught the brilliance of fiery red, an exciting moment to be remembered. Jim carefully placed the stone in a leather pouch, and his search moved ahead with new vigor. In the next couple of hours, Jim had scratched out a few more gemstones, perhaps a dozen or so. Several were large enough to consider taking to some assay office in town, maybe even large enough to use in some kind of setting for Mary Lou. It would be something she could not get from anyone else, if there was anyone else. Sure, she had confided to him that there were no other men she had any interest in. She seemed to really want Jim. Maybe forever?

Time had gotten away from Jim. It had to be break time. The coffee, bread, and bacon tasted better than he imagined. The sorrel drifted over for his company as Jim spread the saddle blanket in the shade for a siesta and a time to think. The trip back into town had been good for him, especially since he had again spent time with Mary Lou. Andy had been great company, friendly, happy, and always helpful. Even the nosey desk clerk was interesting, always trying to dig up anything new to pass on to anyone who might want to know.

Ed was good company for the trip too, but for some reason Ed had seemed a little different, a little edgy, thought Jim. Maybe it was like Andy suggested. Maybe ol' Ed was trying to hide the fact that he was really trying to do something he normally never did, like buying Jim a Christmas present. Of course, Andy was joking, just trying to pull Jim's leg concerning the good-heartedness of his friend, Ed. But then Ed was asking about the new .30-30 Winchester. He knew Jim thought his .30-40 was the better caliber, and Ed himself had his cherished .38-55.

Jim quietly turned over everything that happened in town and during the trip back to the cabin. Things he had overlooked or disregarded were now coming to him. The way Ed acted over the burlap wool bags. Plain edgy over them too. And earlier Jim did have to admit that Ed showed surprise when he told him that Hicks was really Tom Horn. He was even just a little shaken when he discovered Hicks's rifle was a new Winchester .30-30, knowing that several rustlers, or just folks suspected of being rustlers, had been gunned down with a .30-30. Would this be enough to cause Ed to start thinking about how the .30-30 might shoot? Wondering if it had the power and range to do the killings attributed to Horn? Andy's only .30-30 was sold to that kid for cold cash. It wouldn't be available to Ed for any reason. But it was strange that a kid would do that, just walk in and buy a high-dollar rifle and shells without much being said.

The longer Jim rested in the cedar clump, the more he thought about Ed's curious attitude. Things were beginning to come together in Jim's mind: the kid buying the rifle and shells not too long after Ed left the store and the fact that kids don't have that kind of money. Just what was going on? Could it be that Ed and the kid were acting together? Sure! Why not? That could explain Ed's nervous reaction throughout the day and the entire trip! A dozen wool bags don't roll up to that big of a bundle either. Could that bundle contain something else concealed inside, something about the size and shape of a new Winchester .30-30? Then Jim considered ol' Ed not wanting to stay the night at the cabin with Jim, but heading straight out in the dark for his own place, kind of in a hurry to get on home, or in a hurry to get a certain package to his place to put away before anyone knew.

Jim was lost in a daze. Digging for gemstones in the sandstone fissures was not too demanding, and it allowed Jim's mind to drift back to the questions concerning Ed and maybe the new .30-30 rifle. It even came to him that Joe had mentioned that Ed was surely going to kill Rash some day. Jim knew these thoughts would bother him until he proved one way or the other that Ed either did or did not have the .30-30, maybe rolled up in the wool bags. The only way to ever know would be to find those bags at Ed's headquarters without Ed knowing. If Ed did have the rifle, it was rather obvious he did not want anyone knowing about it, and Jim would have to keep still about knowing. At least until he might figure out what Ed's purpose was.

The evening on the bench searching for gemstones proved fruitless, and Jim decided to call it quits. The ride off the bench and across the sage flat to Johnson Draw was pleasant, and dropping down into the bottom was now a well-known trail to Jim and the sorrel. It was homecoming, a good feeling for both. As they came in sight of the cabin, they spotted the familiar roan tied to the hitching post. They had a visitor.

"Ed! Didn't 'spect to see th' likes of you fer some time. You miss me all that much?" Jim said as he got off the sorrel and Ed stepped out of the cabin.

"I jest knowed you'd put it that way, Jim. Always putting me on, ain't you?"

"The least you could have done was do th' cooking, Ed," answered Jim. He unsaddled the sorrel and led him to the corral.

Ed immediately started removing the saddle from the roan, giving the sign that he planned to stay over for the night.

"Jest plumb fergot 'bout cooking, Jim. Should've done it, but jest didn't know if you were coming in or not. Did notice you had some good-looking steak hanging there in the shade. Found your coffee and spuds. Saw you had some onions. Guess I might've been jest planning to do something like settin' me a table. That is, if you didn't show up," Ed commented as he turned the roan loose in the corral with the sorrel. "Guess that means I'm to get two of them steaks off that hindquarter there and get 'em ready fer fixin'."

It was pitch black outside when the two men finally cleared away the few pans and dishes, made a new pot of coffee, and leaned back in the yellow-gold glow of the coal oil lamp to talk.

"Didn't jest come over to put on a feed bag, Jim. Got home th' other day, spent some time checking on th' herders and all. Finally got down to ol' Charley's place on Talamantes Creek there. The jig is 'bout up, Jim. Charley filled me in on some real bad news from Brown's Park, jest 'bout what we thought might happen." Ed was thoughtful as he fiddled with his coffee cup, turning it one way and then another. "You didn't get no note on your door, did you, Jim?"

"A note, Ed? What sort of note? Nothin' here that I know of," said Jim, wondering just what Ed was talking about.

"Weren't none on mine neither, Jim. But maybe we was jest lucky this time." Ed shifted in his chair, looking around as if to check for someone else in the one-room cabin, someone who might overhear just what he was about to say. "First, Jim, I did check on Hicks. He's gone; nobody knows right where. Rash and others that seemed to know ol'

Hicks best jest say he went back to New Mexico to check on his holdings. But jest keep this in mind. He really don't have to've gone nowhere, now does he? Could jest lie low, stay right 'round here, couldn't he? Might jest be over 'round Baggs, maybe Rawlins. Main thing is, nobody really knows." Ed talked in a low voice, one that wouldn't carry very far, surely not beyond the room. If anyone was lurking just outside, he would not be able to pick up the conversation.

"Well, Ed, the way ol' Tom Horn could track and trail, and the way he could slip up on anybody, even Injuns themselves, I'd agree with you. He could jest 'bout be anywhere. Sure, he didn't have to go back to New Mexico. He could've moved off a ways, jest to stay close and watch fer more rustling while certain folks thought he was gone. But what are you saying 'bout notes on doors and stuff?" asked Jim, trying to get back to where the talk started.

"Trying to tell you, Jim. Jest listen. Now, you remember I told you 'bout ol' Horn gunning those folks, but only if they stayed 'round after he give 'em fair warning, like by putting a note on their door to be gone in thirty days or else. If Hicks, or Horn, 'course, had something to do with being a detective fer them big cow men, he'd do jest that after he got th' goods on some fellers fer rustling, wouldn't he?" Ed hesitated, letting that idea sink in on Jim. Then he continued. "Well, notes have been found by a bunch of folks in th' Park, some you wouldn't think Horn would be after. And th' notes didn't show up till Hicks had been gone fer a few days. Nobody even hooks up th' idea that Hicks might be th' one doing it. After all, he ain't 'round to put out no notes, is he? Or is he, Jim? Now I ask you, Jim, could he move back in without being seen? You say he could do 'bout anything without being seen. Night them notes got left, not even any dogs barked. Now that would take some sneaking, wouldn't you say, Jim? Could it be Hicks … er … Horn doing it, Jim? I think me and you knows, and nobody else does!"

"Who all got them notes, Ed? What'd they say?" Jim asked anxiously.

"They could've gone to anybody in th' Park, or any of us, including me. Maybe not you, cause you ain't been here long. Every note said 'bout th' same, be gone in thirty days or else. Funny thing. That Ann and Josie Bassett didn't get none. Don't see how come they wouldn't, 'cept, 'course, they is ladies and all. And far as we know, even ol' Charley Crouse didn't get none. If anybody in th' Park should've got one, it'd sure be ol' Charley!"

"Get to it, Ed! Who got them notes?" Jim asked, a little agitated at Ed for dragging it all out.

"Jim, I'm gettin' to that. Jest hold on now. The first important one was ol' Rash hisself. Then ol' Isom got one clear out at Summit Spring. Joe Davenport and ol' Longhorn Thompson got 'em too. And that young Sam Bassett might've got one—says he's leaving soon as he can. Might even be others. We jest don't know. But that ought to tell us that ol' Tom Horn is sure 'nough out here. Th' folks in th' Park is trying to put this all together, thinking all th' more that it has to be Horn, but not thinking Horn has even been 'round here! But you and me knows ol' Hicks is Horn, and even though he headed out over a week back, he didn't really leave. He must still be somewhere close by. And if these fellers don't get out of th' country, they will end up dead! I reckon we are far 'nough away so ol' Horn don't pay much 'tention to us. Still, we best be on th' lookout fer him. If he shows back up here in a few days, as Hicks, 'course, we both know th' killing will get started!" Ed leaned back, glanced over toward the bunk, and felt exhausted. He couldn't help thinking a worried mind was more tiresome than a worked body.

"Ed, do you think it's safe to keep working them sheep on Cold Spring?" asked Jim.

"Sure, Jim. We didn't get no note, and we don't hardly know Horn," said Ed. "So what we'll do is jest keep on like nothing ever happened. Like we jest don't know nothing 'bout any of this, 'cept what th' folks is telling us. Long as they don't know we are on to this Hicks-Horn thing, we'll be okay, I think."

"Ed, you done got me wide awake! Got to put on 'nother pot of coffee. Ain't no way I can sleep right now," Jim said as he stirred around toward the potbellied stove, shook out the leftover grounds, and searched for another handful of fresh coffee to put on to boil. "Don't you think maybe we best ride together fer a while, maybe be able to fend off any thoughts anyone might have of gunning one of us … er … mostly you, Ed? Something jest might happen over a certain little run-in over jest who could run stock on th' mountain and who couldn't."

"You're right, Jim. Kind of hoped you'd think of that. Least I don't have to bring it up to you myself. Would really like to have you along most of th' time over on Cold Spring, that is, if you have time to hang 'round," answered Ed.

"I'm with you, Ed. Thinking you'd be th' target sort of relieves me of part of my worry. How do you like that kind of thinking? Jest teasing, Ed. I understand. You can count on me. We can head over to your place first light. Then we can jest get on about your sheep business."

CHAPTER 12

It was always delightful to ride out across the hills at dawn, dropping in and out of the aspen groves and around the pine, fir, and blue spruce, through the purple sage, jumping first one bunch of sage grouse and then another, watching the mule deer herds wandering along on their way to bed grounds somewhere up the mountain in the black timber. And out on the lower flats the antelope herds were always moving, dashing one way and then another, stopping for a short bit of grazing, and then off again, playful and full of life, happy to be out in the cool, thin mountain air.

Jim was daydreaming as he and Ed walked their horses out of Johnson Draw, up along the foot of the little bald Bishop Peak, and out of the scattered timber to overlook Beaver Basin, the grazing territory used by Ed, Charley Sparks, and occasionally others. The view was always impressive to Jim. The vast sagebrush country slowly rolled down and away for a mile or two and then up to the rising shoulder of Cold Spring Mountain where the aspen groves filled most of the little draws coming off the slopes, usually with a trickle of a stream in each one. The almost flat-looking horizon, lost in a distant early morning haze, was the dividing line between the laid-back lives of sheepherders and sheepmen and the nervous, watchful lives of the cattlemen of Brown's Park, off the mountain and hard by the constant flow of the mighty Green River.

Beaver Basin was drained on the east end by Talamantes Creek, leading down to Charley Sparks's cabin and on out on the desert into Vermillion Creek, some ten miles or more away. Vermillion made a few circles before heading west and emptying into the Green River down in the Park. The west end of the basin was drained by Beaver Creek, taking its water from the many springs cropping out on the south slopes of Middle Mountain and clear around to the slopes of the Wickiups, where the Ute Indians, cowboys, herders, and ranchers had gathered poles for their lodges and cabins, corrals and fences since time began. The little Two-Bar Creek headed somewhere up in the Wickiups near the Utah line and flowed off the eastern slope to drop into Beaver Creek and on down to the Green. Ed's cabin was just a few hundred yards from the Two-Bar, situated at a good spring that sent its little stream down to join the Two-Bar, all entering Beaver Creek a half mile or so from the cabin.

From the saddle between Bishop Peak and Middle Mountain, Jim could pick up the smoke from Isom Dart's cabin at Summit Springs. When the first fall frost dropped the leaves from all the aspen trees, Jim felt sure he would be able to see Isom's cabin clearly. The temporary sheep camp where Joe Garza was staying at Cottonwood Spring would be off to the east of Isom's a mile or two and a bit more on top of Cold Spring Mountain. This was not visible to Jim. By studying the lay of the land, Jim determined that Ed's cabin was actually farther west than Isom's. This meant there was a considerable amount of grazing on the mountaintop west of Isom, maybe several miles.

"Ed, don't I see some sheep off there to the west, down in the basin there?" Jim called out to Ed, who had moved out ahead by a few yards. "Looks like maybe a few hundred."

"Should be, Jim. Sent Juan out there to get that better grazing fer a few days. Maybe a few weeks. Wanted him to jest work 'em up through Beaver toward them Wickiups and north over toward th' Red Creek country. I had Rudy move his herd off th' desert over to Pine Mountain. Ain't been any stock in there fer a while," Ed replied. "Don't really need herds up there mixing with that Rash bunch. Not with him and Isom trying to push us 'round with too many cattle and all. Used to always put one herd way off toward th' west end of th' mountain, that is till ol' Isom got to using more of that country fer his wild horse operation. Didn't used to have any trouble that way, you see. McKnight, Isom, and me, we always got along sharing that country, till Rash got to gettin' big fer his britches. Troubles sort of jest started. Don't need Juan up there no more, least not fer now."

Jim remembered that McKnight was, or had been, the husband of Josie, down in the Park. If he had been up on Cold Spring with Isom and Matt Rash, maybe he was mixed in with that rustling game too. And perhaps he, too, had received a note on his door, wherever he might be staying.

"Ed, did McKnight get one of them notes from Horn too?" asked Jim as he spurred the sorrel to catch up.

"Don't rightly know, Jim. But he sure should have. At least that's th' way I seen it. But with him and Josie busted up, maybe ol' Horn jest sort of let it go fer right now. 'Sides, ol' Jim McKnight is off over 'round Ashley Valley … er … Vernal. Over in Utah, you know. Them folks can't seem to make up their mind jest what th' name of their town ought to be. That's ol' McKnight's cabin that Isom is in. Even heard tell Isom got hisself some kind of deed. Maybe jest took th' place since it looks like McKnight won't likely be coming back to it. Or maybe that Josie jest up and deeded it straight over to Isom to get even with McKnight." Ed put the roan into a lope. The cabin was not more than two or three miles ahead.

Upon their arrival at the cabin, Rueben learned from Ed that Jim was moving in, at least for a while, and would be riding with Ed mostly on Cold Spring Mountain. Rueben had been worrying about Ed going up on the mountain alone, knowing that Joe Garza thought Ed was laying for Rash, if Rash didn't get Ed first. But now with Jim riding with Ed most of the time, Rueben felt like he could rest easier and get back to doing more ranch work.

Jim took notice of Rueben's relieved attitude. He put up in one of the extra bunks, made a place for his sorrel in the pens, and pitched in as a regular helper on the place. Every few days he would ride out to check on the mare in Johnson Draw, until Ed suggested he just bring the mare over to his place, along with the sorrel. With that done, Jim would only drop in on the Johnson Draw cabin occasionally.

Jim found right off that Ed had the roll of wool bags tucked under his bunk full back against the wall. Usually there would be some other things under there too, making the wool bags a bit hard to see. Jim knew that he would have to inspect those bags before long. They still looked like they just might have something useful tucked in among them, something Ed wouldn't want anyone to know about. To get into those bags, Jim knew he would have to catch a time when both Ed and Rueben were gone. He certainly couldn't risk being caught prowling through them.

That day came sooner than expected when Ed suggested that Jim take time off to attend to things around the cabin. "Jim, you been jest working like a slave from them old days, so today since I ain't going near th' mountain, you ought to jest take off 'round here, do things you need to do, maybe put a new shoe on that sorrel. But you sure don't need to trail 'round with me, 'cause me and Rueben are going out toward Red Creek to visit with Juan and take him some supplies. Got to get on over to see 'bout Rudy too. 'Sides that, you always was a good cook. We'll be back 'fore sundown, jest in time fer a big steak if you got time to get 'em done, that is," said Ed with a twinkle in his eye. "If you jest had to, you might even change that over to some of them trout from down there in Beaver. If you had time to catch 'em, Rueben even left them gunnysack nets down there on th' bank. A pass or two ought to drive a couple dozen right into them sacks. See you 'bout sundown." After that, Ed and Rueben headed out toward Juan's and Rudy's camps.

This was just the break Jim needed for inspecting the wool bags. He watched Ed and Rueben till they were out of sight. Then he ducked back inside the cabin and looked at the wool bags. He backed off to do some thinking. What might happen if Ed suddenly remembered something back at the cabin that he needed to take to Juan? Maybe Jim should wait for a while before pulling out those bags. Let Ed and Rueben get far away, too far for any quick run back. Forget the bags for the time being. Why not get away so as not to be tempted for a couple of hours or more? Just enough time to get down to Beaver and maybe seine up those trout.

When Jim arrived along the banks of Beaver, he soon located Rueben's gunnysack seines, complete with small poles attached, all ready for use. The location was a piece of quiet water with mostly a sand bottom, about ten or fifteen feet wide. At the downstream end it narrowed to less than three feet as it tumbled over rocks and charged down the canyon. Jim set one seine across the downstream end to block the fish from getting by. He took the other seine up as far as he thought he could effectively handle it to push the trout down into the catch basin. There he could bunch the trout up and easily scoop up the number needed for three hungry cowboys. Within less than half an hour, he had two dozen of the fighting little colorful fish, ranging in size from eight inches up to a couple of monsters of fourteen inches. He dressed them on the bank, bagged them in a spare gunnysack, tied them behind the saddle, and headed back to the cabin. There he tied the sack in the cold water just below the spring to keep until cooking time. He was now ready to get on with finding out just what, if anything, Ed had stashed away in those wool bags.

Quickly, Jim had the roll of bags out from under Ed's bunk. Sure enough, there was something stiff-like in the roll. When he unrolled the bags, out came the brand new Winchester .30-30! Inside one of the bags were three boxes of shells, one of which had been opened and half were used up.

So Ed had secretly purchased that rifle! And he had already tested it and got it sighted-in. Now the big question was, just what use would Ed put it to? The connection to Hicks's .30-30 was obvious. Was Ed just trying to get a good idea of the ability of the .30-30, or was he planning something like using it?

Suddenly it all came together as Jim's mind hurriedly put the facts in place. He considered the visit to Rash's cabin and the amount of time spent checking over the cover within a couple of hundred yards around the cabin, places where a man might lie concealed in ambush, and then the trip to town and the secret purchase of the rifle, the same caliber as that of Hicks. And now with notices to Rash and others to leave the area or else, and knowing that the folks down in the Park all knew of Horn's methods of handling suspected rustlers, it really wouldn't much matter who did the killing. The obvious suspect would be none other than Tom Horn!

Jim carefully replaced the rifle, making sure everything was back just as it had been. No use letting Ed find out that someone had discovered the rifle, at least not until Jim could figure out how to handle the situation. He realized that timing would be important, that if enough time went by before Ed did anything, perhaps Horn would finish off Rash first. But could Jim do anything to keep Ed from hurrying the job? The notes gave the rustlers thirty days to leave, so that should mean that Ed must be prevented from doing anything during that time. Any time thereafter, if Rash turned up dead it would easily be blamed on Horn. Of course, it could just happen that Rash might up and leave. If so, everything would work out with no bloodshed.

That would have to be the chance Jim would take. If Rash left, great! If he turned up dead, shot by Tom Horn, just as great! In the meantime, Jim would have to keep Ed away from Rash or Rash's cabin.

The rest of the day went by quickly for Jim, as he now felt that he knew what Ed was up to, knew all the answers, at least for a while. He even felt lighthearted enough to become playful with the sorrel and mare when he released the sorrel back into the corral, taking time to romp with them, if a fellow truly could romp with horses. He ran in circles around the corral with the two animals following in close cadence. Each time he came to the feed room, he would quickly step inside and grab a handful of Ed's private corn, kept for favors Ed gave his best horses. When he bounced back outside, he let each horse have one nibble of the corn before taking off on another run around the pen, this time with the horses staying much closer, looking for another handout. Finally, when Jim tired of the fun and games, he gave each horse a last bit of the special corn and headed back toward the cabin.

Throughout the day Jim kept busy with odd jobs around the cabin and pens, finding time to replace the one bad shoe on the sorrel as well as taking a load of dirt up on the roof to repair a thin spot where Ed had detected a recent leak. He retied and nailed in some loose poles around the corral, and he even had time to do one tub of washing before realizing that Ed and Rueben would soon show up, looking for that big fish fry. By the time he had the victuals about ready, he heard the roan whinny to the sorrel and mare, announcing their return.

Ed and Rueben had put in a long, hard day, riding more than twenty miles delivering supplies and checking the hundreds of sheep. The big steaming meal prepared by Jim consisted of fried fish, potatoes, baked bread, and greens commonly found growing wild along the small streams. Ed suggested that perhaps he and Rueben could use Jim as a full-time kitchen man, doing all the cooking in the future and not riding over the hills at all.

Finally the long day of discovery died out around the old wood stove, a last cup of coffee was savored, and the small talk among the three friends slowed to a trickle. First one and then another tired cowboy gave a long yawn. Ed crawled into his bunk, and Rueben moved to his own. Jim turned out the lamp, slipped off his boots, and called it a day.

The summer days flew by for Jim and Ed. They helped relocate the sheep herds, delivered supplies, kept a sharp eye on the forage and springs, and ensured both feed and water for the animals. They ran across Charley Sparks a time or two, doing much the same. They shared camp meals with Charley, with Joe and Juan, and each other.

Occasionally they gave chase to a nearby coyote, exercising their rifles, knocking off maybe one coyote out of every five they took after. For any cowboy, a coyote chase was a great diversion from many long, boring days of riding the range. If any wily coyote was spotted trotting along, looking back over its shoulder at the cowboys while slinking away into the sagebrush, the chase was on. The coyote knew it was running for its life when the riders cut toward it at full gallop while desperately grabbing for rifles from the ungainly scabbards flopping and slapping against the horses' flanks. If the coyote was lucky, it would be able to drop into a narrow cross draw or arroyo, out of sight just long enough to make a getaway off in a side direction, leaving the cowboys dashing on by. The game played itself out time and time again in those sagebrush hills.

In late June Jim and Ed were caught in a heavy summer thunderstorm, soaking them to the bone before they could make it to a skimpy shelter under some overhanging rocks, just enough protection for themselves but none for the horses. The heavy rain might be good for the grass but not so good for the cowboys and herders. They were forced to hole up for most of two hours, having time to discuss the possibilities of several folks in Brown's Park suddenly packing up to leave, to abide by the notes left on their doors by the suspected Tom Horn. Only Matt Rash and Isom Dart had let it be known that they had too much at stake to run. They were taking up the dare, something that could certainly become very deadly.

"Ed, what do you think those folks that got th' notes pegged on their doors by ol' Tom Horn might do? Think most of 'em will leave? Rash and Isom claim they ain't," asked Jim as they whiled away the time, watching the storm.

"Don't rightly know, Jim. Young Sam Bassett started selling off some of his cattle, like maybe he's gettin' ready to pack out. Joe Davenport I ain't heard much on, but I do know he's sure carrying that gun of his full time. And ol' Thompson ain't been back in th' Park that I know of since that all happened, staying more over on his place close to th' Yampa River. That ol' Isom jest thinks it's too late in life to start running, but sure don't go nowhere alone no more. Keeps someone at th' cabin mostly full time. Ain't even riding th' country checking on his horses and cattle like he ought to."

"Seems like ol' Matt Rash is sort of taking a big stand, like showing folks he ain't scared of nothing. Looks like he jest goes on 'bout his business, maybe thinking there ain't nobody going to stand up 'gainst him," Jim added as he shifted his position to move out of a trickle of water dripping from the overhang.

"He's a fool! Something is sure going to happen to him. Everybody knows he's th' main one doing th' rustling out here. Others might pick up a stray now and then, but ol' Matt jest goes after big numbers," Ed said as he pulled his rain slicker tighter. "Like that Jensen feller out there 'round Powder Wash. Jest getting up his little herd and all, getting his family something fer th' future. They all spent a week back in Cheyenne visiting and then come home and found nothing, nothing at all. No steers, no cows, the only bull they had, all gone. Found their horses out in th' hills a week or so later. Tracks went off a ways till they mixed with another herd. Sort of strange that we seen ol' Matt pushing them cattle up over Limestone during that time, don't you think? Had jest about th' number Jensen lost too. 'Course, by th' time we finally figgered it out, Jensen had packed out. Didn't want his family living in such a place. And that's jest th' sort of thing that's been going on 'round here fer years. Maybe that's jest why I ain't never wanted to be a cattleman 'round these parts."

Ed fidgeted with his slicker, trying to keep water out, before continuing. "Rash is going to get jest what's coming to him, mark my word, Jim. And I ain't so sure it will be coming from Tom Horn neither."

"Maybe so, Ed," said Jim. "Jest you don't get yourself involved in it. If what you say is true, jest be sure you let someone else do th' deed. If it's going to be Horn, there won't be long to wait. Those thirty-day warnings are 'bout up. Won't be surprised to see something start happening, maybe like right after th' Fourth of July. Be 'bout th' right time, wouldn't you say, Ed?"

"If Horn don't get him on th' fourth, jest to celebrate th' holiday ..." Ed answered, letting his words drift off.

"Looks like th' storm is 'bout over, Ed. Maybe we can get on out of here. Nothing like riding wet saddles th' rest of th' day."

Jim stepped out from the overhang and brought up both horses. Ed was still sitting back, deep in thought, hardly noticing that Jim had the horses ready to ride.

"Let's get going, Ed. Can't wait all day. Might be another storm headin' our way," said Jim as he stepped up in the saddle.

By the end of June, Ed had decided to move Juan's sheep herd up onto Cold Spring Mountain but in a very peculiar location, Coyote Springs. That was right in the heart of Matt Rash's grazing grounds, the very country that Charley Sparks used and had told Rash that he planned to continue using. Since Ed had always shared the ground with Sparks, Ed took the stand that whatever Sparks told Rash would also stand for him. While Ed might be right in some ways, Jim knew he was wrong in others. This move would result in overgrazing that area by having three outfits on it at once. When Sparks and Ed were the only ones using it, the country could stand two outfits. But never three. Was Ed doing this to deliberately push Rash into some kind of action? Was Ed spoiling for a fight?

"No, no, Jim, I ain't looking fer no fight," Ed responded when Jim asked about it.

"Then why do it?" Jim asked. "Could at least wait to see jest what Rash might do. Given a bit of time, he might move out. And if not, we think he is out to have real problems with Horn. Don't you see that Rash is going to be nervous and high tempered, all jumpy and 'bout to go off like a cannon at th' least little thing? Moving Juan up there could start something bad!"

Ed glared at Jim with steely cold eyes as he cut him off in midsentence. "You listen to me, Jim! This here is my business. You ain't got nothin' to say 'bout it. You been out here fer all these weeks, months even, and still don't see how we have to handle th' likes of Rash? I'm moving these sheep up there to let him know I ain't 'bout to give that ground up to him. I've made this same move every year since I come here. It ain't nothing new. And jest you remember, Jim, it all started by Rash moving up here on top of me and Sparks. And then using it fer a rustling ground. It ain't going to work. And if it means having it out with Horn, he'll get his chance. Same if he means to have it out with me. One way or another, he's in fer a takedown. If it means killing, so be it!"

Jim had no reply. He knew Ed was right, at least in the law of the land. But he also knew just how close they were to having the Rash problem solved for them by Tom Horn, if things went along as they should. This sheep move could easily ruin it all, forcing Ed to a showdown with Rash. And if that happened, Jim knew that Ed would take Rash from some kind of advantageous spot. Then all the folks down in Brown's Park, knowing of range problems between Ed and Rash, would likely decide that Ed had gunned down their favorite son over land-grazing rights on open range. Ed would be called a greedy, land-hungry bully, wanting it all to himself, not wanting anyone else to have the right to start a competing livestock operation. And killing the president of the cattlemen's association would be hard to defend.

Jim was in a tight spot. He couldn't let Ed know he had found the new .30-30, and he couldn't let him know that he thought Ed was planning to use it on Rash, if indeed he was. At the same time, he was in this thing so deep he couldn't pull out. He had to go along with Ed and help in moving the herd to Coyote Springs, which meant that he would have to side with Ed if Rash put up a fight. The only thing to do would be to pitch in and help make the move go off smoothly, just like it was a common thing, which it was, or had been in the past. Jim was gambling in a big way.

CHAPTER 13

E d had notified Juan to graze his herd back across Beaver Basin and get it up along the shoulder of Cold Spring Mountain as soon as he could. And if he could get it up toward Cottonwood, then both Ed and Jim would be there to help push it on to Coyote Spring, a move of only about a day.

Even Juan wondered why the sudden change. The grazing out toward Red Creek had been good, and they could stay there most of the summer without hurting the grass. But any good herder knew to do only what the boss said, no questions asked.

The first of July found the herd moving by Cottonwood, on the way to Coyote.

"Joe! How you been, amigo?" asked Juan when he drove his wagon into the small clearing around Joe Garza's camp at Cottonwood Spring. "Got them woolies strung out here with the dogs on guard. You seen Mr. Ed and Jim?"

"Juan! Gee, it's sure good to see you, amigo. Get down off that wagon, man. That ain't no easy way to be getting 'round out here, taking your home and all with you," Joe said as he stepped down out of his own sheepherder wagon. "Mr. Ed and Jim is 'round here, just waiting fer you, Juan. They saw you coming earlier today and came on over here. Jest went on a ride back toward Isom's place, seeing where he might be keeping hisself and all. Should be back before long. Coffee is hot, Juan. Come in and let's catch up on what's going on."

Juan set the brake on the wagon, loosened the harness on the old horse, and generally saw to things about the wagon before moving over to Joe's wagon to take the offered cup of steaming coffee.

"Come in, Juan. Still have some hot bacon and fried bread on the stove. Looks like you could use something in your belly," said Joe as he quickly moved a packing box out of the wagon to make more room for the two of them.

As with any group of herders working on the various ranches, they hardly ever got together except at the general roundup that lasted only a week or so and shearing time that might be another weeklong affair. During the rest of the year, they would be out with their herds in remote locations, usually miles apart. Visiting was a rare event, happening only when their herds might cross out on the range.

After a brief meal the two herders passed time renewing old times, finding out about any mail from Mexico that either one might have received and where their friends might have drifted on to. Soon the talk got around to Ed and Jim and why they were taking so much time getting back.

"Juan, I hear you will be up there close to that Rash feller. You get along with him? Ever have any trouble with him?" Joe asked as he poured the last of the coffee in Juan's cup.

"Oh, we do okay. I see him once in a while somewhere out in th' hills, but we never visit much. He doesn't seem too bad. At roundup he does good, always checking over all th' stock. But he don't like our sheep, Joe. He just don't do nothing much out of th' way 'bout it, though. Why?"

"Him and Ed, Juan, they have troubles. A while back Mr. Ed came to my camp, and I sure thought he was going right out after Rash, maybe even kill him. I heard him talk to himself, like maybe he would kill Rash soon," Joe said as he got up.

He started cleaning up the small cabinet area that made up the kitchen in the wagon. As he put away the few utensils they had used, he stopped and looked directly at Juan, as if taking the measure of his friend. "Juan, I'm afraid fer you over there. Afraid you will be caught in th' middle of something bad, very bad. Maybe a shoot-out. Mr. Ed isn't putting you and th' herd over there just fer grazing. I think you are being hurried over there fer some reason. Just this week one of th' Bassett cowboys came by and said most of them were going to Rock Springs fer th' celebration of Fourth of July. A rodeo and parties and all. And Matt Rash is going in too. I think Mr. Ed is getting you over there without Mr. Rash knowing. Doing it while he isn't looking." Joe stopped talking, just staring deep into Juan's face like he was looking at his friend for the last time.

"Joe, what do you mean? You think I'm being used by Mr. Ed fer something? You think he might let Rash jump th' sheep herd, maybe club 'em to death? Maybe doing this move to force Rash into something? Do you really know Ed is trying to kill Rash? Or have you been on loco weed too much, Joe, and things are getting away from you? Ed wouldn't do that." Juan looked bewildered. He was jolted by the things Joe had said, the things Joe had seen. Little did Juan know how bad the blood was between his boss, Ed, and the head of the cattlemen's association of Brown's Park.

Joe could see that Juan wasn't up on all the trouble brewing. "Juan, be careful. If you ever see someone stalking out in th' aspens, maybe with a rifle, you hurry away. Get to th' far side of th' herd. Stay away from all that. If you hear rifle fire, don't run to it. Leave it be. If things get out of hand, jump on that old horse and run like th' wind over here. Mr. Ed gave me more rifle shells and told me that if anything happened, I should leave th' herd with th' dogs and run fer his cabin down in Beaver Basin. Someone there would know what to do. Now, Juan, I'm passing those words on to you. You come here to me, and then we both will run to th' cabin. No use one of us staying up on this mountain if killing should start."

Joe was agitated, and Juan could see it.

"Keep your eyes open, Juan. Be ready fer anything. If nothing happens in th' next month or so, I'll bet Mr. Ed moves you back off th' mountain. That will mean it's over. But until then, watch yourself," said Joe just as the noise of two horses came into earshot.

"Joe, Juan, we're back! Let's get those sheep on their way to Coyote Spring. Can't wait here all day!" Ed called as he led Jim along through the aspens of Joe's little camp.

"Things were awful quiet over there 'round ol' Isom's place, Joe. Looked like he was there. We jest didn't think we needed to go much closer to check on him. He's staying close these days," Ed said as he and Jim moved on out into the sagebrush toward the wandering sheep herd.

"Juan, bring up your wagon. Me and Jim will see to them sheep. You know where we will make camp at Coyote, so jest meet us there 'bout dark." Ed was already pushing on toward the herd, getting their attention, and making them move out.

The herd was led by an old ewe that had been over most of the ground on and around Cold Spring Mountain. She knew all the stock trails and had an idea as to just where the herders might want them to go. As Ed and Jim fell in behind them, they simply started along, the old ewe in the lead. She pointed them east, straight toward Coyote Spring, only a few miles down the trail. The sheepdogs spread out to either side of the herd, keeping them bunched and in line. Ed and Jim's only job seemed to be to just follow along.

"Sheep ain't like cattle, Ed. Don't need no heavy equipment to work 'em with. No big fences, no tall corrals, jest a pack of sheepdogs. I see why you like 'em so much. 'Bout all you got to do is keep some herders and dogs and furnish th' shells fer fighting off them coyotes all th' time," said Jim as the two men started out behind the herd.

"Ain't that so much, Jim. Jest more money in it. 'Course, them cattlemen like to talk 'bout having no predator losses to speak of. Coyotes ain't too bad on them big cows and all. And they don't need a herder out with them cows all th' time like we do with sheep. If you know jest how to get new herders, it really ain't much problem. That's why I keep in touch with all them Mexicans back in town. Hang out in them poor ol' bars off on the edge of town where all th' Mex hang out. They all know I'll hire one of 'em once in a while. Treat 'em good too, Jim. Twenty-five dollars every month and keep, you know." Ed seemed relaxed as they rode easily along.

Ed continued musing. "Been thinking 'bout what you said 'bout getting them sheep too much on ol' Matt Rash up here, Jim. You're jest dead right 'bout pushing him too much. Think maybe I'll have Juan move on down a mile or so to Cold Spring. Then he can sort of keep th' herd between Coyote Spring and Bassett Spring. Put some distance 'tween him and ol' Matt. Coyote Spring is jest too close to ol' Matt's cabin there on N S Creek."

"Ed, I ain't wantin' to interfere in your business none. Jest sure glad you paid attention to what we talked 'bout. Far as I'm concerned, all I'm here fer is to give a helping hand. And maybe jest keep us both out of too much trouble, 'specially if that Tom Horn shows back up. Or if that Matt Rash gets plumb out of hand. You know what I mean." Jim was relieved to find Ed acting sensibly, at least in Jim's own opinion. But even over around Cold Spring, Juan would be right on Matt's grazing grounds. At least it would be another mile away from the cabin.

"Jim, you and th' dogs can get them sheep on over to Coyote without me. I need to take a little detour 'round th' aspen up here, kind of over toward Matt's cabin. Charley told me that Matt and most all them others would be gone fer a few days. Fourth of July rodeo in town, you know. Since we're heading up into ol' Rash's country, maybe I jest better pass by that cabin and see if he ain't in. 'Course, I know he ain't, Jim. Jest need to look around," Ed said in a matter-of-fact way.

"You be careful there, Ed. We jest can't take chances on what others think is happening. Could be that ol' Matt got bucked by some rodeo bronco and came back early. I'll be watching and listening. If any shooting starts, I'll jest head off to Vernal, stop by, get Juan and Joe, and jest keep on going. What do you think 'bout that, Ed?" Jim asked with a big grin on his face all along.

"Well, now, that jest might be th' right way to keep on living. But we all got tp go some day. You jest keep on pushing them woolies. I'll be along. Ought to meet you at Coyote in an hour or two."

Jim watched as Ed cut out toward the breaks along the north side of Cold Spring Mountain, ducking into the first aspen grove a half mile away.

Ed only looked back once, seeing that Jim was still watching after him. Then he put the roan into a lope that would have him near Matt's cabin in no time at all. He needed to scout the place without anyone around.

When Ed was within a quarter mile of Matt's cabin, he drew up the roan to a walk, taking his time on the final approach to the place. There was no sign of anyone. Ed stopped when he was a couple of hundred yards out, stepped off the roan, and started walking carefully from tree to tree, pausing at each to stare at the cabin. He circled around to the south, staying in the cover of the aspens, and then continued to the east, checking the view from every tree or place of concealment. Finally, he returned to the roan and tied him, removed his rifle from the scabbard, and began slipping toward the cabin. He was finalizing a deadly plan.

When Jim and the herd arrived at Coyote Spring, Ed was nowhere around. But since Ed had mentioned going on to Cold Spring, a mile away, Jim decided to help Ed's thinking along and simply push the herd on in that direction. The lead ewe headed right out, the dogs seemed to understand, and Jim didn't have to push at all. He hung back, letting the herd break up a little to graze. All he really wanted them to do was to drift toward Cold Spring to buy a little room from Matt's cabin, a dangerous place in Jim's mind. He knew that Rash was going to have a real chance to meet his maker sometime soon, and he figured it would most likely be near or in that cabin. It was remote, a place where no one would likely hear any shot.

By the time the herd had drifted halfway over to Cold Spring, Jim circled them and put the dogs in charge and headed back to Coyote Spring to meet Ed. He had not been there more than a few minutes when Ed came out of the nearest aspen grove, heading his way. And off to the west, just coming over the horizon, came Juan and the wagon.

"Sort of knowed you'd push them sheep on toward Cold Spring, Jim. You're going to make a real good sheepman." Ed laughed when the two got together at the spring. "See ol' Juan coming on too. Might jest as well take a break here and wait on him. Then we can move on to Cold Spring and help him set up camp. Get something to eat and turn in fer th' night, right there with them woolies."

"What did you find over at th' cabin, Ed?" Jim asked immediately. "Ol' Matt must've not been home."

"Nope. Not in today. Won't be up here till th' rodeo is over in town. I jest needed to get a better idea of th' lay of th' land. Never know when you might really need to know something like that, Jim. Did see, though, jest how ol' Horn could slip up on Rash and gun him down. That is, if he don't decide to leave before too long."

There was only a small patch of aspen near Cold Spring, but it would do for a campground for Juan for a few days or perhaps two or three weeks, until the grass showed signs of overgrazing. The three men made short work of fixing up the camp, eating a meal, and spreading their blankets for the night. Tomorrow Ed and Jim would ride back by Joe's camp and let him know that Juan was camped at Cold Spring. Then it would be back to the headquarters and routine ranch work for the next few days.

CHAPTER 14

July and August were hot months in the high country. It was the time of year that all the cowboys could leave off their long johns and maybe even enjoy taking a bath in the nearest spring or creek. It was also the time that they all began to notice the condition of their clothing, found the worn and torn places, made the repairs, and decided on any need of new or additional clothing before fall set in. The winter clothes were washed and set aside, cleaned and ready for the first frost. Jim and Ed did their share of the spring cleaning, but much of it was passed on to Rueben. As ranch hand and general handyman, those jobs had a way of gravitating toward him. And naturally, both Ed and Jim did still have their riding and checking to do, almost daily.

Ed seemed to need to go up on Cold Spring Mountain too often to check on the herds of both Joe and Juan. And he didn't need Jim along most of the time. With all the cattlemen off to the celebrations and rodeos in the closest towns, Jim figured there would not really be a need for him to stay close to Ed, at least until after the Fourth of July. Ed had found reason to go up to check on the herds on the third, and now on the fourth, he decided to go once more.

"Ed, you don't have to be going up to see 'bout Joe or Juan every day, now do you?" Jim asked as Ed was leading the roan out of the corral.

"Don't get in my business none, Jim. You know we've talked 'bout that, and you know I've got things that need taken care of." Ed was rather abrupt, like he had things on his mind, things like maybe heading up the mountain for reasons Jim wasn't to concern himself with. "When all that bunch of cattlemen get back from them rodeos and all, then you can come along, jest like we talked. Don't need two of us to watch out fer each other when all them is gone, now do we, Jim?"

"Sure, Ed. But we don't want to ferget and ride out alone after they all get back, Since you feel safe going out toward Cold Spring, why don't I jest do some checking fer better grass like off toward the west end of th' mountain today? I'll skirt 'round Isom's place and take a look at jest where anyone might be keeping cattle right now. If things look good, we could jest move ol' Juan off that way before long, couldn't we, Ed?" Jim said in a straightforward way, as though the herds were his own.

Without waiting for an answer, Jim continued. "Probably ought to jest check everthing from Joe's camp west. If you get off in that direction and see a rider, it probably will be jest me, Ed."

Ed nodded without really giving Jim an answer, the customary way of showing agreement out in the ranch country. He then mounted up and jogged off toward Cold Spring Mountain and in the direction of Joe's camp.

Jim moved into the corral to get the sorrel saddled up for his ride.

Ed wasn't concerned about where Jim might think the herds should be moved, and he paid no attention to Jim's idea that Juan might move his herd to the west end of the mountain in the near future. He had bigger things on his mind. He needed to get over near N S Creek to scout out all avenues of escape around Matt Rash's cabin. Escape routes for anyone, Tom Horn, or Ed Cole. He had to be careful. He had to know that no one knew what he was up to.

Halfway up to Joe's sheep camp, Ed turned off, staying just on the north side of Cold Spring Mountain. He was below the rims and could not be seen from Joe's camp. Then he put the roan into a fast lope, cutting across the ridges and draws that fed off the mountain into Talamantes Creek. This would give him the best cover to prevent anyone from seeing him as he closed in toward Matt's cabin. The last mile or two could be ridden in almost complete cover, mostly buckbrush, chokecherry, and aspens. By picking his way carefully, he could approach unseen. If he hurried along, he could make the entire ride in less than two hours, maybe even in one. But to avoid being seen, he knew he would have to ride easy, using routes down deep in the brush, staying off the better livestock and game trails.

Once he arrived near the cabin, Ed checked it out from a distance to be sure no one was there. Then he rode on in, making a circle with an eye to just where a horse could be ridden on a dead run through the aspens with as little chance of being seen as possible. By running right through the thick aspen grove nearest the cabin, it looked like the fast way out would be to hit the sagebrush flats right out on top of Cold Spring Mountain. But that would put a rider close to Juan's sheep herd and close to being seen. Another route would be across the sage north of the cabin, a distance of only about two hundred yards, and into the heavy aspens breaking off the mountain. Then there was always the trail right down N S Creek into the big canyon leading down into Talamantes Creek, some four or five miles away. This would put a rider near Charley Sparks's cabin, a route that just might be useful if things went wrong and a rider had a bullet in him, needing help in a bad way.

Ed considered what route Tom Horn would take if he just happened to put an end to Matt Rash's life right there in the cabin. He would need to get to some town in a hurry to establish an alibi, claiming that he could not have been in two places at once, many miles apart. One route would be right along the top of Cold Spring Mountain, east to Limestone Ridge and over it, out on the desert flats and on to perhaps Powder Wash and Baggs, Wyoming, a distance of some seventy miles. That ride would require several changes of horses if he rode at full speed. Even if he headed across Cold Spring Mountain and down into Brown's Park and out to Lay and on to Maybell, Colorado, he would still have to have extra horses. If the rumors were true that Horn was being paid to handle rustlers by Ora Haley of the Two-Bar Ranch, halfway from Brown's Park to Maybell, horses would undoubtedly be staked out along the way.

Ed put in the whole day in the area around Matt's cabin, contemplating ways to do the killing and avoid getting seen, much less getting caught. He knew that if Horn came in and took care of Rash first, he would not have to worry about it. On the other hand ...

Jim had saddled up and gone up the mountain within the hour after Ed left. Instead of heading directly off toward the west end of Cold Spring Mountain, he cut straight up to Joe's camp. He wanted desperately to know if his suspicions might be right, that Ed was doing some hard looking and planning for gunning down Matt Rash. In Jim's mind, it was all unnecessary. Just wait, let Tom Horn do it, if it would be done at all. There was still a chance that Rash might decide to leave the area, just like the note on his door suggested. But still, Jim knew how Ed thought his grazing rights should be maintained. Had he actually shot down a couple of fellows for moving in too close to his territory? Would he do it again? And this time would it be the president of the Brown's Park cattlemen's association? Jim needed answers if he was going to keep Ed out of this deadly trouble.

Joe wasn't around his wagon, but Jim easily found the sheep herd about a half mile away, and Joe was there tending the herd. Jim could see that Joe wasn't concerned with anything in particular, so things must have been going along in a normal sort of way.

"Joe! Amigo! How's things going?" Jim called out when he saw that Joe had seen him approaching.

"Buenos, good, Mr. Jim. And how's things with you?"

"The same, Joe, the same. I'm jest heading out to scout th' west end of th' mountain to get an idea of th' grazing out there. Kind of thinking 'bout moving Juan out that way 'fore long," answered Jim as he rode up to Joe and his dogs. He stepped down from the sorrel and dropped the reins, and the sorrel immediately started grazing on the abundant mountain grass.

"Have you seen Ed this morning?" asked Jim. "He was heading out this way a little earlier."

"No, Jim. He never came this way. Did he say he was coming up to see me?" Joe asked with a curious look on his face.

"Well, no, Joe. Not directly, at least. But you know how he is and all. Wouldn't hardly get on this part of th' mountain without dropping by to be sure you were doing okay." Jim did not want Joe to know he was checking on Ed too closely, and he sure didn't want to let on that both he and Ed were in the know about Tom Horn. But Jim's concern was readily evident to Joe.

"Jim, do you think maybe he is out checking on where Matt Rash might be? I know he is hunting him, maybe not directly, but hunting him just the same. Jim, I think he is looking for him, wanting to know just where he is at all times. He's going to get him, Jim. Like I told you. He's going to get Rash." It was obvious that Joe was worried about what Ed might be up to.

"If he didn't come by here, Joe, he probably cut off to th' east somewhere. It don't matter much right now, Joe, 'cause ol' Matt is in town doing some rodeoing. They won't get into anything today, at least. I'll bet he is headed over to Rash's cabin, maybe over to see Juan. He sure didn't want my company."

Jim was satisfied with what he had learned. Ed was not out checking on the livestock or the herders. But Jim had tied his own hands earlier by telling Ed that he would be on the west end of the mountain. He couldn't very well go blundering off toward Matt's cabin to see what Ed might be up to now. All he could do was keep to the west end, keep checking on the grass and possible cattle herds, doing what he wasn't much interested in. He could make the big circle in just a few hours, get back down to the cabin, and hope Ed showed up by dark without incident.

"Joe, I guess I might as well let you know straight out jest what I'm thinking. You're thinking th' same way. We've got to watch out fer ol' Ed. Try to keep him from doing something he'll regret. I think he's over there at Matt's cabin, trying to figure out jest how to do away with Matt without seeming to be guilty of nothing. You see th' cowboys drifting 'round the country. You know there were notes left on some doors here and there? You know 'bout Tom Horn? Ever hear of him?"

"Oh, si, Jim, si. Yes, we hear all the stories. Th' way Horn kills anyone he thinks is a rustler. Many drifters come by my camps, hungry. They tell me Horn is after them. They are riding out of th' country, fast. They tell me 'bout friends that turned up dead after Horn warned them to leave. And yes, Jim, I know 'bout the notes on th' doors 'round here. They told me Matt and Isom both got a note. I fear for them." Joe didn't know what else to say.

"If all that is true, Joe, maybe that's jest more reason fer us to try to keep Ed out of Rash's way. If those notes mean anything, maybe Rash will be gone soon, one way or another. Maybe we can keep Ed and Rash apart till something else happens," said Jim. "Keep your eyes open, Joe. Let me know if any stranger shows up 'round here."

With that, Jim caught up the sorrel, mounted up, and headed off toward the west end of Cold Spring Mountain. He wasn't too interested in grazing conditions or livestock. After a brief ride around the high country, he headed back off Cold Spring Mountain and down to Ed's headquarters cabin to wait out the day doing routine ranch work with Rueben. Ed returned before sundown in time to help Jim and Rueben put away the work tools.

On the seventh of July, Ed and Jim had a visitor, young Sam Bassett. Sam had been in Rock Springs to the celebrations and the rodeo and was on his way home to Brown's Park. When he rode up to Ed's cabin near noon, he was invited in for grub and some visiting. Sam was the oldest son of the Bassett family and had started a herd of cattle down in the Park with the rest of the family. He had met Jim at the recent dance and was pleased to find him at Ed's place.

"Sam, jest what on earth are you doing out here all alone? Wouldn't none of them others ride with you?" Ed started off after they had finished the meal and cleaned up the kitchen. "I would've thought you'd be riding with at least a dozen folks."

"I was, Ed. But when I told ol' Matt that we ought to turn in here fer a visit, he wouldn't do it," said Sam. "Talked all the others into just heading on home through Irish Canyon. All that rodeoing plus the long ride back home was getting to him. Said his boot was sure rubbing on that ol' bad foot of his. Ought to just get straight on home 'cause he wanted to go up on Cold Spring Mountain first thing tomorrow morning.

"You guys would be proud of the way ol' Matt did in the rodeo. Finished third in broncos, and would've done real good roping but for that ol' bad foot. Caught his steer fast like, but jumped down and had to hobble out to him, losing lots of time. Finished out of the money." Sam was beaming as he talked about his pal, Matt.

"You say he's heading up on the mountain, maybe to his cabin, early tomorrow?" asked Ed. "Foot must be okay, Sam. But there's sure something more important than hearing 'bout his rodeoing and bad foot, Sam. Jest what 'bout that there note on his door, that note maybe from ol' Tom Horn? Talk's all over th' country 'bout that. Now, jest what does ol' Matt 'tend to do? Get out of th' country? Or sit tight and wait it out? Tell you what, Sam. If it's a note from Horn hisself, jest might not be healthy to hang 'round here." Ed turned straight toward Sam and continued. "Sam, you know Horn kills fer th' enjoyment. Is that what ol' Matt wants?"

Jim stopped putting away his new Boone spurs and the extra spurs he had been cleaning, and he, too, turned directly toward Sam. Rueben was putting on another pot of coffee, but he paused and turned. Everyone was listening alertly, eager for a response.

"Well, gee, fellers. Sure, it could be bad," Sam agreed. "But all I know is I'm not hanging 'round here too much longer. My dad and I have talked it over, and we just don't see much future 'round here if we have to put up with some sort of outlaw problem all the time. Josie and the boys are moving into Craig too. She and Dad decided it would be the best place to raise those two boys, so she's selling out. I've been selling off a few of my cows along for some time now, so it looks like maybe I'll just go ahead and close out and leave. Might join the army just to see the outside world. Been wanting to go up to Alaska to try my hand a gold digging. Might be lots easier than cowboying, don't you think, Ed?" Sam asked.

After a few seconds of thought, Sam continued. "Can't rightfully speak for ol' Matt, though. I know I talked to him just after he let us know 'bout that note. Tried to talk him into getting out too and going along with me up north. But like he said, what with wanting to marry up with Ann and settle down right here in the Park, it just ain't the time to be moving on."

"Don't he have enough sense to know if he don't move on, there jest maybe ain't goin' to be no more time? Have you ever heard of anyone gettin' those notes and then having a long life ahead of 'em, Sam? And ain't it so that his thirty days is up? Why, Horn could be laying fer him right now. Maybe even back at the house, or in Bull Canyon, 'fore he even gets home tonight." Ed was plainly jittery, shuffling around in his chair, even raising his voice a bit.

Jim took this all in. "Why, Sam, I didn't know you ever got a note on your door. Did you? Ain't never heard anyone say you did."

"It's not that, Jim. It's just that I've been thinking of leaving for some time, and like Dad says, this might be th' best time. Notes don't have nothing to do with it. Dad hasn't liked it out here much anyhow, and 'specially since Mom died a few years back. Now getting out seems to be all he talks 'bout any more. The only thing keeping him here is all the kids."

After they downed another pot of Rueben's black coffee, the visiting broke up, and Sam had to hit the trail over the mountain to arrive in the Park before pitch dark. Jim hated to see him go, having taken to him rather quickly as a very enjoyable and engaging young man. Jim remembered Sam's dad, Herb, down in the Park too, and he could envision living with those two fellows as good neighbors if he decided to settle in this country. But he noticed that Sam never quite gave an answer to the question of receiving a note on his door. Could it be …?

Ed stood quietly and watched Sam as he rode out through the

sagebrush heading toward Beaver Creek and then up the side of Cold Spring Mountain and perhaps out of his life, at least for now. He had nothing to say to comments from either Jim or Rueben. He simply walked into the cabin and lay down on his bunk, his hands behind his head, thinking.

Jim asked Rueben what had suddenly gotten into Ed. Rueben said he didn't know, but he had seen Ed get this way before and had learned to simply move on and forget about it. It always meant that Ed had something heavy on his mind. Maybe this time it was something about those notes and just what might be happening sooner or later. Rueben said he always handled it by getting busy around the place until Ed figured out whatever was on his mind.

"If that's th' case, Rueben, what is there that needs tending to?" Jim asked as they walked out from the confines of the cabin into the shed area.

"Well, Jim, I did cut some wild hay last week just up the way about a mile or so, up Beaver Creek. That flat always makes good hay. So every summer we cut all we can fer feeding th' horses in th' winter. Ed got us a horse-drawn mower last year in town. It does th' cutting and raking, so all we have to do is load it and haul it down here. We could just 'bout get one load done 'fore dark, if you want to help," said Rueben.

With that, the two headed up to the hayfield with the flatbed wagon and pitchforks. Within a few hours they had the wagon loaded and were headed back to the corral and the small fenced area used for a hay yard.

The work had given Jim time to think, time to figure out just what Ed might be thinking about. It seemed that Ed was very interested in the fact that Matt Rash had gone down to his headquarters in the Park and would be heading up on Cold Spring Mountain first thing in the morning. Maybe he was worried about just what Matt might do when he found Juan and the sheep herd up on top. Or maybe Matt would go to the west end to Isom's cabin and stay there for some time, maybe a few days, not knowing about Juan and the herd for a while. On the other hand, since he had his own cabin at N S Creek, surely he would go straight there.

That was it! That had to be what was on Ed's mind! He had been scouting out Matt's cabin for several days now, and with Matt's return, Ed might be planning to carry out some scheme he had been working on. Perhaps Ed intended to stalk Matt for a while to find out just how Matt operated when he was staying at the cabin. Then, if Horn didn't show up in a few days and handle the Rash situation, maybe Ed would. In any case, it looked like time was running out. Who would strike first?

Jim thought he knew in his own mind what Ed was going to do. He would probably head up the mountain tomorrow, alone, and spend the day watching Matt Rash from a hideout to get a good idea of Matt's movements. Jim knew that Ed would not make a move until he absolutely knew what Rash's daily routine would be. He had to know just when Rash would be getting up every morning, just when he would be stepping outside to get a bucket of water, just when he would begin saddling up for the day. Then he needed to know just when he would return every evening, just what his routine would be every night. All these details would be necessary for a man who was going to rid the country of a major resident and avoid being accused of the crime. And in view of the ongoing events—those notes on various doors, the rumors of Tom Horn being somewhere in the area—he just might pull it off. The blame would very logically be placed on Tom Horn.

But this was not what Jim wanted to happen. Why should his best friend on the mountain try this when a known killer of rustlers, if given time, might handle it? Why couldn't Ed see Jim's way? Ed could sure be headstrong, even bullheaded. He simply did not have to take everything into his own hands. Jim knew he had done his best to talk Ed into waiting or even perhaps forgetting about trying to remove Rash from the area.

"You two have sure put in an afternoon," Ed called out to Rueben and Jim as they pulled in the gate to the little hay yard. "Bet you could do away with a big steak and anything else, soon as you get that hay unloaded there. I been slaving over th' hot stove all afternoon, just fer you two."

"I'll bet you have, Ed!" answered Jim as he jumped off the wagon and started unloading the hay with the pitchfork. "It must have really been a hot, hard day, sitting 'round in th' shade, thinking 'bout us down there in th' hayfield. Wouldn't surprise me any if all we'd get was hard, cold bread and water. Would it you, Rueben?"

"Oh, Mr. Jim, Ed wouldn't do us like that. He's too good fer that. 'Course, when we all left, he was sort of lying on th' bunk," replied Rueben with laughter in his voice.

As they unloaded the hay, they could see Ed scurrying around in the kitchen, getting things ready for a big meal. He seemed very happy, like the bed rest had cured his ailment, whatever that was. Jim remembered seeing him in just that mood before, after reaching some major decision.

Ed talked incessantly all through the evening meal, the kitchen cleanup, and the final two pots of coffee before bedtime. Neither Jim nor Rueben could figure why Ed might be in such good spirits, but they felt happy for him. It would do Ed good to feel this way, and it would surely make everyone else's time much more pleasant. Ed and Jim teased Rueben about his huge Spanish rowels on his spurs, and they all talked about the fine B. Boone spurs Jim had purchased from the nice lady, Jody, back in Denver. Ed even offered to trade his ranch to Jim for those spurs, all in jest.

It was late when the yipping of the coyotes and the lonesome howl of a faraway wolf put the three cowboys to sleep. The bunk was soft and warm following a day in the hayfield for Jim. He hardly remembered something waking him toward dawn, but he was too comfortable to give it any thought. He instantly went back to sleep.

CHAPTER 15

The morning of the eighth of July dawned bright and clear. Jim and Rueben awoke to notice the coolness of morning in the gray light and then turned over to fall back to sleep, something they had not had the luxury of doing in many weeks. They intended to wait for Ed to roust them out and maybe even have coffee ready.

"Ed? Rueben? Anyone awake yet?" called Jim, knowing the morning had gone by more than he had planned. "Ain't anybody got up yet? Rueben! Get out of there. Ed? Ed?"

Jim crawled out and took a look around. The sun was well up over the rim of Cold Spring Mountain, meaning that it was moving on toward midmorning. Rueben was beginning to come around, just sitting up in the bunk. But Ed's bunk was vacant. Maybe he was out getting water or maybe feeding the stock, getting ready for the day. Jim got dressed, slipped on his boots, and went to the door to look outside for Ed. He was not anywhere in sight. Jim proceeded to walk out to the shed, where he noticed Ed's saddle missing. Then out in the corral he found the roan gone. Something was up. Ed was already gone.

"Rueben, did you know Ed left early this morning?" asked Jim when he returned from the corral. "His roan is gone, and it looks like he left while we slept in. Do you reckon maybe he's up checking on th' hay in th' field, since we brought in that load last night?"

"Not much telling, Jim. I guess that's what woke me a little sometime last night or likely early this morning. Thought I heard someone moving 'round in here. Just didn't pay much attention. Sleeping too good. Just thought it was one of you getting up to go out to the outhouse. Heck, Jim, he didn't even make us no coffee." Rueben was fully dressed and beginning to get started in the kitchen.

It wasn't like Ed to pull out without saying anything to anyone and leave before light. Must just be somewhere nearby, maybe checking the fence around the place, or maybe had to get up to push the stock out of the new hay. Maybe the hay yard fence wasn't too good. Jim kept wondering about it as he poured the last of the water from the bucket into the wash pan. When he bent over to wash his face, he was staring straight at Ed's bunk. And just under the edge he saw the ruffled wool bags. They had always been carefully kept back, completely out of sight. Someone had gone through them.

Quickly, Jim turned and glanced around for Rueben, who was in the kitchen busily stirring up breakfast. Then he made his move toward Ed's bunk and the wool bags. He unrolled them, knowing in advance what he would—or would not—find. The new Winchester .30-30 was gone, and one new box of shells was missing.

Instantly Jim knew what the sounds in the night were, why the roan was gone, and exactly what the missing .30-30 meant. Ed was making his move on Rash!

"Rueben! Get out and saddle up my horse! Hurry! I've got to ride out 'fore it's too late. Ferget that breakfast. Move, man, move!" cried Jim as he ran for his gun belt and Colt .45. By the time he had his gun strapped on, he was out the door. Rueben had his saddle off the tree and was putting feed in the trough to bring in the sorrel.

"What's up, Jim? Why all of a sudden are you in such a rush?" asked Rueben as he caught up the sorrel and slipped the bridle over his ears. "Do you know something 'bout Mr. Ed?"

"Maybe, Rueben, maybe. Jest could be too late. I think he's making his move on Matt Rash! Couldn't wait. Jest couldn't wait! Jest had to take matters into his own hands. The ol' hardheaded fool knew we had a better idea. Couldn't wait! If I put my horse in a good lope, and keep it up all th' way, maybe I've got a chance to find him 'fore it's too late. Jest don't know …"

Jim tossed the saddle over the back of the sorrel and drew up the cinch. He checked his rifle and scabbard and made sure his field glasses were in the saddlebags. He looked for extra ammunition there too and hurriedly led the horse out of the shed.

"I'll go by Joe's camp and let him know to watch fer anything going on. And to be ready to run down here with you if he has to," Jim explained to Rueben.

He stepped up on the sorrel and turned once more to Rueben. "I'm going to try to stop Ed from killing Rash, or getting killed by Rash, whichever way it might turn out! If my thinking is right, he'll be setting it up at Rash's cabin. It'll be close to noon before I can get up there. Now, don't you open your mouth 'bout none of this! Stay right here at th' cabin and don't dare leave. Could be that Joe and Juan might jest come running in later, and they'll need you here. If things work out okay, I should be back here with Ed by midafternoon, or anyhow by dark. But if not, there most likely will be some shooting up there, and I don't want any of you headin' up that way, least not till tomorrow. If we don't come in tonight, if it's that way, you go down and get Charley Sparks to ride up with you. Be careful, Rueben!" Jim hurriedly stuck his spurs into the sorrel and dashed out across the sagebrush flats toward Cold Spring Mountain and destiny.

The excitement of the sudden run caught on with the sorrel as he loped easily along, taking long strides that covered the country quickly. Jim knew he could put the horse into a full gallop, but that would wear him down long before reaching the cabin at N S Creek. He would head straight to Joe's camp and give the sorrel a couple of minutes rest there, but then it would be nonstop to the cabin, if they needed to go that far—a thought that entered Jim's mind as he charged up the slopes of Cold Spring Mountain.

What if he showed up during an all-out gunfight between Ed and

Rash? What would happen if Jim arrived after it was over and Rash was alive? Would Rash shoot Jim too, since he surely knew he was a partner with Ed? Would Jim then have to kill Rash, maybe in self-defense? And just what would Jim say to Rash if they met up out on the range before anything had happened? He would simply have to turn Rash back off the mountain in some way. Maybe he could tell him that he had seen Tom Horn on the mountain headed toward Rash's cabin. Sure, why not? That just might save the day.

Three miles put Jim and the sorrel well up along Cold Spring Mountain, not far below Joe's camp. From a point, Jim saw the sheep herd off the mountain overlooking Talamantes Creek. Just the break he needed. No need now to go clear up on top to the camp, for Joe should be down with the herd. Cross a couple of more draws and he would be at the herd.

"Joe! Joe! Have you seen Ed?"

"Ed? No, Jim. Should I? Was he coming up to see me?" Joe replied, noticing that Jim's sorrel had worked up quite a lather.

"I don't have time to fill you in, Joe! Have you seen him at all? Maybe before light this morning?"

Joe hesitated, thinking that maybe he did remember something early. "No, Jim. I haven't seen him, but maybe he did come by very early. Before light th' dogs all got up, barking and carrying on. Wasn't anything out there, Jim. I thought it might have been a wolf or something, but then th' dogs gave up. Not what they would do if it was a wolf, don't you think, Jim?"

"It was Ed, Joe. Had to be. He's headed over to Rash's cabin. Looks like trouble coming up, Joe. I want you to watch out. If anything unusual happens, be ready to take off to th' cabin in Beaver. Rueben will be there. And if Juan comes running into your camp, jest load on that ol' horse and run fer th' cabin, both of you. I'll tell you 'bout it later. Got to run!" And Jim was off again toward Rash's cabin.

Having to drop down in every draw and cut coming off the mountain was hard on the sorrel and slowed him down. Jim thought that perhaps they should go toward the top to get on more level ground, which would make traveling much easier, although it would take a little time to climb up. He touched the sorrel on the offside neck with the reins, just enough to turn him angling up toward the top of Cold Spring Mountain and easier travel. They could still stay in the edges of the aspens to have cover in case anyone might be working up there. No use letting anyone know.

By the time they reached the clear top, the sorrel was blowing hard. Jim realized that he could not push the horse too much and slowed to a walk. He would let him walk for a few minutes until his breathing got back to normal, and then he would be able to push him as hard as necessary for the full distance to the cabin. Jim figured that if he got within one mile of the cabin without incident, he had best slow down and use caution. Rash could be running from Ed and maybe in the aspen somewhere. Or could be the other way around. And if Rash happened to have gotten the best of Ed, there sure would be nothing to gain by rushing in on Rash and becoming the second cowboy to lose the day.

Suddenly Jim saw a lone rider a half mile ahead, just entering the patch of aspen that ran all the way to Rash's cabin. In the few seconds that he was in view, Jim could not recognize the horse or the rider, but he knew it wasn't Ed. He reined over into the nearest aspen grove, still watching the rider that he could see from time to time in the trees. He was moving very slowly, as though stalking something or someone.

Jim quickly dug out his field glasses and started watching for the rider. In a few seconds he came out in a small clearing, stopped, and looked all around. Jim found him in his glasses, made a fine adjustment, and when the rider next turned toward him, he recognized him as James Hicks … Tom Horn … one and the same. He was back and had come for Matt Rash, stalking him right through the same aspen grove that Ed would probably be in too.

Jim's head was spinning. Who would get to Rash first? Or would the two stalkers run into each other? And now with Jim in there too, what would be the final outcome? Three was definitely a crowd.

Jim slowly backed the sorrel into a thicker clump of brush, keeping a view of the tree area where Horn was. Now he knew he had problems. He could no longer charge in toward where Ed might be, couldn't simply get between Ed and perhaps Rash, if in fact Rash was there. With Horn in play, Jim would have to try to stay out of his sight but still find Ed before anything broke loose. If Horn did get to Rash and then found that Ed was there, and perhaps Jim too, Horn would be forced to eliminate all three of them. He never left witnesses.

Jim knew it would be all but impossible to move into position to see the cabin, to verify that Rash was there, and to also find Ed. He would have to find Ed's roan. The horse would be somewhere short of the cabin, tied in a concealed spot. If Jim could do that, he still had a chance of getting to Ed before anything started.

Jim wished he had gone with Ed more when Ed was scouting out Rash's cabin. He at least would have learned the lay of the land, perhaps where Ed might make his approach to the cabin. But as it now stood, Jim only knew what he had learned on that earlier trip to the cabin to check on hides without brands. He remembered how Ed had left him and made a big circle, studying every place that someone watching the cabin could use. Or even places from which a rifle shot would not miss anyone near the cabin.

Horn had moved deeper into the aspens. Jim could only get a glimpse of him once in a while, and that was only through the glasses. Without them, he would have lost Horn entirely. He had to move to a better location, someplace where he could see what Horn's intentions were. He spotted a depression ahead of Horn, and perhaps while he was down in it, Jim could move across to higher ground, still in thin aspens. Maybe from there he could get a better view of Horn and still not be seen. It was a desperate chance he had to take. If it worked out, he might even have a view of the cabin.

The sorrel moved along quietly, as though he sensed the need to step lightly. By the time they had covered several hundred yards, Jim saw the cabin ahead through the trees. He stood for a long while, studying the area where he expected to again see Horn. Minutes seemed like hours as Jim used his glasses to ferret out some sign of where Horn might be. Then he picked up the flick of an ear, the swish of a tail. Finally, he made out the shape of a horse, tied in thick brush—Tom's horse. Horn was on foot, probably making his final, sneaking approach to the cabin. Jim knew it would be unlikely that he could find him again.

Quickly Jim turned his attention back to the cabin. Was there anyone there? Through the glasses he could see a horse in the small pole corral attached to the cabin. It had to be Rash's horse. He was home.

Jim still had no idea just where Ed might be. Was he even here? Maybe he wasn't out to get Rash today after all. Maybe just wanted to set up the real date a little later. And maybe he, too, had seen Tom Horn. If so, he would have surely backed off to let Horn do the dirty deed, just like Jim had tried to convince him earlier.

Suddenly the sorrel turned his head and pointed his ears alertly. Jim was ready. He always used his horse's great senses to keep him out of trouble. Jim watched where the sorrel was pointing. Then he saw it—the rear end of Ed's horse. The roan was standing almost out of sight, only fifty yards away. With the glasses, Jim made out the saddle, and Ed wasn't in it. The roan was tied. Ed had to be on foot, making some kind of stalk toward the cabin just like Horn was doing.

Jim quickly stepped down from the sorrel, tied him, looped the field glasses to the saddle horn, pulled out the .30-40 rifle, and slipped off toward the cabin in hope of somehow finding Ed. It was now a race, but a slow and cautious race, one that could end in any of a dozen different ways. And it seemed to Jim that he just might be the odd man out, nerves on edge, sweat running down his forehead.

When Jim could again see the cabin through the thin brush and aspen trees, he was only a hundred yards from it. And there was Ed, just rounding the corner of the cabin, rifle in hand, one step into the doorway. The first shot ripped through the mountain air. Then a second shot.

Instantly, Jim hunkered down behind a fallen aspen log, in disbelief at what he had seen. Just as suddenly, from only forty yards to his right, he heard a cracking of brush followed by a clatter of rocks and heavy footsteps heading back away through the cover. Jim whirled, frightened by what it had to be, knowing that it was Tom Horn, too close! His natural reactions threw the rifle up in the direction of the disruption, just in time to glimpse Tom Horn running away through the trees toward his horse. Horn had been just as startled by the two shots as Jim! Within seconds, the sound of horse hooves pounding through the woods and on out into the sagebrush told the story. Tom Horn was breaking out for distant parts.

It took Jim a few seconds to recover. Then, just as he stood up he saw Ed step around outside the cabin and fire one last shot. And Rash's favorite horse fell dead.

Jim was shocked. He didn't know what to do. He had realized that this could all happen, but he was not prepared for it. He had no idea that he would witness this killing, no idea that he would see Tom Horn run away, not taking part in the affair at all, and no idea what to do next.

In the confusion of the stupor he was in, Jim simply backed further into the aspens, moved to his horse, untied him, and walked him over to Ed's roan. There the three stood, waiting. Jim's mind was blank. He had no plan for this situation.

Ed hurried back into the patch of trees toward his horse. He had completed what he set out to do and was confident that no one had seen it. No one could witness against him. And he was sure that ol' Tom Horn could be used as the scapegoat, since everyone around had come to believe that only Horn could have placed all those notes on the doors and gates telling those fellows to leave or else. His plan was airtight, he thought. A few yards into the trees and brush, Ed came to a sudden halt. There before him stood his roan, the familiar sorrel belonging to Jim Keaton, and Jim himself. •

"How long you been here, Jim?" were Ed's first words. "Jim, I'm talking to you! How long you been here?"

"Just long enough, Ed. Just long enough," Jim responded, still much in a daze over the whole show. "I guess we better get moving, and fast."

Without another word, Ed dropped the new Winchester .30-30 into the scabbard. The two men stepped up in their saddles, turned their horses back, and started walking quickly out of the aspens and out of Matt Rash's territory, and life.

"Ed, we better get out of here fast as we can. Don't want anyone knowing we had time to be here when Rash … when Rash was killed." Jim was slowly regaining his senses. He was beginning to understand the enormous problems that could confront the two of them if anyone tied together the timing of the killing with their presence on the mountain. "Joe knows we're out here. Had to go by his camp trying to find you earlier. Got to get back to him and tell him something that might make sense to keep him from seeing that you were over at Rash's place!"

Ed had nothing to say. He was shocked that someone could have slipped in and caught him in the act he had planned so well. All he did now was follow along with whatever Jim said, not thinking, not trying to plan a way out. And above all, he was not thinking clearly enough to even wonder how Jim was on to him or how he came to suspect something might be happening up there at Rash's cabin.

They covered the first two or three miles as fast as the horses would carry them, ducking in and out of cover, trying to stay as far down off the clear mountaintop as possible, but still in good fast-traveling country.

Jim had time to get his thoughts straightened out while they rode. It even crossed his mind that he ought to get Ed down to Charley Sparks's place and put him under arrest for murder. But how could he do that to Ed, his best friend, the man that had taken him under his wing, clearly showing that he would do anything in support of Jim? No, he couldn't do that to Ed. But protecting him would make Jim an accessory to murder.

When they got within a mile of where Joe might be, Jim reined up, raising his hand to indicate to Ed that they needed to stop. "Ed, I'm jest going up there to see Joe and tell him that I found you halfway over to Rash's. I'm going to tell him that you were out early checking on th' possibility of putting in a dam at that spring back in that rough little canyon there. And you had been planning on keeping water there for th' sheep so we could stay more off th' mountaintop. Maybe he will believe that you finally listened to me 'bout staying clear of Rash." Jim was staring hard at Ed, making sure he understood that he was setting Ed an alibi, and Ed would be expected to make it work.

"Now, Ed, you jest ride along easy-like, right on off th' mountain. Get down in th' basin looking like nothing ever happened. If Joe is where I think he will be, he jest might see you, and if you ain't looking too excited, maybe he won't think any more 'bout it."

Jim turned the sorrel up the mountain, heading up to visit with Joe. Ed turned down toward the bottom where he would break out in open sagebrush where anyone could see him—in particular, where Joe could see him if he happened to look down in the basin.

Jim's ride up the mountain alone gave him more time to think. It looked to him like he just might have a workable plan that would cover for Ed, but at the same time it would incriminate himself. If he simply passed on the story to Joe, and if Joe believed it, things would sure be easier for Ed. Then he could fill Ed in on the fact that Tom Horn had been there and seen the killing too, and that he had turned tail and run. Jim thought that Horn probably realized that he would get blamed for the death of Rash and that he had better get out of the area just as he had doubtless planned. And maybe even collect a killer's fee from those greedy big ranchers, the cattle barons that everyone suspected of hiring Tom Horn to eradicate the range of all rustlers. With luck, Ed would not even be considered as a possible suspect.

Jim was still frustrated with his efforts to think clearly. After all, he had just witnessed a murder. He had to report it … or did he? Rash was an outlaw, rustler, the sort that often got shot or strung up to some tree by any rancher catching up with him. The law would then normally excuse ranchers, after a brief hearing. How was Ed's situation any different? Proof of Rash being a true rustler might be hard to come by if Ed were taken in. Sure, Jim saw the evidence; so did Ed. But others down in the Park seemed to support Rash, even making him the president of their cattlemen's association. Jim had too much to consider. Did you have to report all killers? Even best of friends? There was no time for this kind of thinking, especially not right now.

"Joe! Sure glad you didn't move too far, made my ride easier," Jim called out as he approached Joe and the herd. "Needed to get back up to let you know there wasn't no need to worry 'bout jest where ol' Ed was this morning. Found him looking over that spring over there in that bad little canyon there. He's been thinking 'bout putting a dam 'cross it fer holding a little water fer th' sheep. Found him walking off th' distance needed fer doing th' dirt work. Sure was surprised to see me come running up to him! Couldn't jest let him know I was worried 'bout him moving in on ol' Rash. Had to jest tell him I was hurrying 'cause I'd overslept."

Joe was relieved. He was sure that Ed was after Rash, and that this was the day he planned to do the killing, in view of Jim's hard ride out to try to catch up with him earlier that morning.

"So it was Ed that came by in th' dark this morning causing th' dogs to go to barking. Ain't seen Mr. Ed out that early before," said Joe as he moved over toward Jim. "He must have decided you were right 'bout leaving ol' Matt Rash alone, eh?"

"Joe, he finally said I was right 'bout waiting out whatever might happen 'bout them notes on all th' doors. He could see that if ol' Matt didn't leave, maybe Tom Horn would come back to see him. He does think that would be th' best way now." Jim could see Joe relaxing, a sure sign that he was buying the idea. "He's off down there in th' basin now, heading back to th' cabin. Wants me to help him get some paint ready fer marking several new lambs up here. I best get moving if I'm going to catch him before he gets clear back home."

When Jim turned toward the basin, he saw Ed quietly riding along. He looked back at Joe, got his attention, and pointed toward Ed. Joe looked and nodded, letting Jim know that he, too, had seen Ed. This would surely help build Ed's alibi.

Jim joined up with Ed before reaching Beaver Creek. As they rode along, Jim could tell that Ed was still confused, that he still couldn't believe that anyone had been on to his plan, let alone in that aspen grove and witnessing the shooting. If Ed didn't get his thinking back before reaching the cabin, Rueben was sure to see that something awful had truly taken place, and he would know.

"Ed, you jest don't know how close you come to either gettin' to miss out on Rash or to gettin' yourself killed too!" Jim had to get things straight with Ed before they reached the cabin. "You didn't even know you had company back there in those trees, now did you?"

Ed turned to stare at Jim. "No, Jim, no. Sure didn't. Never thought you'd try sneaking up on me like that."

"Don't start that kind of thinking, Ed. It weren't me I was talking 'bout!" snapped Jim. "If you hadn't been so headstrong 'bout gettin' ol' Rash yourself, you'd have seen th' company you were gathering. You could've jest sat back and enjoyed gettin' to see ol' Tom Horn finish off Rash hisself!"

Jim's comments startled Ed.

"Tom Horn? Jest what are you trying to get at?"

"Ed, when I was hurrying to cut you off, I seen a rider ahead in th' trees. It was James Hicks … Tom Horn. If you could've waited five minutes, Horn would've done that killing fer you!"

Ed drew the roan to a sudden stop. He turned toward Jim with a fully amazed look on his face. "You mean Tom Horn was in them trees with me? And you were in there too?"

"You finally got it, Ed. We almost had ourselves a party! I lost Horn in th' trees till you fired that first shot. Horn jumped out of his skin jest forty yards from where I was sitting. Turned and ran to his horse, loaded on, and ran like th' wind out of there. He never knew either one of us was there till you shot. He was there to take care of Matt hisself, Ed." It was plain now to Jim that Ed was coming back to reality.

"How'd you know I was coming up here fer ol' Matt? Been coming up here most every day. Why did you figure out that this was the day?" asked Ed.

Jim could see that Ed was now simply full of questions, just the way he wanted to see him. Jim knew he was going to be okay.

"Ed, I knew you had that new Winchester .30-30 since you brought it home. This morning I seen you pulled it out of them bags and didn't get them back right. And I sort of seen how your eyes lit up last night when young Sam Bassett told us Matt would be up to his cabin today. It jest all added up, Ed," said Jim.

"Now I've got to see to it that your alibi holds up," Jim continued. "That's why we need to get to talking 'fore we get back there to see Rueben. Joe looked like he bought th' idea that you were only up there looking fer a place to dam up some sheep water. Now when we get back to Rueben, you got to make that same story fly. Ain't no one knows 'bout Matt, and if luck holds out, they might not know fer some time. And right now, I bet ol' Horn is busting his britches trying to get some ground 'tween hisself and this mountain. He knows well 'nough th' blame is going to be put straight on him. And we intend to do all we can to help it along," Jim said, with just a little twinkle in his eyes. After all, if Ed didn't carry it off, Jim would be just as guilty. And if locals decided to hold a rope party, there might be two guests.

"Don't ferget, Ed. You got to get that .30-30 back in its place without Rueben seeing it. Or maybe jest plain get rid of it. If they figure out that ol' Rash got it from a .30-30, most folks 'round here ain't never seen one. Anyway, they know what you and me shoot, and there is some who probably remember that James Hicks carried a new .30-30. Could be they might jest start hooking all that together and finally decide who Hicks really is. Fer right now, though, Ed, you got to keep Rueben from knowing 'bout you having that .30-30." Jim could see that Ed was back to normal, understanding everything he was telling him.

When they got to the shed at the cabin, Ed pulled the .30-30 out of the scabbard and hid it among some salt blocks and wool bags. He then pulled his trusty .38-55 from its hiding place behind some fence posts and replaced it where it belonged in the scabbard.

Jim stepped into the kitchen where Rueben was busy making fresh bread and asked him to put on the coffee.

"Where did you find Ed? Did you catch up with him in time?" asked Rueben, obviously somewhat amazed that neither Jim nor Ed appeared nervous or excited.

"Jest jumped to conclusions too quick this morning, Rueben," Jim replied. "Jest knew that ol' Ed was out after Rash, but I was wrong. Ought to let that be a lesson not to make up your mind over something you are worrying 'bout. Found him up there in th' rough little canyon beyond Joe's herd, jest measuring out a place fer a new water dam. Won't work, though. Not enough dirt there in them rocks. Anyhow, I done that runnin' fer nothing. Ed knows I was right, says we can wait and see if maybe Rash leaves, or jest lets hisself get killed by ol' Tom Horn!"

Jim got out the tin cups and could see that Rueben was relieved as he started the new pot of coffee. And Jim couldn't help but feel a bit smug, but nervous, since he now seemed to have convinced both Joe and Rueben that Ed didn't make it all the way over to Rash's cabin.

CHAPTER 16

Back on the mountain, Joe was very pleased that Ed had not been after Rash and that Jim had found him checking out a new water hole for the sheep. By moving the herd closer to a patch of aspen trees, Joe had a nice shady place to spend the afternoon. He was over a half mile from the wagon and had carried himself a small lunch of tortillas and jerky. After a short siesta he got out his knife and spent some time cutting his name and date in the largest aspen tree, a mark that would stand until the tree died, maybe fifty years.

Joe's job of sheepherding was not too demanding. The only real problem always came down to predators—coyotes and wolves and maybe a mountain lion or bear once in a great while. If he kept the herd on good grass and near good water and then bunched them up some for the nights, he had it made. Cottonwood Spring was ideal, leaving Joe lots of time to make his camp better or to improve the spring or just anything else he might be inclined to do. Time was always on his hands.

As he was putting the finishing touches to the carving, he heard a horse approaching.

"Wake up, Joe!" It was the voice of his herder friend, Juan. "You been resting too much!"

"Juan! What are you doing so far from your herd? Something wrong?"

Juan stepped off the old herder horse and let the reins drop. He moved into the shade with Joe and squatted down to talk. "Joe, you know what Ed and Jim told us: if anything unusual happened we were to let them know. Well, just today near midday, I had th' herd near Coyote Spring. Just over the rise in that little rocky place where someone at th' spring couldn't see th' herd. I was getting out my tortillas, when suddenly I hear two shots come from over 'round Matt Rash's cabin, over in th' aspens. Then in a minute I hear another shot. I did what you and Jim said and started to move to the far side of th' herd. There were three or four cedar trees there where I could hide and be above th' herd, looking out across th' country. No one could see me. Soon a rider comes from that way. Riding fast. Looking back a lot. Running from something, I think. Maybe he had been chasing coyotes, but didn't look like he was." Juan's eyes were wide with excitement at reliving the story for Joe.

"Who was it, Juan?" asked Joe, cutting in on the story.

"I do not know for sure, but I think I have seen him on th' mountain, maybe a long way off, with Matt Rash. I think it was Matt's roundup cook. Maybe that new man, Hicks. Th' horse looked like th' one Hicks had. But he was too far for me to know when I saw him, many weeks back. It might not have been th' same man. Maybe just a stranger. But he was in a big hurry. I watched him into th' thick cedars going off th' mountain, off toward Brown's Park. He never came in sight again. After taking care of th' herd good, I decided to come tell you so you could tell Mr. Ed or Jim, like they said."

Joe thought it over for a moment. "Maybe he was chasing coyotes, but you are right, Juan. I will pass it on to Ed and Jim th' first time I see them."

The two herders made small talk for a few minutes before Juan bid Joe adios and headed back to see after his herd.

The next day Jim and Ed moved up to Joe's camp with some sheep marker to leave with Joe for his several new lambs. They were also making their alibi look better by announcing that they were heading over to the spring in the rough canyon to again check the site for dam-building dirt, necessary for any new work. While they visited, Joe related the story from Juan to both men. They agreed with Joe that it might have looked unusual, but it could have been someone chasing coyotes, as Juan said. And on top of that, Rash's roundup cook had been gone for a month or more. In any case, since the rider was gone, there was nothing more to it.

"Joe, jest what time of day did Juan say this rider was seen?" asked Jim.

"Oh, Jim, it must've been noon 'cause Juan said he had his tortillas with him, jest fixing to eat," answered Joe.

"Must've been 'bout th' time me and Ed was leaving from here to go to th' cabin, don't you think, Joe? That would be why we didn't hear any shots. We was down here in th' basin." Jim spoke convincingly, aiming to get Joe's agreement with what the time must have been, to build on Ed's alibi.

"Si, Jim, that would be th' time. I was getting ready for my lunch. Moved th' herd just a little and ate in th' shade of th' first aspen grove. I could see you and Ed down in th' basin before time to eat, not yet noon. Juan heard th' rifle shots at noon."

Jim was satisfied. He looked over toward Ed and gave just a hint of a nod, letting Ed know that what Joe said would be mighty important when ol' Rash was found, whenever that might be.

After a few more minutes of small talk, Jim and Ed continued toward the rough canyon where they were supposed to be looking over a future dam site. They rested there for a long while, thinking over the events of the last two days. They couldn't just head back to the cabin, not if they were to make Joe and anyone else think they were seriously thinking of building a dam to retain some water for sheep.

"Ed, this little draw really is too rocky for any dam building. We couldn't get enough real dirt loose from 'round here to fill a bushel basket, let alone build any kind of dam. We'll jest have to tell Joe and any others that we think we can find a better location, maybe on along toward Chokecherry Draw, or maybe more up on top where there might be plenty of dirt. Joe knows this country. He will understand why we changed our minds 'bout puttin' in a dam here." Jim rambled on, simply idling away time before they would head back to the cabin.

"Did you say something, Jim? I was sort of lost in thought."

"Get up, Ed! Ain't no use faking it up here no more. We're jest letting our thoughts get too heavy on one thing. And you know we done made up everything we 'tend to tell anyone 'bout ol' Rash or 'bout jest where we was on th' day Juan saw that strange rider and heard them shots. Let's head in," Jim said as he moved to gather in the horses.

After getting back to the headquarters cabin, Jim and Ed rounded up the fence tools and started walking the fence around the home place with Rueben. Now and then they would tighten a wire, drive in a couple of new staples, tamp in a loose post or two, and generally work to repair the fence for the coming winter. The section around the haystack got most of their attention as they discussed putting up one more wire and making the fence maybe six feet high in hope of keeping out a few of the smaller deer that would surely try to get in to feed on the fresh hay. When snows arrived in the fall, deer would show up in big numbers. There was room on each post to add one wire, but to do the job right they agreed they needed to put in taller posts. This would be a tough job, digging all new post holes, setting the posts, and stretching new wire. But it had to be done, and Ed indicated that he wanted to work Jim as long as he was around.

Jim thought the hard work would keep the Rash affair off Ed's mind. Even at that, though, every time Rueben left to get more tall poles, Ed nervously brought up the problem of just how long it might be before someone found ol' Rash.

"Ed, we got our story all worked out, so jest you don't get too jumpy 'bout it. Ain't nobody else was up there 'cepting ol' Horn, and he wasn't there any too long! Likely, when they find Rash, word will run like wildfire. We'll hear 'bout it as quick as anyone. Main thing we got to do is jest keep it backed off in our mind by gettin' lots of this work done.

If I don't miss my guess, good ol' Juan has us covered with what he saw. All we got to do is push that idea along." Jim did his best to keep Ed calm, assuring him that the story was good and would work. At the same time, Jim quietly worried about the fact that he had witnessed the murder but wasn't going to report it.

Summer could be hot out in the high sagebrush country, and the morning of the tenth of July was the beginning of another hot day, not at all unusual. Jim, Ed, and Rueben had started early with the fence work. Even though deer could get over most six-foot fences, the three men hoped to keep out some of the smaller animals come winter and deep snow. They would need every scrap of hay to make it through to spring.

"Rueben, looks like me and Jim can get th' rest of these posts up. Only need two or three more. Why don't you head on to th' cabin and rustle up them victuals, see what we got. Won't take too long. Maybe we can get th' wire up after we chow down. Then maybe we can cool off a bit when this ol' sun gets too hot fer working."

"Sure thing, Mr. Ed. I put on a new pot of beans early, before we got started. Ought to be done. And we got plenty of bread made up, and some good brisket left over. Won't take long," answered Rueben as he dropped his tamping bar and turned toward the cabin.

As soon as Rueben was out of sight around the cabin, Ed turned to Jim. "Something must be going on up there on Cold Spring, Jim, don't you think?"

"Ed, we got our plan. There ain't nothing going on nowhere. You got to ferget about it. I got it on my mind too, Ed, but if we let it eat on us, it's goin' to show. That cabin up there is left alone most always, so nobody might not go up there fer some time yet. It don't matter when they find ol' Rash—we know they will be spreading th' word faster than an antelope can run. Somebody will be getting down here to let us know. We jest got to remember not to let on. Got to be surprised right out of our skin." Jim was getting more agitated with Ed's continual talk about Rash.

Ed worried that he had been caught doing the deed on Rash by two fellows, Jim and Horn, without even knowing it. Could someone else have seen the event too? Of course, if others had seen him, they would surely have had the law on him before now. They would have gone off that mountain in a gallop, and there would have been folks up to Rash's cabin that same afternoon. And they would have been after Ed before dark.

"You're right, Jim. Jest got to simmer down more. Sure, if anyone was up there, we'd know it by now. Like you say, ain't too many folks go up to Rash's place every day. This here fence work sort of keeps Rash off our mind, don't it?" Ed agreed as he pounded the dirt in one more post hole. "You got th' last one going, do you, Jim? I'll get th' new wire, and maybe we can get it along before Rueben calls us in."

Rueben spread a good lunch for the three of them, and an hour later they had the hay yard fence finished. After putting away the tools, the three men retired to the front porch of the cabin for a siesta in the shade from the early afternoon sun.

Most cabins were arranged to face toward the early morning sunrise to utilize its warmth to start the day, and the afternoon sun would then cast shade over whatever front porch there might be. The porches were appreciated by residents or visitors in both summer and winter, providing a place to rest in the cooler breezes that drifted across them in the summer and a sheltered place out of the snow and mud of winter, a place to deposit muddy or wet chaps and heavy coats before entering the snug cabin for the company of the potbellied stove.

"Ed, you really picked a good place fer this cabin. Jest look how far we can see there, out across Beaver Basin and Beaver Creek, and even 'way on down toward that Talamantes Creek. I always like to be able to see out across th' country. Jest don't like being closed in by black forest," said Jim as he relaxed, fully stretched out on the porch with his head propped up a bit on a fire log covered with a rolled-up wool bag. "We could 'bout spend th' rest of th' day doing this, don't you think, Rueben?"

"Might could, Jim, but looks like we might be having company soon," answered Rueben. "Been seeing dust down there a couple of miles. Don't look like dust devils."

"Now, Rueben, I been here looking 'bout th' same direction as you fer jest 'bout th' same time, and all I seen was dust devils here and there. Either you're loco, or you sure got good eyes. Is it true that you brown-eyed Mexicans can really see better than us whites, even if we have brown eyes too?" Jim asked as he casually glanced out across the sage-covered valley.

Ed roused up alertly, peering far out across Beaver Basin. "By golly, Rueben, you're right. I see it too. Gone now, Jim. Wait and keep watching down there. It'll show directly. Ain't no dust devils. Ol' Rueben been out in th' open sage most of his life, Jim. That's how he learned how to see. Dust devils always send dust straight up. Riders leave dust low to th' ground, jest drifting gently on whatever little breeze there might be."

Now all three men were sitting up, watching, wondering just who might be coming to visit.

"There he is! Jest one lone rider, Ed. Looks like he's in a hurry. Jogging right along straight our way. Looks like we might jest as well get th' coffee pot back on th' stove, Rueben," Jim said. He stared intently across the sage while Rueben stepped into the kitchen.

In only a few short minutes the rider had closed the distance to less than a half mile.

"Why, Jim, that's one of ol' Charley's men coming! Hope Charley ain't got no trouble down his way," Ed said.

"Careful, Ed. Could be some kind of news we been thinking 'bout. Don't let on if it is. If they found ol' Rash, we got to be real bad surprised," said Jim almost under his breath, trying not to let his voice reach Rueben in the kitchen.

Jim glanced quickly at Ed and saw his face suddenly drop without reply. If this cowboy had word of finding Rash, Jim's plan would have to work. Could they put on a good enough act? Would Ed be able to carry it off? Would their alibi hold, and would both Joe and Juan speak up to support them?

The rider came on, now waving to Ed and Jim.

"Jamie! Man, what's th' big hurry? Riding up here like your pants is on fire!" called out Ed as soon as the cowboy bailed off his horse at the hitching bar. "Ain't seen you in a big hurry in a while, Jamie."

"I know, Ed, and this time is different! We jest got word from that George Rife feller and th' Meyers kid that ol' Matt is dead in his cabin up there on Cold Spring Mountain! Charley sent me flying up here to get you and any of your men to beat it up there quick as you can. Charley left right out. If what the kid said is right, Charley's got to do something. He done sent another rider out to all th' sheep camps on th' mountain to get them herders over there, and another rider headed over to get Bill Finch. Said some of them herders might be th' only fellers with any idea 'bout what might have happened." Jamie was so excited he couldn't deliver the news fast enough.

"Now, now, Jamie. Jest slow down. We ain't deaf neither! Did you say ol' Matt might be dead? Or did you say he surely was dead? Up on th' mountain there, in his line cabin?" Ed asked, looking for the world like he was in total disbelief.

"Dead, Ed! Dead! George said he was plumb dead. Dead fer some time, looked like. Had flies all over him. Stinking! Said blood was all over th' place, all dried out. And that Meyers kid, Felix. He jest 'bout collapsed right then and there. Got plumb sick! Came off th' mountain with George, but sure ain't worth much, all pale and can't much talk. They jest went in to say hello to ol' Matt, and there he was. Dead on his bunk. They think he was all shot up!"

"That can't be, Jamie!" said Jim, doing his best to look just as startled as Ed. "Ain't nobody would do that to ol' Matt! You got to be wrong, man!"

Ed cut in. "Jamie, man, you're shakin' all over! Simmer down. Get in here and sit a minute. Get yourself calm. When we seen you coming, we got th' coffee ready. Looks like you could use something more than coffee. Rueben, pour him a big slug of hot coffee. Got to settle him down and get this story straight." Ed was pulling off the act so well that Jim was amazed.

It did not take long for Jamie to relate everything he knew about the death on the mountain. The four finished off the coffee quickly, and Jamie left to complete his check of any camp or riders in or around Beaver Basin before heading back to Matt's cabin himself.

Rueben caught up the horses while Ed and Jim gathered a few necessities they thought they might need when they got up to Matt's cabin: a shovel and the bottle of Cat Claw whiskey. Within minutes all three riders were heading across the sage, across Beaver Creek, and on their way up Cold Spring Mountain toward Matt Rash's cabin.

At Cottonwood Spring, Joe was getting his things together. He already had the sheep herd moved to a good location where they would settle in without him watching over them. He had his old horse saddled and was just about to step up when Ed, Jim, and Rueben came into the little camp clearing with all three horses blowing hard.

"Ed! Looks like you got th' word too! One of Charley's riders came up just a little bit ago telling me something 'bout maybe Matt Rash got hisself killed! Said you would be heading up here and Charley had to have all of us up there as quick as we could make it." Joe turned his horse, put his left foot in the stirrup, and stepped up into the saddle.

"Sounds like you got the same story we jest got from Jamie down at th' cabin, Joe," replied Ed as he reined in the roan. "They don't seem to know much 'bout what happened. They think he could have been dead up there fer several days. Let's not run off too quick yet, Joe. Give these horses a few minutes 'fore we start." As Ed finished, all riders dismounted to give their horses what little rest they could.

"Joe, Jamie said Charley thought maybe jest you herders would likely know anything 'bout what happened. Did you have any idea?" Jim asked as he dropped the reins and moved over near Joe.

"No, Jim. I don't know what might have happened, 'cept maybe Juan might know something. You remember he came running to my camp a couple of days ago telling me he heard shots over that way and then saw a rider running away from there or from somewhere over that way."

"By golly, Joe, you don't think Juan might've jest been that close to some lowlife, yellow-bellied killer, do you? When you told us 'bout it, we jest thought it was probably some young feller out after coyotes. Ain't been none of us over that way much in several days now, has there, Joe? You ain't been up to see Juan or nothing?" Jim carefully brought up the details he wanted Joe to recall, details that would place himself and Ed away from the bloody scene on that day.

"Since you mention it, Joe, didn't Juan think that lone rider looked like it could've been that feller, Hicks?" Jim continued setting the stage. "'Course, we all thought he was gone out of th' country, but sure ain't nothing keeping him from sneaking back. Ed, you been all over this country. Could ol' Hicks sneak back and nobody would know?"

"Sure, Jim. That wouldn't be too much of a thing to do. He was 'round here long enough to get a good lay of th' land. Could've jest as easy as not come back in here without anyone knowing," said Ed with a faraway look in his eye, a look that might make Joe remember even more than really happened. "Let's get on up there. Maybe somebody else jest might've seen that rider too!"

With that, the four headed out in a fast jog, strung out, not talking. They were eager to see what had been found.

On their arrival at Rash's cabin, Ed's little crew was surprised to find several others besides Charley Sparks already there, including Bill Finch. But on second thought, they realized that several hours had passed since Charley had sent out his runners to spread the word. A look around disclosed that no one from Brown's Park was there, but any ride down to the Park would take a lot of time. It might be that Charley would wait for some of the Bassetts or Davenports or perhaps Sam Spicer to get up to the cabin before proceeding with any official hearings. Charley was the closest thing to an official in that part of the county, designated to act as deputy sheriff without pay. It would fall to him to hold any inquest, which meant he would have to interview everyone around to try to find evidence of just what took place and when.

"Been a long time since I smelled death this strong, Ed," said Jim as they dismounted and tied their horses in the shade.

"Glad to see you made it, Ed," Charley said. "Need to have you and Jim as well as Joe and Rueben go in the cabin and take a look. I need all of you to get a good view of what it all looks like for the inquest. Need your thoughts on what you think might have taken place." Charley was trying to keep calm and rational, but both Ed and Jim could see that even he had been badly shaken by what took place inside the cabin. "I've been keeping the fellers back from the area so we can later do a search around to see if something might be found that would help us figure out what happened. Just step careful over there, don't touch anything inside. Oh, you might want to cover your nose with something. I brought along some carbolic acid to soak your nose cloths in. Can't stand the death odor in there."

After everyone had viewed the death scene, the group moved upwind from the cabin a few yards, built a campfire, put on coffee and jerky, and settled in for a long afternoon. Jamie and two other riders returned with word that they had not found any other cowboys or herders. Charley then took Bill and Ed aside and formed a search group to carefully go over the immediate grounds around the cabin, looking for anything unusual that might be a clue to what had happened there several days earlier. They had to reenter the cabin and make a quick search there too.

Bill Finch was in the cabin when he made a discovery and called out. "Charley! Come look what I found! Jest might be th' shells from th' rifle that put poor ol' Matt away!"

Both Charley and Ed moved quickly back inside the cabin, conferred briefly with Bill, and just as quickly stepped back outside with two empty rifle shells in hand.

"Fellers, looks like Bill here found what we've been looking for! These two shells are 'bout new, and both come from a .30-30 rifle. Matt never owned one. Who do any of you know that owns and shoots one?" Charley asked.

A murmur went through the tight little group near the campfire. Several commented that they had never even seen a .30-30. One by one, they started discussing various folks around the area and just what caliber of rifle each one used. Then they began to bring up fellows who only traveled through the Park area, and finally the name of James Hicks popped up.

"I never knew jest what he used, Charley. But come to think of it, I did notice that he had a good-looking, new rifle in his scabbard. Noticed 'cause none of us could ever afford to have one!" said Jamie.

Suddenly, Jim stood up, looked all around. How could a better chance ever come along? "Well, since you mention it, Jamie, I did see that too. And since I like my .30-40 so well, I noticed that new-looking rifle in Hicks's scabbard, and it was a .30-30! Noticed 'cause I ain't never seen one outside a hardware store, never knowed any rider to have one!"

"That one don't count, fellers, cause Hicks has been gone back to New Mexico for several weeks. We need to know who might have a .30-30 and be around here now," said Charley.

"Mr. Sparks, you ain't heard what Juan seen a few days ago." Joe said. He was not used to being in such serious circumstances and was somewhat reluctant to voice any opinions or make statements without being asked. "He seen a rider. Ask him. He'll tell you."

"Is that right, Juan? What about a rider?" Charley's curiosity was aroused. He had to have more information than they had thus far turned up. There were folks back in town who would not hear of a common herder saying anything important. But Charley and the other ranchers and cowboys who lived and worked every day with them respected and depended on them as equals and knew they were very observant. "What did you see, Juan?"

"It may not be important, Mr. Sparks. We thought it most likely was jest a coyote hunter. But he was running his horse fast. And kept looking back, back toward where I had jest heard three rifle shots. That's why we thought it was only a hunter. I can't be sure, but the rider looked like that fellow who cooked fer Mr. Rash in the roundup." Juan was obviously uneasy. "But later when I told Joe, and Joe told Mr. Ed, I found out that th' cook had left th' country weeks earlier. He was gone. But that rider sure looked like him."

Then Joe spoke up and filled in the details, even mentioning that Ed and Jim had visited him and headed off the mountain toward their cabin before the time that Juan heard the shots and saw the rider. Neither Jim nor Ed had anything else to say about their whereabouts on that day. Joe had covered for them without even knowing it.

"Fellers, it sounds like Juan probably saw th' killer of poor ol' Matt, but we don't know who it might have been. He thinks it looked like Hicks, and I'll keep that in mind, but since Hicks is gone, it most likely was not him. Not much way he would be around without someone knowing. Now, we all know Matt got that note on his cabin telling him to leave the country or else. So now, based on that, it looks like the most likely killer would be whoever wrote the note. Folks down in the Park all think it had to be ol' Tom Horn, but no one has ever seen him around here. Or maybe no one would know him if they saw him! We do know, however, that Horn does his shooting with a .30-30, according to the other lawmen that I've talked with." Charley hesitated, waiting for someone else to offer any better ideas.

"Charley, jest a thought fer you to chew on," Bill Finch said as he moved close to Charley and Ed and Jim. "You remember how fast that Hicks feller made that long ride over to Ashley Valley … er … Vernal back when Jim McKnight got hisself shot up? Made that run, maybe forty or fifty miles, in less than five hours. Seems that might jest mean that a feller like that could be most anywhere in no time at all. What I'm gettin' at is that maybe ol' Hicks could be around. Jest 'cause he left fer New Mexico sure don't mean he had to go to New Mexico, now does it? Could jest move out in th' hills, or over to some resting place, and hang out fer a while, and then move back in here without anyone knowing no better. Besides all that, ain't nobody knows much 'bout Hicks. Jest who is he anyhow? And thinking 'bout it all, he wasn't jest a poor drifter neither. Always had a decent outfit, good saddle … and that nice new rifle."

Charley took it all in, and then he turned to Ed and Jim. "Bill is right. We never did know much about Hicks. And he did hang out almost all the time with Matt. He never talked with anyone much. Maybe I'll get a wire off to some of the lawmen down toward New Mexico and see just who knows Hicks. Bill may be on to something. At the same time, I don't think it would hurt anything to wire around and see if anyone can account for Tom Horn during these last few days." Charley hesitated, looked at the cabin, and nodded toward a clear spot close by. "Ed, get some of the fellers started digging a grave about right there. If we don't get that body buried pretty quick, we won't be able to get near it."

It was near sundown before all the work of burying Matt Rash was finished. A few of the men gathered for their last cup of hot coffee before heading for their respective cabins, while some got busy rounding up the horses that had drifted off a few hundred yards to graze.

"Charley! Got a rider coming up from the Park. Looks like one of them Bassett cowboys," called out Jamie as he was catching up his mount.

Within minutes the rider was among the group, greeting most of the men and moving toward Charley. Everyone recognized him as Pete, one of the Bassett riders.

"Hello, there, Pete. Wasn't looking for anyone from the Park. You must have 'bout run that horse all the way up here!" said Charley as he stuck out his hand to welcome Pete into the gathering.

"Wasn't that much of a run, Mr. Sparks. I jest happened to be th' first one to leave after your man came in with th' word 'bout Matt being killed. Ain't none of us believed it. Took some time to sink in. Then when that little Ann got started screaming and bawling and carrying on and all, I jest decided I needed to get on out of there and up here to see what happened. That Ann is sure letting it out. Can't much blame her, what with everyone kind of knowing 'bout them two maybe marrying and all. Is it true, like she says, that ol' Hicks is sure enough the killer?"

"No, no, Pete. There isn't anyone that knows anything about the killing yet. We've heard from all the herders and cowboys that might have been on the mountain when this thing happened, and not much evidence is here. I don't think Ann would know any more 'bout it than we would. She just happened to have some troubles between herself and Hicks before he left. Makes it easy for her to jump on him, 'specially with him being gone." Charley was the steady influence among the men, keeping things under control.

Charley continued providing details to Pete. "The fellows will tell you that we heard that one herder saw someone riding across the range, actually running his horse maybe full out, from the direction of three gunshots from around Matt's cabin a couple of days ago. Fits in with what the killing looks like. We did pick up a couple of new .30-30 shells from inside the cabin. And some say that Hicks had a new .30-30. But with him out of the country, it doesn't look much like he could have been up here too. Matt's body wasn't in any condition to look at, so we had to hurry and get him in the ground there," said Charley as he pointed out the new grave. "We're just shutting down and about to head home, Pete, but I'm sure you can find a scrap or two of jerky and maybe a cup of coffee."

Ed and Jim moved toward their horses, away from the group. "I can't believe how this thing is working out," Jim said very quietly to Ed. "Let's get ourselves off this mountain and leave them to build th' case 'gainst ol' Hicks, and Horn!"

CHAPTER 17

Jim and Ed both knew that Charley Sparks would make a trip to Rock Springs to report the official findings of the Rash murder to the sheriff. He would also send off telegrams to other lawmen in Wyoming trying to get a handle on just where Tom Horn might have been for the last few weeks or months. In addition, he would surely wire some officials down in New Mexico to try to get a lead on just who Hicks might really be. Then Charley would have to make a long trip over to Hahn's Peak to the county seat to give the evidence to the Routt County sheriff, since the killing took place in Colorado and not Wyoming. That would all take time, maybe a week or more.

"Jim, we got things to do 'round here to get ready fer winter. Got to get more of that basin hay cut and brought in. Plenty of things to do over th' range too. Got to be sure some of them herds of woolies is doing okay and get th' fellers some supplies. Looks like I might be riding th' rest of th' summer," Ed said as he and Jim sat on the cabin porch whiling away time, thinking.

Jim wasn't paying too much attention, still lost in thoughts of the last few days. "I got things needing done over in Johnson Draw too. That little horse pasture ain't any too tight. Jest a brush fence, 'cepting th' corners where I set in some good posts. Probably don't need more than a couple of days to get that caught up. Been dragging a few aspen

logs over along the fence line, thinking I might end up with enough to
start setting some more permanent posts along.

"Ed, you know we might start seeing more grazing open up there
on th' mountain now that ol' Rash ain't up there," Jim continued.
"Somebody is bound to get his cow herd handled. That would only leave
ol' Isom Dart up there, wouldn't it? And I bet that Isom ain't gettin'
any too far from his cabin after Rash got gunned."

"Ain't doing nothing but getting th' range back to where it was
before Rash started trying to take over. Me and Charley always had
plenty of room till then," Ed answered without much thinking. "Then
got to remember that even ol' Isom weren't there till that Rash got
to moving 'round. No need in Isom even being here. Takes up some
grazing that ought to be ours."

"But, Ed, don't you think ol' Isom might jest get out since he got
th' same note on his door? He surely ought to get to thinking that what
happened to ol' Matt is likely to happen to him next," said Jim, not
giving any thought to what Ed might be leading up to.

"He's had his chance. He ain't showing much sense," Ed said as
he sat staring out across the vast sagebrush basin, lost in his thoughts.
"If that Horn would get hisself back here, I'll bet ol' Isom would find
hisself next in line."

Jim turned and looked at Ed, who was mostly talking to himself,
thinking a bit out loud. Could it be that Ed would just as soon get rid
of Isom too, like he did with Rash? If the Rash killing was blamed
completely on Horn, would Ed try his hand at getting Isom off the
range too? Surely not, but something to consider. Maybe Ed learned
something from the Rash episode, since he came within only a couple
of minutes or so of not having to do the killing himself. If he wanted
Isom gone, he might just wait Tom Horn out, assuming Horn would
return to finish the job. These thoughts worried Jim.

In spite of all that had happened recently, Jim liked Ed and could still
feel relaxed with him. He appreciated all the things Ed had done for him,
the Johnson Draw cabin, use of Ed's spring wagon, the introductions

to folks in the Park, and now full use of Ed's headquarters. The things that true friends always do.

But now the words of Andy Ewing, back in town, began to bother Jim. Andy's warning about watching Ed, something about how cold-blooded the man could be to his enemies, while being the best of friends to those he liked. How would Jim know which side of the fence he was on, now that Ed realized that Jim knew he had killed Matt Rash?

Confusion was setting in. Maybe he didn't belong there any longer. Maybe it was time for him to just pack out, get on back down to Texas, back somewhere along Devil's River, a more peaceful place, a place where folks didn't plot to kill their neighbors over the use of public ground, a place where all the ground was properly deeded and becoming fenced. A civilized place.

"Ed, since things look quiet 'round here fer now, I think I'll jest head on over to my cabin and get some work done. That is, if you don't need me, if you and Rueben can handle things here. 'Course, if you can't get along without me ..."

Ed continued staring out over the country as though he had not heard a word Jim had said.

"Ed! Wake up, man. Listen to me," Jim said. "You ain't heard nothin' I've said fer th' last hour, have you?"

"Oh, sure, Jim. Jest that I was thinking. Sure, if you need to get on over there, go ahead. Me and Rueben can do okay. We got plenty to keep us busy fer a while. There won't be nothing going on 'round here till Charley gets his duties done and gets back to fill us in on what he learns. Ought to be able to make the Hicks-Horn connection hard and fast by then, don't you think, Jim?"

"He sure ain't going to find anyone named Hicks down in New Mexico! And I bet he ain't going to find out where Horn has been these last few weeks neither. And if he gets much description on ol' Horn, it'll fit Hicks like a glove. Ed, this thing is working out too good to be true!"

Jim stood up, stretched, and headed for the shed. He called in both the mare and sorrel, snapped a lead rope to the mare's halter, saddled up, and rode off with a final wave to Ed and Rueben. He could feel the tension draining out of him as he crossed the basin, cut around Bishop Peak, and dropped down into Johnson Draw.

Somehow the Johnson Draw cabin didn't look as snug and serene as it always had in the past. Maybe he had been away too much lately. The setting now seemed to be too confining, set in too narrow a canyon. Jim began seeing things that had been of no importance before. What if someone wanted to set up an ambush for him in that closed-in cabin? He could sit on the high canyon sides almost anywhere and have a perfect view of any movement Jim might make. The distance would be close.

When Jim turned the mare and sorrel loose in the small pasture, the thought entered his mind that there really wasn't enough grazing enclosed for any livestock to speak of. It was interesting how he had not noticed this fact before. As he stared up and down the two draws making up the cabin grounds and pasture, he saw that any livestock herd would have to be turned out on top of the divide, on the land being used by Ed. To get any more grazing down in the two draws would require a lot of timber cutting, a lot of hard work that might take a couple of years or more. And the little creek that flowed in front of the cabin was adequate for the cabin and maybe the two horses, but would it flow enough for any sizable cattle herd? Would the springs flow year-round? Why hadn't he noticed these things before?

Jim busied himself inside the cabin doing a bit of housework to get the place straightened up for the next few days. He built up the fire in the cast-iron stove, set water on for coffee, and stretched out on the bunk to think. Those fleeting ideas concerning the cabin location and grazing grounds bothered him. Surely they were being brought on by fatigue and worry about the events of the last week or more. But while lying there trying to get his mind straight, he began to see that the worries might be real.

Jim could now see that setting up a full ranch-style life would require more room than the Johnson Draw cabin and pasture offered.

And now he had doubts about getting any land from Ed, since it was abundantly clear that a man who would kill over words would not hesitate to do so again, and even more quickly over land. Could Jim continue his thoughts and ideas of settling down anywhere near Brown's Park and Cold Spring Mountain? Had he gone too far in his friendship and loyalty with Ed? Maybe his friend, Andy Ewing, was turning out to be more of a friend than he ever thought. After all, Andy had tried to warn him and, in fact, did warn him about the possibility of Ed's thin character, that he had killed with little pretense in the past and ought to be watched if any serious matters ever came up. And what could be more serious than Jim catching Ed in the act of murder?

Jim worked hard for the next few days tightening the pasture fence with the addition of more substantial brush and tree limbs. He even cleared a couple of clumps of heavy buckbrush from the middle of the draw to give the sparse grass a better chance. But his mind just wasn't in it. He couldn't drive himself like he had in the past to try to clear more and more land to make more grass. He just wasn't sure any longer that he would ever really need more grass.

Staying at the cabin was not giving him the peace of mind he had had in days gone by. What he needed was a real change, maybe a trip to Rock Springs and a visit with that green-eyed beauty at the Cat Claw. Maybe Mary Lou was what he really needed.

He made up his mind quickly, and this time he would not let Ed or anyone else know that he was going into town. He needed to find out if being with Mary Lou would clear his mind about the actions he needed to take concerning Ed, the Johnson Draw cabin, his future ranching dreams, and even Mary Lou herself. He would take the gemstones from the diamond field and make a deal with a jeweler for something special for someone special. Within the hour he had saddled the sorrel, packed necessities in the saddlebags, and was making dust toward Rock Springs.

The next day before midmorning, Jim checked in at the Valley House, putting up with the talkative clerk who bubbled over with news concerning the murder of Matt Rash out in Brown's Park. Jim allowed that he did know about it but that he simply knew little more than that. The clerk rattled on, giving Jim details that were obviously making the rounds in town.

Finally, Jim broke off from the clerk and headed out to find the only jeweler in town. He had the little leather bag with all the precious stones from the diamond field tied tightly inside.

"Yes, sir! These seem to be fine stones, Mr. Keaton. Just where did you say they came from?" asked the jeweler.

"Brought them up with me from Texas. They were in my family fer years, so I finally decided they ought to be put to good use. Need 'em mounted 'round some good diamond you might have. Got to be nice fer someone special like," said Jim, unwilling to open up any discussion about the real background of the stones.

"Well, Mr. Keaton, seems you just might know more about high quality stones than any of these coal miners 'round here. I've got a special diamond here that few folks have ever seen the likes of. When I've shown it to the few who showed any knowledgeable interest, they didn't believe it was real. But, Mr. Keaton, I can assure you that this stone beats any I've ever had. Let me show it to you." The jeweler went to a small safe, spun the dial a time or two, opened it, and produced a stone the likes of which Jim himself could hardly believe: a natural, yellow-amber diamond.

"Not many of these are ever found, Mr. Keaton. And when they are, the mine owners keep most. Had I not known the diamond dealer quite well, he would never have shown this to me, let alone sold it to me. I'm a lucky jeweler, and you are a lucky customer."

Jim studied the stone closely, even borrowing the jeweler's glass through which he studied the diamond for internal flaws, finding none. "Gee! This does seem to be something different. If it is really this rare, is th' price going to be too high fer jest a cowboy to afford?" asked Jim, wanting to do some price bargaining like Mary Lou had taught him a few weeks earlier. "I'd want you to set it in something like a ring, maybe surround it with all these stones of mine. Make it really different from anything else around."

"Mr. Keaton, I can do just that. Won't take but maybe overnight … er … maybe even late today, if you think you could see it clear to pay the value. Somewhere 'round maybe one hundred dollars?"

Jim could see that the jeweler was testing the water, just like Mary Lou told him any good salesman would do. But Jim knew he had to have that diamond set in that particular ring. He had to put on a show.

"Why, that's almost robbery, mister! Ain't nobody in his right mind going to pay that much! That'd be more than three months of wages!" Jim said in his most serious manner.

"I knew right off, Mr. Keaton, that you were a smart fellow. Knew you would be able to see that the regular price could be negotiated some. Tell me, just what do you plan to do with this ring? Not being nosy, you understand. I keep the confidence of my customers, if you know what I mean, Mr. Keaton. Maybe if I knew who it might be for?"

"Do you know Miss Mary Lou Garrett at the Cat Claw?"

"Miss Garrett? Why, Mr. Keaton, you don't mean you and her?" The jeweler was beside himself with surprise. "I would have never known! Miss Garrett has been my best customer in town for years, Mr. Keaton. Don't you worry 'bout that price. Let's see here. Yes, maybe I could do a lot better. How about just fifty dollars? Cash, of course. Really, now, I'd 'bout be giving it away. But for you and Mary Lou … er … Miss Garrett, I would be happy to do that!"

"I've got the cash, and I'd want it finished before sundown," answered Jim, knowing that he had just made a terrific deal. Now if Mary Lou only accepted the deal he planned to offer her, sometime just after sundown.

Jim spent the morning making the rounds, looking in all the shops, passing time until he could get over to see Andy at the hardware store. Most of Andy's business would be over before noon. Sure enough, when Jim walked in, Andy was more than happy to tell the other clerks to take over while he and Jim went to the Valley House for lunch.

"Jim, I can't hardly wait to hear your side of the story 'bout that killing of ol' Matt Rash!" Andy blurted out as they quickly departed from the store. "Ain't been this much talking going on fer years! Man, was you right there? Did ol' Horn jest shoot him down right there?"

"Can't tell you much more than you already know, Andy," said Jim. "And no, Andy, I wasn't right there. Wasn't nowhere near there. See, me and ol' Ed was looking over a place to build a new water hole 'bout th' time ol' Matt must have got hisself killed. Ed's herder saw some rider runnin' away from that area jest a little later. Said it looked like that cook of Rash's, guy named Hicks. Charley Sparks was coming to town with all th' details fer th' sheriff. Don't know nothing else, Andy. So now tell me what you think you know 'bout it all."

"Sure 'nough, Jim. Charley did come in. Had a long meeting with the sheriff. Some deputies were in there too. They got off wires to all over. Spent the day jest sending and receiving all them wires. That night them deputies all told everbody in town jest what went on. They say nobody knowed jest where ol' Horn was all last month. He weren't anywhere 'round his usual hangouts. And that man you call Hicks. Ain't no Hicks nowhere down in New Mexico! At least none with that name that was gone out from their places during the last month. By the time all that stuff got put together, the sheriff and ol' Charley both seemed to jest know the killer had to be Tom Horn. And ol' Horn jest 'bout had to be Hicks! Now don't that jest 'bout beat it all, Jim?" Andy seemed to have all the details and more.

"So now jest what is th' sheriff going to do?" asked Jim. "He knows he can't much cross th' state line."

"That's jest it, Jim. There ain't much more he can do. But since ol' Horn is living in Wyoming, the sheriff thinks he can enter the case now that they discovered Horn was absent from his regular places fer the same time that your feller, Hicks, was showing up in Brown's Park. If them is the same feller, then our sheriff thinks he jest might get in on making an arrest. At least sometime down the road. After all that time here, ol' Charley left on his way to Hahn's Peak to give the same word to the sheriff over in Colorado. They seem to think the sheriff over there won't much care 'bout ol' Matt getting killed. Don't think there will be much investigating from there," said Andy as both men entered the Valley House.

The noon hour stretched into the early afternoon as Jim and Andy exchanged stories and ideas concerning the killing and the notes that were tacked on several doors of folks down in Brown's Park. Some of them had already packed up and moved out, and others, like Isom Dart, were still hanging on, watching their backsides at all times, worried even more now that the first of their kind had seen the fulfillment of the posted contract.

"Andy, you remember when you said something to me 'bout watching out 'bout ol' Ed?" Jim asked, wanting to get off the Rash stories and on to things that might involve Jim more directly. "If I remember right, you said he sometimes treated his enemies sort of rough."

"Sure, Jim. Lots of us know 'bout ol' Ed. He's all right when you are on his side, but watch out if you're not! Seems not to have any sort of feelings 'bout folks at times. Followed that sheep rustler out on the sagebrush desert and jest plain killed him. 'Course, that ain't too unusual in stock country, but then he went after that feller that tried to homestead up there in Beaver Basin. Ed jest called him out and killed him too. Then came that poor old miner in the diamond field. Ol' Ed jest killed and buried him right there. Never even lost no sleep over it. 'Course, nobody ever proved anything 'gainst him. And like you mentioned to me back a while, we don't really know fer real sure that he done any of this. But, Jim, like I said, jest watch him. Long as you're in good with him I don't think he'd do you no harm at all. Would stick up fer you too!"

"Andy, I've got to tell you something. Something I might ought not tell anyone. But it's been eating on me fer a while, and you being 'bout th' only feller I know well enough to trust with much of anything, well, looks like I jest got to tell you." Jim tensed up, trying to decide just what and how much he could afford to tell his friend.

"I jest ain't telling you all I know 'bout that killing of ol' Rash. Don't ask me nothing 'bout it. But I do want to tell you that I'm getting a funny feeling 'bout good ol' Ed. See, he jest was sort of talking 'bout having Isom Dart up there on that mountain th' other day. Said Isom didn't have no business being on that land, public land, you see. And now with Rash gone, more grazing is going to be open. Then he said jest enough 'bout ol' Isom to give me that funny feeling. You don't think ol' Ed would try to do in Isom fer th' grazing, do you, Andy? Jest th' thought makes my hide crawl."

"You mean ol' Ed's thinking of maybe jest plain killing poor ol' Isom? Man, I'd get far away from anything like that, Jim. Jest how many folks can ol' Ed do away with 'fore he gets caught? Or 'fore someone beats him to the punch? We've all known to watch out 'round ol' Ed, Jim, but since you been getting on with him so good like, I had no idea he might even be making you nervous." Andy leaned far back in his chair, staring intently at Jim.

"What I'm getting at, Andy, is that if I get to knowing too much 'bout some of ol' Ed's dealings, would he go after me?" Jim was uneasy and knew it was showing.

"Jim, you wouldn't be telling me this if you weren't scared of ol' Ed, now would you?" said Andy as he turned pale from hearing what Jim had said. "I jest sure do wish you weren't down there 'round all that, Jim. You ain't been in this country long enough to get mixed up like that. And if you're telling me now that he knows something 'bout the killing of ol' Matt, and if you happen to know he knows you know, I jest think you ought not to even go back out there! I ain't too sure you understand hard men like ol' Ed. Why, he jest don't bat an eye when he kills. Least that's how it looks to some of us!"

"You're right, Andy. Guess I never really wanted to admit that to myself, but you're right. It ain't that I'm plumb scared, Andy. Jest that now I find that I'm beginning to watch my backside and wonder. If he is as cold as you say, why he could set up above my cabin and I'd never know." Jim was quiet for a moment, and then he said, "I want you to know, Andy, if anything happens to me. After what you've told me today, I ain't staying out there much longer."

Jim felt like he could relax after admitting to himself and Andy that he was not staying in the Johnson Draw cabin much longer. He could now get his mind off Brown's Park and back to more important things.

"Andy, I've got things planned that could make my own personal life better than I ever thought in my wildest dreams," said Jim. "And it sure don't include Brown's Park!"

Andy perked up. "Why, Jim, jest what do you mean?"

"This ain't th' best time or place, but I might jest as well tell you. I'm having that jeweler do me up a special ring today. Picking it up in a little while. Then heading straight over to th' Cat Claw."

"A ring? You mean a ring like a feller might give to a wife?" Andy stuttered, hardly believing what Jim was getting at.

Jim turned a little red and looked all around like he might be overheard. "If she will have me, Andy."

"My gosh, Jim! This is the best thing I've heard all year! Why, what do you mean, if she will have you? That lady has the blues full time when you're gone out in them hills. We can't even get her to be close or friendly with none of us! Jest a smile and business. When is all this? Tonight, you say? She don't even know yet?"

"Andy, if it works out, I won't even need that sorrel to get me back out to th' Johnson Draw cabin. I'll jest jump up there on some ol'cloud and ride it back and never touch th' ground! Won't take me long to close out any dealings I've got out there. Might stay long enough to help ol' Ed finish gathering some winter hay. Maybe get things set fer th' winter, but I ain't planning to be out there fer th' first snow. Made my mind up. Might be going back to Texas, if Mary Lou agrees. Jest needed to get my mind cleared, and today you've done that fer me," Jim answered. "She'll know soon enough, Andy. Now don't you say a word 'bout all this. You think ol' Ed is rough, you ain't seen nothing if I find out you told anyone what we jest talked about!"

It was dusk when Jim left the jewelry shop with the beautiful, fully custom ring done up in a small, leather-covered box. Jim was floating, his boots hardly touching the sandy, coal-dust-laden streets, heading straight toward the Cat Claw.

"Jim! Oh … Mr. Keaton … I mean. We've been looking all over for you! I mean, Miss Mary Lou, she sent us all over looking for you. Everyone knew you were here in town!" Wanda gushed like a fountain, bubbling over, hurrying to grab Jim by the arm, and almost dragging him back toward a quiet corner table somewhat away from the boisterous crowd. "You just sit right here while I get upstairs to tell Mary Lou you're here!" She was off, dashing toward the back stairs, taking them two at a time, scurrying up to the inner balcony and Mary Lou's private entry.

Jim suddenly felt that everyone in the Cat Claw was looking at him. He glanced around. Not a cowboy, drifter, drummer, or gambler was paying the slightest attention to him. The hustle and bustle of the place had shielded the excitement shown by Wanda. Only Wanda's best girlfriend, Jeanie, noticed Jim, giving him a sly wink and a slight head motion toward the upper balcony. Jim looked up, and there stood Mary Lou in her best form-fitting red gown, flared a bit at the knee, dangling earrings twinkling in the dim light of the dozens of oil lamps surrounding the barroom floor. For a long moment neither knew just what to do. Then Wanda started down the stairs, motioning to Jim to come on up. When he passed her on the landing, she whispered that she would send Jeanie up with a bottle of the best whiskey in the house, on her!

Their embrace in the dim light of the upper balcony was warm and close. Jim instantly knew that he had picked the best night possible for his planned romantic moment. No one knew the few quiet words that passed between the two as they entered Mary Lou's private domain, quietly closing the door to the rest of the world.

The next afternoon Jim left the Cat Claw, going out the back way, down the outside stairway, and up the street to the hotel. Most of the ranch hands and other visitors to Rock Springs were taking a siesta, a Spanish custom that everyone thought was well deserved. Even the talkative little desk clerk was snoozing as Jim quietly got by him and went up to the room he had rented but not used the day before. He slipped off his boots and stretched out on the bed, thinking about the whirlwind affairs of these recent few days and Mary Lou in particular, soon to become Mrs. Keaton.

Back in the Cat Claw all the girls had been buzzing around, stopping to exchange a few words from time to time with each other. The bartender kept up his front, that he was not interested in whatever the girls were up to, even though he also knew all about the visitor to Miss Mary Lou's room the evening before. Wanda and Jeanie and all the other girls were betting on whether Mary Lou would remain single when the visit was over. They knew how Mary Lou felt about the handsome fellow who treated them all too politely. But all they could do was wait.

Late in the afternoon Mary Lou hurried down the stairs in her businesslike manner. The girls quickly became busy, and the bartender had glasses to shine and stack. Then Mary Lou called them all to the large table reserved in the rear for special parties. When they had gathered around, Mary Lou simply laid her left hand out on the table for everyone to see. The yellow-amber diamond was breathtaking. And the questions started.

"Yes, we are" was Mary Lou's first answer. "Within the next couple of months" followed. "Either in Texas or perhaps right here in Rock Springs. Where we will live will be strictly up to him."

Then the question from the bartender came, more business oriented, to which Mary Lou answered, "I don't know that we will sell out the Cat Claw. We might just decide to stay right here and run the show! I can fit in most anywhere, running this fine saloon or being a rancher's wife. Makes no difference at all to me!"

Mary Lou gave quick, short, and decisive answers to the dozens of questions directed at her, just as her business background had taught her. When the questions slackened, Mary Lou announced, "The drinks are on the house for everyone!" And the party began.

The streetlamps were just being lit when Jim slipped over to find Andy locking up the store.

"You rascal, you," said Andy when the place was secured and the two relaxed and started talking. "You jest up and popped her the question, and she said sure, and that was all there were to it?"

"Word must fly 'round here, Andy. I wanted to break this to you first. How'd you know 'bout it this quick?"

"Jim, you sure don't think something as big as all us losing that pretty little Mary Lou would go by unnoticed, do you?" replied Andy with a grin on his face big enough to sink a ship. "Why, the minute them girls at the Cat Claw got the word they jest ran all over spreading it to high heaven. You'd think some of them was getting hitched up, the way they was acting. And the party they set off is tearing up the whole town by now. That Cat Claw ain't never seen this much business fer nothing else that ever come by!"

"Did Mary Lou really start a party over there? Last night she said she jest might throw th' biggest fling ever seen. Said I'd best be there too!" said Jim as he looked around nervously. "I must have gone to sleep up there in th' room a bit. Meaning to get down here and buy you a big steak tonight. Think we can still make it, Andy?"

"Only if we do it at the Cat Claw. I wouldn't dare be caught taking you away from all them folks. They been waiting fer you so they can see jest what the two of you look like together. Jim, we might jest as well get on over there and make it a party too. Besides, that Mary Lou can get that cook of hers to turn out a steak that makes all them others look like bone soup!"

It was after midnight before Jim, Andy, and Mary Lou could get together to enjoy just a bit of private, personal talk, the kind that happened only among the best of friends, without anyone to interfere. There was never a question about loyalty concerning whatever was discussed, and the three soon got off into serious talk.

"Jim, does Mary Lou know 'bout the way things are out in Brown's Park?" asked Andy when all the cowboys and drummers and others had drifted off.

"Andy, I don't know that I've told her everything, but sure, she knows 'bout things. She hears things here in th' Cat Claw that folks jest don't think 'bout when they say 'em. She don't know 'bout what I might know 'bout that killing of poor ol' Matt, but she don't need to know neither. Why?"

Andy ignored Jim's question and moved on to direct his discussion to Mary Lou. "I really think Jim is in a bit of a spot out there in Brown's Park, Mary Lou. He done got hisself involved kind of deep in some things that ain't none of his affair, and I worry 'bout him getting hurt out there. Them folks can be jest plain mean. They done things out there that we don't even think any civilized folk would ever do. So I jest might as well tell you that he knows too much 'bout that Rash killing. Won't tell me nothing more 'bout it, maybe he told you?"

"I know, Andy," said Mary Lou in her usual quiet manner. "He doesn't tell me all those things, but then maybe I don't really need to know. He should try to close out down there and move up here as soon as he can. Thinks he owes Ed some help before winter sets in, so he might hang around down there the rest of the summer. But, Andy, you know now that I've got something I've always wanted, I really don't want him to go down there and not come back!"

"Jim, what we are both trying to say is that neither of us trusts your friend there, ol' Ed." Andy sounded stern and continued. "We both seen him do things to folks that jest ain't right. Sure, if he likes you, and it sure looks like he does, things might jest go along real good. Thing is, though, he could kill you and never look back. We'd never know. And if what you said to me 'bout Rash means you even know maybe that Ed was in on it, Ed would kill you, Jim! He ain't got no feelings. Why don't we all get together and go back down there and close out any of your affairs. With several of us, I don't think anything would be done 'gainst you."

Jim knew they were right. He had no real problem, though, with Ed. And Ed wouldn't know that Jim and his friends were even thinking about Ed as a killer. But Jim knew.

"I've got to get on back down there," said Jim, "and alone too. There won't be no trouble. Ed and I do real good, and I feel like I owe him fer letting me have th' use of th' cabin all this time. Besides, there's always some of his cowboys 'round most of th' time. Rueben is a good one. He wouldn't let nothing happen if he knew it was in th' makings. Besides, if Ed were to jest up and offer me a bunch of that country north of him and tell me he would pitch in and help get me started, I'd sure trust him. It would get me up this way, away from Brown's Park, and he could jest go on with his business down there. I would be out of th' way. And if it don't really look right, maybe Mary Lou and I will jest move up here and keep running th' ol' Cat Claw! Or maybe even jest sell out and head off down there to those peaceful waters of th' Texas Devil's River!"

With that, Mary Lou perked up. "Jim, I could really go for something like that! But don't you take too long to see how things are going. I don't want you down there around that Park bunch any more than you have to be."

It was getting late, and Andy had to open the store early in the morning. He shuffled back his chair, looked both Jim and Mary Lou over, smiled, and said, "Mary Lou, you could have picked me and not had all these problems. Would you like to change your mind?"

"Why, Andy, you never ask at the right time! We've been here in the Springs all these years and never shared an afternoon or evening together alone," she said in her beguiling way as she snuggled up closer to Jim.

CHAPTER 18

It was a very long ride from Rock Springs back out to the cabin in Johnson Draw. Jim had business on his mind, the kind he never dreamed of having when he first left Texas to check on the will left by his brother. The old stories of the salted diamond field had proved to be true, and the beautiful country for ranching had also proved out. But he never dreamed of the personalities that would be involved in this lonesome country. The lawlessness was like stepping back in time, back to the early days when white men first thought of moving into Brown's Hole. Those men were independent, ruthless, and lawless. Jim never saw that sort of thing in Texas, and the only thing close to it was what he had witnessed as a soldier back in Arizona.

The whinny of the sorrel was the first announcement that they had arrived back in their own territory in Johnson Draw. It got an immediate response from the mare, far up the draw in the little horse pasture. Jim knew the mare would be delighted to have them back. He had begun spoiling her a bit with handouts, feeling a little guilty in not using her more.

But this time Jim did not simply ride straight up to the cabin as in the past. He found himself hesitating slightly behind each clump of brush, looking up the canyon walls, studying the trail for any sign of visitors. When he had only another hundred yards to go, he drew up the sorrel, quietly pulled his field glasses from the saddlebags, and started combing over each and every rock and dark cedar thicket up above the cabin. It was clear to him that hiding places were abundant in most any direction. Anyone could set up an ambush. But this time he found no sign of anyone around. He noticed, too, that the sorrel's whinny had received only the one response from the mare. No return whinny had come from up above on the plateau where someone might tie a horse, out of sight.

Quickly Jim put away the glasses and spurred the sorrel toward the cabin. He scolded himself for showing signs of fear, signs of concern, at least. At the same time, however, he knew he had to be more observant of what was going on around him, more cautious, vigilant. After all, he had certainly seen how sly and cunning Ed had been in making his move on Matt Rash.

Jim stayed in Johnson Draw for several days, but he did not set right in to build the permanent fences he had been planning earlier. He wasn't working on long-term projects. He spent most of his time reflecting over the recent weeks and trying to come up with some little passing thing that might now indicate any bad blood between himself and Ed. Nothing showed up. He saw nothing that would even begin to indicate that Ed might turn on him. Actually, he saw only things that would sustain their friendship.

It was time to get on with life, get back to help Ed prepare for fall and winter. And figure out how to tell Ed that he was soon to become a husband, meaning that he could be moving on to better things. How would Ed take to the idea of Jim leaving? Maybe good ol' Ed would insist on Jim taking up land close by, maybe even offering him lands that Ed had used over the years. After all, he seemed to have the same respect for Jim that he had always had for Charley Sparks and more recently for Bill Finch. If this were true, Jim could easily see being neighbors with Sparks and Finch, and Ed.

Jim had even discussed this very possibility with Mary Lou, and she was in agreement, if it worked that way. But her hope was more along the idea of setting up ranching close enough to Rock Springs to allow her to continue with the Cat Claw until she could find a buyer at top price. And she thought they would be better off moving north of Erickson's, even up to the Pretty Water country or around Aspen Mountain, leaving all the Brown's Park problems far behind.

Setting the fantasies aside, Jim called in the sorrel, saddled up, and rode off toward Ed's cabin.

"Rueben, you're all alone up here? Where you got ol' Ed?" asked Jim as he dismounted and turned the sorrel loose in the pen.

"Jim! Man, is it good to have you back! Ed's out on th' mountain, up toward Isom's, I think. He's been riding a lot since you've been gone. I've had to do all th' chores by myself too. Carrying supplies out to th' camps, bringing in extra wood for th' coming winter, keeping up th' fence. We kind of came to lean on you, man! The minute you were gone, we both knew you had been doing a lot of work up here. Thought maybe you had caught on and jest up and left!" said Rueben as he stepped out of the cabin and moved out to the pens.

"No, Rueben. I jest had to get some things done over in Johnson Draw. You missed me but didn't even come over to see if th' coyotes might've chewed me up?"

"We jest ain't had no time fer watching over you, Jim," said Rueben. "Besides, we sort of wanted to stay 'round here to be in on anything that might go on with that killing of Matt Rash. Had several cowboys drifting up fer a change. They all wanted to know what we knew, and we wanted to know what they knew. Jest a standoff, I guess. Didn't learn a thing."

Jim heard Rueben out. "Well, Rueben, I got caught up over there and took a ride into town. Heard lots of things 'bout th' killing in there. Seems they jest 'bout have th' thing pinned on Tom Horn. Found out that Charley Sparks went over to Hahn's Peak to give all that information to th' sheriff there, but ain't nobody thinks much will be done."

"That's right, Jim. Charley did just that, and he thinks nothing more will get done there. That little Bassett lady has sure been busy trying to get everybody thinking ol' Hicks is th' killer. She don't understand that th' law seems to think Hicks and Tom Horn could be th' same feller. Jest yesterday one of them Bassett cowboys come by and told me over hot coffee that somebody down toward Maybell, 'round Lay, I think, was taking pictures of antelope and seen a rider 'bout sundown, riding hard across the hills. Said the feller looked a lot like Hicks. That was the same day that Juan saw that rider that he thought looked like Hicks too. Looks like the time would work jest right fer that to be th' same rider." Rueben filled Jim in with everything that had happened while Jim was gone. "Word got off to Rash's people down in Texas too. They will be up right away to get Matt out of th' ground and take him home. We all been sort of taking care of Matt's cattle, waiting fer th' family to get up here and decide what to do with them."

Jim and Rueben made the rounds of the headquarters, pens, and outbuildings, making small talk about the work needed before winter set in. Before sundown, Ed came riding in from Cold Spring Mountain. Jim knew Ed would be happy to have him around again, and Ed quickly asked if he planned to be available to help with the ranch work, getting ready for fall. Jim said he planned to be, but he wasn't sure he would be around for the winter since he might be looking for a place to buy between Cold Spring Mountain and Rock Springs. Ed knew Jim would probably want his own place. He even volunteered to help Jim find a place, as time might permit. When the talk died down, Jim wondered why no one had brought up the fact that Jim might become a married man. Maybe word had not yet spread all the way down from Rock Springs. And Jim saw no reason to let the word out just yet.

Jim moved in with Rueben and Ed, and they all pitched in trying to get things ready for fall. During the next few weeks they cut several tons of hay, moved it into the hay yard, and improved the fences to help keep the wild game out of the stack. Jim was sent out a time or two with supplies for the camps, and those camp boys kept him up on all the rumors of the range. When Rash's father and brother came up from Texas to recover Matt's body, everyone on the mountain showed up to help them all they could. Jim and Ed helped with the digging, along with Isom Dart. They all showed great remorse concerning the death of Matt, and all promised to do everything they could to find the killer.

It wasn't long before Jim noticed that Ed was doing a lot of early morning riding up on Cold Spring Mountain. And for some reason he seemed to always bend around toward Isom Dart's end of the mountain, maybe just doing some coyote searching, trying to keep the predators down and perhaps backed off from his sheep herds. Usually he was back before midmorning, ready to head out to one of the camps. And it seemed to Jim that Ed always had something to occupy both Jim and Rueben around the headquarters early, while he left for the mountain long before first light. On his return, things always carried on normally, jobs to be done everywhere, trips to be made to the camps, water holes to be checked. Jim's curiosity soon got the best of him.

"Ed, you sure must have lots of them coyotes or something up there on th' mountain to get you out so early ever day. What takes you off up there?" Jim asked at the first opportunity.

"Not that so much, Jim," answered Ed. "Jest got to watch out fer how many steers and all ol' Isom might be turning on th' mountain since Rash ain't up there. They pretty much got all of Rash's herd off and sold, so th' mountain ought to have more room fer other stock, don't you see? Thing is, Jim, looks like maybe ol' Isom is even putting out a few more head every day. Really don't look like too many more cattle, but sure is a lot more wild horses. Maybe he's breaking out a bunch to take to town."

"He ain't moving over on th' grounds that Rash was using, is he?" asked Jim rather quietly. "I know you used to make use of most of that country 'fore Rash moved in and all. Used to use most of what Isom's got too, didn't you?"

"They neither one should've moved up here, Jim. That all used to be mine and Charley's. We didn't have no kind of trouble then. But when ol' Jim McKnight split out from that Bassett gal, and even fer a long time before, things started changing. McKnight weren't much trouble.

Then along came Rash and then that Isom. Now that Isom's got it all, he jest might want to push us others off th' mountain."

"Ed, I didn't realize Isom was much problem. Th' little I've seen of him, seems to be okay. Jest seems to keep his business off on th' west end of th' mountain," Jim commented.

"Ain't that, Jim," said Ed. "Thing is, he jest don't belong up there. Me and Charley opened that country up fer our use. Now we ain't even been allowed th' freedom to graze where we used to. Graze where we always had rights. Isom jest don't belong."

Jim knew he was getting into something that was of primary interest to Ed. The earlier comments he had heard from Ed about Isom not belonging made Jim wonder if Ed might try to eliminate Isom just like he did Rash. But maybe Isom might up and leave since Rash was gunned down. Maybe it was time for Jim to pay a visit to Isom.

Within the week, Jim got his chance. Ed had gone out on the desert to check camp locations he would use come winter. He would be gone for the day or longer. Jim made the excuse to Rueben that he was going to take the opportunity to do some coyote shooting on the mountain, saddled up the sorrel early, and turned him toward Isom's country.

The ride was enjoyable, as always, on the slopes of Cold Spring Mountain just after sunup, the morning mist burned off by the early golden rays of sun. The wildlife was still out grazing, a few antelope here, a few deer there, and, of course, a coyote scampering across the sage-covered hills from time to time. But Jim had no intention of shooting at coyotes even though that was his stated mission. He wanted to get on to Isom's cabin before he might be out and gone.

Before long, Jim could make out a trace of smoke from the cabin where Isom might be eating breakfast. When he entered the small aspen grove, he saw that Isom had not yet left the cabin, and the horses were still in the pen waiting to be fed to start the day. The cabin was all closed up, but Jim could see Isom moving around inside through the single small window. Then he saw a second person inside and wondered who might be there with Isom and why.

"Hello, there, Isom! Coming up out here! You open fer company yet?" Jim called out to let Isom know that he was not a stranger or a shadowy drifter, someone that just might make good on the posted threat on Isom's door a dozen weeks or so earlier. Jim and the sorrel moved on slowly to the hitching post but waited for Isom's reply.

The plank door opened just a crack, and the muzzle of a rifle slowly came into view. Then with a wider opening, Jim made out the figure of someone checking him out. And suddenly the door popped wide open, the rifle dropped, and out stepped young Sam Bassett.

"Why, Jim … Jim Keaton! What on earth you doing way up here? Get down and get in here fer breakfast! Isom and me was jest wishing we had good company to chow down with." Sam turned and called Isom out. "Look who's here!"

Jim was made welcome and immediately ushered inside. The door was closed and bolted shut. The table was all set, and Isom simply added another plate and cup as they sat down to a breakfast of biscuits, gravy, fried grouse, bacon, and coffee, a meal the likes of which Jim never expected. They exchanged small talk about the range, whether the water holes were holding out, if there had been any problems with any livestock, and how all their acquaintances were. When they had kicked around all the normal stockmen's concerns, cleared the dishes, and poured the last cup of coffee, talk turned to the recent problems they all shared—the killing of Rash and the suspicions of just who might have done it.

"Isom, I guess you heard 'bout all them lawmen thinking that your ol' friend, Hicks, is really Tom Horn?" asked Jim. "They checked all over th' country and couldn't find a Hicks missing from New Mexico, and then they couldn't determine just where ol' Horn had been fer th' last few weeks. Looks like they is th' same feller!"

"That news traveled faster than th' wind, Jim. But I ain't wanting you to ever get any idea that Mr. Hicks was a friend of mine. No, sir! That man belonged to Matt. He weren't no good. Easy to see. I stayed clear of him. But he did come up here a couple of times, jest looking 'round. Said he was checking fer cattle," said Isom as he pulled up a chair after getting the kitchen in final shape.

"Tell me, Isom, why do you bolt this door? We ain't had no bears up here in years, at least not too many. You ain't scared of 'em, are you?" questioned Jim.

"Oh, no, Jim. Not fer bears. No, no. We jest got to watch out fer who might be 'round. I know that note me and ol' Matt both got jest might be real. Now that Matt done got his, looks like maybe my time is getting close to being up too. We keep that door bolted hard. Even keep th' little window bolted. And after last week, we ought to even put something over th' window. But then, we need to see out too. We cut out some of th' chinking from th' logs on every side of th' cabin here. Gives us a hole to maybe shoot through. And we can even peek out through them holes too. See, Jim? There's one behind you in that wall, and there is one on th' front wall." Isom was nervous, but he wanted to talk.

"What do you mean, after last week? What happened?" asked Jim.

Isom hesitated, thought for a minute, and then looked straight into Jim's face. "Jim, you have a good reputation 'round here. You don't belong in none of these bad things here. The only reason I'm telling you all this is that folks think you can be trusted. But more than that, you jest ain't part of these bad things. Last week I got out to go to th' spring a bit early. I always look th' place over hard 'fore I move out in th' open." Isom glanced out the small window and then continued. "That morning things looked okay, so I went to th' spring. Then something told me I weren't alone. Your hair jest stands up on your neck, Jim. When I looked 'round, there was a rider off in them quaking asp trees, trying to stay out of sight, hiding like. We was being watched! I didn't let on that I knowed, jest walked on back inside th' cabin. Through them gun holes I seen th' feller sneak out of them woods, maybe quarter mile, maybe more, out there. Lost him then. Never could see who it was. Think maybe it was Hicks or Horn. But now we know someone is watching."

This surprised Jim, but it surely made sense. This was just how Ed had been watching Matt's cabin before taking him out.

Isom was obviously nervous as he continued. "Me and Sam, here, we both are being watched, don't know who, jest being watched. We started staying together then, not going off alone. There are a couple of other fellers th' same way. They come up any time we need to get much work done. They know to come and go together too. Sometimes we all jest stay here in th' cabin fer days. We ain't scared, Jim, but we sure don't know what else to do. A couple of th' fellers say they is leaving, getting out of this country. Even Sam here is going to move out. But I been here too long, moved too many times, got too much going on here. Jest don't want to run no more."

Jim was quickly adding things up. Ed had been heading out to the west end of the mountain early and far too often. And now Jim knew that rider in the aspen trees had to have been Ed. He hadn't been out looking for any coyotes. He'd been stalking poor ol' Isom. And here again, he almost got caught! Jim couldn't believe how Ed thought he could slip out here and spy on Isom, do the same thing he did with Rash, get on to Isom's habits, and one day just plain shoot him to death with that same .30-30 he'd used on Rash! The old fool must think that he was invincible or that nobody would investigate enough to ever catch up to him. By directing all the blame to Tom Horn for what he'd done to Rash, he must be thinking he could do it again.

Jim knew he would have to confront Ed in some manner, figure out some way to prevent Ed from going after Isom. But for now he would try to talk Isom into leaving and staying alive.

"Isom, we ain't knowed each other much, but I don't want to have to dig th' hole to be putting you in neither!" Jim said. "You're right. This don't seem to be much my business, but I'd sure feel better 'bout you if you would jest up and leave fer a while, keep your skin, man! You wouldn't have to be gone ferever. Get out fer a few months, till something changes. Wouldn't have to be gone a year, fer sure, Isom. Why, some of us would watch after things fer you. You know them

Bassetts would keep your stock and have it ready fer you when it all blows over. If Horn is th' one doing all this, you know some day some 'puncher will get th' drop on him and finish him right off. Won't be no need to be gone then. Could jest come home and get back to living. If you stay here, ol' Horn jest might sneak in and plug you! You'd never know what hit you!"

Isom had nothing to say. Sam fidgeted around, nothing to say, wishing he were somewhere else. Things got quiet; only the sound of burning logs in the potbellied stove could be heard.

Finally, Isom broke the silence. "Jim, I knows you is right. And I hope young Sam here pays 'tention to what you jest said. Ain't no use him risking his life fer nothing. Sam, you paying 'tention? Me and your ma kind of raised you together. She ain't here no more, but I is, and I sure don't want to lose you fer something like this. You jest got to get your things and get out, get off this mountain, out of th' Park, go somewhere. Stay away, like Jim says, till maybe something can happen to them fellers like Horn. Me? Well, I been running most of my life. Jest tired of it."

Jim knew he had done all he could to try to talk sense into them. He sure couldn't let on that the real killer most likely wouldn't be Tom Horn, but probably Ed. Maybe Jim could find a way to keep Ed from continuing on the death march. He had tried before Ed got Matt, but he could not convince him to drop it. Now, with Isom the target, could he do anything to protect Isom? And after Isom, would there be others? Would there never be an end?

"Isom, Sam, I've said my piece," Jim said. "Don't want nothing bad to happen to neither of you. Fer now, I came out this way to shoot a few coyotes. Better get on my way. If you hear some shots from off that way, it will be me, getting after them coyotes."

Jim gathered his vest and gloves and bid the two men farewell. When he stepped up on the sorrel, he heard them bolting the cabin door.

Jim enjoyed the ranch work and cowboying for Ed, and he had

come to like all of Ed's camp men, especially Rueben, Ed's right-hand man. Jim noticed that Rueben had started confiding in him, talking about the things he had seen Ed and others do while he was working there on the mountain. Rueben knew that all the ranchers watched for any maverick calf, lost without a branded mother cow around, and that they all caught up the little ones and applied their own brand as quickly as possible. No neighboring rancher ever questioned that practice, since it was not one that would ever significantly build a herd. But it still boiled down to rustling.

Jim knew, too, that Rueben had been around when one rancher or another showed up with a dozen or more new calves, all with freshly burned-on brands, and that Matt Rash and Isom Dart brought in more than anyone. The camp boys kept Rueben informed of others doing the same, including some of the Bassetts. Jim could see that rustling was a way of life in Brown's Park, and it had spread up on Cold Spring Mountain. He was just far enough away, in Johnson Draw, to be out of that sort of operation for the most part. Best he could tell, rustling was not much of a factor on north toward Rock Springs. And, of course, that was why Mary Lou had talked about Jim perhaps finding a ranch closer to Rock Springs. Even she knew the boundary of the major rustling.

CHAPTER 19

All through the month of August and into the early part of September, Jim felt that he was right at home and in his element, doing all the jobs necessary to get things ready for winter. He knew he could always find time for the pleasurable things like taking off an afternoon to catch a few dozen trout out of Beaver Creek or chase after a few wily coyotes. And he really enjoyed searching out some special mule deer buck that would carry antlers three feet wide, a trophy on which he would like to line up the sights of his trusty .30-40. It was the time of year, too, when big antelope bucks started rounding up their harems for the breeding season. The antics of those bucks chasing off all the younger, smaller ones were always interesting to Jim and the camp boys, and they spent a lot of time just watching the chase. Then it would be back to whatever job was at hand, cutting hay, loading the wagon, digging post holes, setting new posts, shoeing horses, repairing harness, and even doing a little housework.

Mixed in with all this, Jim just had to see Mary Lou as often as he could. He still saw no need to advertise the fact that he and Mary Lou were making plans for the future. He knew word would get to the mountain soon enough. And there was no use in talking about leaving the country, even though he had told Ed he might not stay the winter. He did tell Ed he would be interested in a permanent place north of Cold Spring Mountain. Ed even mentioned a place or two

that he thought Jim might be able to get title to and offered to help, if
he could.

Jim volunteered to go to town for the least little thing, always looking
for an excuse to see Mary Lou. He took the spring wagon in once, alone,
to start bringing back supplies for the long winter. Ed wanted to go, but
he was busy preparing an outlying camp location for the winter grounds
for a herd. Jim hurried off before Ed could say anything.

On Jim's return, Ed did have a few things to say. "Jim, you sure
packed off in a hurry fer town th' other day. You got something going on
in there with one of them Cat Claw gals? Or is it one of them senoritas
from 'cross town? I know you ain't jest wantin' to get in there to visit
with ol' Andy. But fer some woman, well, most of you young bucks
would find a way fer that, now wouldn't you, Jim?" Ed was quite testy.
"Still, glad you got it done fer me. If I took off to go in, that camp would
still not be shaped up fer th' winter. I might get time fer one trip myself
'fore th' snows get too much started."

"Ed, you know I don't chase 'round with all them ladies in town.
Got more business on my mind than that. Sure, I did get over to th' Cat
Claw. You ain't hearing nothing 'bout that clear out here, now are you,
Ed?" Jim put out the feeler to see if Ed was keeping back something the
drifting cowboys might have passed on to him.

"Jest know what I'd be doing if all them ladies fell all over me like
they seem to do fer you, Jim! Seen how you and that pretty thing that
owns th' Cat Claw was getting along. Wouldn't blame you none at all
if you got roped in by something like that. But any time you hook up
with a woman, things don't never go too good. They get to telling you
jest when and what you can do."

Jim knew no word of his connection with Mary Lou had reached
Ed as yet.

"Let's get them oats and corn put in th' barn. And them parts fer
th' mower need to be put where we can know jest where they is when
we get th' thing drug down here fer winter. Got to get it repaired and
ready fer next spring. Two or three cutter blades is bad. One is gone.

All that grub goes in th' cabin there. Rueben can give you a hand." Ed seemed to always be looking ahead, preparing for the future.

When Jim carried in some of the grub boxes, he took a quick peek under the bunk to see if the rifle that had been rolled up in extra wool bags was still there. While he was not sure he would be around when and if anything ever happened to Isom Dart, he knew that if that rifle ever was moved, Ed would be off to do another ugly deed. If the rifle stayed put, Isom should be okay. But could Jim always be around to try to stop Ed from removing Isom from the mountain?

A few nights later, the first freeze of winter came on. It started early in the afternoon when clouds rolled in from the west, followed by a cold mist that turned into sleet after sundown. By daybreak the ground was frozen a bit, the water troughs were frozen over, the water bucket had nearly an inch of ice in it, and all the horses had a fine sheen of frozen mist on their backs. Rueben was up early putting kindling in the potbellied stoves in both rooms, adding a few pieces of split logs, and stoking roaring fires. Jim and Ed rolled out by the time the chill was leaving the rooms, and Rueben had the aroma of freshly made coffee drifting from the kitchen.

"This feels like maybe winter done got here!" Jim said as he pulled on his boots and wandered into the kitchen with Ed and Rueben.

"You been down there in Texas too long, Jim. This here is jest our first notice that we best be done with all our summer work! Won't have no more cold fer a few days. Next one may last two or three days, and then the next cold spell ought to bring in th' snow. Why, ten years back, or so, me and Rueben got caught up here in th' first of that bad winter when so many folks lost everthing they had. We got no early notice! Jest started in all of a sudden like. Then kept at it fer four straight days. Snowed so hard we couldn't get out more than jest to th' barn. Caught th' boys bad up on th' mountain too. Nothing we could do. When it broke, we only got 'bout a week, and it hit again. Then th' snow stacked up, and we didn't have clear ground till spring." Ed was enjoying reliving the past for Jim's edification.

"Folks down in th' Park didn't do too bad. Most made it all th' way through without any loss. Them up toward Rock Springs, they lost it all. Some dumb cows froze solid jest walking along, trying to find a place out of th' wind and ice. Rife told me he had to go out in th' spring and push them frozen cows over so he wouldn't be counting them as live! Erickson, th' same. Up from them, some nesters snowshoed out, got to town, caught th' first train out, and never come back!" Ed was impressing Jim with just how bad the winters could be.

"Well, now, Ed. We ain't got left out of them kind of winters down in Texas neither," countered Jim. "Them fellers up in th' panhandle sure 'nough lost stock, jest like up here. 'Course, you're right enough 'bout me maybe being down there too long. Missed seeing all this country fer all those years. Missed getting to meet some mighty fine folks up here."

"Rueben, ain't it jest like I been telling you 'bout Jim here? He don't belong back down there, belongs right out here with us. He's got th' makings of a mountain man!" said Ed as he pushed back from the table and shuffled around, getting ready to move on for the day.

"Sure, Mr. Ed. I agree. We ought to do everything we can to get him to stop thinking 'bout leaving jest 'cause winter is coming on. Right now we need him to help us get th' camps moved off th' mountain and out on th' desert fer th' winter," replied Rueben, as he, too, started clearing the kitchen and getting ready for the day.

"Jim, let's me and you ride up to see 'bout getting Joe to start his herd down off th' mountain pretty soon. Got him a good winter ground picked out, not far from Dry Creek, out there on th' desert where you and me rode back when you first come out here," Ed said to Jim after they had moved out on the porch. "Ain't going to be cold any today. Sure nice up here, this time of year, Jim."

Jim caught up the sorrel, saddled up, and rode off behind Ed and the roan. The frost was thick on the sage, and the aspen and pine pockets showed heavy frost on the branches, sparkling in the early sun. The ride up to Cottonwood Spring took no time at all, and they found Joe's camp in neat order, but Joe had already gone off with the herd.

"He probably got them woolies over 'round that Chokecherry Draw there, toward ol' Charley's place," Ed said. "We best see what all Joe will be needing fer th' trip off th' mountain, got to have him plenty of grub, some oats and stuff fer th' horse. While we are here, we can look th' wagon over too. Always something broke on them wagons, Jim. Maybe we can even get th' thing fixed up fer him today."

Ed stepped down, loosened the cinch on the saddle, and allowed the roan to graze off. Jim did the same with the sorrel, and he started looking around for anything that he might give attention to that would help Joe get off to a good start in a few days.

The wagon seemed to be in good shape, and Ed made a list of supplies that Joe was short of. "We sure got to ask Joe 'bout his winter clothing too, Jim. These fellers don't seem to ever think 'bout how long and cold it's going to be out there. Since we got things going pretty good, we might stoke up th' fire a bit and put on th' coffee, don't you think, Jim?"

"Sure thing, Ed. Then we can sort of stretch out under th' aspens and do some talking, planning," Jim replied. "Joe jest might drop back up here 'round noon. Or he might be able to see that we are here from where he has them sheep, do you think, Ed?"

"Oh, yeah, them herders always watch back if they can. Got to keep an eye on their camps too, you know," said Ed as he got out two cups and waited on the pot to boil. It was still warm from earlier in the morning and was again boiling in jig time. With their cups of fresh, hot coffee, Jim and Ed stretched out on the ground and leaned back against convenient aspen trees and enjoyed the bright morning.

"Ed, I been worrying 'bout you lately," Jim started. He was savoring the coffee, keeping the cup between his hands and using it as a hand warmer, a habit of all range cowboys. "You been riding out a lot to hunt coyotes, but we ain't seeing no empty cartridges, not hearing no shooting. Matter of fact, Ed, you always seem to return from over 'round Isom's place. You surely ain't spying on ol' Isom none, now are you, Ed? You ain't planning on doing him in?" Jim hesitated, not sure just how to open up any discussion about Isom.

Ed straightened slightly and diverted his stare away, looking out over Beaver Basin. A long, heavy silence fell over both men. Jim knew Ed was trying to get his thoughts together before answering such a question. Maybe Jim should not have started it. Maybe he was guilty of jumping to conclusions, not justified. But as long as he knew about Ed watching Isom and almost getting caught in the act by Isom, Jim felt he owed it to Ed to let him know that he was aware of at least some of his actions.

"Ain't nobody but you would ever hook any of this up to me watching ol' Isom, Jim. Rueben, he don't know. None of these herders know. Not even Joe. I been careful 'bout getting up there without anyone knowing. You're right, Jim. I ain't been shootin' coyotes much. Rode right through a whole pack a week or so back, didn't even think 'bout it till too late. All them critters got plumb away. Jest had my mind on what I was doing. Weren't watching fer coyotes. Watching fer cowboys, drifters. Don't want to have someone knowing I been up toward ol' Isom's. Should've knowed you would know, though. Jest like when you knowed all along 'bout ol' Rash! Can't get much by you, Jim. Guess that's really why I took a liking to you right off. You ain't like all them other fellers 'round. And that's why maybe you jest don't belong out here. You ain't part of none of this."

Jim sat still and kept silent, not knowing how far Ed might go in his talking now that he had started.

"With you knowing all 'bout me and Rash, and then th' way you set me up with an alibi that put all them lawmen on to ol' Hicks and Horn, I knew you was different. Wouldn't have to kill you."

Jim's hair suddenly seemed to stand on end. Goose bumps came up, and his jaw went slack. Did he just hear Ed mention the idea of killing him? Jim instantly realized how close to death he might have been ... and did not know!

"Now you know well as I do that ol' Isom can't jest stay up here like he owns this mountain. Got up here 'cause of ol' Rash. Now Rash is gone. So now Isom has to be gone. Some of them other rustlers done gone since getting notes on their doors. Been waiting fer ol' Isom to get out. Now it don't seem he wants to go. Th' last chance is fer Horn hisself to get up here and do in ol' Isom 'fore someone else has to do it fer him!" Ed was rambling, talking about things Jim did not need to know.

"Jim, you jest still don't understand how we all see things out here," said Ed as he turned more toward Jim. "Me and Charley, we been here fer years. We staked out our country. We get along. Down in th' Park, some of them folks been there even longer. Thing is, Jim, none of our kind is jest going to let outsiders move us off our land. We been building things fer th' future. We cleared out them redskins. You notice when ol' Rash come in, a sort of big-time rustler, you see, ain't none of us giving him our ground. Why, them Parkers even pushed him off up here on us! They didn't want to give him ground, neither did us up here. Well, he jest kept pushing." Ed rambled on, and Jim was careful not to interfere.

"Now, Jim, we always handle our own problems out here. Seems ol' Charley sort of wanted th' laws to handle Rash, but that might've been three, four years away. We couldn't wait. Somebody had to do something. So I done the job. You been a big help in this fer me, Jim, but you still don't belong. No need in you getting involved in killings. Let us alone, leave us handle our own things. We want you 'round here as a good neighbor. We all want to help you get a place, north of here, a place that would keep you from getting in all this bad stuff. This started 'fore you come along. Ain't none of your business now!"

Jim was stunned. Ed was pouring out his guts to him. If anyone else knew just what Ed was saying, Ed would be lynched before sundown! The Bassetts would have quickly brought up the past killings around Cold Spring Mountain and tied them to Ed the minute they found that Ed had cold-bloodedly shot their friend and ally, Matt Rash. Ed would not have lived through the day.

"Now, Jim, I know you got it in your head that I plan to do in ol' Isom, jest like ol' Rash. You really don't know that, now do you? 'Course not! So you best jest stay away, stay out of it. You don't need to know what happens out here." Ed turned toward Jim, relaxed, shuffled around a bit, and waited for Jim's reply.

Jim could hardly believe how open Ed was about handling rustlers and outlaws and his ideas concerning Isom. "Don't do it, Ed. You can't always keep gettin' away with these things, even when you and some others think it's right. You had no idea back there a couple of months ago that you had two witnesses to you gunning down Rash! You thought you had it all planned, no one would be 'round. Then you couldn't believe it when you got to your horse and found me standing there. Couldn't believe that Horn was watching you too! So now what makes you think you can pull off th' killing of Isom without no one knowing?"

"Don't need to hear this, Jim!" Ed was visibly agitated.

"Ed, I sort of got caught up in that killing of ol' Rash. Can't say anything to nobody 'bout it," said Jim. "Felt like it maybe was part my fault 'cause maybe I could have stopped you. If I could've held you off jest one day, even maybe jest one hour, ol' Horn would've done it fer you! Then I saw that Horn was th' one that should've been th' killer, not you. So there I was, with an alibi fer you, and in position to see to it that th' herders sort of put th' blame on Hicks too. But now ol' Isom? No way!" Jim was now talking fast, talking more than he intended.

"I jest can't sit by and let you do this!" Jim continued. "If you jest wait a while, why Horn will either be back, or maybe he will think all th' rustling has stopped. Then he would be gone, and Isom would have to stop rustling or gamble on having Horn return to finish him off. I hear he is scared out of his skin right now. Keeping close to his cabin, and always has some others 'round him fer protection. Ain't been no rustling since Rash was killed. We jest don't know but what maybe Isom is 'bout to leave on his own. There sure ain't no need in hurrying 'round, trying to get Isom off th' range any sooner." Jim pointed out anything that entered his mind in an effort to get Ed to back down, knowing just how hardheaded and stubborn Ed could be.

"Another thing, too, Ed." Jim kept on with his attempts at persuasion. "You're moving th' herds to th' winter grounds, and if ol' Isom elects to stay up here on th' mountain fer th' winter, he jest may decide to move back down permanently with them Bassetts. They might need him, if what I hear is right. Young Sam is one of those that plans to get off th' range soon as he can. And you know Josie is selling out, leaving. Them that's left will need th' likes of Isom!"

"Jest ain't your business, Jim! Don't need none of your advice!" Ed's hardheadedness was beginning to show.

"Ed, if you jest keep this up, I'll help you move th' herds, but I can't live out here knowing you might do ol' Isom in. Don't know jest what I'll do if Isom comes up dead while I'm still 'round here. Folks would start asking me what I might know. Maybe I best jest hurry on, soon as them herds is off th' mountain." It was Jim's last chance to get Ed to consider a change of heart.

"Ed! Jim! That you up there at th' wagon?" The call came from the aspen grove a couple of hundred yards away. Both the sorrel and roan perked up their ears, pointing toward the grove. Then a dog barked, and out of the trees came Joe, riding his sheep wagon horse and accompanied by one of his sheepdogs.

"Si, amigo!" called Jim. "We been waiting fer you to get up here fer coffee!"

As soon as Joe arrived the talk turned to moving the herd off the mountain for the winter. Joe knew of the camp that Ed had arranged out near Dry Creek. Joe chatted some with Ed concerning the things that would be needed for the winter camp, and he asked if Jim would be going out with him to help get the woolies on the desert.

"No, no, Joe. Jim ain't going out with you. You can make it jest like always. Maybe me or Rueben might be along. Got things fer Jim to do. 'Sides, he's thinking he ain't going to stay 'round here, winter jest too bad." Ed had cut in, volunteering that Jim was leaving.

By the end of September the mountains were ablaze with the golden leaves of aspens as they picked up their brief, fall colors. Nights dropped down to freezing most of the time, and the days had the crispness of fall. It would soon be winter on the mountain.

Ed had the herds moving toward the winter grounds, but he had not needed Jim's help at all. Ed seemed to want to keep Jim at the headquarters doing odd jobs. Jim was becoming frustrated with what he considered inactivity, and he started thinking about clearing up his business in Johnson Draw and heading into town to be with Mary Lou for the rest of the winter, and longer.

On the first day of October Jim decided to tell Ed that he was leaving. He would first go to Johnson Draw and make the cabin tight for winter and have it in top shape in return for Ed allowing him to use it for the past few months.

"Jim, I jest don't know how to let you up and leave after all we been through and planned fer th' next few months. Been looking fer a place fer you to take up too. Are you sure you know what you're doing? Ain't leaving ferever now, are you, Jim? Soon as spring gets here I think we can get that place up there 'bout twenty miles north of Erickson's. Be a fine place fer you to put down stakes. Room fer a good herd, either sheep or cattle," said Ed in a warm and friendly manner that had Jim yielding to the friendship that had developed out in the mountains. "Jest think 'bout it fer a few days, Jim. Get over there to th' cabin, and I'll shake loose 'fore you move on. You say you won't be heading out from Johnson Draw fer 'bout ten days?"

"That's right, Ed. It'll take a while to get things done over there. Want th' two horses to have a few days to fatten too, 'fore riding 'em out to Rock Springs, maybe fer th' winter," Jim replied. "When we get a break in th' weather from time to time, I'll drop out fer a few days. Maybe we can decide more on that place you know 'bout. If I can get it financed. Ol' Kendall and me, we is great friends there at th' bank!"

Both men broke into laughter.

Jim felt somewhat satisfied that Ed had not gone after Isom since their talk on the mountain. He had, however, checked on the hidden rifle most every day, just to be sure it was not about to be put to use. Maybe Ed had at least heard part of what Jim was trying to get over to him, and if so, perhaps Isom would be okay. Maybe he would decide to move off the mountain. In any case, Jim knew he could not do any more to help.

Late in the afternoon Jim bid Rueben and Ed adios and rode the sorrel out across Beaver Basin, perhaps for the last time. He couldn't ride away as usual with the sorrel's fast jog. That would be too quick. He simply put the sorrel in a comfortable walk, giving himself time for thinking about serious things—remembering what Andy and others had told him about Ed's nature, the fact that he could be ruthless, cold-blooded, and even cruel at times. But then he could be totally protective of those he liked, maybe even overprotective. All folks agreed that Ed would never harm a true friend, and it seemed that Jim would fit in that category. Thus, he should not have any worries about Ed trying to eliminate him.

The day after Jim departed, Ed sent Rueben out to help Rudy move the last of the sheep out to the desert. Rueben was happy to get a break from headquarters work, a chance to spend time with his Mexican herder friends. He loaded a bedroll and a few minor supplies behind the saddle and rode off toward the herd.

CHAPTER 20

Ed had been keeping track of the comings and goings of Isom Dart as much as he could. He got out early in the mornings and checked to be sure Isom had spent the night in his cabin, usually riding close enough to the cabin to observe any trace of smoke coming from the chimney. And he tried to check the corral to be sure Isom's favorite horse was there. He had determined that Isom was staying close to his cabin, almost always with someone. At times he had several cowboys staying with him, perhaps expecting safety in numbers and thinking Tom Horn would surely not try to carry out the threat of the note on the door with any witnesses around. Horn never had witnesses.

Rueben had been gone several hours, indicating that he would not be returning for some forgotten item, when Ed pulled the .30-30 out from under the bunk, all wrapped in wool bags. It was loaded in the magazine just as all ranch rifles were kept, even though there had been three shells fired from it a few weeks back. He checked it over, loaded in three fresh cartridges, shouldered it a few times. He then took it out behind the barn and test-fired it on a target some hundred yards away. It was right on. The time had come. Ed was ready to make his move.

Long before first light on the third of October, Ed had the roan saddled and was making his way up Cold Spring Mountain. He needed to leave the roan some distance from Isom's cabin, since there were not many hiding places close by. And he did not want the roan whinnying if some other horse discovered him. Ed would walk the last mile in, taking the narrow cover of the only thicket leading into the stand of timber near the corral.

It was nearly pitch black in the patch of trees near Isom's corral where Ed decided he could stay hidden until first light. He could easily check the cabin for anything unusual. He had been over the plan many times. If too many other fellows happened to be in the cabin, he could easily slip back out through the trees and brush, undetected, he thought. There would be another day. But so far, everything looked good.

Not long after the sky lightened in the east, Ed detected movement in the cabin, maybe 150 yards away. The door opened only slightly, and someone reached out and fetched a couple of pieces of firewood from a small stack kept very close to the door. Before long the chimney emitted a curl of smoke, and it was light enough for accurately aiming and firing a rifle.

Ed planned on Isom following his daily routine of coming out to the corral to saddle up early for the day. As he waited, the chill of the frosty October morning crept through his heavy, wool-lined coat. How long would it be before Isom headed up the path toward the corral? He thought about what Jim had told him, about being watched the day he shot Matt Rash. And he thought about the fact that Jim had not only caught on to the Rash situation, but he had been on to what he was doing this minute, waiting in ambush for Isom Dart. If Jim could figure this out, and even slip up close during the act, why couldn't someone else do the same?

Ed looked all around, now nervous, but maybe just cold. He noticed the extra horses around the corral, probably some of Isom's wild herd. There were no other horses or horsemen in sight, and the broken sage out past the pocket of trees could not hide a coyote, much less another man. Only the narrow thicket leading back toward the roan would offer any concealment at all. Ed needed this strip of cover for his escape. If anyone were on to his game, he would be in that strip of cover. And if Ed got the killing done, then he would likely run face to face into whoever it might be. Ed knew of only one man that could do that—Jim Keaton! And Jim had even told him he would not stand for another killing. As soon as word reached Jim that Isom was dead, would Jim come after Ed?

Now doubt ... and cold ... set in on Ed. Had he thought this thing through? What if Isom had several men with him and they decided to fight it out? How many could Ed handle before one of them might get him? He had only the one full magazine, seven cartridges, for the .30-30. Then he would have only his Colt .45, six shots.

A man's mind could play tricks on him under a strain and in the cold of a new dawn. Ed knew this. He just had to concentrate on the job at hand. That meant that if more than three or four fellows happened to be with Isom, he would be a fool to try to get Isom this time around. He would have to lie low until they all caught up their horses, saddled up, and rode out—and hope they would not go out near his roan. But his first plan just had to be the best. He had made the plan without being under this strain, made it while he rested under the aspen trees in the warmth of the sun, went over it too many times. It had to be the right way to go, and all these other worries had to be no more than nerves showing.

Suddenly the cabin door popped open wide and out came the youngster, George Bassett. The show was underway! Then out stepped Isom himself, followed by a local cowboy named Yarnell. The three started up the trail directly toward the corral, closing the distance between themselves and Ed but not knowing what lay in store.

Ed checked the .30-30 and slowly raised it alongside the big pine tree trunk. He would take Isom as soon as he had a perfect shot. Only two other cowboys to contend with. The distance closed rapidly. Only a few more steps. Ed had the sights aligned squarely on the forehead of Isom. Abruptly from the cabin stepped another cowboy, but Ed was too far along to divert his attention to him. As he applied pressure to the trigger, the sharp crack of the hard-shooting .30-30 split the cold morning air.

Isom dropped like he had been pole-axed. Ed quickly worked the lever of the rifle by reflex and fired again, not really an aimed shot, just a follow up in case the first didn't finish the job at hand. George Bassett broke and ran, first toward the corral and then back toward the cabin. Ed suddenly became aware of others appearing from the cabin. One was Sam Bassett. Another was a cowboy named Seger, and there was yet another, a part-time partner of Isom, John Dempshire. Men were coming from everywhere! Ed had no idea how that many men could have been in that small cabin. Yarnell made a run for the corral fence and then turned back to dash for the cabin. The last three to appear started to run toward Isom and then lost their nerve and broke back over each other, all trying to gain entrance to the cabin at the same time. The Bassett boys circled around the cabin before finally finding the door and bursting inside.

Ed couldn't believe what he was seeing. Why didn't all those fellows simply start shooting in his direction? Was he that well hidden? Were all those fellows so scared that they completely forgot to try to defend themselves?

Then Ed turned his attention back to Isom, who had not moved at all. He kept the rifle on him for a few seconds before deciding the head shot had indeed hit home. When he again glanced back to the cabin to see whether he was going to be fired on by any of the other five cowboys, he saw the door tightly closed, undoubtedly bolted.

Ed knew he could not relax. At any minute those fellows might locate him and come busting out with their guns blazing. He thought again, how could all those fellows have been in that cabin on that very morning? Then he noticed he was trembling, beginning to understand how close he had come to fouling up, one more time. And Ed knew those fellows were not cowards, yet there they were, herded into a tight little cabin like a bunch of sheep. It just had to be the fear of Tom Horn. But now it was time for Ed to ease back out of there, back to the roan, and get off the mountain as quickly as he could without being seen.

Inside the cabin the four men and young George cowered in various corners, trying to get down so that any shots through the door or window would not likely hit them. They were caught in total fear and completely off guard. None had carried their guns with them when they walked out of the cabin. Now they were each lost in panic, with their confused thoughts. Would they be gunned down in the next few seconds or minutes? How many men were out in the trees waiting for them to try to escape? Or was there only Tom Horn? Those who had received notes tacked to their doors were now second-guessing their own actions. Why had they agreed to hang around Isom? Why hadn't they packed up and left the country along with a couple of the others? Sweat was pouring from their brows.

Several minutes passed before any one of the men could talk. Then John Dempshire took over. "Everybody got a gun? Get shells in those chambers! Be ready fer anything. We don't know what those killers might do next! Looks like they done killed ol' Isom. Anybody see anything out there? How many are there?"

No answers came. Slowly the other four started moving around, reaching for their guns, getting situated for what might come next.

"Get on over to them peep holes, them gun ports! See if you can see anyone out there. Yarnell, you take th' one looking out back. Sam, take a look out 'round th' corral. And none of you show yourselves 'round that window, 'less you want shot!" John was organizing the best he could.

"Looks like ol' Isom is dead, all right, John," said Sam after he searched the sage and tree areas for a couple of minutes. "He ain't moved any since he went down. Looks like a big pool of blood all 'round him too!"

Then Yarnell spoke up. "Ain't nobody out this way, at least it don't look like there is, John. But I sure ain't 'bout to stick my nose out of here! They jest could have us surrounded. They sure got us pinned in here. We don't want to make no move till we know what's going on out there."

Seger joined in. "I ain't going to be th' first one out any door! They is going to shoot him fer sure!"

"The only couple of shots fired so far seemed to both come from th' same spot, didn't they, fellers? I thought they come from them trees up by th' corral there," said John. "Maybe if it is Horn, maybe he is alone up there. We need a way out th' back! If we can get out at all."

It took more than an hour before the fellows made a survey of how they stood in the cabin. They had only one bucket of water, half enough firewood for the evening and night, but enough food for several days. Their ammunition was limited to what they had in their gun belts. It came to them that whoever might be out there just might decide to set fire to the cabin.

"Sam, get that axe there and give it to George. I need you to stay on watch while some of us cut a hole in this back wall. Seger, you get that meat saw. We're going out after dark, if not sooner. But ain't no use trying to use that front door." John got the men busy, knowing that if they simply sat around and let their thoughts get carried away, they might do something drastic like try to make a run for it right out the door to their deaths.

If they did not spot anyone lurking out in the trees by midday, they could hope to escape. And since their horses were still in the corral, they probably would find that only one man had done the killing and pulled out immediately. But they couldn't take any chances.

CHAPTER 21

The sun was just peeking over Cold Spring Mountain when Ed returned to his cabin, hid away the .30-30, packed up a few items in the saddlebags, and headed out again. If he could hurry out toward one of the desert camps, he would get there early enough to provide himself with an alibi, if it ever became necessary. He would push the roan along as fast as he could for the first few miles, only slowing enough to let him cool down before arriving at the camp.

Joe and Juan had taken their herds off the mountain and joined up together down below Charley Sparks's place and then moved out toward Dry Creek. Somewhere out in that country they would split the herd again, moving apart by a few miles to allow best grazing for the winter. Ed had sent Rueben off with Rudy, moving out of the Pine Mountain, Red Creek, and 4-J Basin country toward Vermillion, and he didn't want to show up so soon over there. That might make Rueben wonder what was going on. By getting out to Joe and Juan first, he could easily move on later, making it look like he was simply making his first round of all the winter camps.

Ed's plan worked out just right, meeting up with Joe and Juan near the juncture of Talamantes and Vermillion. They were grazing their herds along slowly, taking advantage of all the upper-level grass they could prior to reaching the low country for winter. The weather had not yet changed much. The days were bright and warm, allowing the sheep to graze for a few more days en route to the Dry Creek winter grounds.

"You sure left early this morning, didn't you, Ed?" called out Joe as they joined up.

"Yep. Sure did, Joe. It was still dark. Jest wanted to get here in case you needed me. Sort of like to jest be out with th' herds too. Ain't much going on back 'round th' place. 'Specially with that Jim leaving," said Ed, wanting to be sure the herders knew Jim had pulled out.

Juan joined in. "Ain't he coming back, Mr. Ed? We got lots of good help from him."

"No, Juan. Looks like he ain't never coming back. Jest thought it gets too cold up here in th' winter. Said he was heading back to Texas. Wants to get hisself a ranch on some place called Devil's River. Not far from th' ol' Mexican border, you know." Ed was setting a plan in motion, and only Ed would know the final outcome.

Back in Johnson Draw, Jim was getting the place shaped up for winter. The horses were enjoying the small pasture where the grass had grown deep and was rich enough to put several pounds on their frames before Jim had to pack them up and head out for Rock Springs. Even though he was concerned about what Ed might do back on Cold Spring Mountain, he had stopped thinking so much about how he could be ambushed from the steep sides of the draw, places where a rifleman could pick off anyone around the cabin. His open discussion with Ed, telling him just how things could work out without Ed doing anything against Isom, seemed to have had some effect. And if it did, then perhaps Jim and Mary Lou could get a place, maybe toward Rock Springs, and still use the Johnson Draw cabin when they were down in the Cold Spring Mountain area visiting.

But Jim had trouble forgetting the comment Ed had made about not needing to kill him. Maybe that was Ed's way of simply clearing the air, admitting to Jim that he was now considered a true, lifetime friend. Ed was even helping him look around for a place to buy, volunteering to help him get a loan from the bank. Perhaps Jim shouldn't disregard what Andy and others had told him, that if Ed took a liking to you, you couldn't want a better friend. And just look how well Ed got on with Bill and Marge Finch, right in the country he ran stock on.

Late in the day of the fifth of October, Jim heard his horses whinny in the pasture, telling him something was around. Jim checked his .30-40 rifle and stood it near the door of the cabin. Then he watched the two horses to see just what they were worried about. They were pointing up the mountain where the trail came off. He heard a few rocks turn over, heard steel against rock, all indicating a rider was coming in.

"Hello, down there! Anybody home? Coming on in!" It was a vaguely familiar voice, one he had not heard often.

Jim called out, "Come on in! I'll get th' coffee on!" He knew whoever was out there was coming in friendly-like.

Within minutes the rider came into view, rode up to the hitching bar, and stepped down. It was one of the Bassett cowboys Jim had met briefly at the burial of Matt Rash a few months back. Jim only knew him as Pete.

"Jim! Surprised to find you out here. One of th' herders up there, works fer Sparks, said Ed's man told him you were quittin' this country. Too cold, heading back fer Texas," said Pete in his friendly manner.

"Gosh, Pete! Been a while. Didn't know I was leaving! Them herders sure can get their stories mixed up. What gets you off down in this country?" asked Jim as he stepped out from the doorway.

"More business than pleasure, Jim, even though it's always pleasure when I know I'm heading this way," answered Pete as he loosened the cinch on the saddle, indicating he might be there for the night. "Be all right if I turn my horse loose in your pasture, Jim?"

"Sure, Pete," answered Jim. "Been needing some company. Got some roasted brisket, a pot of fresh-made beans, some bread. 'Bout anything we might need fer a spread. Even got some oats left there in th' shed fer th' horse, jest to make him feel at home. Set your saddle up on that extra saddle tree there. Cabin's in nice shape too. Been trying to get it ready fer th' winter," said Jim as he moved out to help Pete get settled.

With the small chores done around the shed, Jim and Pete entered the cabin and poured the coffee.

"Pete, you said something 'bout coming down here maybe fer business," Jim started off. "Nothing too serious, I hope. Least not like th' last time we met!"

"'Fraid so, Jim. There's been 'nother killing up on Cold Spring. I ain't no good at breaking bad news. But here it is, jest straight out. Poor ol' Isom Dart got done in! Buried him this afternoon. Bassetts sent me out to spread th' word and see if anyone might've seen anything out of th' way in th' last couple of days. Ain't nobody at Ed's place, and looks like th' herders all headed fer th' winter grounds."

"Isom? Surely not, Pete! Not Isom," stammered Jim, not wanting to believe what he was hearing.

"Let's pour another cup of this coffee, and I'll fill you in, far as I know," answered Pete.

Jim moved to the coffee pot, refilled both cups, and sat down eager to hear just what might have happened. Could it have been Tom Horn returning?

"Jim, best we could all make out, Isom was gunned down maybe 'bout on th' third. He was up at th' cabin with five other fellers that was helping him with his cattle and horses. When they walked out to saddle up that morning, somebody was hid out in them trees there by th' corral, shot twice, hit ol' Isom square in th' head. Dead 'fore he hit th' ground. Them five fellers ran back to th' cabin, all scared they was going to be next. Took 'em some time to come to their senses. Stayed all day locked in, maybe scared in. Know that's how I'd be."

Pete was sure down to earth with the story, well beyond too much excitement, thought Jim.

"They cut a hole in the back wall, trying to get out and stay out of sight of anyone up near th' corral. After dark, one of 'em scouted up toward th' corral. Things looked clear, so they took their horses and slipped out of there. Made a long circle. Still scared that maybe th' killer was ol' Tom Horn, like Charley and th' law was thinking 'bout ol' Matt. Didn't get down to Bassetts till th' next day." Pete was swirling his coffee around in the cup nervously.

"Then by th' time we all got some fellers together to go back up there, we had to wait till today. Got up there early and found poor ol' Isom jest lying there, most of his head blowed off. Stiff as an old buck deer left over a rock to drain overnight. Must have been awful cold up there at night. Isom wasn't hardly even startin' to stink." Pete hesitated before continuing. "Josie went up with us. She sure thought a lot of that ol' black man. That little Ann jest broke down and wasn't no good to nobody, so Josie jest plain told her she couldn't go along. Jest didn't want her up there screaming and raving. Well, Josie picked out th' place to lay ol' Isom away, and we dug th' hole good and deep so no varmints can dig him up."

Jim wanted the whole story, and Pete seemed to have it.

"We decided to search 'round up there in th' timber and see if we could find any trace of th' killer. Sure 'nough, Jim, we found two new .30-30 empty cases right there beside that big pine tree. We found th' boot tracks leading out of there too. Able to track 'em back to where he had his horse. Followed th' horse till we lost it in a bunch of other tracks."

Pete continued. "Then 'fore Josie had me head out to find any herders or cowboys that might know anything, we had us a big talk. Seems that little Ann jest might be more right than we give her credit fer. She been claiming ol' Hicks was Matt's killer all along. Well, seems some of th' fellers knowed Hicks was carrying th' only new .30-30 ever seen on th' mountain or down in th' Park. Now that we found these .30-30 shells, and they is th' same as what was found in Rash's cabin, well, jest looks like a cinch. Hicks done both killings! Then if what Charley and them lawmen think is true, Hicks and Horn is th' same feller!" Pete spoke straightforwardly in a matter-of-fact manner.

"I didn't want it happening. No reason fer it, Pete," said Jim. "I was up there visiting with Isom not long back. Tried to talk him into jest leaving, get out fer a while. No use him hanging 'round up there. Most of them folks that got notes on their doors was leaving. With ol' Matt done killed, why should Isom risk staying any longer?" Jim was upset. He knew, or sure thought he knew, who had done the shooting. It had to have been Ed.

"Pete, I been here fer a couple of days. There ain't been any drifter this way that I know of. If it really is Hicks … er … Horn, don't he most always head over toward Lay, maybe over to Baggs?"

Pete thought about that for a moment. "That's what I understand, Jim, but them tracks we was following didn't seem to be heading out that way. Lost 'em kind of coming off th' north side of Cold Spring. 'Course, smart as that Horn is, he jest might have made that trail fer us to foller. Then cut back toward Boone Draw, over to Lay, maybe on up to Baggs. Last we knew of his working was 'round Baggs, and even more north and east."

So, Jim thought, they had trailed the horse off toward Beaver Creek, off the north side of Cold Spring Mountain. That would have been Ed, for sure. The old fool didn't even think about anyone trying to track his horse! Jim's mind was racing. Ed might figure how to get a killing done, but he sure wasn't very smart in planning a getaway.

Jim found it hard to enter into small talk, or even serious talk, as the evening went along. Pete talked on about how several fellows were either already gone or were packing up to leave in view of the troubles and the notes left by Tom Horn. Thompson had not been back to Brown's Park since he received a note, and he was staying close to his lower ranch down toward Lay. Sam Bassett had made up his mind to get out, head up to Rock Springs, and join the army. Another fellow had suddenly decided the winters were just too cold in that part of the country and was on his way to Missouri. It was beginning to look like a mass movement to other faraway places.

"But, Pete, how 'bout folks like you? Ain't heard of none of you leaving," said Jim, after a long pause in the rambling stories.

"Jim, there's lots of us that jest ain't in all this. We ain't nothing but drifting cowboys. Here today, gone tomorrow. Ol' Tom Horn ain't after none of us. Least we hope he ain't! Charley tells us we don't really need to think 'bout it none 'cause we ain't doing no rustling. He says ol' Horn never bothers no one but them rustlers, so we can jest go on 'bout our business." Pete was obviously at ease with his decision to simply stay put. "Now, Jim, you sure ain't leaving 'cause you got to get out from ol' Horn?"

"Why, heck no, Pete! I'm jest 'bout like you. Drifted in here looking maybe fer some place to light. Now, jest drifting on, maybe. You say some of Charley's men told you I was leaving, heading back to Texas?" Jim wanted to know more about any rumors spreading around.

"Well, Jim, them herders said that is what Mr. Ed's been telling them. Ed passed that on to one jest a day or two back. That was th' herder I saw after leaving poor ol' Isom in his grave. That's why I was surprised to find you still here."

Why would Ed be out there spreading the word that Jim would be gone, wouldn't be around any more? Sure, Jim had told Ed that he was leaving, but probably not leaving the entire country, and not leaving permanently. They had even discussed the fact that Jim would be back down to talk more about getting the ranch up toward Rock Springs, even hitting up Kendall at the bank for a loan. Maybe Ed was just disappointed in losing him and was trying to convince himself that he couldn't count on Jim coming back. Just being remorseful and not wanting anyone to see his true sadness.

"Well, Pete, you can see that I'm still here. But right now I'm jest too tired to keep thinking 'bout poor ol' Isom. Let's hit the sack. We can talk more 'bout this tomorrow. Stick one good log in that stove there, Pete, and I'll close the damper. Won't get too cold here that way." Jim needed time to think.

Jim slept little, tossing and turning most of the night. On several occasions he sat straight up, wide awake from some drifting thought concerning Ed's motives for starting rumors about his leaving the country. Long before first light the yapping of the coyotes had both Jim and Pete up to start a new day. Pete pitched in, stoked up the fire, and had the coffee ready before Jim got the bacon and biscuits done. With Pete for company, Jim put on the dog and made up a pot full of thick gravy, complete with bits of antelope and deer jerky added. That, with a scoop of wild berry jam, should keep them going for the day.

"Pete, if you jest insist on going on with your job, you can find Rudy and Rueben out 'round Vermillion with one herd, and you might catch up with Joe and Juan out there toward Dry Creek somewhere. 'Least that's where we all talked 'bout taking 'em last week. Ed must have gone out with one or th' other of 'em too," Jim said as Pete saddled up before the sun had shown down in the draw. "If you get all that done and happen back by, jest move on in. I'll be 'round somewhere. Unless somebody else tells me I ain't here no more! Don't think any of Ed's boys can be of any help to you by knowing anything 'bout Isom. They might have seen something, but I bet not. They can put you on to any other herders 'round th' area. You might talk with them, might find out something," Jim allowed.

Pete stepped up in his saddle, turned his horse down Johnson Draw, and headed on his way.

Somehow, Jim felt eerily alone. He knew in his own mind that Ed was now a double killer, not to mention other killings that folks thought Ed had pulled off in earlier years. Jim now knew Ed had no feelings about killing anyone, just like Andy had warned him. The sheep rustler, a poor old prospector, a homesteader, a grazing rival, Matt Rash, and now poor old Isom Dart. Who's next? Surely he wouldn't now take aim at Jim? But then why not? Jim was the only one that knew for a fact that Ed was guilty of killing Matt Rash. He had used that new .30-30 for the second time. Could it be that Ed planned to use it a third time—on Jim?

Jim's first thought was to hurry to Rock Springs and turn Ed in to the sheriff. Jim alone had the evidence needed to hang Ed for killing Rash. But when the Brown's Park folks found out that Jim had really provided Ed with the alibi to cover one murder, making him an accomplice, would they suddenly turn on him? He knew how Brown's Park folks handled their own problems. What would prevent them from suddenly forming a rope party with both Ed and Jim as guests? After all, Matt Rash had been their cattlemen's association president, and Isom Dart had been a favorite of the Bassett family. Could Jim take such a risk?

As Jim turned back to the cabin, he scanned the canyon walls, checking each clump of cedar, each thick aspen grove, each rock outcrop, anywhere a killer might conceal himself for a shot at his next victim. He stepped quickly into the confines of the one-room cabin and noticed he had even blocked the door, something he had never done in the past. He heard the slightest sounds: the scratching of a small field mouse, the rustle of aspen leaves quaking in the slight movement of the canyon air, the muted call of a magpie somewhere along the draw. The cabin began to feel stuffy. Jim found himself glancing out the small window too often. He needed to think out his options.

Jim realized he was in a fix. He knew too much about the murders on Cold Spring Mountain. He knew he could go to the authorities and report what he knew about Ed, and the result would be the removal of a killer from the range. But in doing so, he would run the risk of being caught up in the web if he had to admit to helping Ed with the alibi when Rash was shot down. He was an accomplice in the eyes of the law. They might just as easily put Jim in prison or worse. Even at best, he would have to go through the trial as a witness, subjecting Mary Lou to the hardship, and forced to stay in the area for many months. And just the idea of being branded an accomplice to murder left him cold. Anything might happen.

It soon became obvious to Jim that there was only one thing to do. He would leave things alone, let them work their own way out, avoid the risk of being caught up in the murders. He would pack out of the cabin at first light tomorrow and go immediately to Rock Springs, taking everything he might want or need from the cabin, leaving nothing of his behind. He had slowly come to recognize that Rash and Isom had both been rustling, and the killing was something many ranchers would call justified. Out in this remote ranch country, things like that were often excused, even by the law. Rustlers were not tolerated. So maybe ol' Ed only did what others would have done, under the circumstances. And from this point of view, Jim could live with what Ed had done.

Within the hour Jim could not stay in the cabin any longer. He needed to get out somewhere for a while. Some place to relax and calmly figure out his immediate future. Maybe head up to the diamond field, out in the open. That's where he was at peace during his first few days in the area. First, though, he would make the cabin ready to close and then pack a lunch in the saddlebags. The sorrel would take him up to the flats where the salted gemstones were resting in rock crevices. A place to think, a place to while away the afternoon of the last day he planned to be on the mountain.

When Jim reached the diamond flats he unsaddled the sorrel and turned him loose to graze. He could call the sorrel when he was ready to head back. He moved down into a small wash leading off into a fair-size canyon, only dropping a few yards off the flat. The cedars were scattered, giving shade and perhaps a windbreak, if needed. This was where his brother had maintained a small camp many years before, leaving just enough sign for Jim to discover.

Jim quickly built up a small fire, put on the coffee pot, and warmed up a good-size piece of backstrap from the last antelope left hanging in the shade near the cabin. He broke out a roll of fine fried bread kept over from the day before. Soon he was relaxing in the shade of a cedar, resting peacefully on his saddle blanket, and thinking. Then, quietly, like the subtle blooming of a cactus flower after a desert rain, Jim relaxed with his decision fully made. He leaned back in the shade, rested his head on the saddlebags, and faded into a deep sleep.

Fall was the most beautiful time of the year in the mountain country. The nights were cool, even crisp, and the days were bright and rather warm, at least when out of the wind in a sheltered place like the little draw off the diamond field flats where Jim had secluded himself. The aspens had turned gold, and their leaves fell in gold and brown piles throughout the groves, leaving some trees looking like skeletons, all gray in their upper reaches, with black scars on white trunks down below. The once proud green waves of new grass had all turned yellow and dried, their seeds blown by the winds to new places for next spring's growth. The new mating season was on, and all the antelope bucks gathered their harems, as did the bull elk and to a lesser extent the buck mule deer, in an effort to reproduce their kind for the coming year. Overhead, the migration of waterfowl heading south to warmer climates was a constant sight.

It was in this fall splendor that Jim roused to some little unknown sound and then just as easily dozed back off to sleep. He had made his decision and felt good about it.

Moments later Jim was roused again, this time by the whinny of his sorrel. He stirred slightly, turned over, and was almost asleep again when his instincts set in from old days. If his horse woke him, it was for a reason. His eyes popped open to the sight of someone standing over him, staring down, quietly, not wanting to awaken him.

"Don't mean to startle you none, Jim. Jest seen you here, looking like you was sleeping off something."

Jim realized that it was Ed Cole himself. But how could it be? Ed should be off out on the desert with one of his herds. And how could he have known Jim was out here at the diamond field? It was like the first time they had met, the time Ed slipped up on Jim while Jim was on the high point overlooking the field, being watchful. Even then, Ed had surprised him.

"Ed! My gosh, man! You sure can sneak up …" Then Jim saw that Ed was holding his Colt .45 pointed directly at Jim's midsection. "Ed! What is this? Why?"

The roar of the big .45 was deafening at that close range. So close that the flash from the muzzle stung and blinded Jim, still lying on his saddle blanket.

Jim took the awful pounding of the big lead slug as it hit him squarely in the middle, tearing at his insides, burning and ripping on through, and finally leaving his body. He felt himself struggling, trying to gain his footing, unable to get his legs to go where he intended. He couldn't believe what had happened: Ed was getting rid of the only viable witness to the Matt Rash killing.

Jim glanced down and saw that the front of his shirt had turned blood red. His blood was streaming out, warm, dripping fast to the ground around him. He looked up at Ed, just standing there with his .45 cocked once more and still pointed at him, even though he was down and could not move his legs to get up.

"Ed, Ed! What for, what for, Ed?" said Jim, realizing he could not move the lower half of his body. "What for?"

"Sure did hate doing this to you, Jim. But like we was talking back up there on th' mountain one day. You remember, don't you, Jim? We talked 'bout getting killed by ambush, never knowing jest who done it. Like I said back then, I jest thought it was best to get it from a friend, one that would jest give it to you straight, right up front. You'd know then that you would be treated right, not jest left fer th' coyotes to eat on." Ed was staring hard at Jim. "You had to know I couldn't jest let you go off telling strangers what you and me both knowed 'bout ol' Rash. Then when you figured out 'bout me and Isom ... well, jest can't let it go."

Jim wasn't thinking clearly, still trying to get to his feet, struggling on the ground, and getting muddy from his blood mixing with the yellow and gray dirt. He was surprised at the amount of his own blood flowing out from the big wound in his belly. He put his hand over the gaping hole, trying in vain to stem the flow.

"Don't use yourself all up, Jim. Jest lie easy. Won't take long. I brung a shovel here. Sure don't need to give you 'nother bullet. But I want you to know, I'll treat you th' best, Jim," Ed said as he put away the .45 and turned to a small clearing next to the cedars. "This looks like a soft spot here. Look okay to you, Jim? Better than where I put that ol' prospector a few years back, didn't get him deep 'nough in th' ground. Coyotes come and got him. Weren't but over there, other side of them cedars. Ground was hard. He weren't no friend, Jim. You is. I'll take good care of you. Won't let them no good coyotes get you."

Jim could hear the gravel scraping onto the shovel as Ed started digging. The first few shovelfuls were mostly gravel, with all the grinding sound. Jim noticed that he lost sight of Ed at times, even though he was staring right at him. He also lost his hearing at times. Must be what happens when a big .45, handled by a friend, drains too much blood out, he thought.

"You're going fast now, Jim, getting pale. Sure sorry 'bout that. Told all them folks you was leaving. Told 'em you was heading fer Texas, not coming back. They won't be looking fer you. I'll kill your two horses in some deep draw so nobody will find 'em and start asking questions. Got it all planned out, Jim. But sure would like to have them Boone spurs of yours there, Jim, if you don't mind? I'll jest tell th' boys you give 'em to me fer a goin' away present."

Jim could hear most of what Ed was saying and could hear the shovel digging deeper into the ground. He managed to open his eyes enough to see the dirt pile getting higher. He couldn't raise his hands and was having some trouble breathing. But he suddenly realized what Ed had been saying about planning it all out so that no one would miss him.

With the last flicker of life that was left in him, Jim managed a call to Ed. As Ed turned to hear him out, Jim gasped a last few words. "You don't know … Mary Lou … she's waiting … she'll be looking … She will … get … you." Jim could no longer see light and felt no more pain as he relaxed into death.

Ed looked puzzled, and turned away.

EPILOGUE

A search for Jim Keaton was commenced from Rock Springs by Andy Ewing and friends of Mary Lou Garrett. Inquiry to the sheriff in Del Rio confirmed that Jim never returned home, and the Denver law firm had not heard from him. The search party then went to Brown's Park to check all the ranchers and cowboys for anything they might know. Charley Sparks thought it unusual that Ed claimed Jim was gone, but later Pete had spent the night with Jim in the Johnson Draw cabin. When they found Ed was wearing Jim's Boone spurs, Ed told them the spurs were a going away gift from Jim. Andy and Mary Lou knew Jim would not part with those spurs, but they had no way of proving it. Everyone suspected Ed of doing one more killing, but hard evidence was not found and no charges could filed.

During the months of October and November Ed took several of Isom Dart's abandoned wild horses and started breaking one to ride. On Christmas eve Rueben found that horse standing near Ed's headquarters with the saddle askew and one of Ed's boots hung in a stirrup with the Boone spur tangled in the cinch. Rueben backtracked the horse and found Ed's dead body, badly broken and torn. He had obviously been bucked from his horse and dragged to death in a wild run. He was less than a mile from his cabin.

No one was ever apprehended for killing Matt Rash. No one was brought in for killing Isom Dart. And Tom Horn never again returned to Cold Spring Mountain. He was later accused of killing Willie Nickell, the young son of a rancher near Iron Mountain Station, Wyoming, tried, convicted, and hanged to death on November 20, 1903.